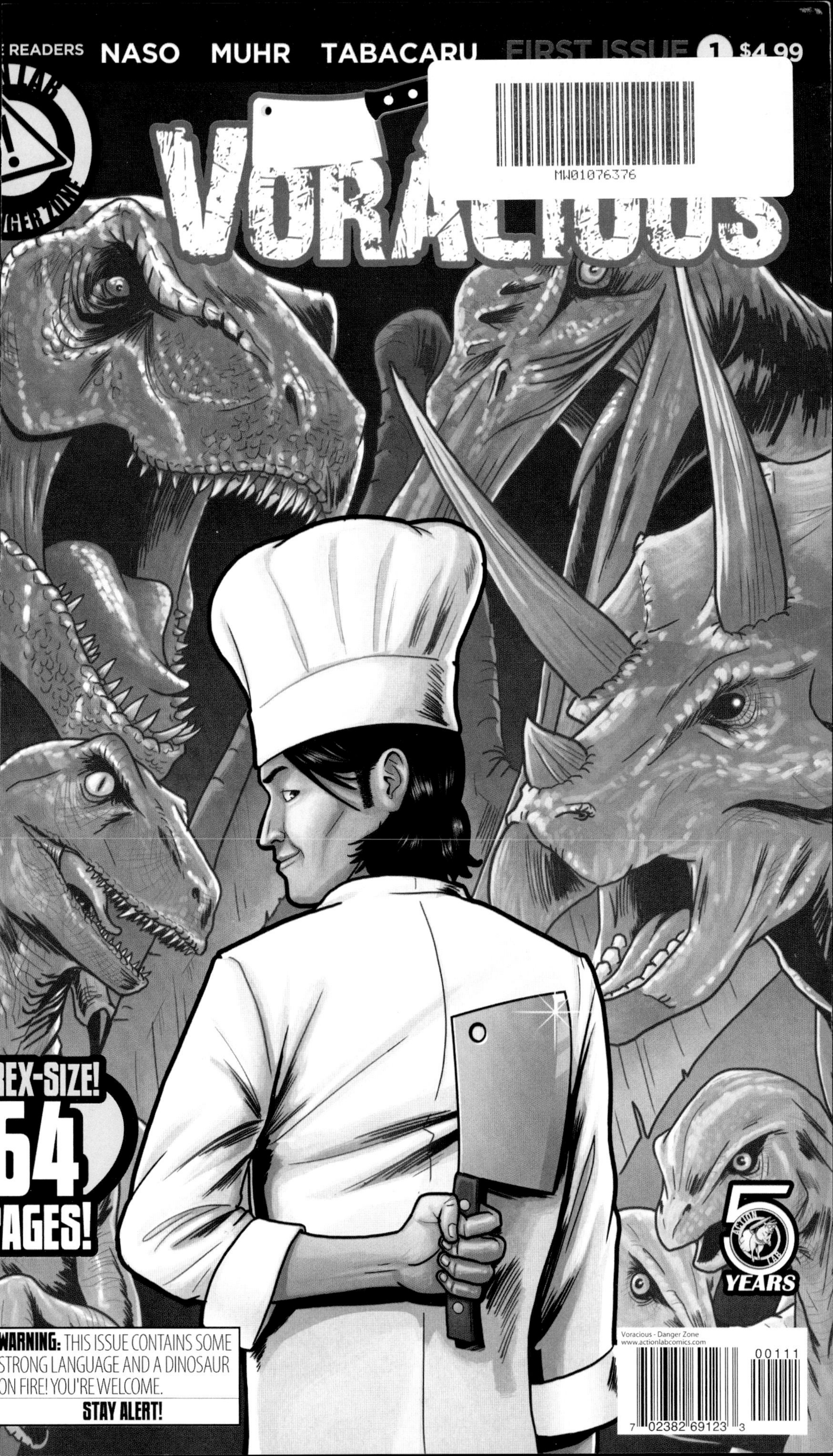
E READERS
NASO MUHR TABACARU
FIRST ISSUE 1 $4.99
VORACIOUS
REX-SIZE!
64
PAGES!
5 YEARS
WARNING: THIS ISSUE CONTAINS SOME STRONG LANGUAGE AND A DINOSAUR ON FIRE! YOU'RE WELCOME.
STAY ALERT!
Voracious - Danger Zone
www.actionlabcomics.com
00111
7 02382 69123 3
MW01076376

ACTION LAB: DANGER ZONE PRESENTS

VORACIOUS

TYRANNOSAURUS-SIZE 1ST ISSUE!

CHAPTER 1
ALL THINGS PASS WITH TIME

CHAPTER 2
THE LEAVES THAT DIE EACH FALL

Written by
MARKISAN NASO

Art, Lettering & Design by
JASON MUHR

Color Art by
ANDREI TABACARU

VORACIOUS created by
NASO & MUHR

JASON MARTIN - PUBLISHER
KEVIN FREEMAN - PRESIDENT
DAVE DWONCH - CREATIVE DIRECTOR
SHAWN GABBORIN - EDITOR IN CHIEF
JAMAL IGLE - VICE-PRESIDENT OF MARKETING
JIM DIETZ - SOCIAL MEDIA DIRECTOR
COLLEEN BOYD - SUBMISSIONS EDITOR

Find Markisan Naso at www.markisan.com.
Find Jason Muhr at www.jasonmuhr.com.

ACTIONLABCOMICS.COM/DANGER-ZO

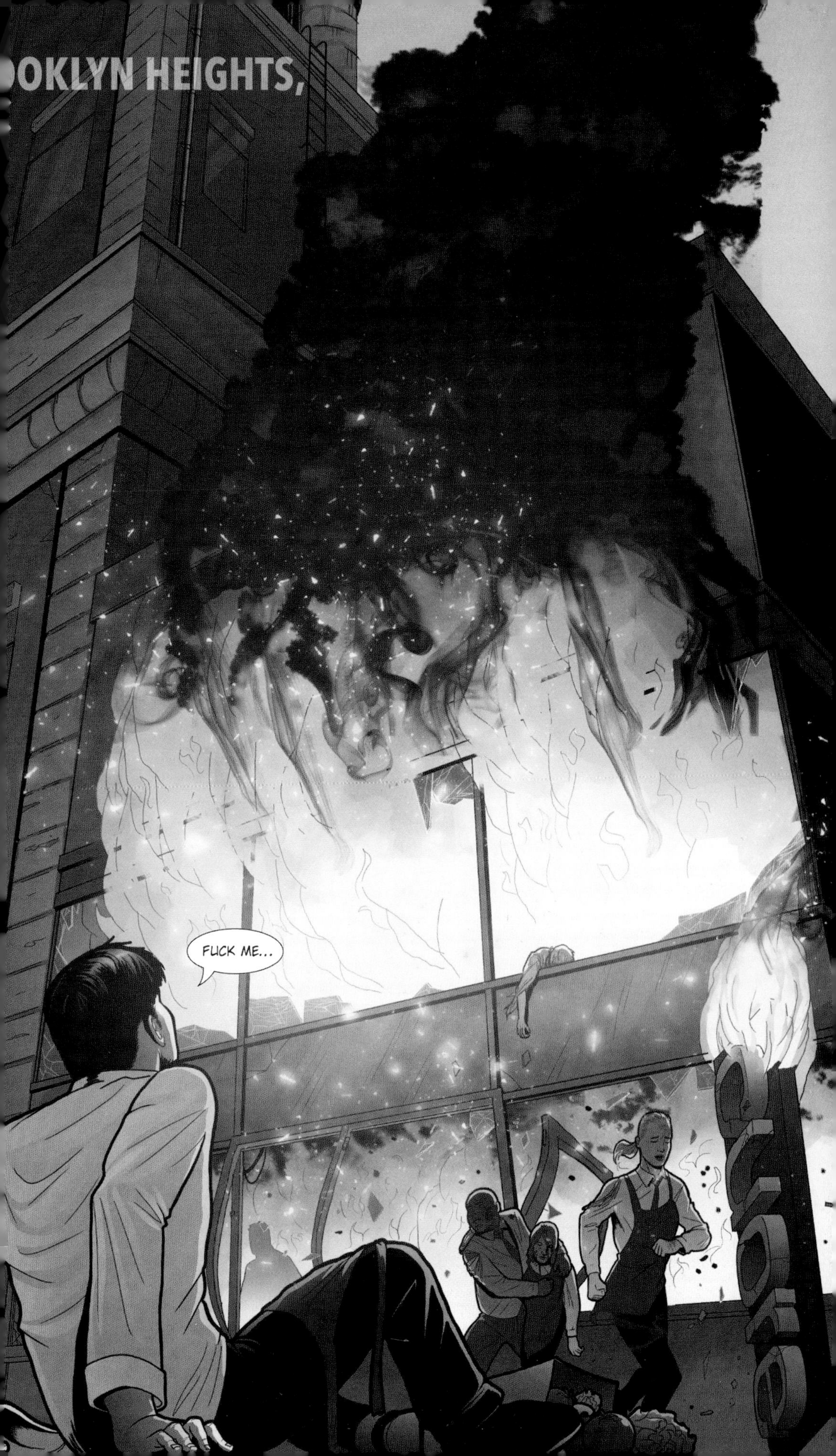
OOKLYN HEIGHTS,
FUCK ME...

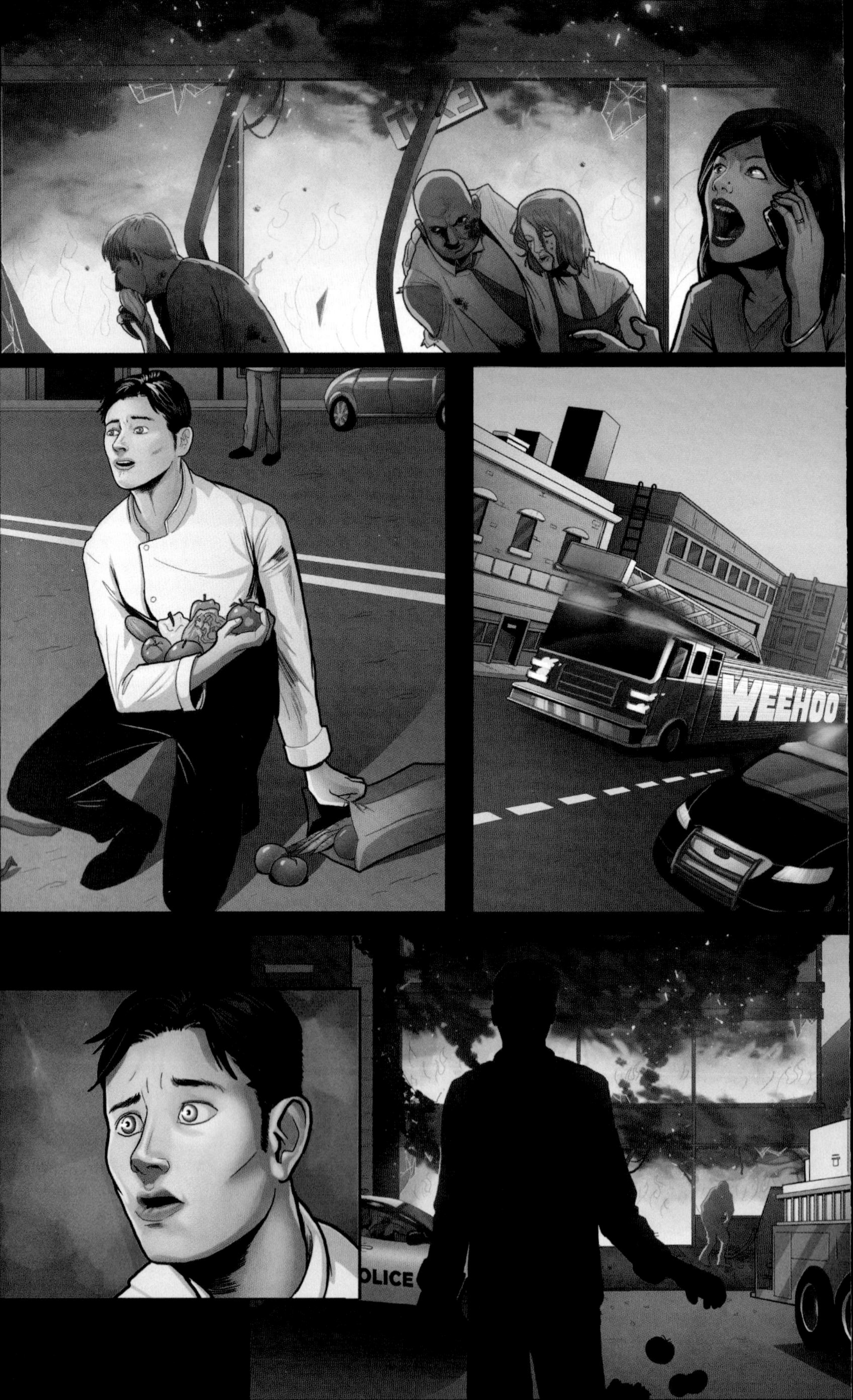
WEEHOO
OLICE

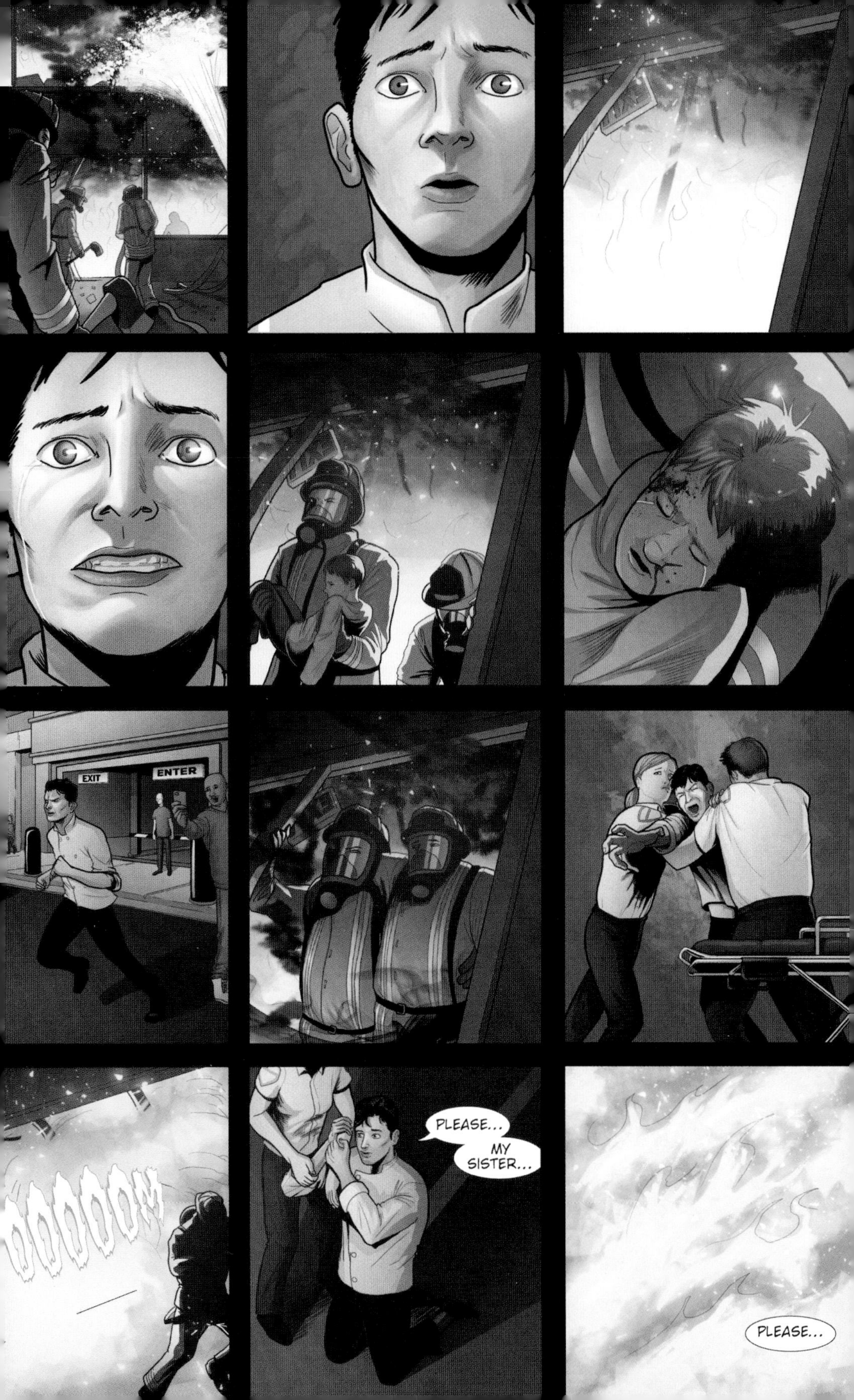
EXIT
ENTER
PLEASE...
MY SISTER...
PLEASE...

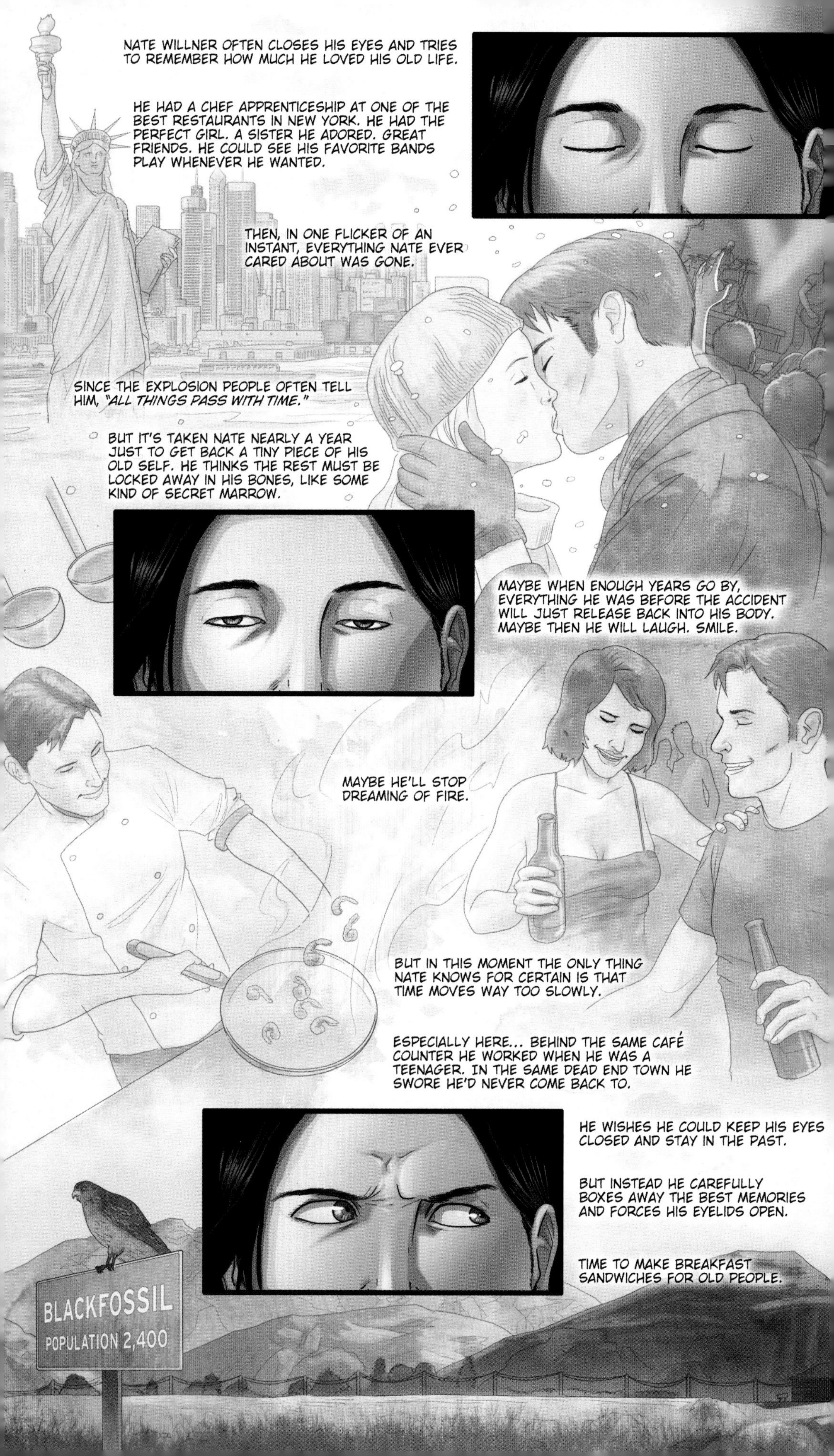
NATE WILLNER OFTEN CLOSES HIS EYES AND TRIES TO REMEMBER HOW MUCH HE LOVED HIS OLD LIFE.
HE HAD A CHEF APPRENTICESHIP AT ONE OF THE BEST RESTAURANTS IN NEW YORK. HE HAD THE PERFECT GIRL. A SISTER HE ADORED. GREAT FRIENDS. HE COULD SEE HIS FAVORITE BANDS PLAY WHENEVER HE WANTED.
THEN, IN ONE FLICKER OF AN INSTANT, EVERYTHING NATE EVER CARED ABOUT WAS GONE.
SINCE THE EXPLOSION PEOPLE OFTEN TELL HIM, *"ALL THINGS PASS WITH TIME."*
BUT IT'S TAKEN NATE NEARLY A YEAR JUST TO GET BACK A TINY PIECE OF HIS OLD SELF. HE THINKS THE REST MUST BE LOCKED AWAY IN HIS BONES, LIKE SOME KIND OF SECRET MARROW.
MAYBE WHEN ENOUGH YEARS GO BY, EVERYTHING HE WAS BEFORE THE ACCIDENT WILL JUST RELEASE BACK INTO HIS BODY. MAYBE THEN HE WILL LAUGH. SMILE.
MAYBE HE'LL STOP DREAMING OF FIRE.
BUT IN THIS MOMENT THE ONLY THING NATE KNOWS FOR CERTAIN IS THAT TIME MOVES WAY TOO SLOWLY.
ESPECIALLY HERE... BEHIND THE SAME CAFÉ COUNTER HE WORKED WHEN HE WAS A TEENAGER. IN THE SAME DEAD END TOWN HE SWORE HE'D NEVER COME BACK TO.
HE WISHES HE COULD KEEP HIS EYES CLOSED AND STAY IN THE PAST.
BUT INSTEAD HE CAREFULLY BOXES AWAY THE BEST MEMORIES AND FORCES HIS EYELIDS OPEN.
TIME TO MAKE BREAKFAST SANDWICHES FOR OLD PEOPLE.
BLACKFOSSIL
POPULATION 2,400

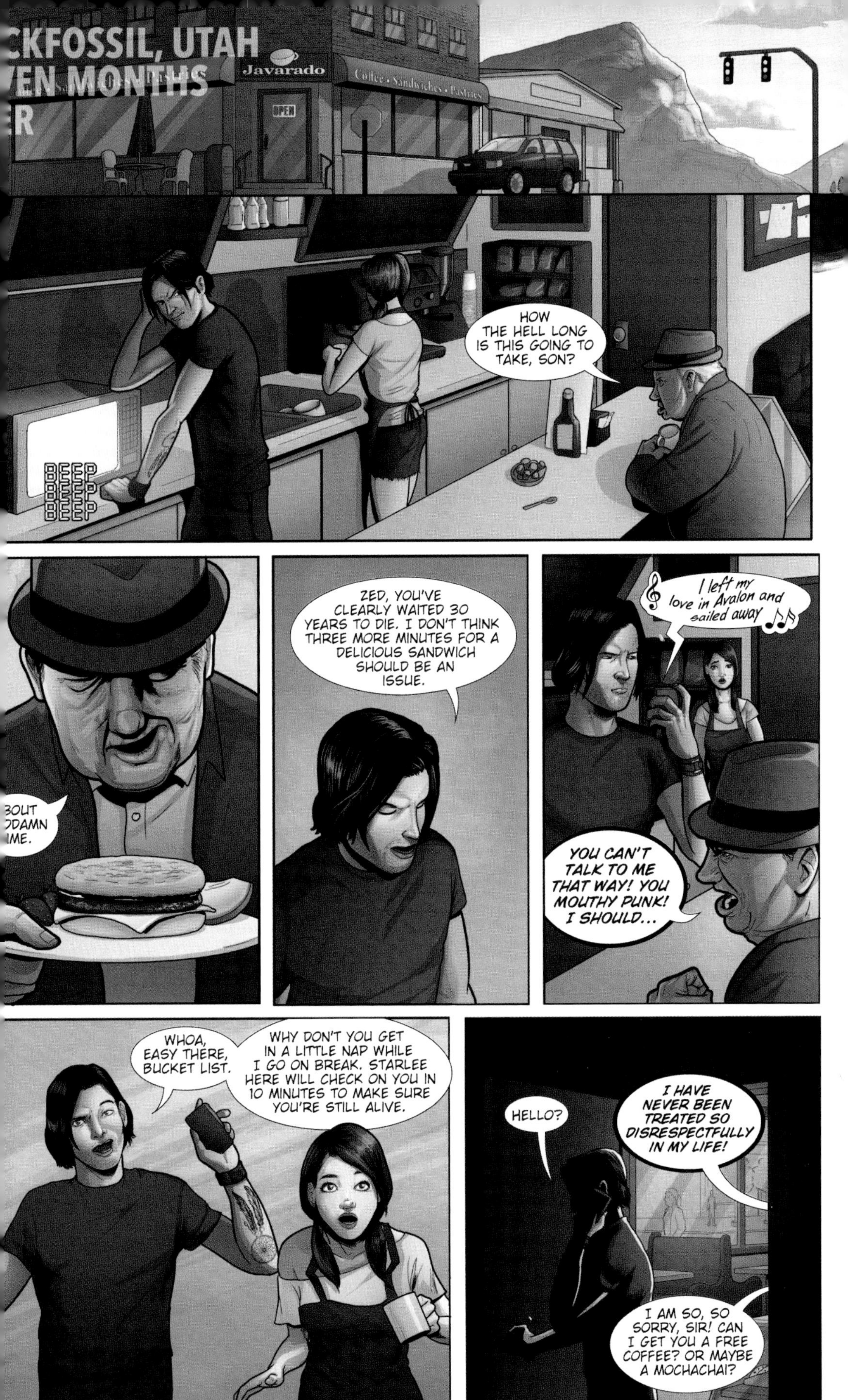
CKFOSSIL, UTAH
VEN MONTHS
Javarado
Coffee • Sandwiches • Pastries
OPEN
HOW THE HELL LONG IS THIS GOING TO TAKE, SON?
BEEP BEEP BEEP
BOUT DDAMN IME.
ZED, YOU'VE CLEARLY WAITED 30 YEARS TO DIE. I DON'T THINK THREE MORE MINUTES FOR A DELICIOUS SANDWICH SHOULD BE AN ISSUE.
I left my love in Avalon and sailed away
YOU CAN'T TALK TO ME THAT WAY! YOU MOUTHY PUNK! I SHOULD...
WHOA, EASY THERE, BUCKET LIST.
WHY DON'T YOU GET IN A LITTLE NAP WHILE I GO ON BREAK. STARLEE HERE WILL CHECK ON YOU IN 10 MINUTES TO MAKE SURE YOU'RE STILL ALIVE.
HELLO?
I HAVE NEVER BEEN TREATED SO DISRESPECTFULLY IN MY LIFE!
I AM SO, SO SORRY, SIR! CAN I GET YOU A FREE COFFEE? OR MAYBE A MOCHACHAI?

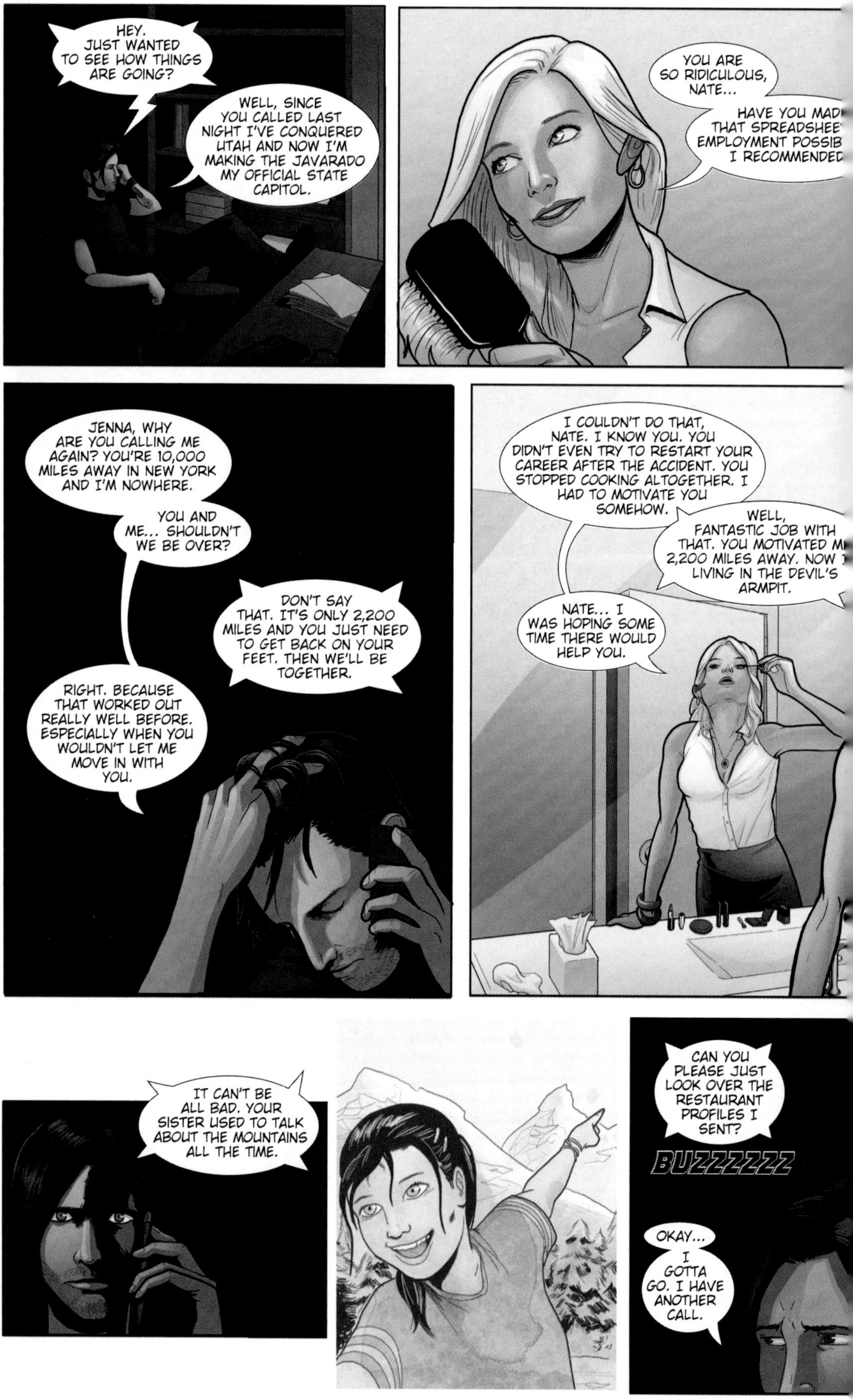
HEY. JUST WANTED TO SEE HOW THINGS ARE GOING?
WELL, SINCE YOU CALLED LAST NIGHT I'VE CONQUERED UTAH AND NOW I'M MAKING THE JAVARADO MY OFFICIAL STATE CAPITOL.
YOU ARE SO RIDICULOUS, NATE...
HAVE YOU MAD THAT SPREADSHEE EMPLOYMENT POSSIB I RECOMMENDED
JENNA, WHY ARE YOU CALLING ME AGAIN? YOU'RE 10,000 MILES AWAY IN NEW YORK AND I'M NOWHERE.
YOU AND ME... SHOULDN'T WE BE OVER?
DON'T SAY THAT. IT'S ONLY 2,200 MILES AND YOU JUST NEED TO GET BACK ON YOUR FEET. THEN WE'LL BE TOGETHER.
RIGHT. BECAUSE THAT WORKED OUT REALLY WELL BEFORE. ESPECIALLY WHEN YOU WOULDN'T LET ME MOVE IN WITH YOU.
I COULDN'T DO THAT, NATE. I KNOW YOU. YOU DIDN'T EVEN TRY TO RESTART YOUR CAREER AFTER THE ACCIDENT. YOU STOPPED COOKING ALTOGETHER. I HAD TO MOTIVATE YOU SOMEHOW.
WELL, FANTASTIC JOB WITH THAT. YOU MOTIVATED M 2,200 MILES AWAY. NOW LIVING IN THE DEVIL'S ARMPIT.
NATE... I WAS HOPING SOME TIME THERE WOULD HELP YOU.
IT CAN'T BE ALL BAD. YOUR SISTER USED TO TALK ABOUT THE MOUNTAINS ALL THE TIME.
CAN YOU PLEASE JUST LOOK OVER THE RESTAURANT PROFILES I SENT?
BUZZZZZZ
OKAY... I GOTTA GO. I HAVE ANOTHER CALL.

YOU'RE KIDDING ME. I'LL COME RIGHT OVER.

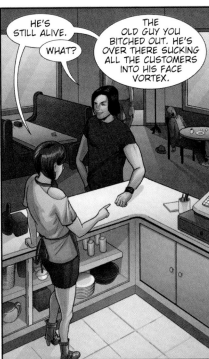

HE'S STILL ALIVE.

WHAT?

THE OLD GUY YOU BITCHED OUT. HE'S OVER THERE SUCKING ALL THE CUSTOMERS INTO HIS FACE VORTEX.

WHOA. HIS MOUTH IS GIGANTIC.

SNOOORRRRR

YEAH! AND LOOK AT THAT PUDDLE OF DROOL!

HEY, STARLEE, TO LEAVE RLY.

WHY? YOU JUST GOT HERE.

I KNOW. BUT SOMETHING REALLY WEIRD HAS COME UP. BESIDES, THIS PLACE WILL BE DEAD FOR HOURS. AND YOU ALREADY HANDLED THE THANAGARIAN SNORE BEAST OVER THERE.

THANKS STAR. I'LL COME BACK IN A BIT. PROMISE.

OKAY, BUT I CAN'T GUARANTEE THIS GUY WILL BE BREATHING WHEN YOU GET BACK.

SNOOORRRRR

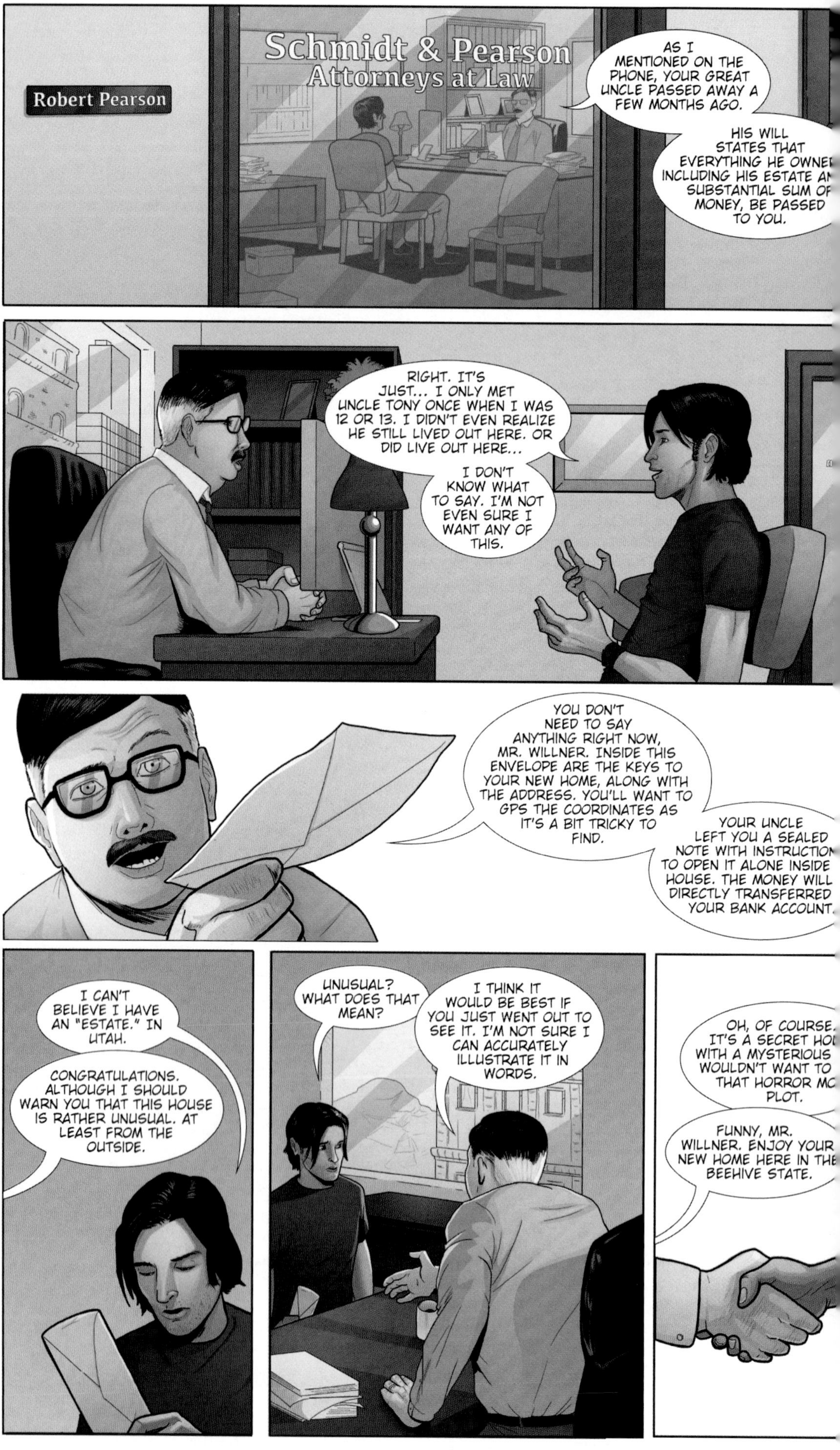
Schmidt & Pearson
Attorneys at Law
Robert Pearson
AS I MENTIONED ON THE PHONE, YOUR GREAT UNCLE PASSED AWAY A FEW MONTHS AGO.
HIS WILL STATES THAT EVERYTHING HE OWNE INCLUDING HIS ESTATE A SUBSTANTIAL SUM OF MONEY, BE PASSED TO YOU.
RIGHT. IT'S JUST... I ONLY MET UNCLE TONY ONCE WHEN I WAS 12 OR 13. I DIDN'T EVEN REALIZE HE STILL LIVED OUT HERE. OR DID LIVE OUT HERE...
I DON'T KNOW WHAT TO SAY. I'M NOT EVEN SURE I WANT ANY OF THIS.
YOU DON'T NEED TO SAY ANYTHING RIGHT NOW, MR. WILLNER. INSIDE THIS ENVELOPE ARE THE KEYS TO YOUR NEW HOME, ALONG WITH THE ADDRESS. YOU'LL WANT TO GPS THE COORDINATES AS IT'S A BIT TRICKY TO FIND.
YOUR UNCLE LEFT YOU A SEALED NOTE WITH INSTRUCTIO TO OPEN IT ALONE INSIDE HOUSE. THE MONEY WILL DIRECTLY TRANSFERRED YOUR BANK ACCOUNT.
I CAN'T BELIEVE I HAVE AN "ESTATE." IN UTAH.
CONGRATULATIONS. ALTHOUGH I SHOULD WARN YOU THAT THIS HOUSE IS RATHER UNUSUAL. AT LEAST FROM THE OUTSIDE.
UNUSUAL? WHAT DOES THAT MEAN?
I THINK IT WOULD BE BEST IF YOU JUST WENT OUT TO SEE IT. I'M NOT SURE I CAN ACCURATELY ILLUSTRATE IT IN WORDS.
OH, OF COURSE. IT'S A SECRET HO WITH A MYSTERIOUS WOULDN'T WANT TO THAT HORROR MC PLOT.
FUNNY, MR. WILLNER. ENJOY YOUR NEW HOME HERE IN THE BEEHIVE STATE.

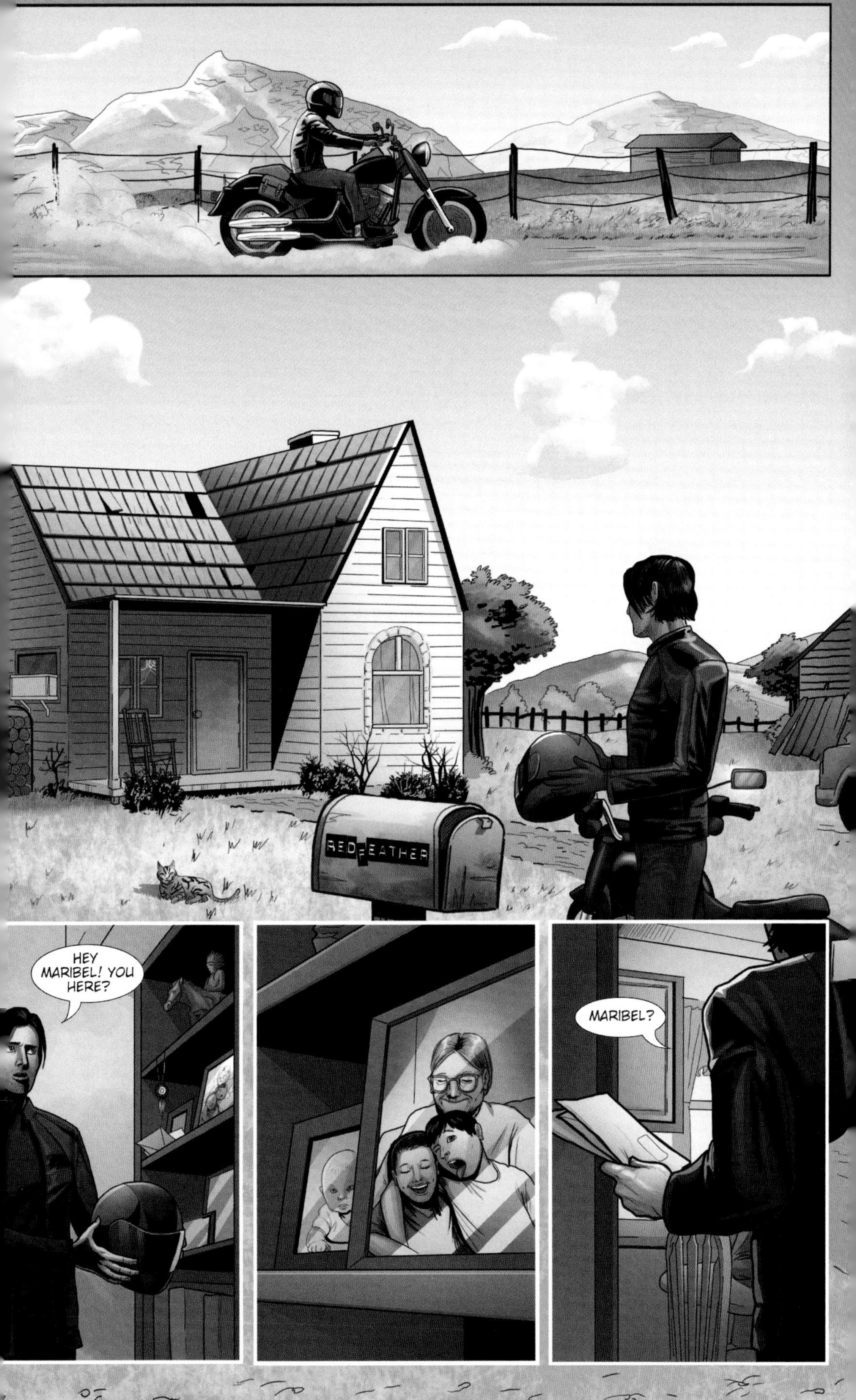
RED FEATHER
HEY MARIBEL! YOU HERE?
MARIBEL?

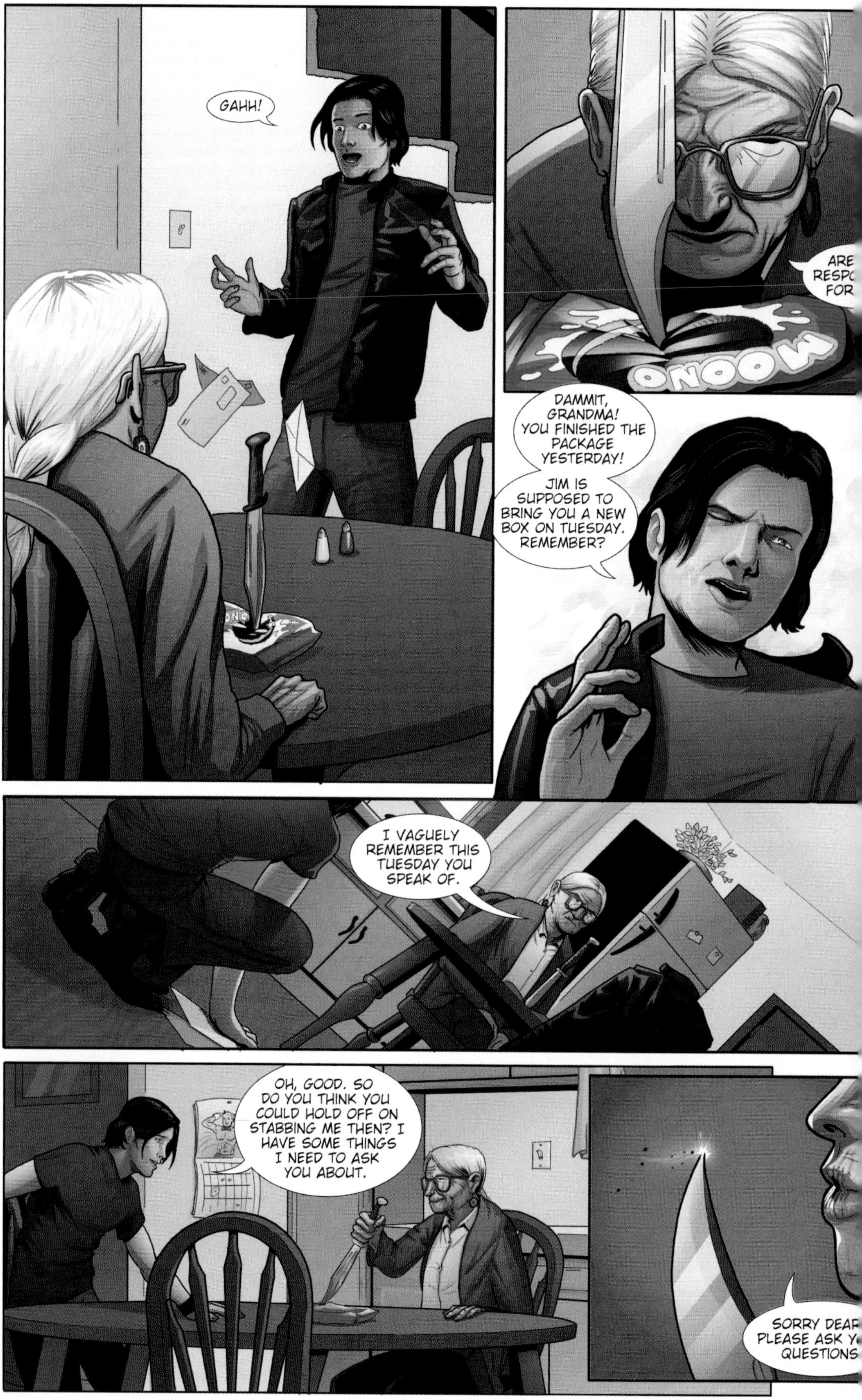
GAHH!
ARE RESPO FOR
DAMMIT, GRANDMA! YOU FINISHED THE PACKAGE YESTERDAY!
JIM IS SUPPOSED TO BRING YOU A NEW BOX ON TUESDAY. REMEMBER?
I VAGUELY REMEMBER THIS TUESDAY YOU SPEAK OF.
OH, GOOD. SO DO YOU THINK YOU COULD HOLD OFF ON STABBING ME THEN? I HAVE SOME THINGS I NEED TO ASK YOU ABOUT.
SORRY DEAR PLEASE ASK Y QUESTIONS

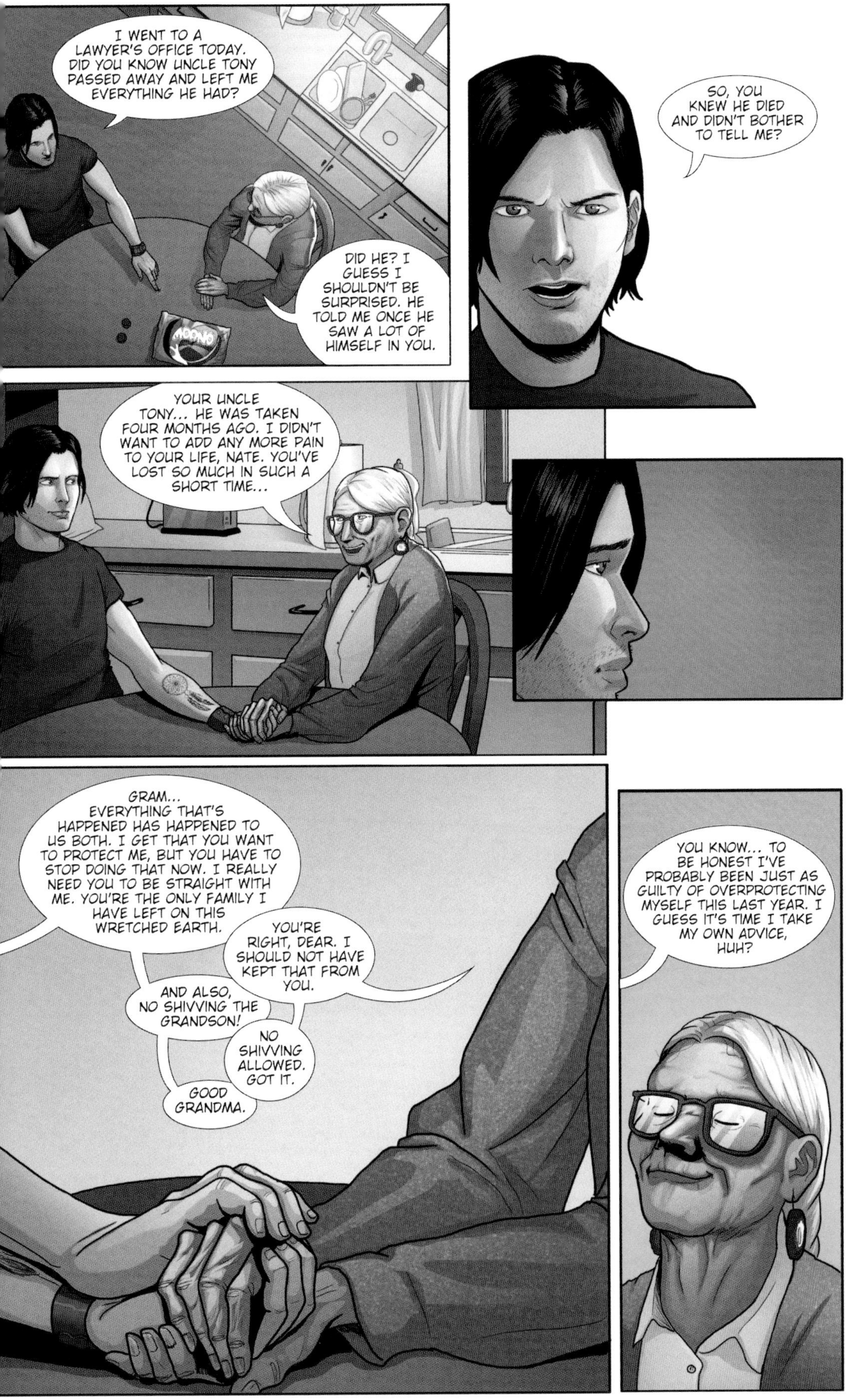
I WENT TO A LAWYER'S OFFICE TODAY. DID YOU KNOW UNCLE TONY PASSED AWAY AND LEFT ME EVERYTHING HE HAD?
DID HE? I GUESS I SHOULDN'T BE SURPRISED. HE TOLD ME ONCE HE SAW A LOT OF HIMSELF IN YOU.
SO, YOU KNEW HE DIED AND DIDN'T BOTHER TO TELL ME?
YOUR UNCLE TONY... HE WAS TAKEN FOUR MONTHS AGO. I DIDN'T WANT TO ADD ANY MORE PAIN TO YOUR LIFE, NATE. YOU'VE LOST SO MUCH IN SUCH A SHORT TIME...
GRAM... EVERYTHING THAT'S HAPPENED HAS HAPPENED TO US BOTH. I GET THAT YOU WANT TO PROTECT ME, BUT YOU HAVE TO STOP DOING THAT NOW. I REALLY NEED YOU TO BE STRAIGHT WITH ME. YOU'RE THE ONLY FAMILY I HAVE LEFT ON THIS WRETCHED EARTH.
YOU'RE RIGHT, DEAR. I SHOULD NOT HAVE KEPT THAT FROM YOU.
AND ALSO, NO SHIVVING THE GRANDSON!
NO SHIVVING ALLOWED. GOT IT.
GOOD GRANDMA.
YOU KNOW... TO BE HONEST I'VE PROBABLY BEEN JUST AS GUILTY OF OVERPROTECTING MYSELF THIS LAST YEAR. I GUESS IT'S TIME I TAKE MY OWN ADVICE, HUH?

SO, HE LEFT YOU EVERYTHING?

THAT'S WHAT LAWYER GUY SAID. I NOW HAVE $500,000 AND A HOUSE IN THE MOUNTAINS THAT MAY OR MAY NOT BE A VAMPIRE CRYPT. HEY, HAVE YOU EVER BEEN TO UNCLE TONY'S PLACE?

I HONESTLY DON'T REMEMBER. IT'S BEEN A LONG TIME SINCE I'VE SEEN HIM.

I WASN'T GIVEN MUCH TO GO ON, BUT IT SOUNDS LIKE THIS HOUSE IS PRETTY HARD TO FORGET. YOU *SURE* YOU HAVEN'T BEEN THERE?

OH NATE, I HAVE NO COOKIES I'M GETTING TIRED. YOU MAKE ME SOME O SPECIAL TEA OF YO BEFORE I LIE DOWN?

SURE, GRANDMA.

I JUST REALLY WISH I KNEW MORE ABOUT HIM, YOU KNOW? I CAN'T BELIEVE I'M INHERITING EVERYTHING FROM A GUY I MET ONCE.

ANYWAY, I'LL STOP BABBLING NOW. SPECIAL TEA COMIN' UP.

Shining Wate

NATE?

WHATEVER YOU DO WITH THAT HOUSE AND MONEY, DO IT FOR YOU. PLEASE DON'T WORRY ABOUT ME. USE THOSE GIFTS FOR SOMETHING THAT WILL MAKE YOU HAPPY.

SLSSH SLSSH

THE EARTH ISN'T ALWAYS A WRETCHED PLACE, YOU KNOW.

WHATEV YOU SA MARIBE

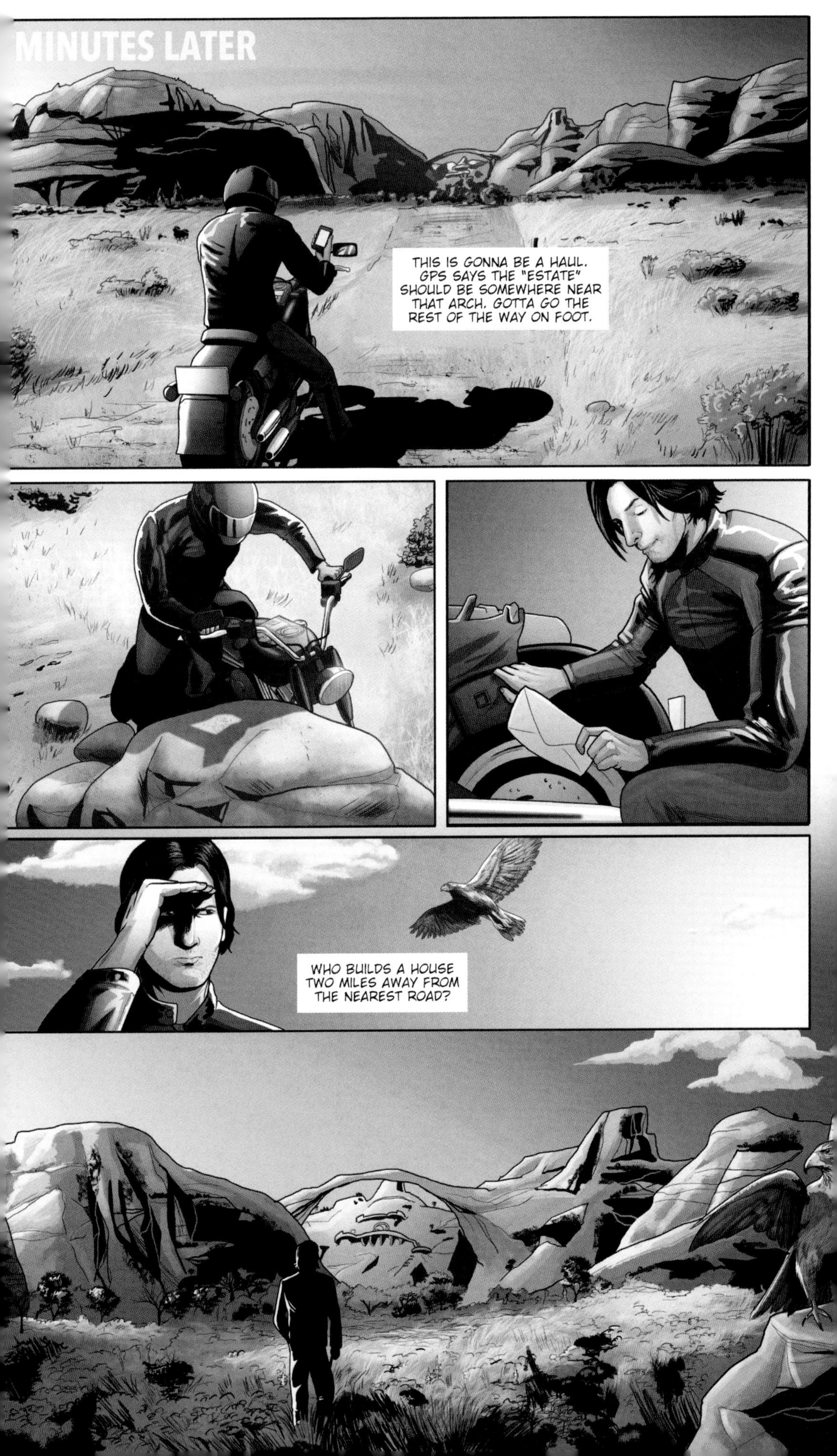
MINUTES LATER
THIS IS GONNA BE A HAUL. GPS SAYS THE "ESTATE" SHOULD BE SOMEWHERE NEAR THAT ARCH. GOTTA GO THE REST OF THE WAY ON FOOT.
WHO BUILDS A HOUSE TWO MILES AWAY FROM THE NEAREST ROAD?

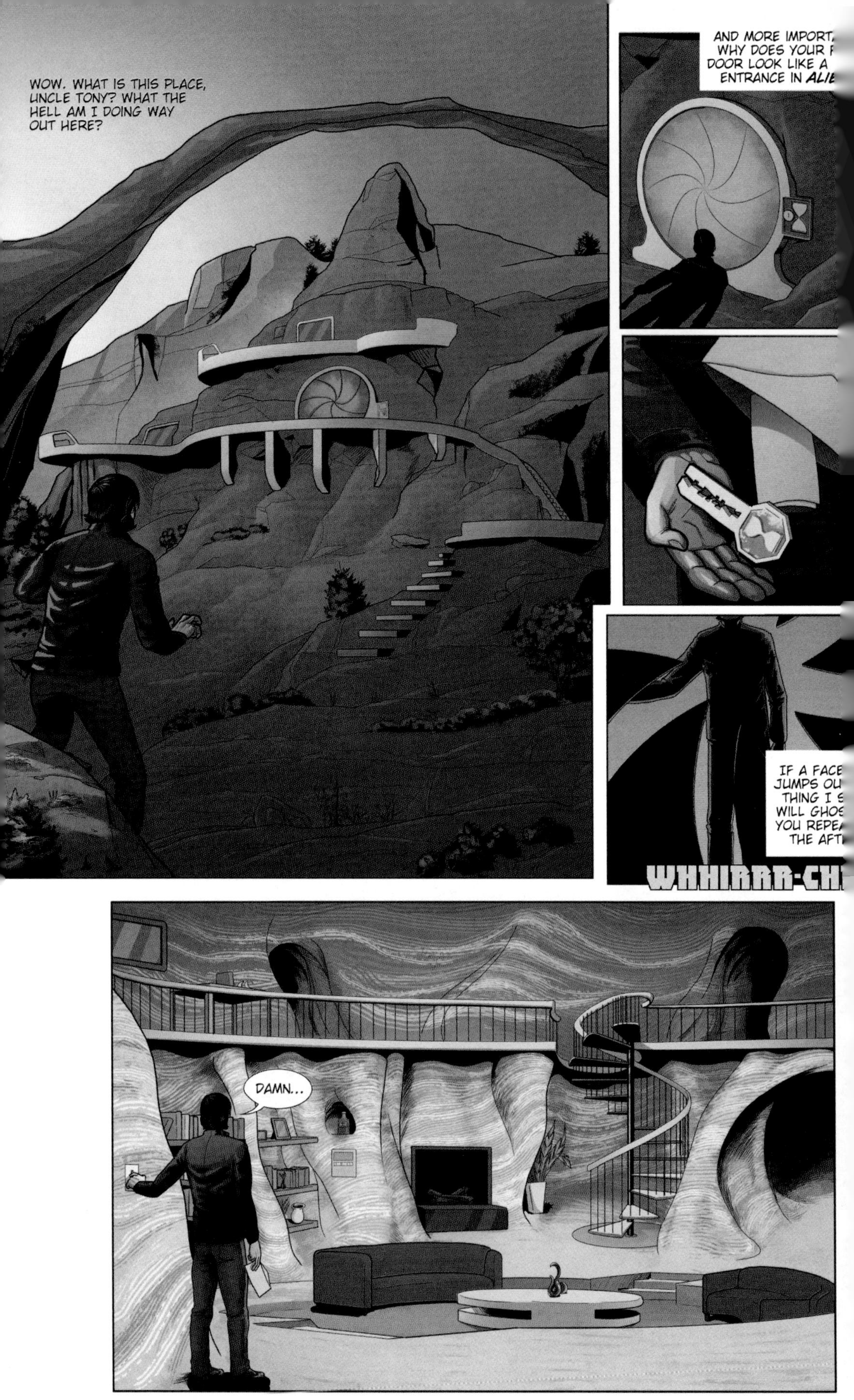
WOW. WHAT IS THIS PLACE, UNCLE TONY? WHAT THE HELL AM I DOING WAY OUT HERE?
AND MORE IMPORT WHY DOES YOUR DOOR LOOK LIKE A ENTRANCE IN ALIE
IF A FACE JUMPS OU THING I WILL GHOS YOU REPEA THE AFT
WHHIRRR-CH
DAMN...

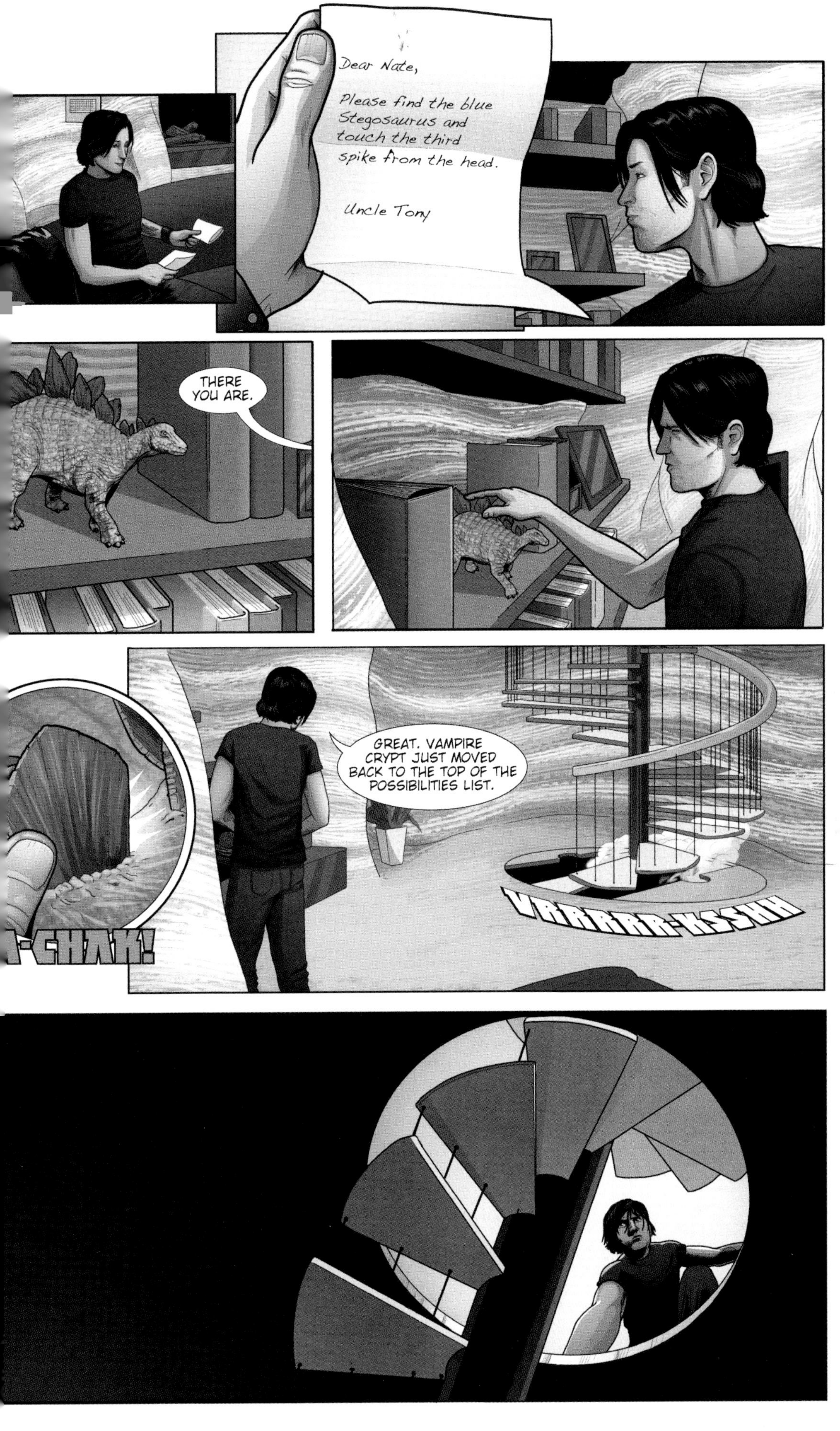
Dear Nate,
Please find the blue Stegosaurus and touch the third spike from the head.
Uncle Tony
THERE YOU ARE.
-CHAK!
GREAT. VAMPIRE CRYPT JUST MOVED BACK TO THE TOP OF THE POSSIBILITIES LIST.
VRRRRR-KSSHH

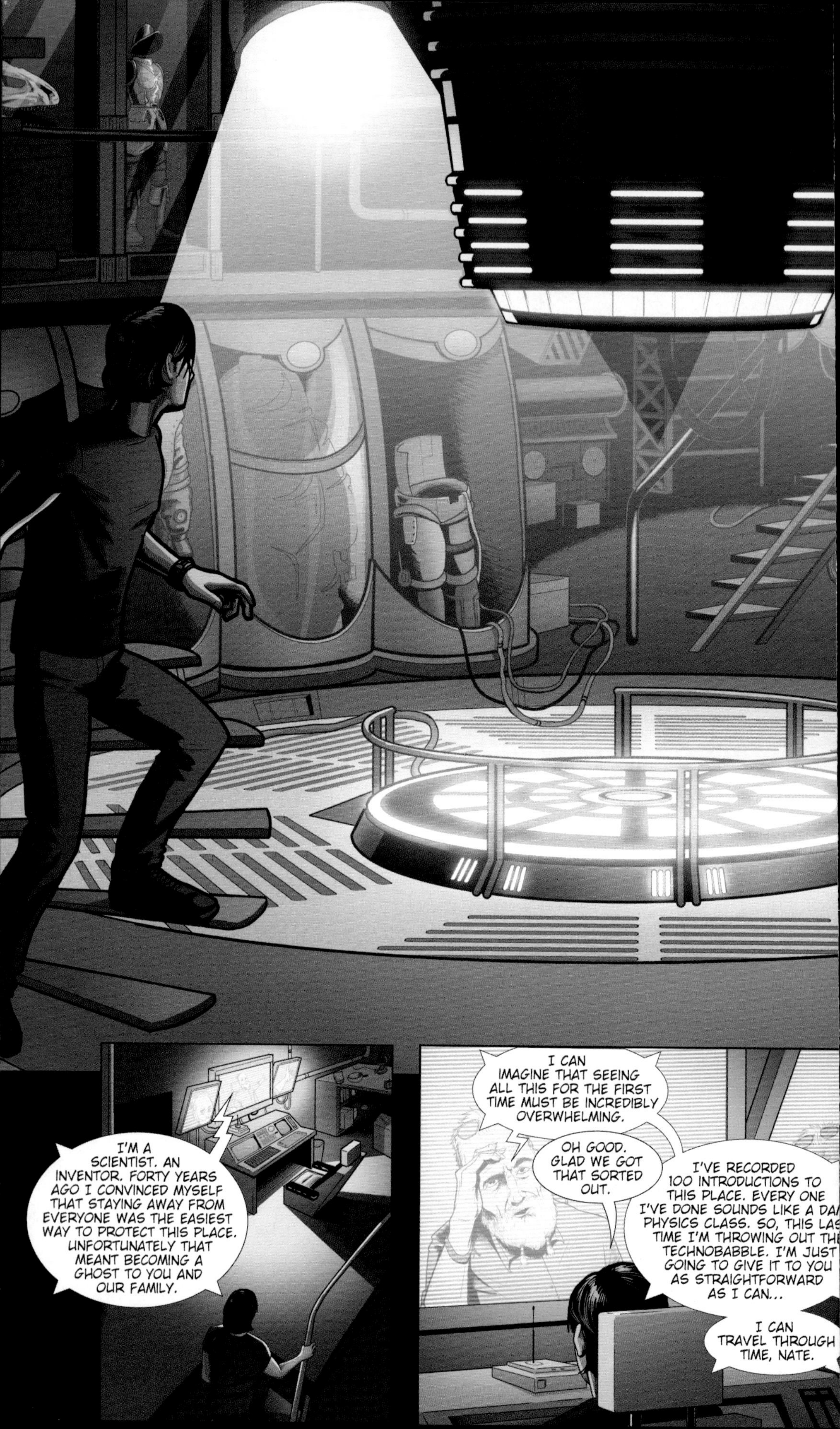
I'M A SCIENTIST. AN INVENTOR. FORTY YEARS AGO I CONVINCED MYSELF THAT STAYING AWAY FROM EVERYONE WAS THE EASIEST WAY TO PROTECT THIS PLACE. UNFORTUNATELY THAT MEANT BECOMING A GHOST TO YOU AND OUR FAMILY.
I CAN IMAGINE THAT SEEING ALL THIS FOR THE FIRST TIME MUST BE INCREDIBLY OVERWHELMING.
OH GOOD. GLAD WE GOT THAT SORTED OUT.
I'VE RECORDED 100 INTRODUCTIONS TO THIS PLACE. EVERY ONE I'VE DONE SOUNDS LIKE A DAM PHYSICS CLASS. SO, THIS LAS TIME I'M THROWING OUT TH TECHNOBABBLE. I'M JUST GOING TO GIVE IT TO YOU AS STRAIGHTFORWARD AS I CAN...
I CAN TRAVEL THROUGH TIME, NATE.

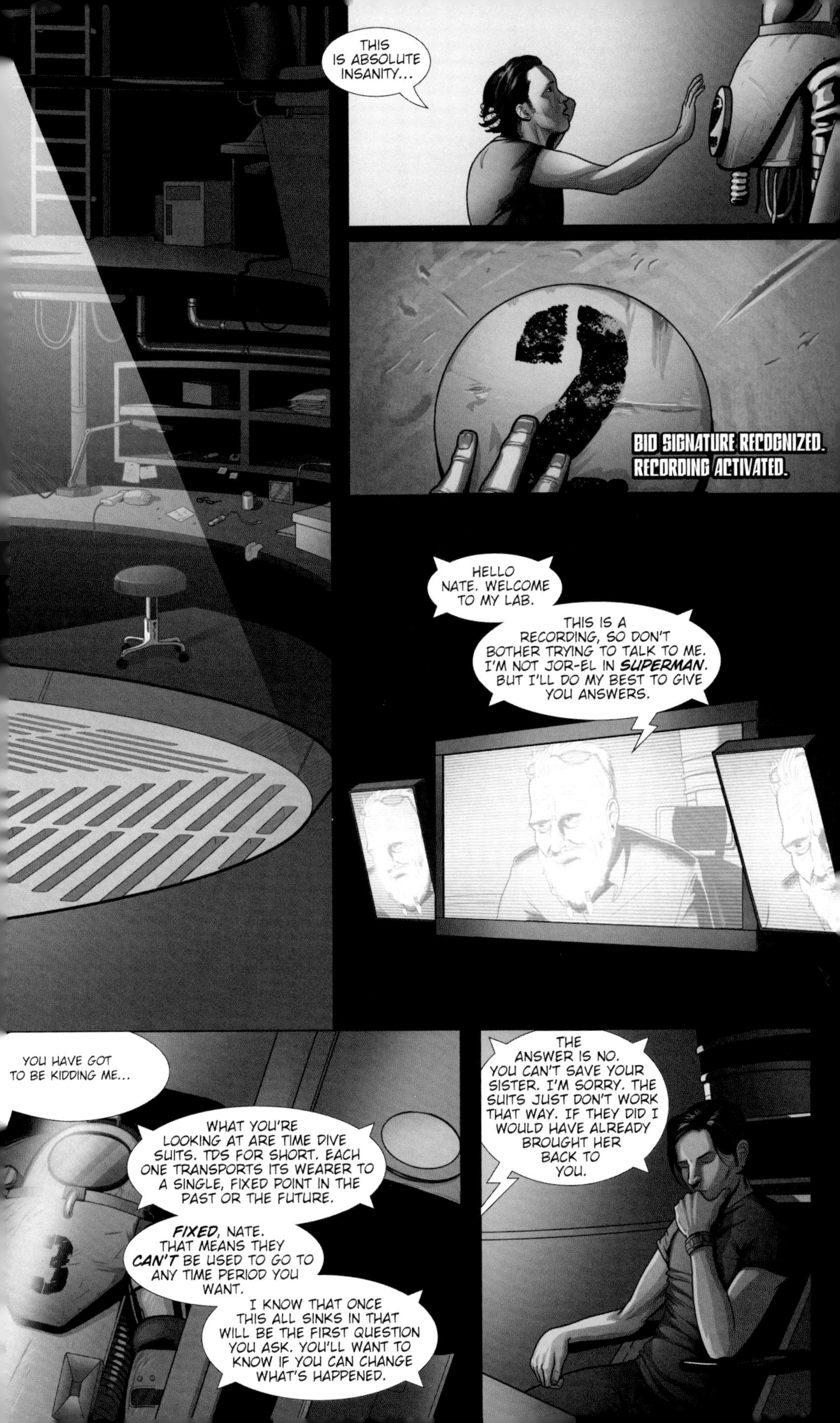
THIS IS ABSOLUTE INSANITY...
BIO SIGNATURE RECOGNIZED. RECORDING ACTIVATED.
HELLO NATE. WELCOME TO MY LAB.
THIS IS A RECORDING, SO DON'T BOTHER TRYING TO TALK TO ME. I'M NOT JOR-EL IN SUPERMAN. BUT I'LL DO MY BEST TO GIVE YOU ANSWERS.
YOU HAVE GOT TO BE KIDDING ME...
WHAT YOU'RE LOOKING AT ARE TIME DIVE SUITS. TDS FOR SHORT. EACH ONE TRANSPORTS ITS WEARER TO A SINGLE, FIXED POINT IN THE PAST OR THE FUTURE.
FIXED, NATE. THAT MEANS THEY CAN'T BE USED TO GO TO ANY TIME PERIOD YOU WANT.
I KNOW THAT ONCE THIS ALL SINKS IN THAT WILL BE THE FIRST QUESTION YOU ASK. YOU'LL WANT TO KNOW IF YOU CAN CHANGE WHAT'S HAPPENED.
THE ANSWER IS NO. YOU CAN'T SAVE YOUR SISTER. I'M SORRY. THE SUITS JUST DON'T WORK THAT WAY. IF THEY DID I WOULD HAVE ALREADY BROUGHT HER BACK TO YOU.
3

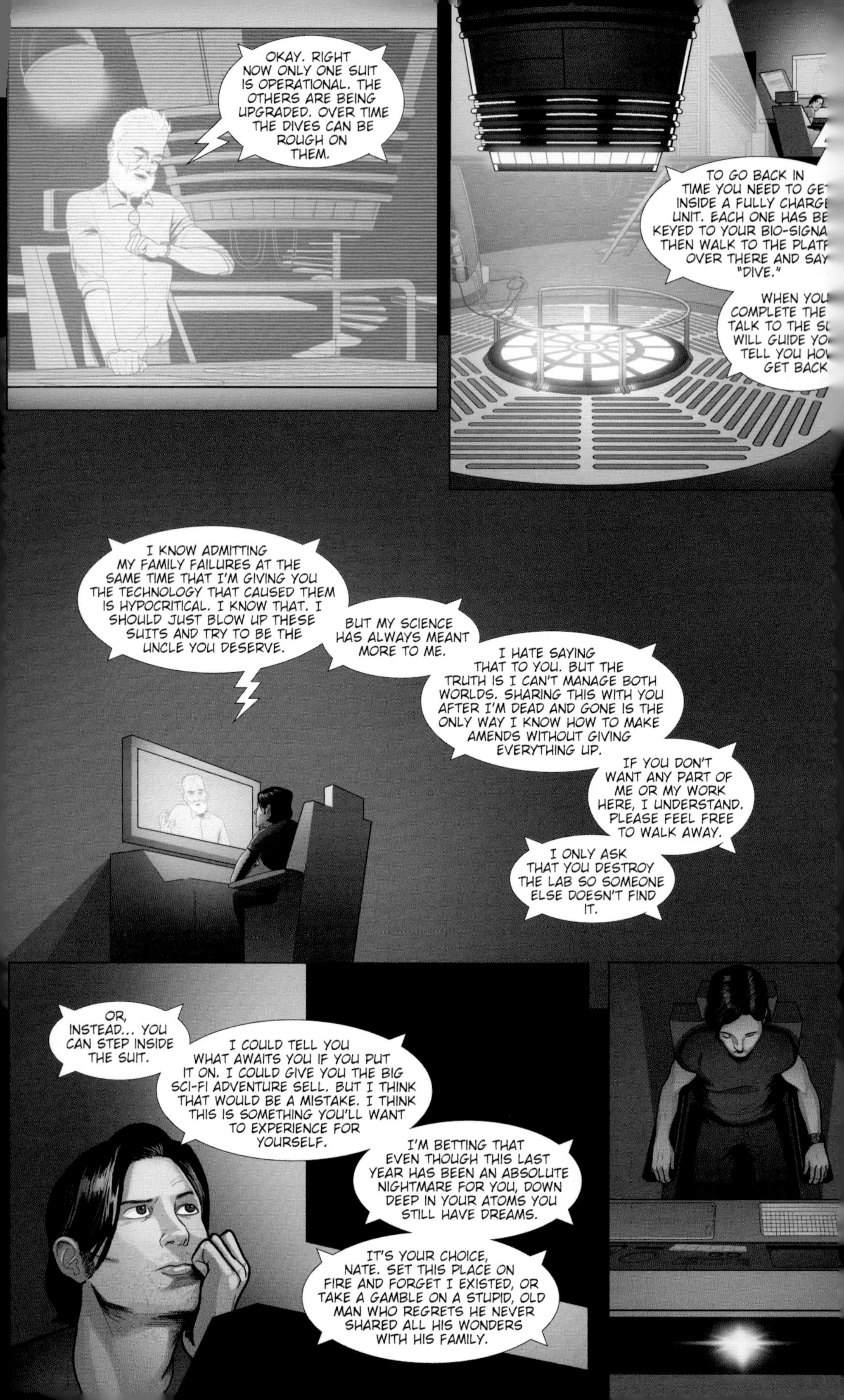
OKAY. RIGHT NOW ONLY ONE SUIT IS OPERATIONAL. THE OTHERS ARE BEING UPGRADED. OVER TIME THE DIVES CAN BE ROUGH ON THEM.
TO GO BACK IN TIME YOU NEED TO GE INSIDE A FULLY CHARG UNIT. EACH ONE HAS BE KEYED TO YOUR BIO-SIGNA THEN WALK TO THE PLAT OVER THERE AND SAY "DIVE."
WHEN YOU COMPLETE THE TALK TO THE S WILL GUIDE YO TELL YOU HOW GET BACK
I KNOW ADMITTING MY FAMILY FAILURES AT THE SAME TIME THAT I'M GIVING YOU THE TECHNOLOGY THAT CAUSED THEM IS HYPOCRITICAL. I KNOW THAT. I SHOULD JUST BLOW UP THESE SUITS AND TRY TO BE THE UNCLE YOU DESERVE.
BUT MY SCIENCE HAS ALWAYS MEANT MORE TO ME.
I HATE SAYING THAT TO YOU. BUT THE TRUTH IS I CAN'T MANAGE BOTH WORLDS. SHARING THIS WITH YOU AFTER I'M DEAD AND GONE IS THE ONLY WAY I KNOW HOW TO MAKE AMENDS WITHOUT GIVING EVERYTHING UP.
IF YOU DON'T WANT ANY PART OF ME OR MY WORK HERE, I UNDERSTAND. PLEASE FEEL FREE TO WALK AWAY.
I ONLY ASK THAT YOU DESTROY THE LAB SO SOMEONE ELSE DOESN'T FIND IT.
OR, INSTEAD... YOU CAN STEP INSIDE THE SUIT.
I COULD TELL YOU WHAT AWAITS YOU IF YOU PUT IT ON. I COULD GIVE YOU THE BIG SCI-FI ADVENTURE SELL. BUT I THINK THAT WOULD BE A MISTAKE. I THINK THIS IS SOMETHING YOU'LL WANT TO EXPERIENCE FOR YOURSELF.
I'M BETTING THAT EVEN THOUGH THIS LAST YEAR HAS BEEN AN ABSOLUTE NIGHTMARE FOR YOU, DOWN DEEP IN YOUR ATOMS YOU STILL HAVE DREAMS.
IT'S YOUR CHOICE, NATE. SET THIS PLACE ON FIRE AND FORGET I EXISTED, OR TAKE A GAMBLE ON A STUPID, OLD MAN WHO REGRETS HE NEVER SHARED ALL HIS WONDERS WITH HIS FAMILY.

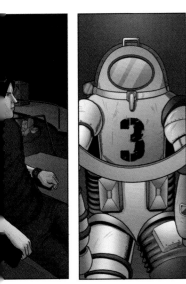

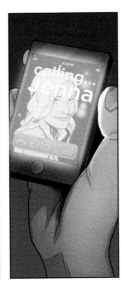

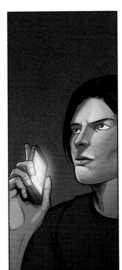

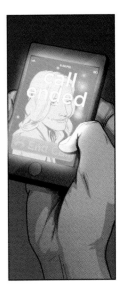

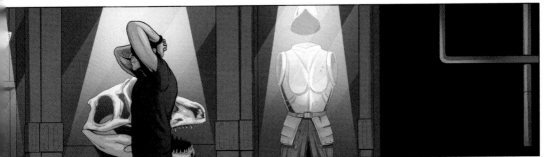

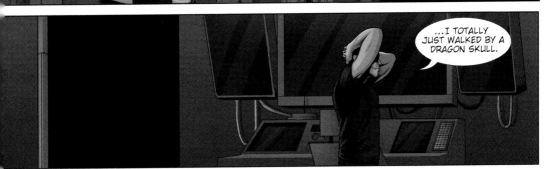

calling... Jenna
call ended
...I TOTALLY JUST WALKED BY A DRAGON SKULL.
Look, Nate! I'm flying to Saturn!

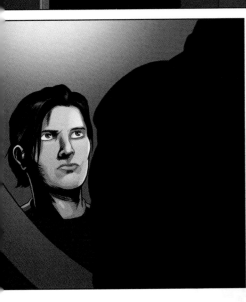

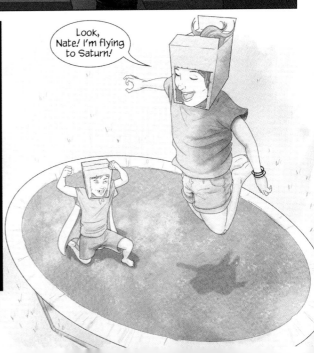

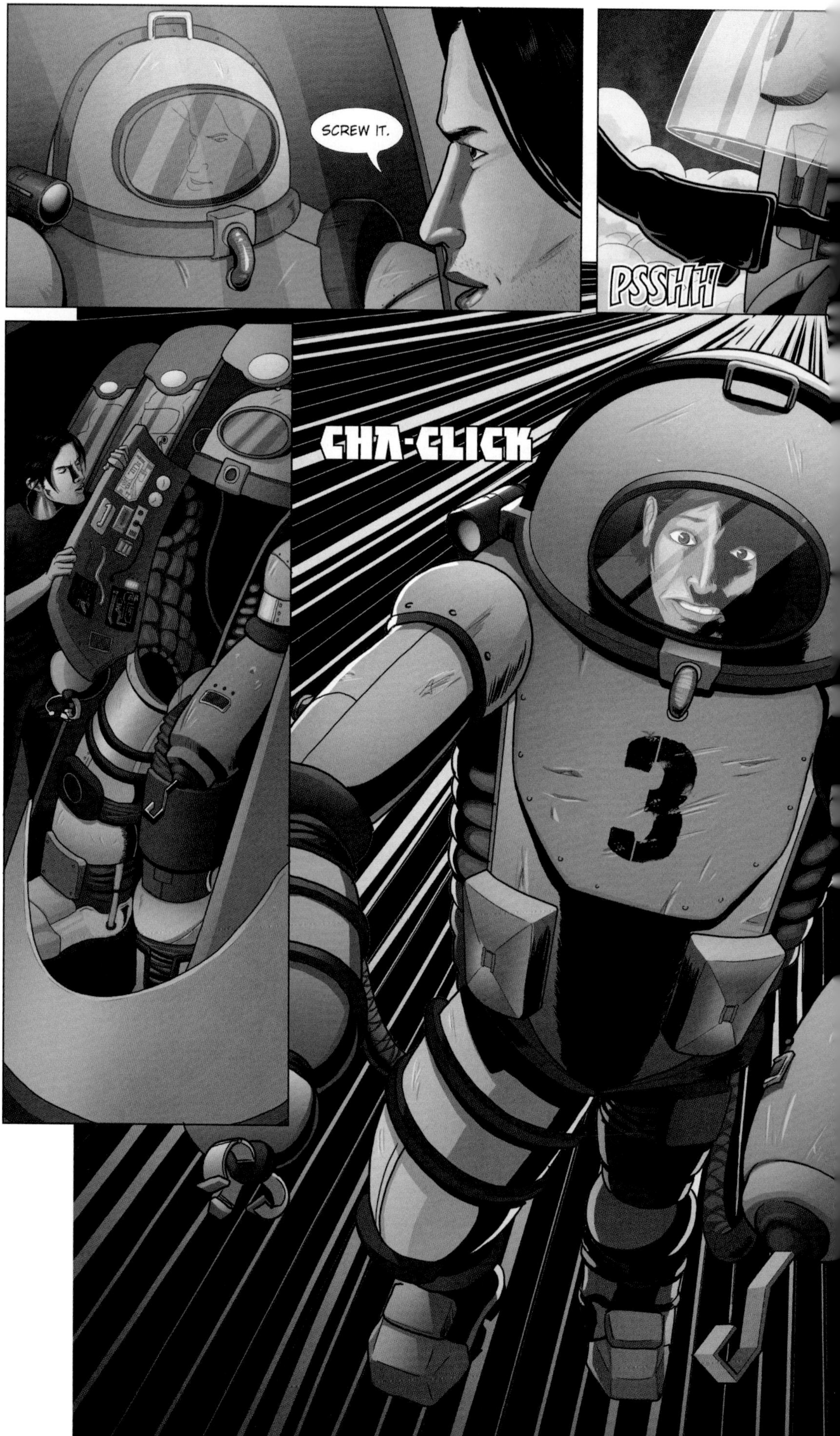
SCREW IT.
PSSHH
CHA-CLICK
3

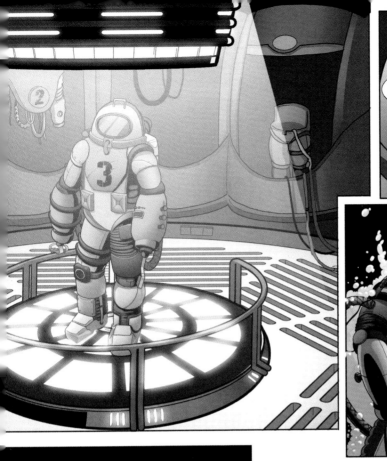

DIVE?

FAWOOOOSH

VRRRRRVVVV

NATE WILLNER OFTEN CLOSES HIS EYES AND TRIES TO REMEMBER HOW MUCH HE LOVED HIS OLD LIFE.

HE HAD A CHEF APPRENTICESHIP AT ONE OF THE BEST RESTAURANTS IN NEW YORK. HE HAD THE PERFECT GIRL. A SISTER HE ADORED. GREAT FRIENDS. HE COULD SEE HIS FAVORITE BANDS PLAY WHENEVER HE WANTED.

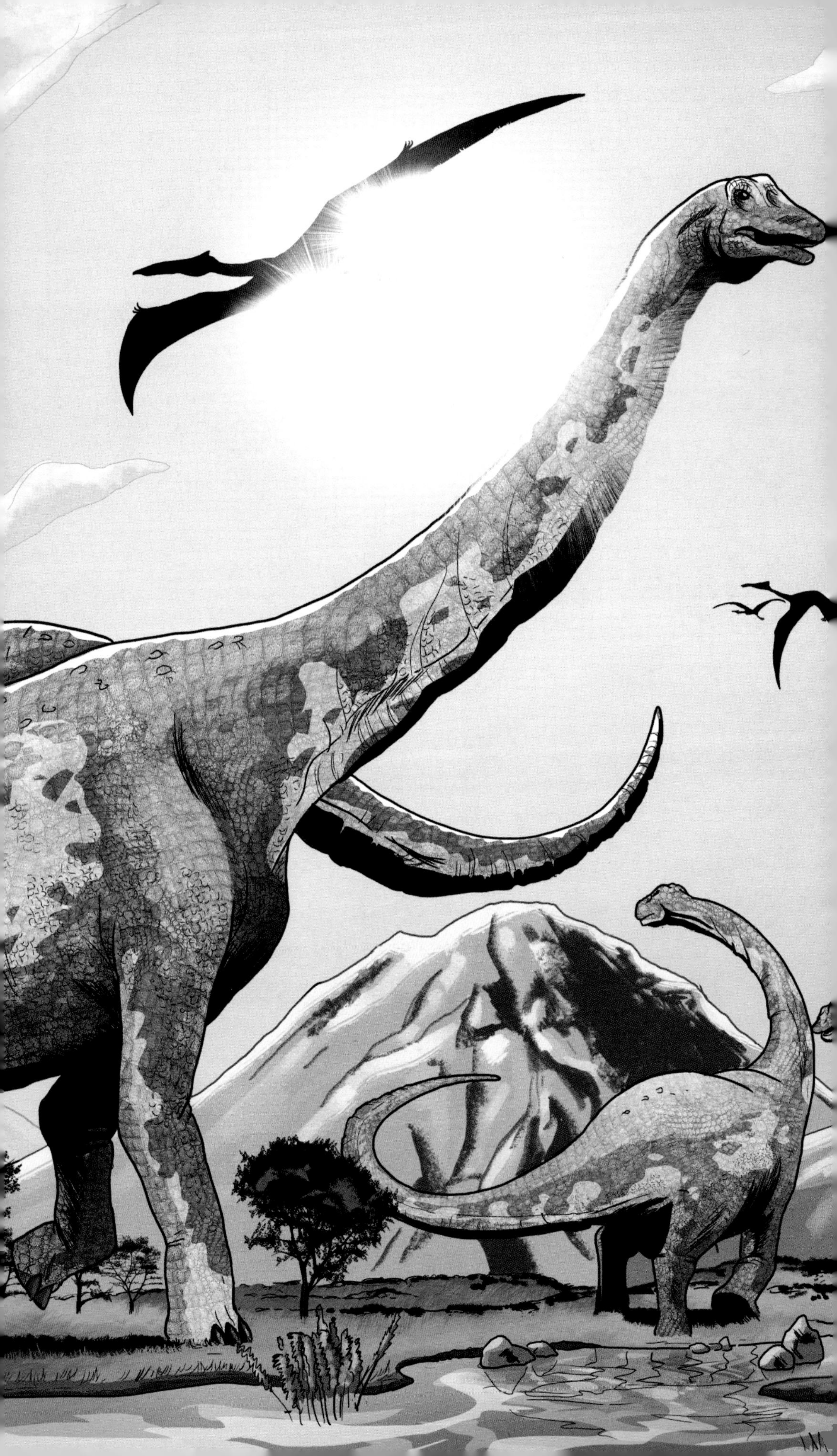

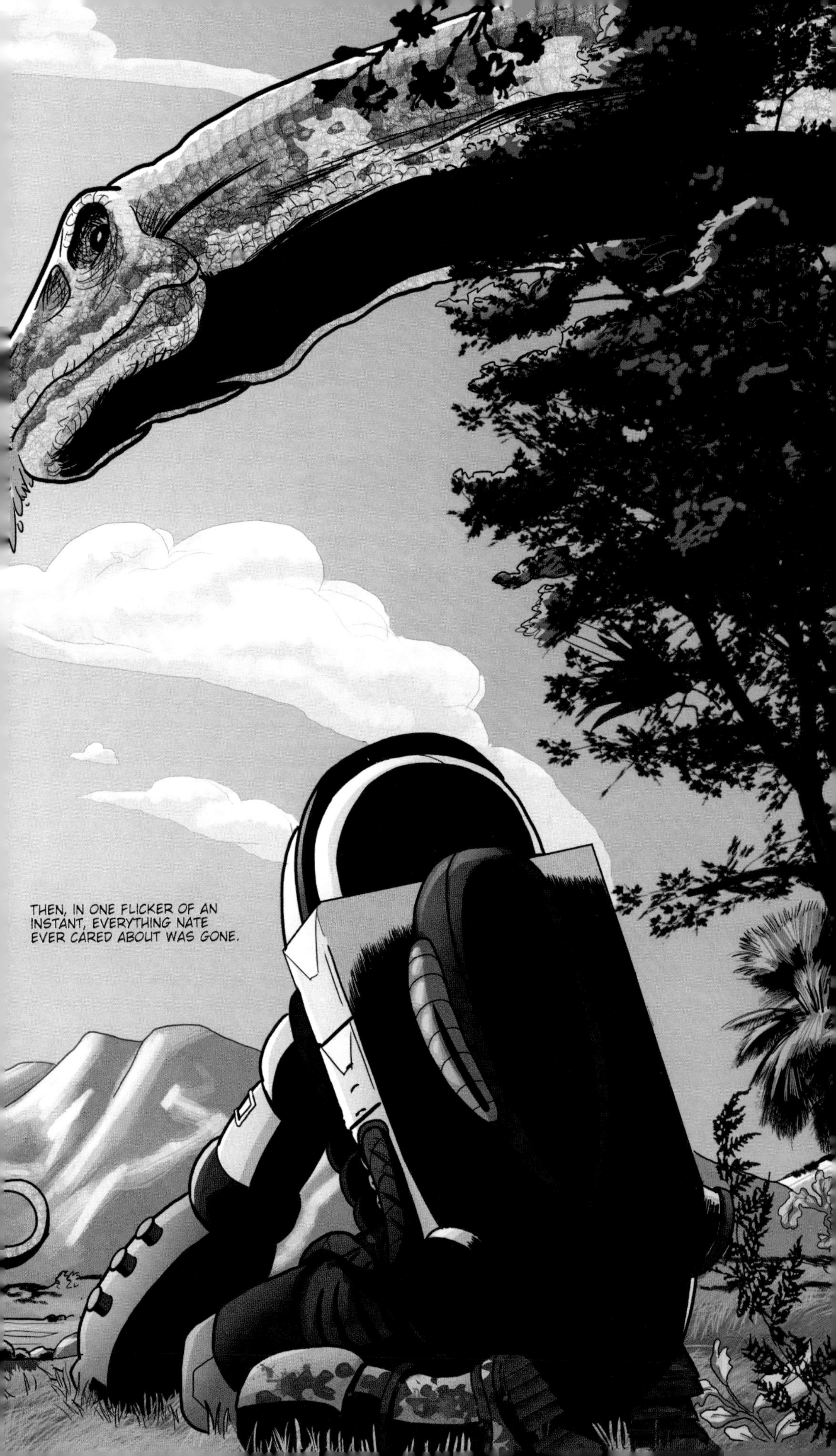
THEN, IN ONE FLICKER OF AN INSTANT, EVERYTHING NATE EVER CARED ABOUT WAS GONE.

THIS CAN'T BE REAL...
DON'T GET EATEN! DON'T GET EATEN!
CLANK
CLANK
KLINK
TNNG
KA-THUD

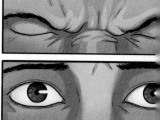

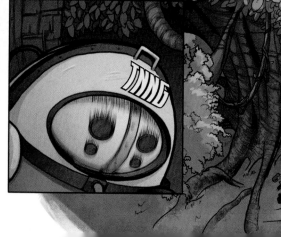

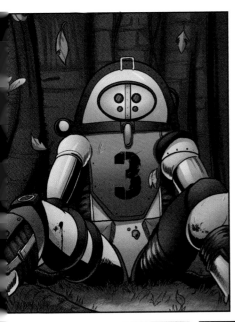

SHINK

WHAT THE...

///T INTEGRITY 99%.
) DANGER DETECTED.

NO
ER DETECTED?
E ARE FREAKIN'
SAURS! DANGER
S DETECTED!

PLEASE RESTATE COMMAND.

HOW ABOUT
YOU GET ME THE
HELL OUT OF HERE,
GOOGLE TALK!

PLEASE RESTATE COMMAND.

HOME!
TAKE. ME.
HOME!

"HOME" KEYWORD RECOGNIZED.
TDS POWER AT 13%. RETURN
DIVE IN 6.3 HOURS.

SIX
RS! HOW AM I
DSED TO SURVIVE
ASSIC PARK FOR
SIX HOURS!?

ATION CORRECTION:
CRETACEOUS PERIOD.
OXIMATELY 70 MILLION
YEARS AGO.

PERFECT.
I'M TWO SECONDS
AWAY FROM BECOMING A
VELOCIRAPTOR TREAT AND
MY ROBOT SUIT IS A
SASSY ASSHOLE.

CORRECTION: DINOSAUR CLASSIFICATION:
GENUS: ALAMOSAURUS.
SPECIES TYPE: ALAMOSAURUS SANJUANENSIS.

THAT'S
IT. YOUR NAME IS
SASSHOLE FROM
NOW ON.

OKAY, THIS IS NOT FUN.
HEY, IS THERE A GOOD PLACE TO HIDE WHILE YOU CHARGE UP? WHERE SHOULD I GO?
"GO" KEYWORD RECOGNIZED. TRANSLATION: DESTINATION. RECOMMENDED DESTINATION: RIVER. 1.3 MILES SOUTH.
RIVER? AH, RIGHT. I BET I NEED TO BE UNDERWATER TO DIVE BACK.
ER... PLEASE CONFIRM.. IS WATER REQUIRED TO GET HOME?
TRANSFER MEDIUM NECE
WATER REQUIRED FOR
GOT IT. AND WHAT ABOUT THESE THINGS? I CAN MOVE THE FINGER CLAW, BUT DOES THIS HOOK DO ANYTHING?
WUMP
WUMP
WUMP
POOM
FWIP
OH. THIS CANNOT BE GOOD.
GAAHHH!
GRAPPLING HOOK ACTIVATED.
I REALLY, REALLY SHOU HAVE SET YO ON FIRE.

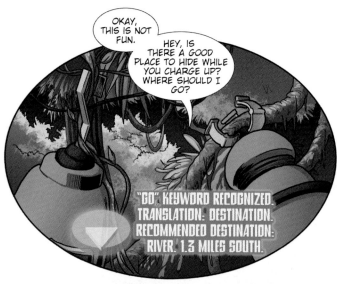

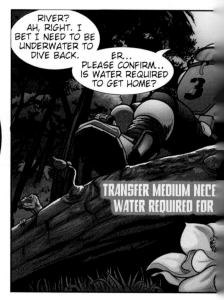

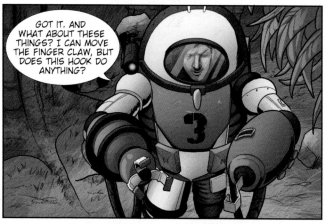

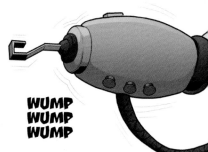

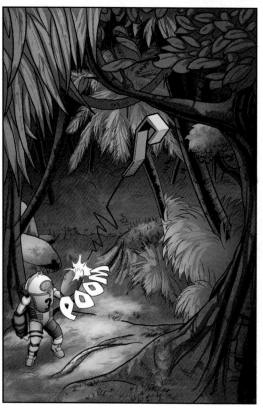

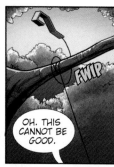

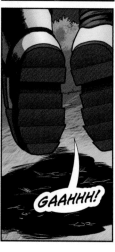

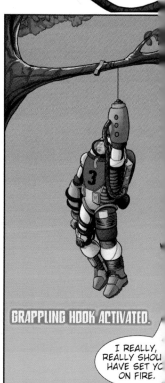

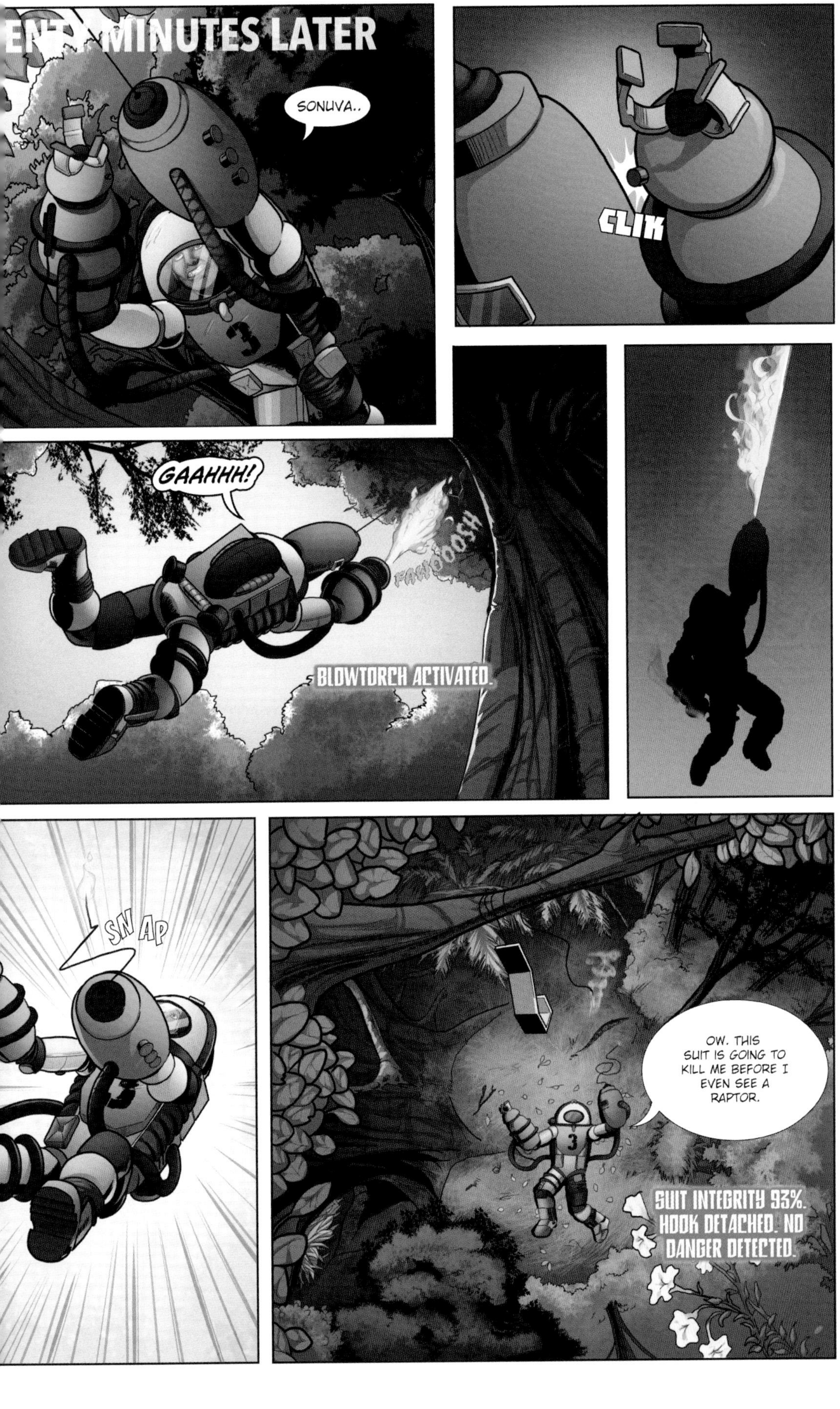
ENTY MINUTES LATER
SONUVA..
CLIK
GAAHHH!
FAWOOOOSH
BLOWTORCH ACTIVATED.
SNAP
OW. THIS SUIT IS GOING TO KILL ME BEFORE I EVEN SEE A RAPTOR.
SUIT INTEGRITY 93%. HOOK DETACHED. NO DANGER DETECTED.

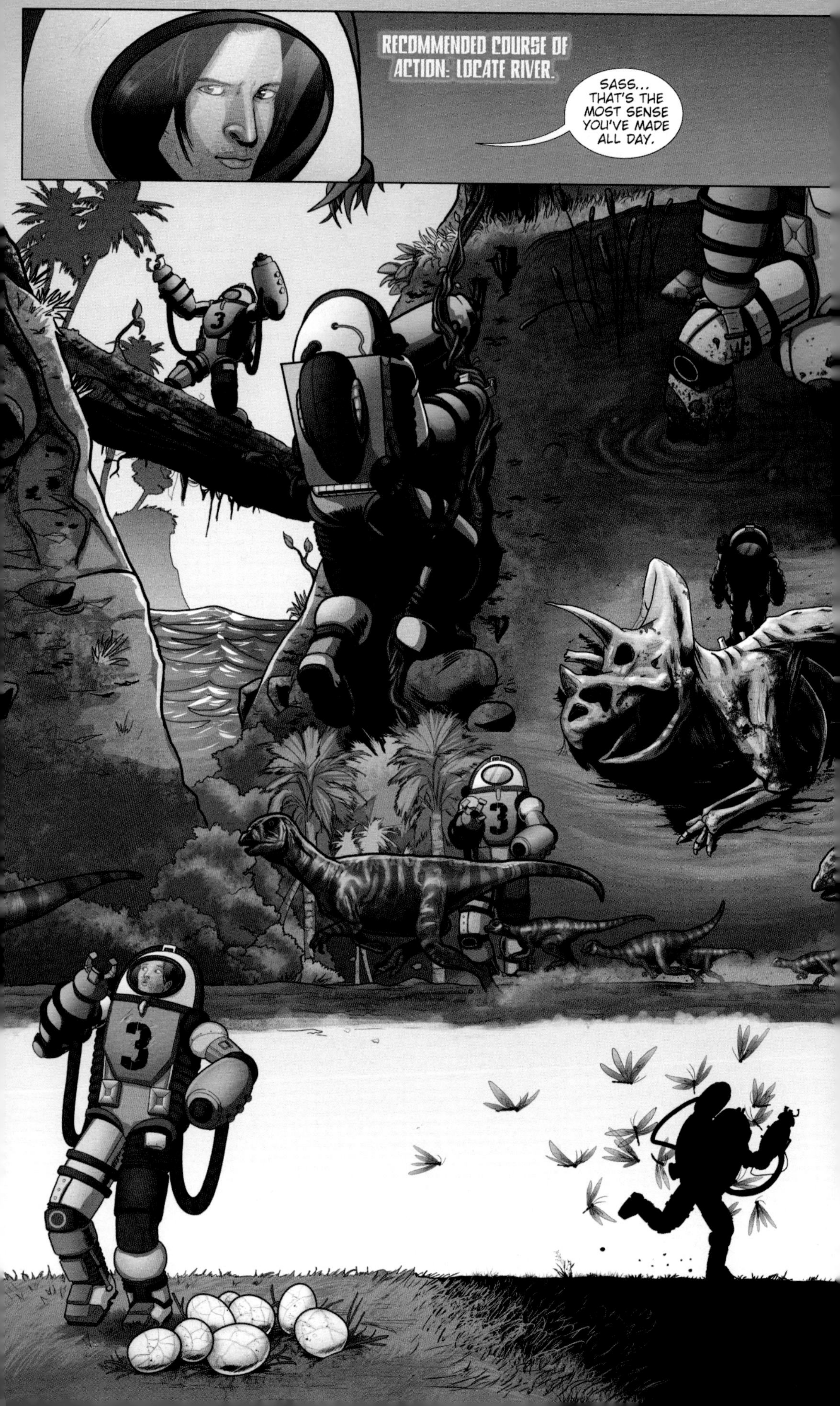
RECOMMENDED COURSE OF ACTION: LOCATE RIVER.
SASS... THAT'S THE MOST SENSE YOU'VE MADE ALL DAY.

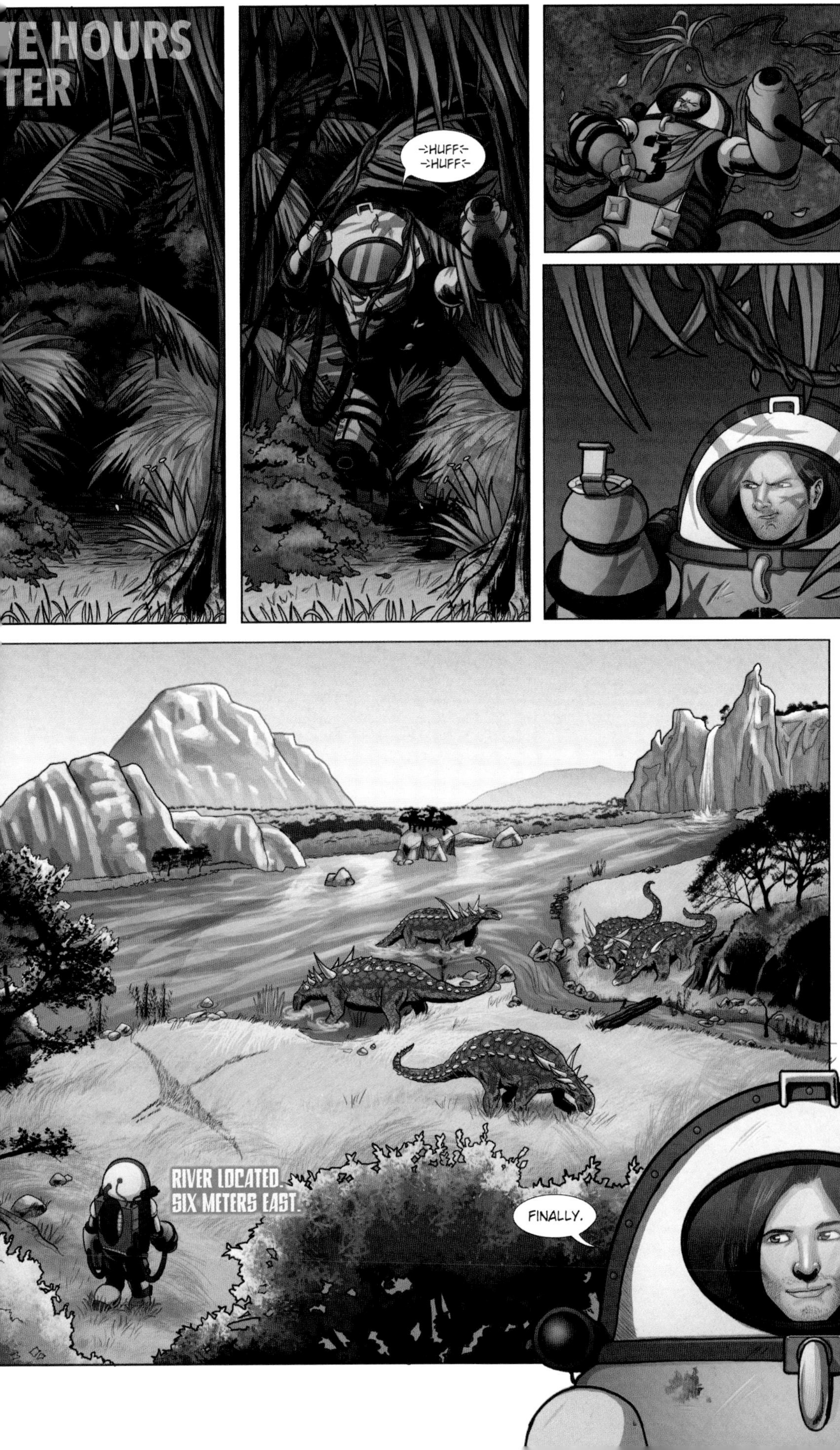
VE HOURS
TER
HUFF
HUFF
RIVER LOCATED.
SIX METERS EAST.
FINALLY.

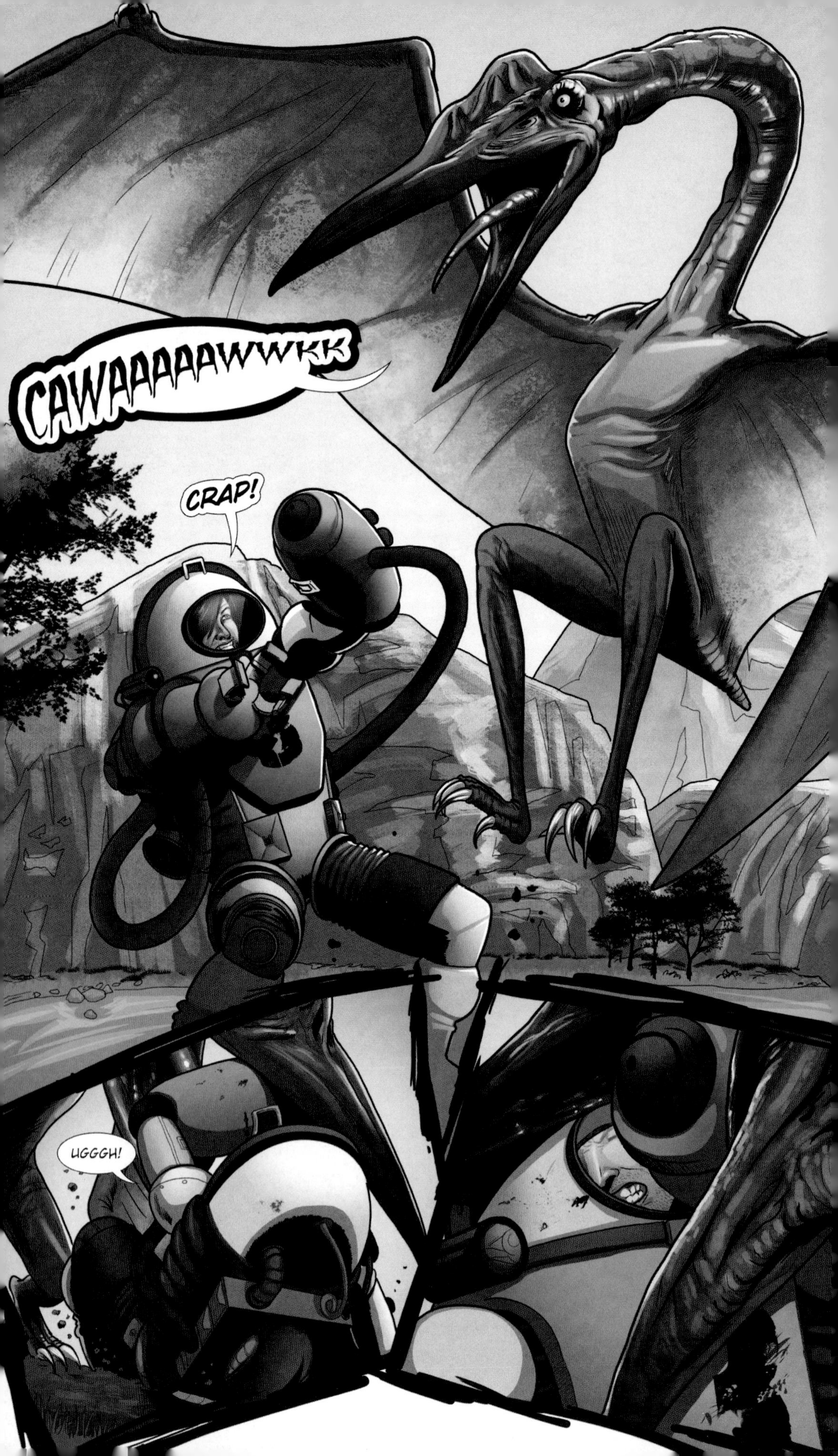
CAWAAAAAWWKK
CRAP!
UGGGH!

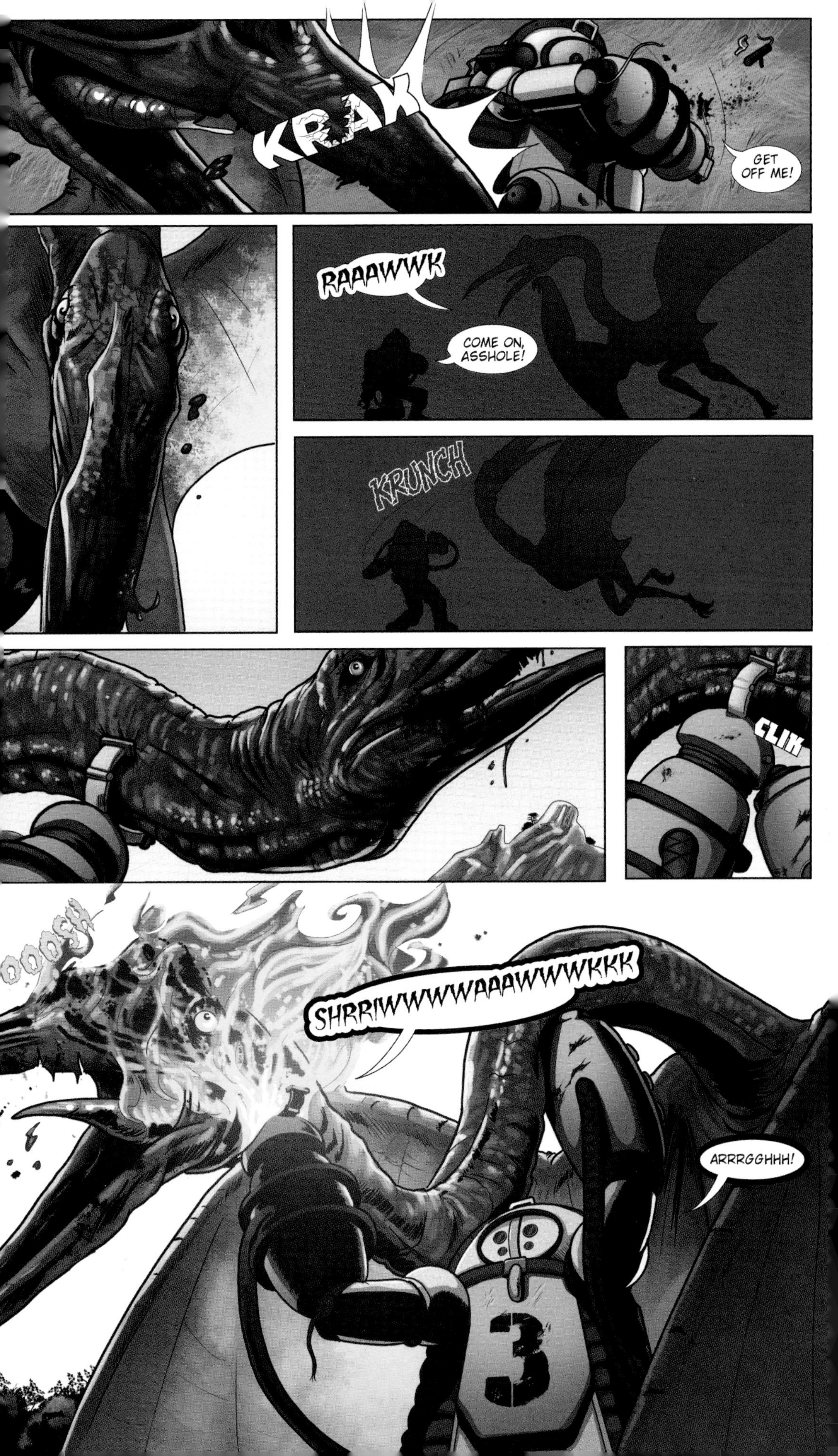
KRAK
GET OFF ME!
RAAAWWK
COME ON, ASSHOLE!
KRUNCH
CLIK
OOOSH
SHRRIWWWWAAAWWWKKK
ARRRGGHHH!

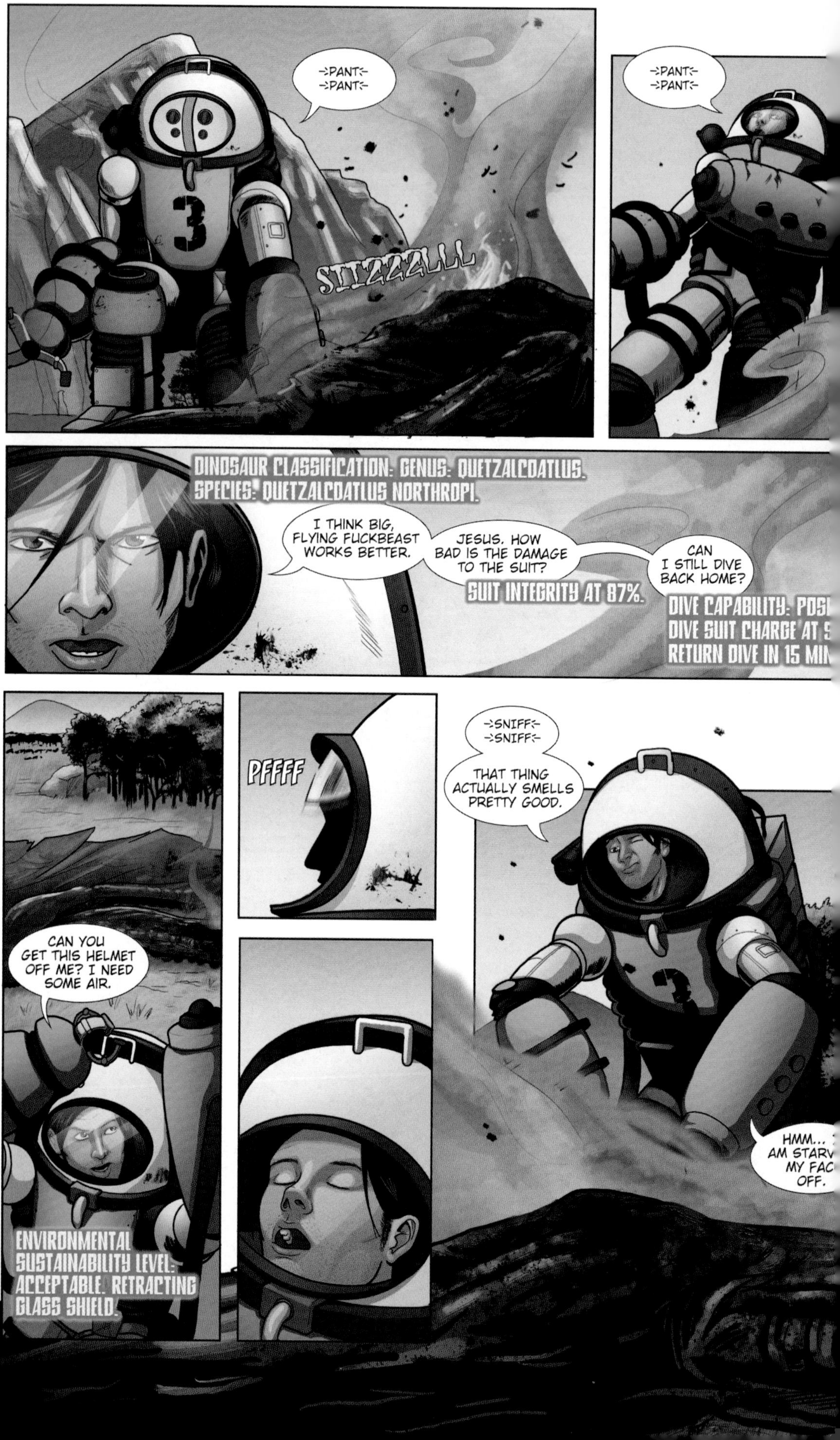

-PANT-
-PANT-
SIIZZZLLL
-PANT-
-PANT-
DINOSAUR CLASSIFICATION: GENUS: QUETZALCOATLUS. SPECIES: QUETZALCOATLUS NORTHROPI.
I THINK BIG, FLYING FUCKBEAST WORKS BETTER.
JESUS. HOW BAD IS THE DAMAGE TO THE SUIT?
SUIT INTEGRITY AT 87%.
CAN I STILL DIVE BACK HOME?
DIVE CAPABILITY: POS
DIVE SUIT CHARGE AT
RETURN DIVE IN 15 MI
CAN YOU GET THIS HELMET OFF ME? I NEED SOME AIR.
ENVIRONMENTAL SUSTAINABILITY LEVEL: ACCEPTABLE. RETRACTING GLASS SHIELD.
PFFFF
-SNIFF-
-SNIFF-
THAT THING ACTUALLY SMELLS PRETTY GOOD.
HMM... AM STARV MY FAC OFF.

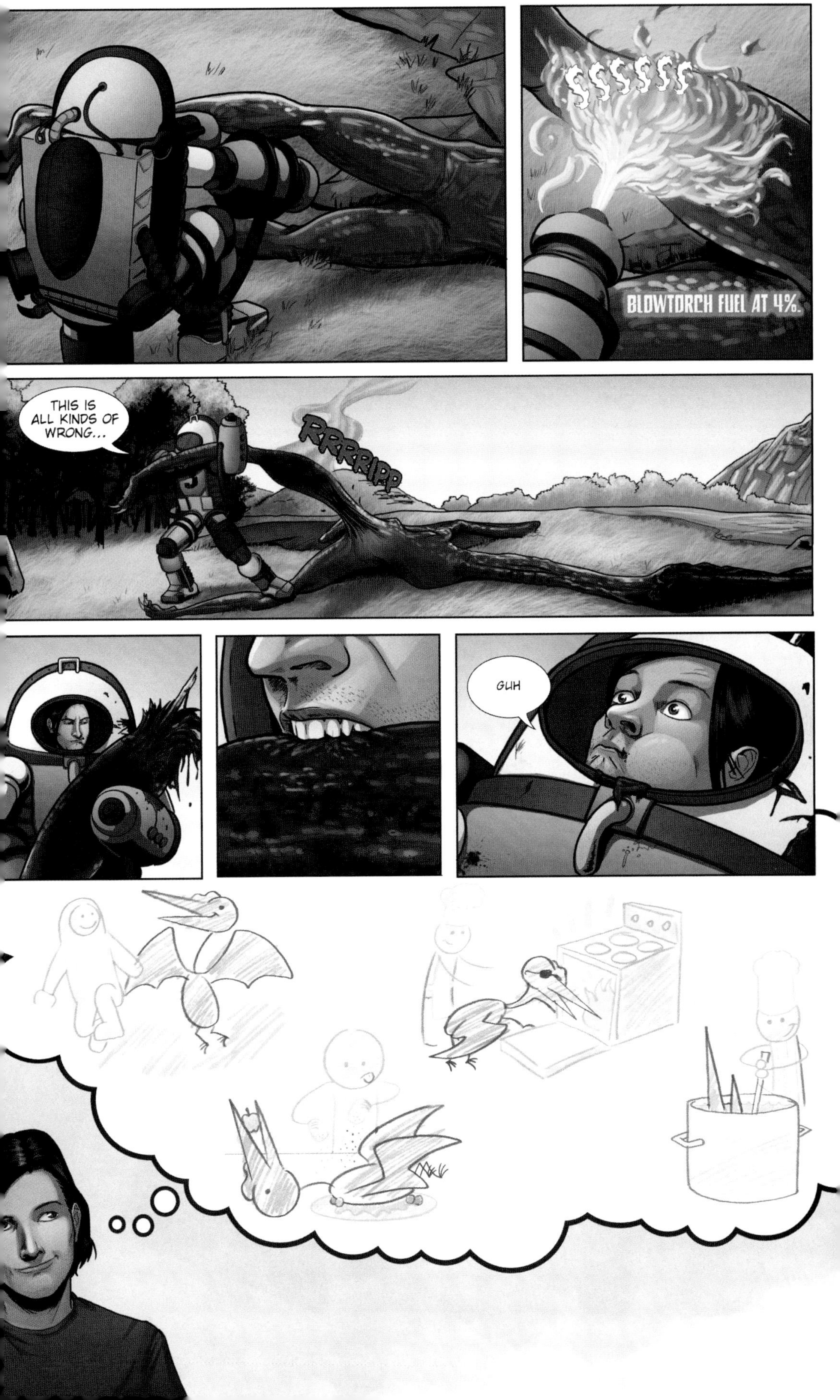
SSSSSS
BLOWTORCH FUEL AT 4%.
THIS IS ALL KINDS OF WRONG...
RRRRRIPP
GUH

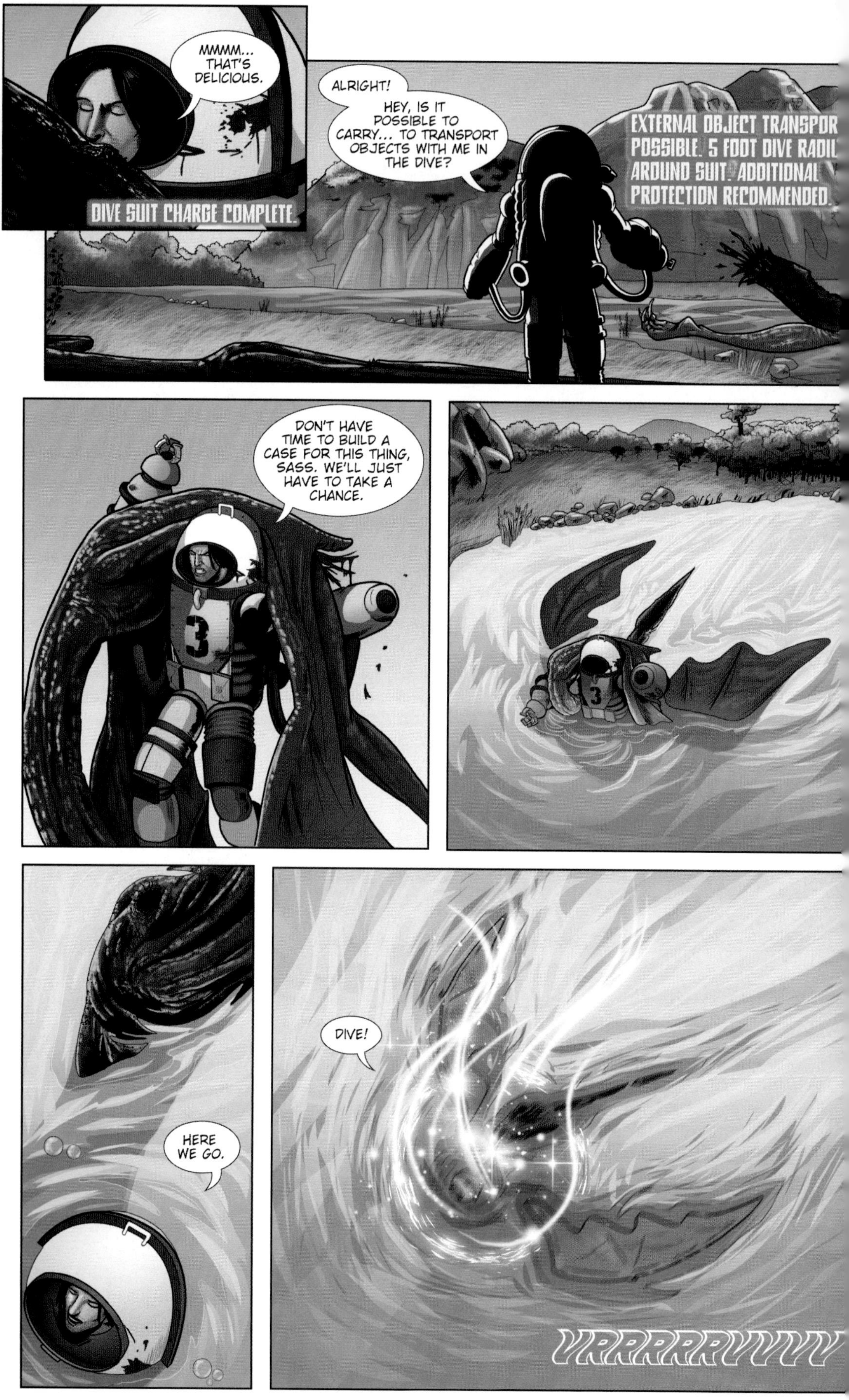
MMMM... THAT'S DELICIOUS.
DIVE SUIT CHARGE COMPLETE.
ALRIGHT!
HEY, IS IT POSSIBLE TO CARRY... TO TRANSPORT OBJECTS WITH ME IN THE DIVE?
EXTERNAL OBJECT TRANSPOR POSSIBLE. 5 FOOT DIVE RADIU AROUND SUIT. ADDITIONAL PROTECTION RECOMMENDED.
DON'T HAVE TIME TO BUILD A CASE FOR THIS THING, SASS. WE'LL JUST HAVE TO TAKE A CHANCE.
HERE WE GO.
DIVE!
VRRRRRVVVV

MAN, YOU REALLY WEREN'T KIDDING ABOUT THAT RADIUS.

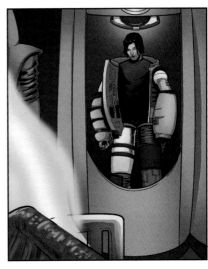

TO THE KITCHEN WITH YOU.

NNNNUGGHHH!

-:HUFF:-
-:HUFF:-

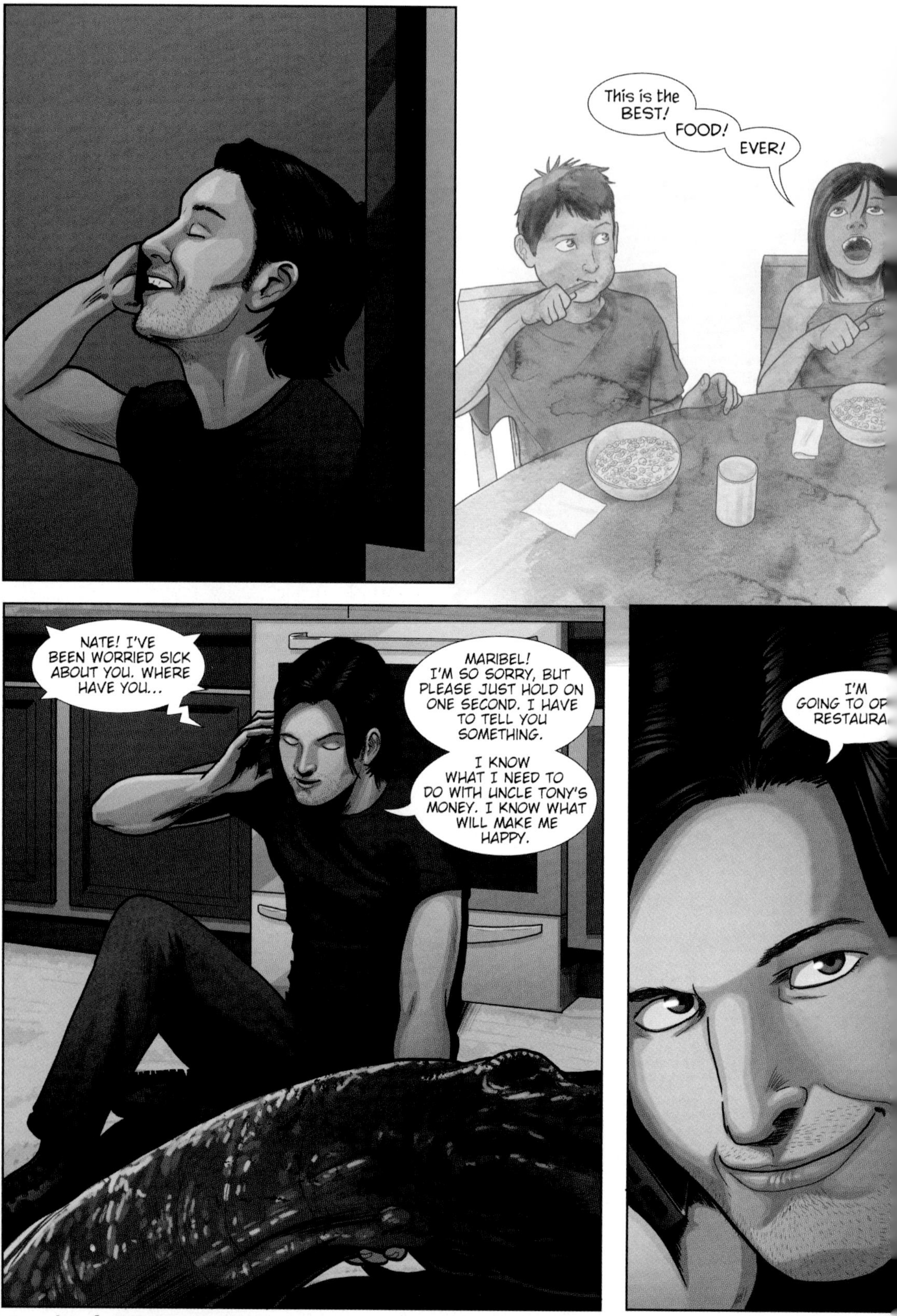
This is the BEST! FOOD! EVER!
NATE! I'VE BEEN WORRIED SICK ABOUT YOU. WHERE HAVE YOU...
MARIBEL! I'M SO SORRY, BUT PLEASE JUST HOLD ON ONE SECOND. I HAVE TO TELL YOU SOMETHING.
I KNOW WHAT I NEED TO DO WITH UNCLE TONY'S MONEY. I KNOW WHAT WILL MAKE ME HAPPY.
I'M GOING TO OP
RESTAURA

End of **CHAPTER 1**
ALL THINGS PASS WITH TIME

Writer **MARKISAN NASO**
Artist & Letterer **JASON MUHR**
Colorist **ANDREI TABACARU**

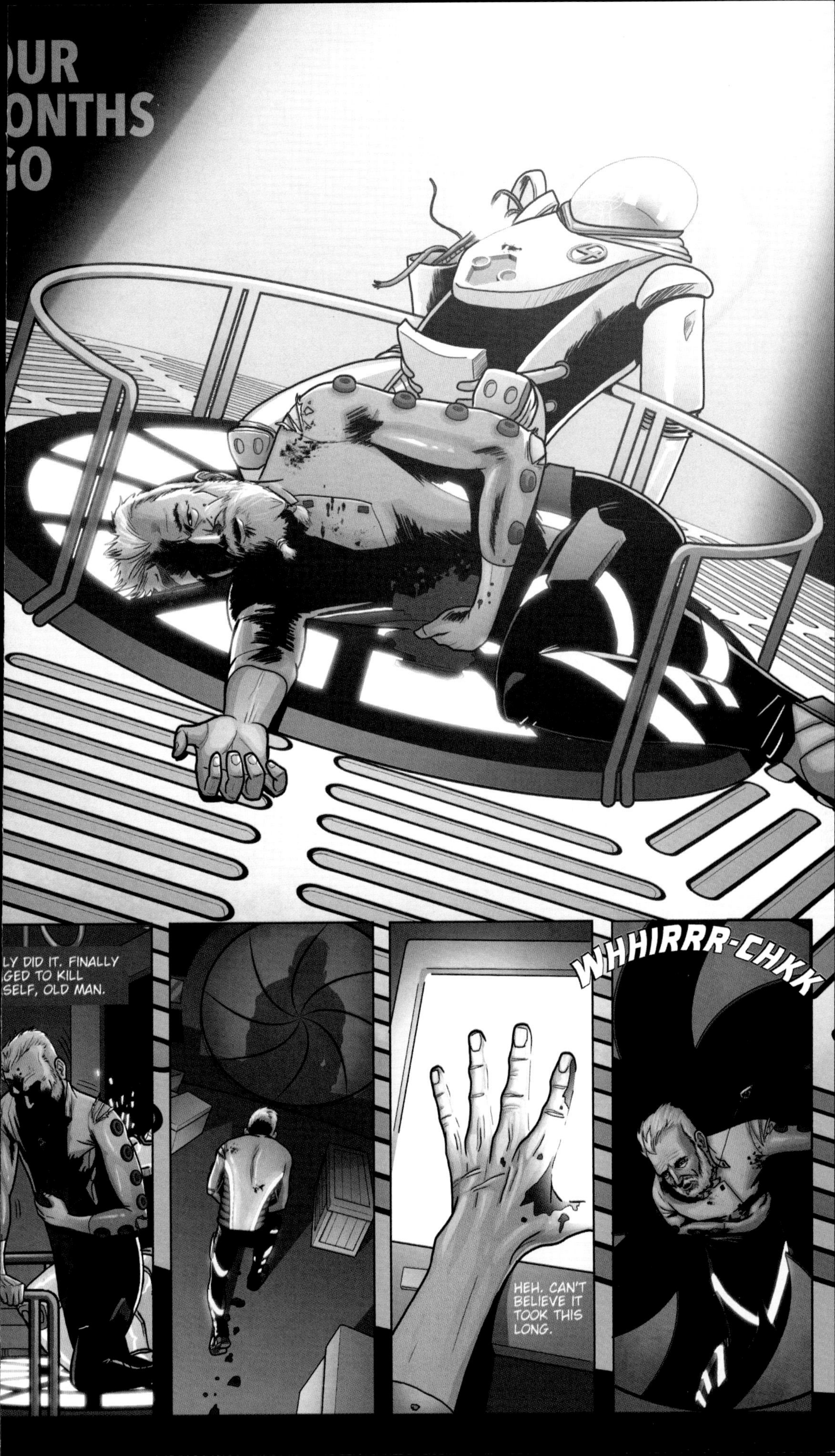
OUR
ONTHS
GO
LY DID IT. FINALLY
GED TO KILL
SELF, OLD MAN.
WHHIRRR-CHKK
HEH. CAN'T BELIEVE IT TOOK THIS LONG.

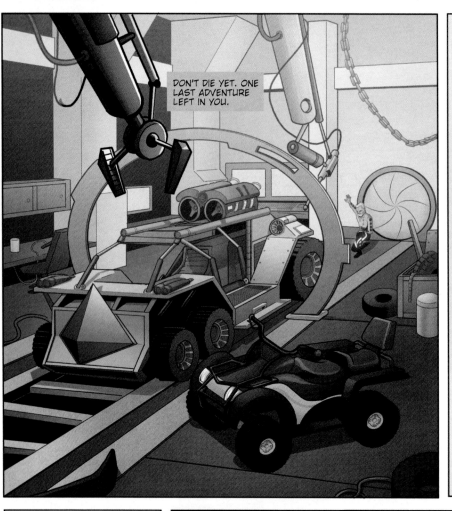

DON'T DIE YET. ONE LAST ADVENTURE LEFT IN YOU.

MOVE DA...
MOV...

BBRRRMM

VRRROOMM

SKAAREEECH

PLEASE...
STAY AWAKE.
STAY AW...

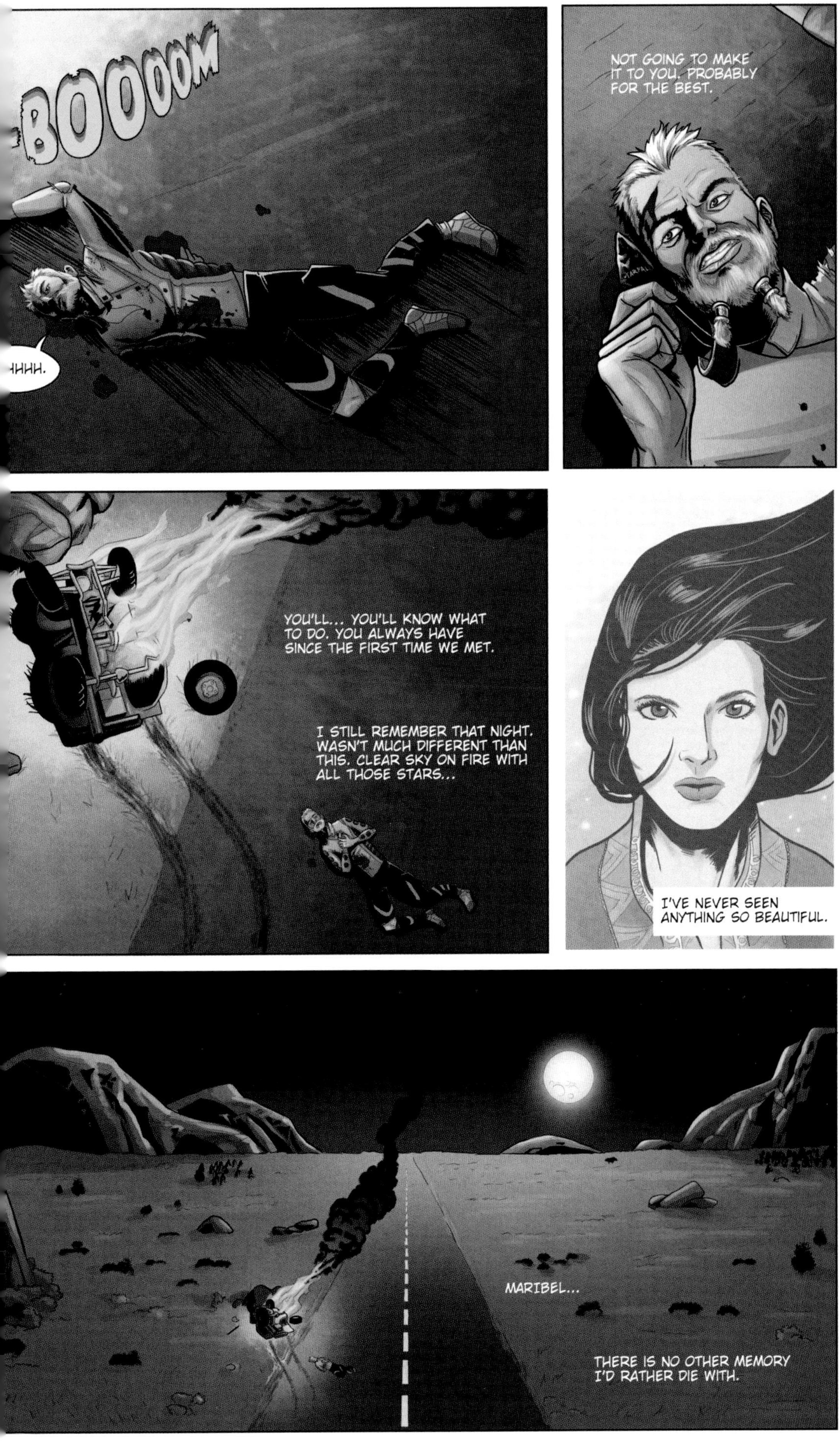
BOOOOM
HHHH.
NOT GOING TO MAKE IT TO YOU. PROBABLY FOR THE BEST.
YOU'LL... YOU'LL KNOW WHAT TO DO. YOU ALWAYS HAVE SINCE THE FIRST TIME WE MET.
I STILL REMEMBER THAT NIGHT. WASN'T MUCH DIFFERENT THAN THIS. CLEAR SKY ON FIRE WITH ALL THOSE STARS...
I'VE NEVER SEEN ANYTHING SO BEAUTIFUL.
MARIBEL...
THERE IS NO OTHER MEMORY I'D RATHER DIE WITH.

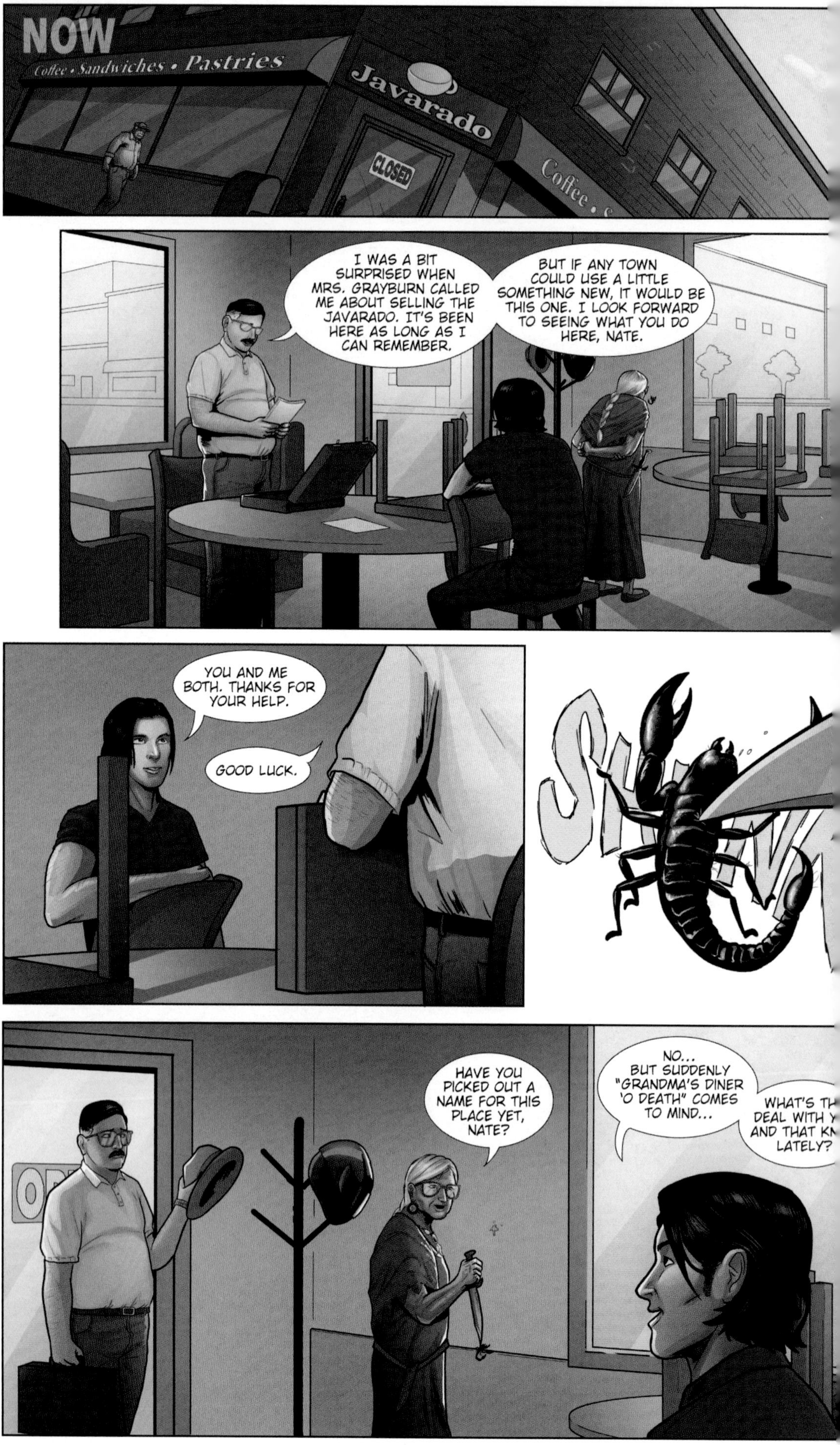
NOW
Coffee • Sandwiches • Pastries
Javarado
CLOSED
I WAS A BIT SURPRISED WHEN MRS. GRAYBURN CALLED ME ABOUT SELLING THE JAVARADO. IT'S BEEN HERE AS LONG AS I CAN REMEMBER.
BUT IF ANY TOWN COULD USE A LITTLE SOMETHING NEW, IT WOULD BE THIS ONE. I LOOK FORWARD TO SEEING WHAT YOU DO HERE, NATE.
YOU AND ME BOTH. THANKS FOR YOUR HELP.
GOOD LUCK.
HAVE YOU PICKED OUT A NAME FOR THIS PLACE YET, NATE?
NO... BUT SUDDENLY "GRANDMA'S DINER 'O DEATH" COMES TO MIND...
WHAT'S TH DEAL WITH Y AND THAT KN LATELY?

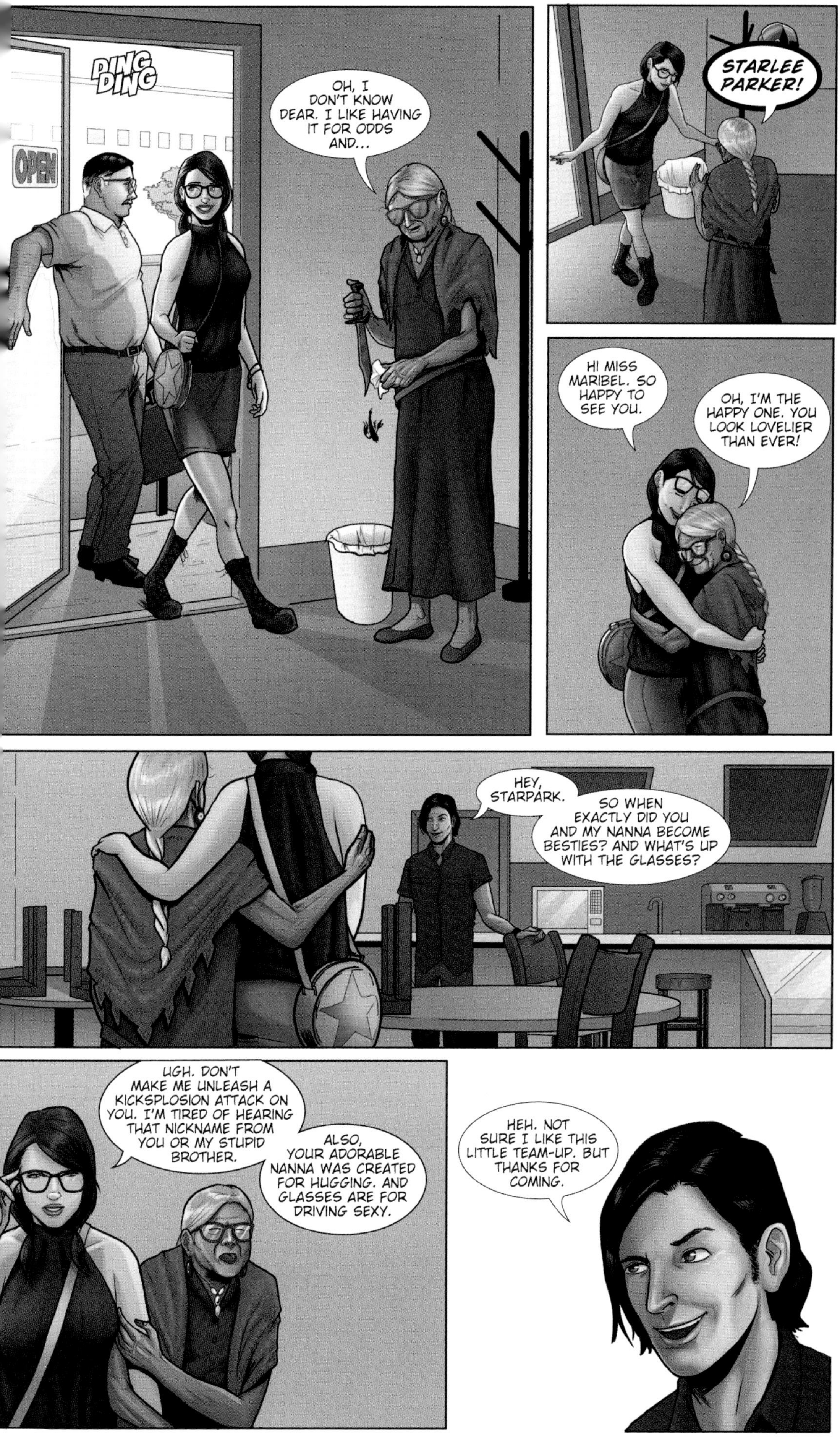
DING DING
OPEN
OH, I DON'T KNOW DEAR. I LIKE HAVING IT FOR ODDS AND...
STARLEE PARKER!
HI MISS MARIBEL. SO HAPPY TO SEE YOU.
OH, I'M THE HAPPY ONE. YOU LOOK LOVELIER THAN EVER!
HEY, STARPARK.
SO WHEN EXACTLY DID YOU AND MY NANNA BECOME BESTIES? AND WHAT'S UP WITH THE GLASSES?
UGH. DON'T MAKE ME UNLEASH A KICKSPLOSION ATTACK ON YOU. I'M TIRED OF HEARING THAT NICKNAME FROM YOU OR MY STUPID BROTHER.
ALSO, YOUR ADORABLE NANNA WAS CREATED FOR HUGGING. AND GLASSES ARE FOR DRIVING SEXY.
HEH. NOT SURE I LIKE THIS LITTLE TEAM-UP. BUT THANKS FOR COMING.

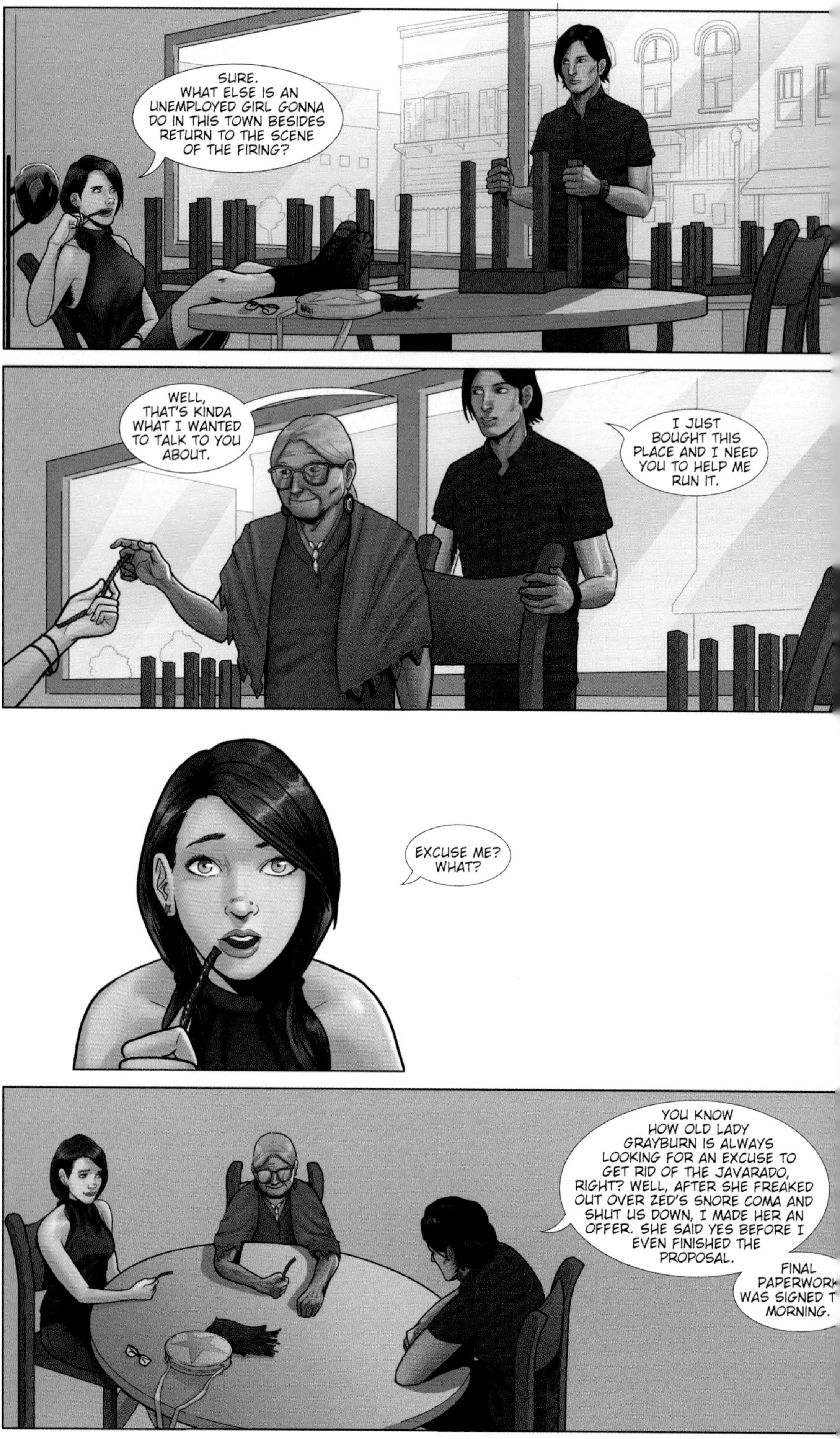
SURE. WHAT ELSE IS AN UNEMPLOYED GIRL GONNA DO IN THIS TOWN BESIDES RETURN TO THE SCENE OF THE FIRING?
WELL, THAT'S KINDA WHAT I WANTED TO TALK TO YOU ABOUT.
I JUST BOUGHT THIS PLACE AND I NEED YOU TO HELP ME RUN IT.
EXCUSE ME? WHAT?
YOU KNOW HOW OLD LADY GRAYBURN IS ALWAYS LOOKING FOR AN EXCUSE TO GET RID OF THE JAVARADO, RIGHT? WELL, AFTER SHE FREAKED OUT OVER ZED'S SNORE COMA AND SHUT US DOWN, I MADE HER AN OFFER. SHE SAID YES BEFORE I EVEN FINISHED THE PROPOSAL.
FINAL PAPERWORK WAS SIGNED T MORNING.

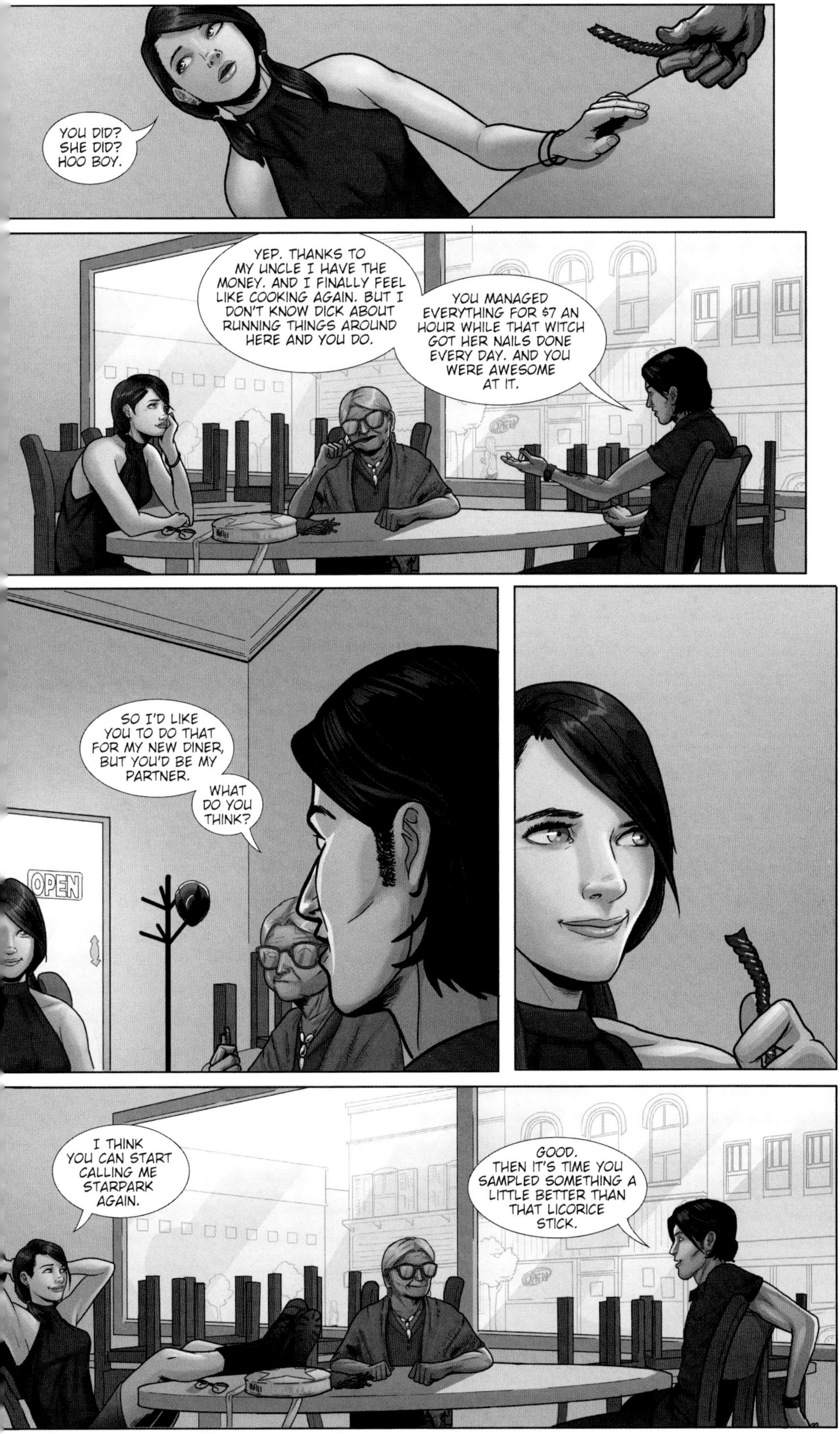
YOU DID? SHE DID? HOO BOY.
YEP. THANKS TO MY UNCLE I HAVE THE MONEY. AND I FINALLY FEEL LIKE COOKING AGAIN. BUT I DON'T KNOW DICK ABOUT RUNNING THINGS AROUND HERE AND YOU DO.
YOU MANAGED EVERYTHING FOR $7 AN HOUR WHILE THAT WITCH GOT HER NAILS DONE EVERY DAY. AND YOU WERE AWESOME AT IT.
OPEN
SO I'D LIKE YOU TO DO THAT FOR MY NEW DINER, BUT YOU'D BE MY PARTNER.
WHAT DO YOU THINK?
OPEN
I THINK YOU CAN START CALLING ME STARPARK AGAIN.
GOOD. THEN IT'S TIME YOU SAMPLED SOMETHING A LITTLE BETTER THAN THAT LICORICE STICK.
OPEN

THREE AND A HALF MONTHS AGO
BLIP BLIP BLIP BLIP
TONY! DON'T TRY TO MOVE! YOU'RE IN THE HOSPITAL. SOME KIDS... THEY FOUND YOU ON THE ROAD. THE DOCTORS SAY YOU ARE VERY WEAK. THEY SAY...
STOP TONY! YOU NEED TO LEAVE THAT ON. LET ME CALL SOMEONE...
BEEP BEEP BEEP

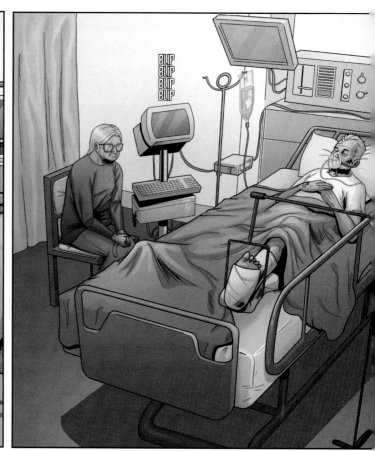

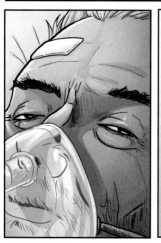

MAR.. MARIBEL... LISTEN. DID YOU GET THE ARROWHEAD? DID YOU...

YES, IT'S RIGHT HERE.

GOOD. GOOD. FOUND A WAY... -:COUGH:- TO GIVE YOU WHAT YOU WANT.

USE THAT... -:COUGH:- USE IT TO...

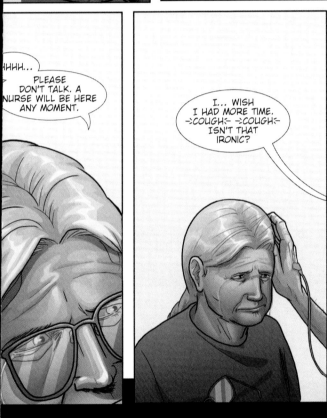

HHHH... PLEASE DON'T TALK. A NURSE WILL BE HERE ANY MOMENT.

I... WISH I HAD MORE TIME. -:COUGH:- -:COUGH:- ISN'T THAT IRONIC?

IT COULDN'T BE ANY MORE SO.

HEH -:COUGH:- HEH...

GOODBYE.

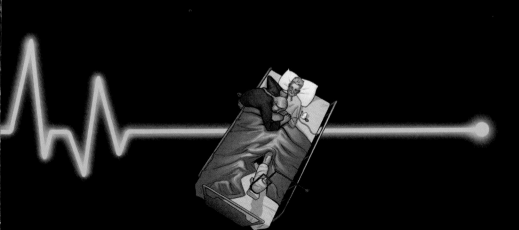

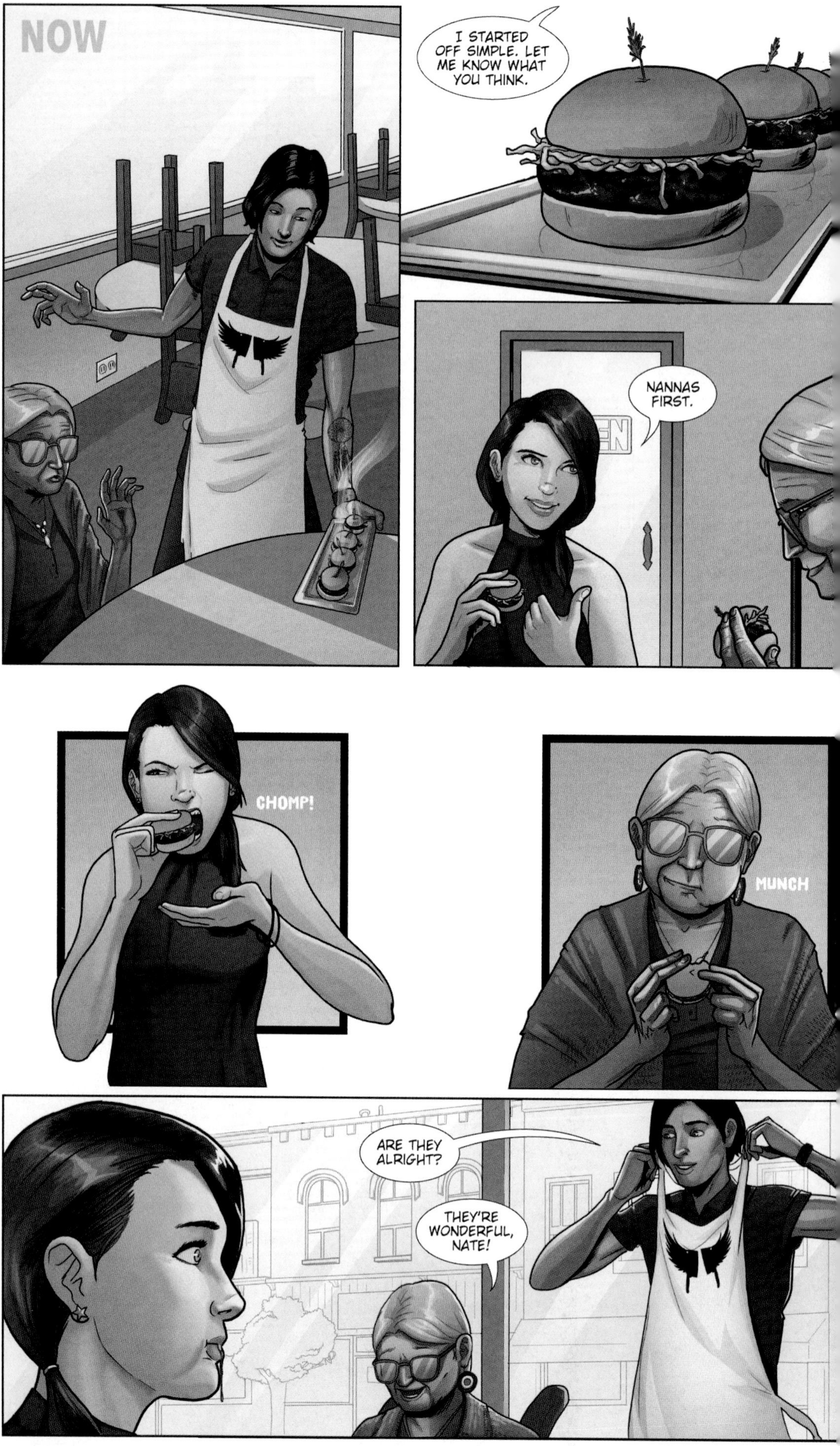
NOW
I STARTED OFF SIMPLE. LET ME KNOW WHAT YOU THINK.
NANNAS FIRST.
CHOMP!
MUNCH
ARE THEY ALRIGHT?
THEY'RE WONDERFUL, NATE!

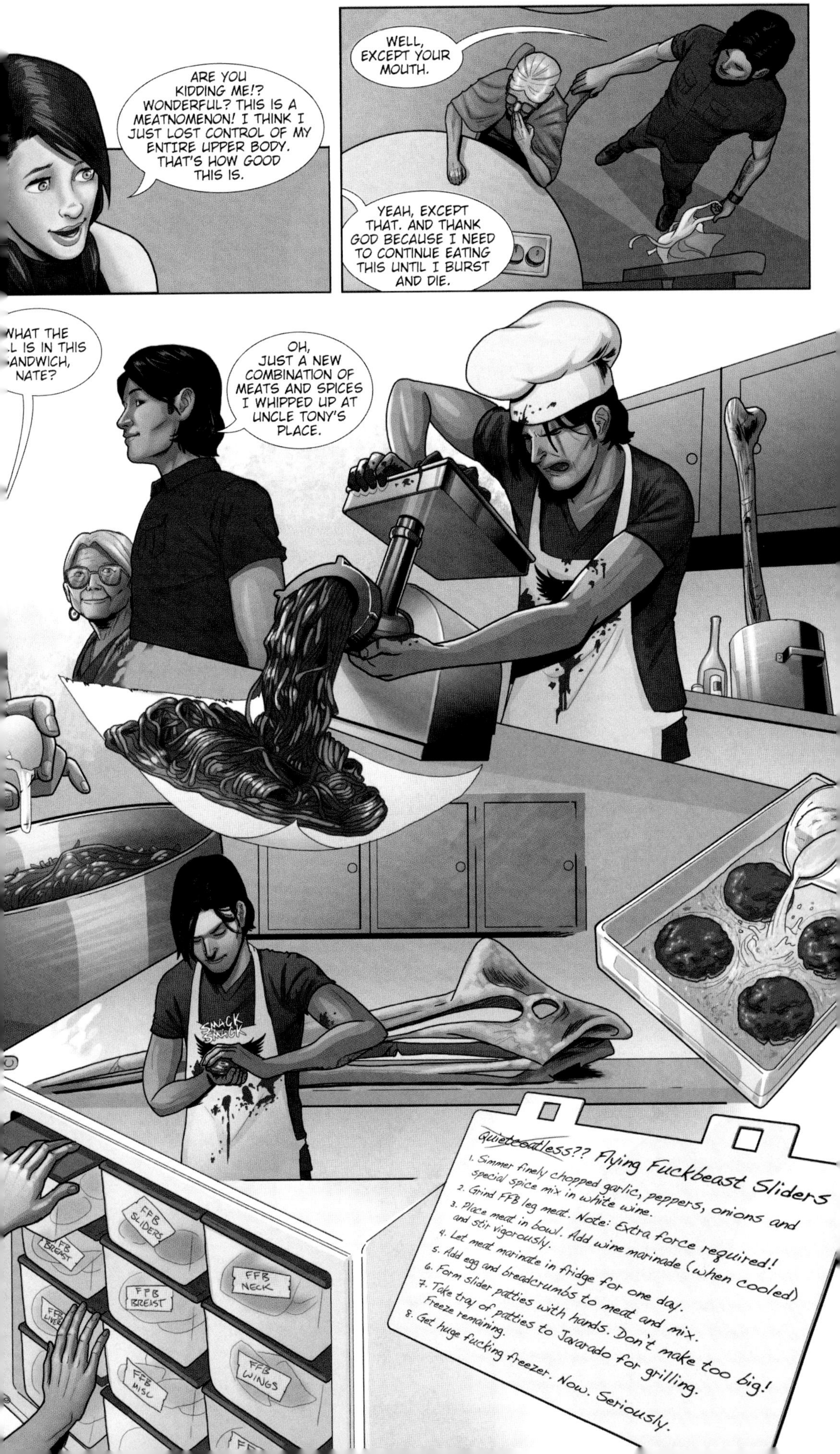
ARE YOU KIDDING ME!? THIS IS A WONDERFUL? THIS IS A MEATNOMENON! I THINK I JUST LOST CONTROL OF MY ENTIRE UPPER BODY. THAT'S HOW GOOD THIS IS.
WELL, EXCEPT YOUR MOUTH.
YEAH, EXCEPT THAT. AND THANK GOD BECAUSE I NEED TO CONTINUE EATING THIS UNTIL I BURST AND DIE.
WHAT THE
L IS IN THIS
ANDWICH,
NATE?
OH, JUST A NEW COMBINATION OF MEATS AND SPICES I WHIPPED UP AT UNCLE TONY'S PLACE.
SMACK SMACK
~~Quietcoatless~~?? Flying Fuckbeast Sliders
1. Simmer finely chopped garlic, peppers, onions and special spice mix in white wine.
2. Grind FFB leg meat. Note: Extra force required!
3. Place meat in bowl. Add wine marinade (when cooled) and stir vigorously.
4. Let meat marinate in fridge for one day.
5. Add egg and breadcrumbs to meat and mix.
6. Form slider patties with hands. Don't make too big!
7. Take tray of patties to Javarado for grilling. Freeze remaining.
8. Get huge fucking freezer. Now. Seriously.
FFB SLIDERS
FFB BREAST
FFB NECK
FFB BREAST
FFB LIVER
FFB WINGS
FFB MISC

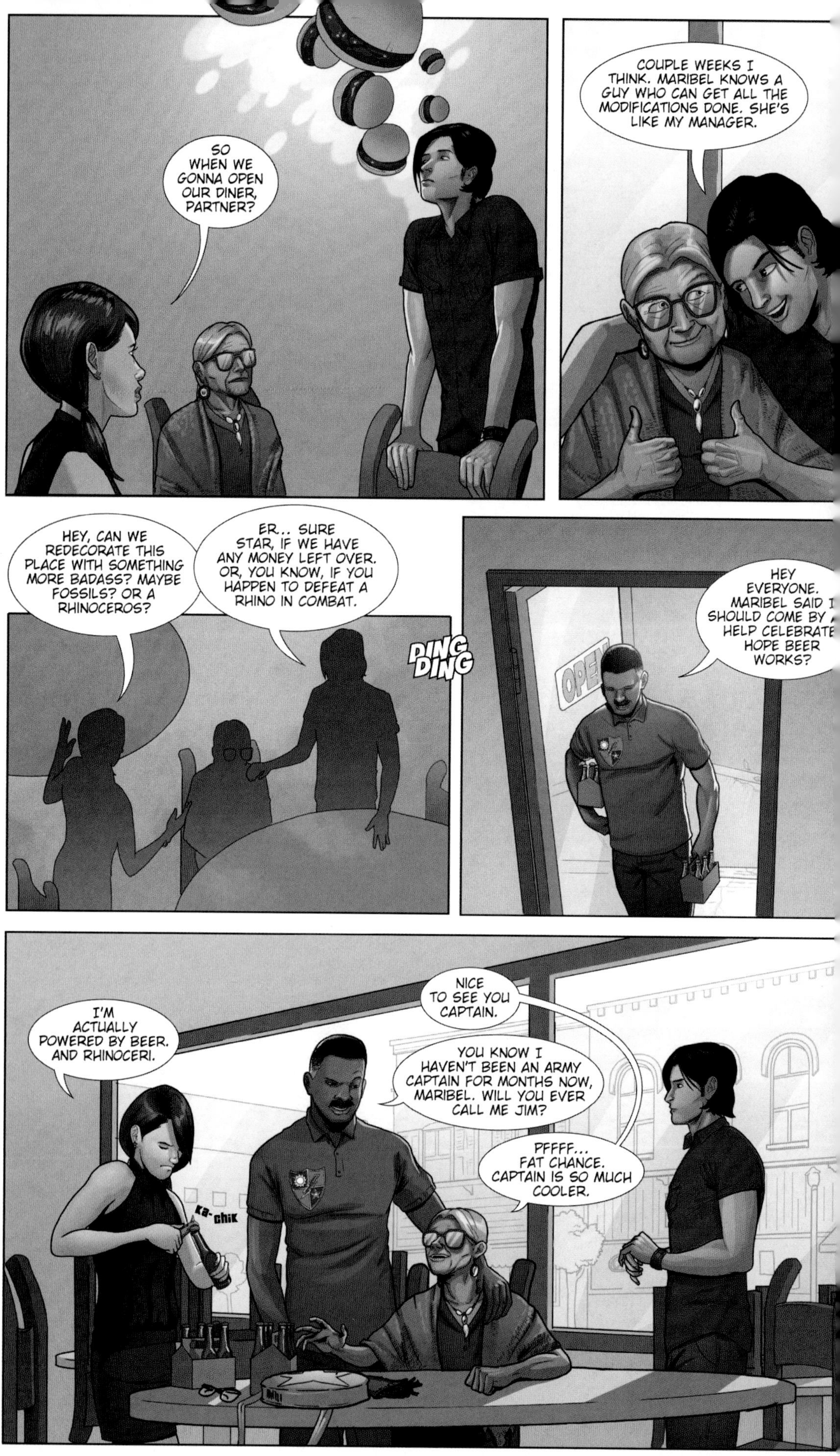
SO WHEN WE GONNA OPEN OUR DINER, PARTNER?
COUPLE WEEKS I THINK. MARIBEL KNOWS A GUY WHO CAN GET ALL THE MODIFICATIONS DONE. SHE'S LIKE MY MANAGER.
HEY, CAN WE REDECORATE THIS PLACE WITH SOMETHING MORE BADASS? MAYBE FOSSILS? OR A RHINOCEROS?
ER... SURE STAR, IF WE HAVE ANY MONEY LEFT OVER. OR, YOU KNOW, IF YOU HAPPEN TO DEFEAT A RHINO IN COMBAT.
DING DING
OPEN
HEY EVERYONE. MARIBEL SAID I SHOULD COME BY HELP CELEBRATE HOPE BEER WORKS?
I'M ACTUALLY POWERED BY BEER. AND RHINOCERI.
NICE TO SEE YOU CAPTAIN.
YOU KNOW I HAVEN'T BEEN AN ARMY CAPTAIN FOR MONTHS NOW, MARIBEL. WILL YOU EVER CALL ME JIM?
PFFFF... FAT CHANCE. CAPTAIN IS SO MUCH COOLER.
KA-CHIK

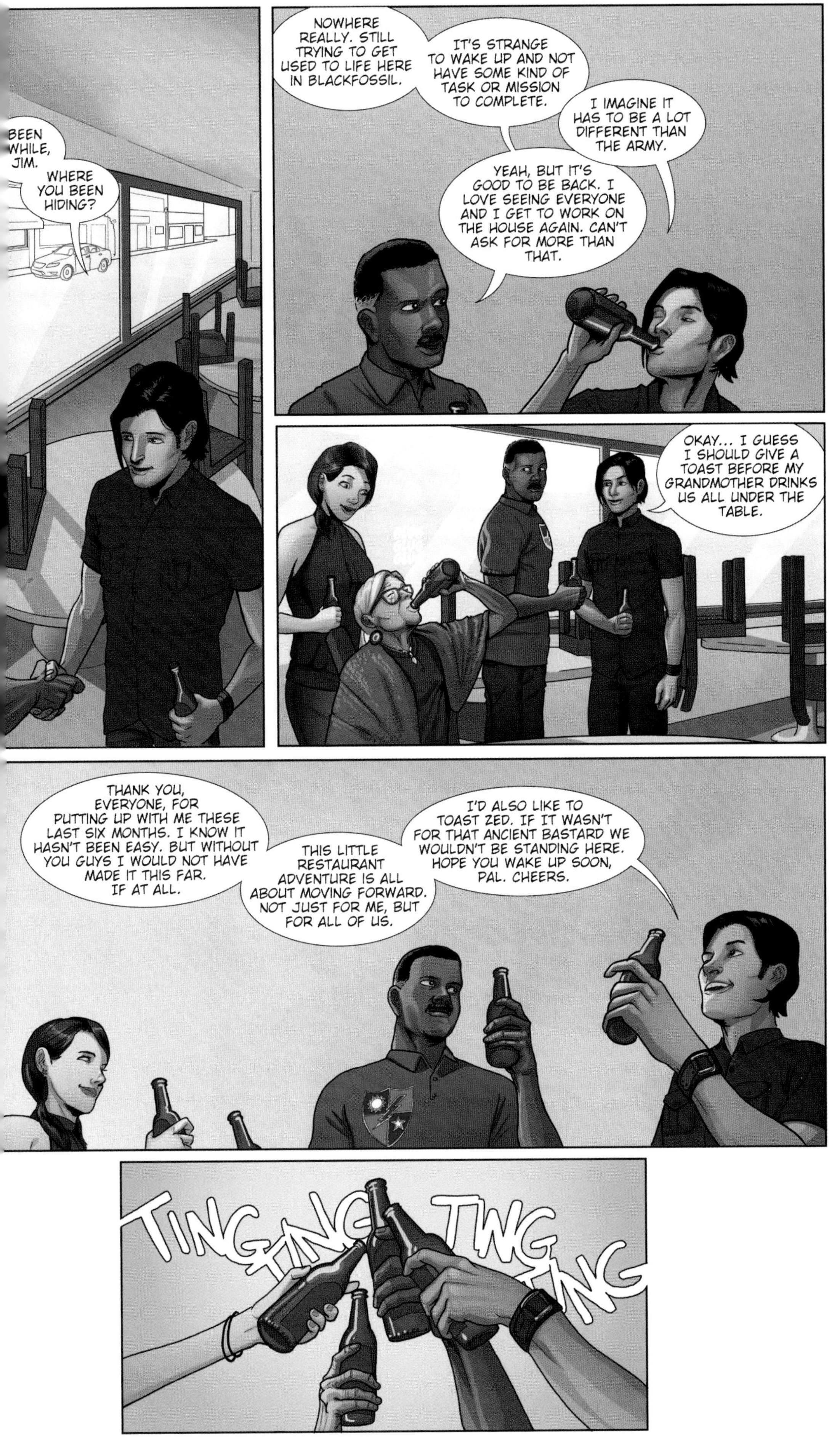

BEEN
WHILE,
JIM.
WHERE
YOU BEEN
HIDING?
NOWHERE REALLY. STILL TRYING TO GET USED TO LIFE HERE IN BLACKFOSSIL.
IT'S STRANGE TO WAKE UP AND NOT HAVE SOME KIND OF TASK OR MISSION TO COMPLETE.
I IMAGINE IT HAS TO BE A LOT DIFFERENT THAN THE ARMY.
YEAH, BUT IT'S GOOD TO BE BACK. I LOVE SEEING EVERYONE AND I GET TO WORK ON THE HOUSE AGAIN. CAN'T ASK FOR MORE THAN THAT.
OKAY... I GUESS I SHOULD GIVE A TOAST BEFORE MY GRANDMOTHER DRINKS US ALL UNDER THE TABLE.
THANK YOU, EVERYONE, FOR PUTTING UP WITH ME THESE LAST SIX MONTHS. I KNOW IT HASN'T BEEN EASY. BUT WITHOUT YOU GUYS I WOULD NOT HAVE MADE IT THIS FAR. IF AT ALL.
THIS LITTLE RESTAURANT ADVENTURE IS ALL ABOUT MOVING FORWARD. NOT JUST FOR ME, BUT FOR ALL OF US.
I'D ALSO LIKE TO TOAST ZED. IF IT WASN'T FOR THAT ANCIENT BASTARD WE WOULDN'T BE STANDING HERE. HOPE YOU WAKE UP SOON, PAL. CHEERS.
TING
TING
TING
TING

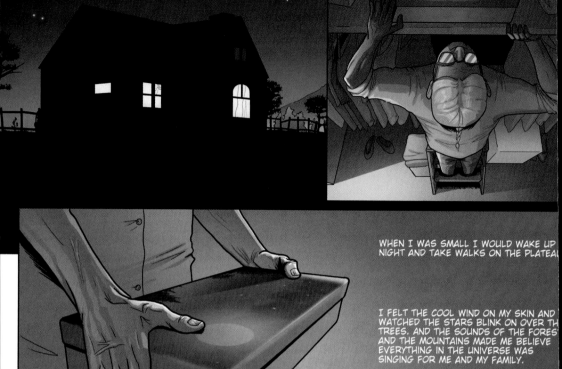

WHEN I WAS SMALL I WOULD WAKE UP
NIGHT AND TAKE WALKS ON THE PLATEA

I FELT THE COOL WIND ON MY SKIN AND
WATCHED THE STARS BLINK ON OVER TH
TREES. AND THE SOUNDS OF THE FORES
AND THE MOUNTAINS MADE ME BELIEVE
EVERYTHING IN THE UNIVERSE WAS
SINGING FOR ME AND MY FAMILY.

THAT'S WHEN I FELT REAL.
WHEN I KNEW EXACTLY WHO I
WAS AND HOW I MATTERED.

I'M NOT THAT GIRL NOW. I
HAVEN'T BEEN FOR A LONG TIME.

THE EARTH TAUGHT ME TO FOR
MYSELF, JUST AS MELTED SNO
FORGETS ITS LIFE.

AS IT SHOULD

BUT NOW I CAN'T STOP REMEMBERING.

NEARLY EVERYONE I'VE LOVED IN THIS LIFE IS GONE NOW.

MY MIND HAS BECOME A SPIRALSCOPE, WINDING THROUGH MY DEEPEST MEMORIES. SEARCHING. TAKING ME BACK TO THE START.

I FEEL THE OLD, NIGHT WINDS SHIFT AND ROAR IN MY HEART. I HEAR THE WAIL OF THE THUNDERBIRDS.

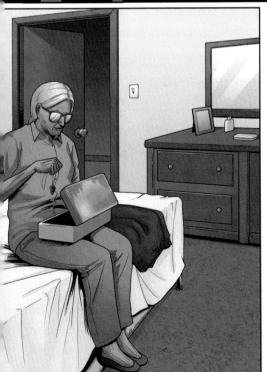

PLEASE EARTH... GIVE ME THE COURAGE TO STAY HERE A WHILE LONGER. AND FORGET IT ALL AGAIN.

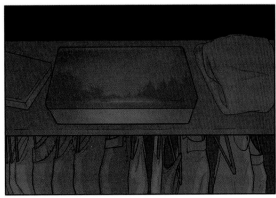

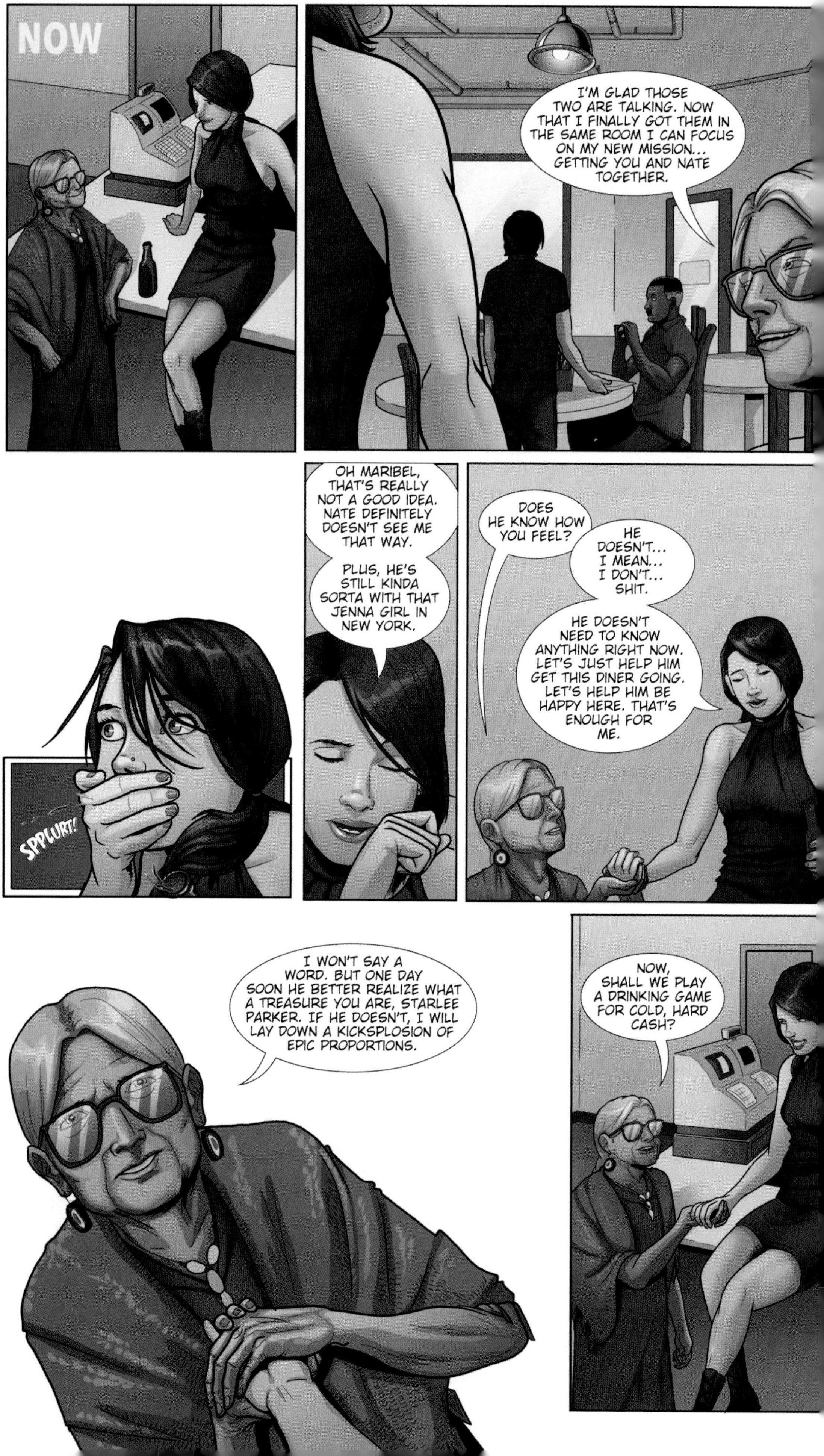
NOW
I'M GLAD THOSE TWO ARE TALKING. NOW THAT I FINALLY GOT THEM IN THE SAME ROOM I CAN FOCUS ON MY NEW MISSION... GETTING YOU AND NATE TOGETHER.
SPPLURT!
OH MARIBEL, THAT'S REALLY NOT A GOOD IDEA. NATE DEFINITELY DOESN'T SEE ME THAT WAY.
PLUS, HE'S STILL KINDA SORTA WITH THAT JENNA GIRL IN NEW YORK.
DOES HE KNOW HOW YOU FEEL?
HE DOESN'T... I MEAN... I DON'T... SHIT.
HE DOESN'T NEED TO KNOW ANYTHING RIGHT NOW. LET'S JUST HELP HIM GET THIS DINER GOING. LET'S HELP HIM BE HAPPY HERE. THAT'S ENOUGH FOR ME.
I WON'T SAY A WORD. BUT ONE DAY SOON HE BETTER REALIZE WHAT A TREASURE YOU ARE, STARLEE PARKER. IF HE DOESN'T, I WILL LAY DOWN A KICKSPLOSION OF EPIC PROPORTIONS.
NOW, SHALL WE PLAY A DRINKING GAME FOR COLD, HARD CASH?

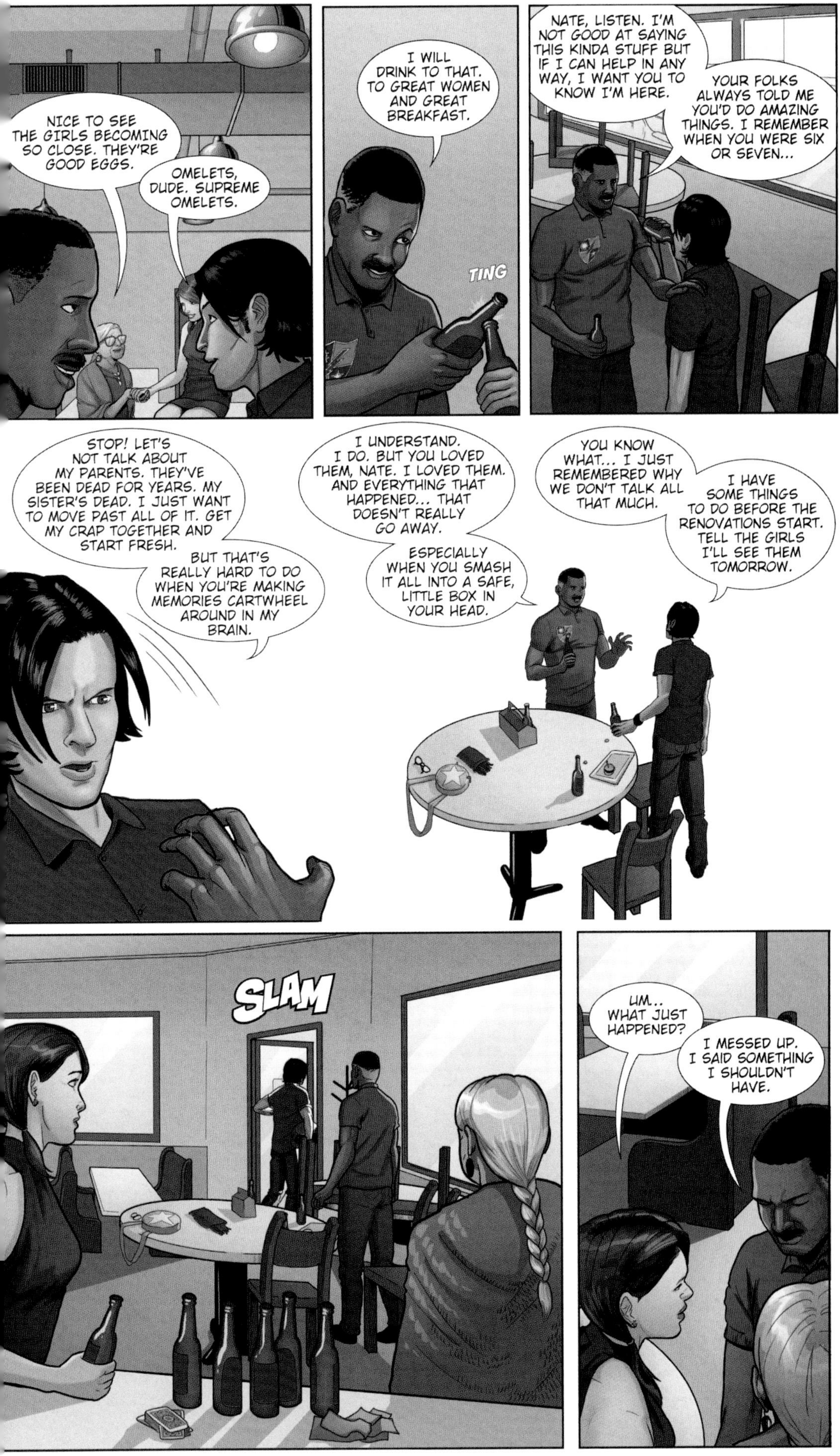
NICE TO SEE THE GIRLS BECOMING SO CLOSE. THEY'RE GOOD EGGS.
OMELETS, DUDE. SUPREME OMELETS.
I WILL DRINK TO THAT. TO GREAT WOMEN AND GREAT BREAKFAST.
TING
NATE, LISTEN. I'M NOT GOOD AT SAYING THIS KINDA STUFF BUT IF I CAN HELP IN ANY WAY, I WANT YOU TO KNOW I'M HERE.
YOUR FOLKS ALWAYS TOLD ME YOU'D DO AMAZING THINGS. I REMEMBER WHEN YOU WERE SIX OR SEVEN...
STOP! LET'S NOT TALK ABOUT MY PARENTS. THEY'VE BEEN DEAD FOR YEARS. MY SISTER'S DEAD. I JUST WANT TO MOVE PAST ALL OF IT. GET MY CRAP TOGETHER AND START FRESH.
BUT THAT'S REALLY HARD TO DO WHEN YOU'RE MAKING MEMORIES CARTWHEEL AROUND IN MY BRAIN.
I UNDERSTAND. I DO. BUT YOU LOVED THEM, NATE. I LOVED THEM. AND EVERYTHING THAT HAPPENED... THAT DOESN'T REALLY GO AWAY.
ESPECIALLY WHEN YOU SMASH IT ALL INTO A SAFE, LITTLE BOX IN YOUR HEAD.
YOU KNOW WHAT... I JUST REMEMBERED WHY WE DON'T TALK ALL THAT MUCH.
I HAVE SOME THINGS TO DO BEFORE THE RENOVATIONS START. TELL THE GIRLS I'LL SEE THEM TOMORROW.
SLAM
UM.. WHAT JUST HAPPENED?
I MESSED UP. I SAID SOMETHING I SHOULDN'T HAVE.

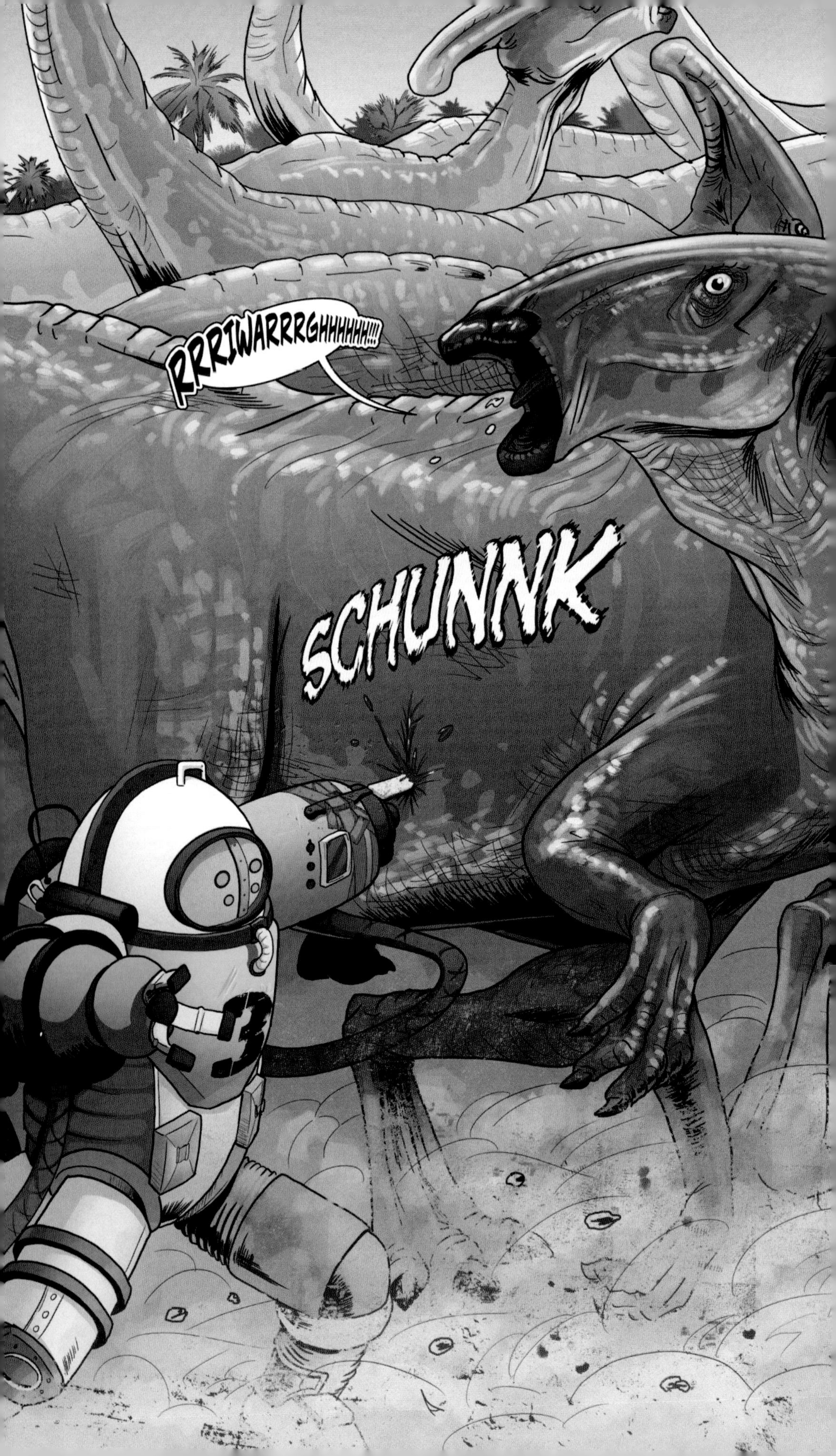
RRRIWARRRGHHHHHHH!!!
SCHUNNK

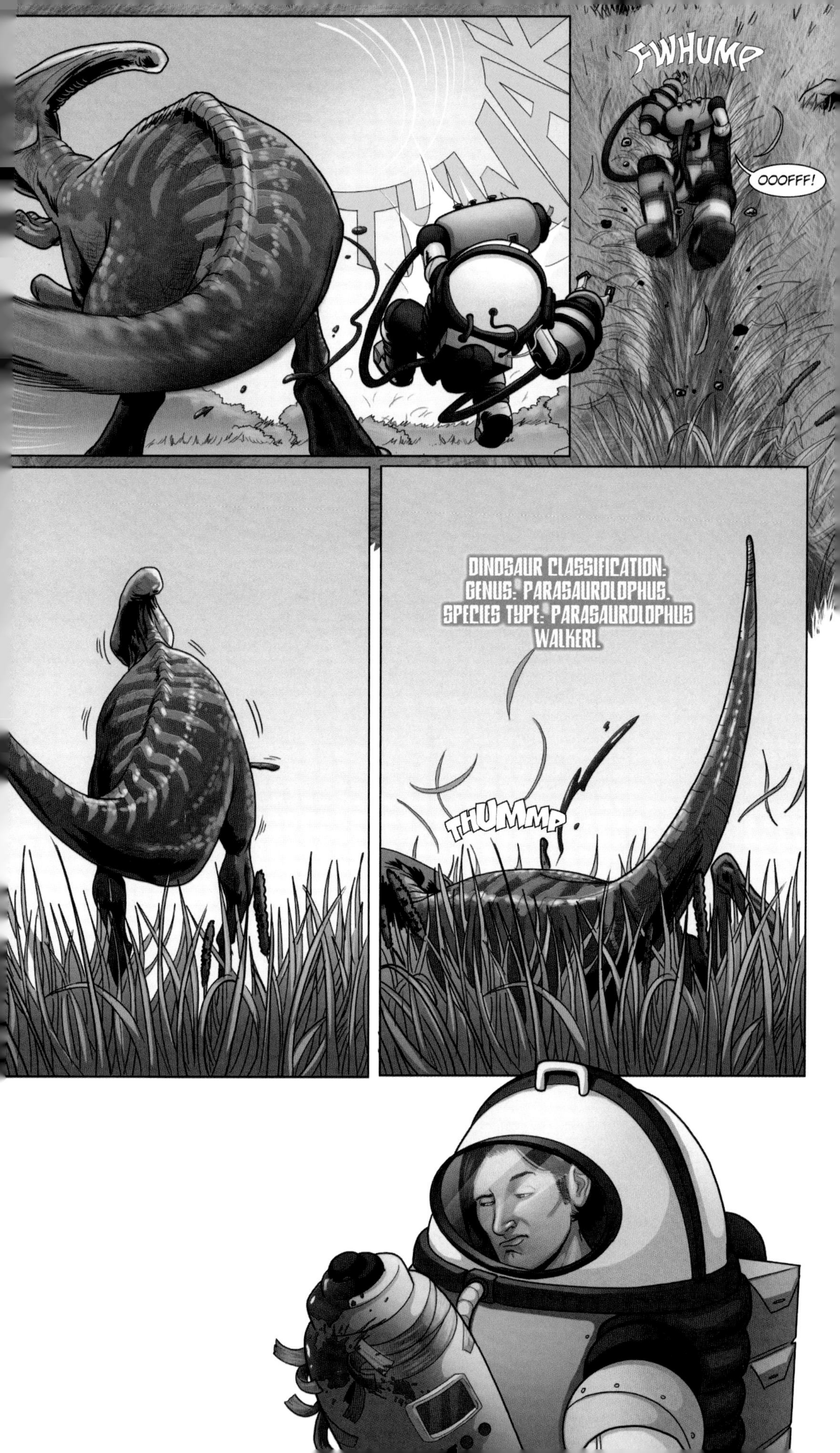
THWACK
FWHUMP
OOOFFF!
DINOSAUR CLASSIFICATION: GENUS: PARASAURDLOPHUS. SPECIES TYPE: PARASAURDLOPHUS WALKERI.
THUMMP

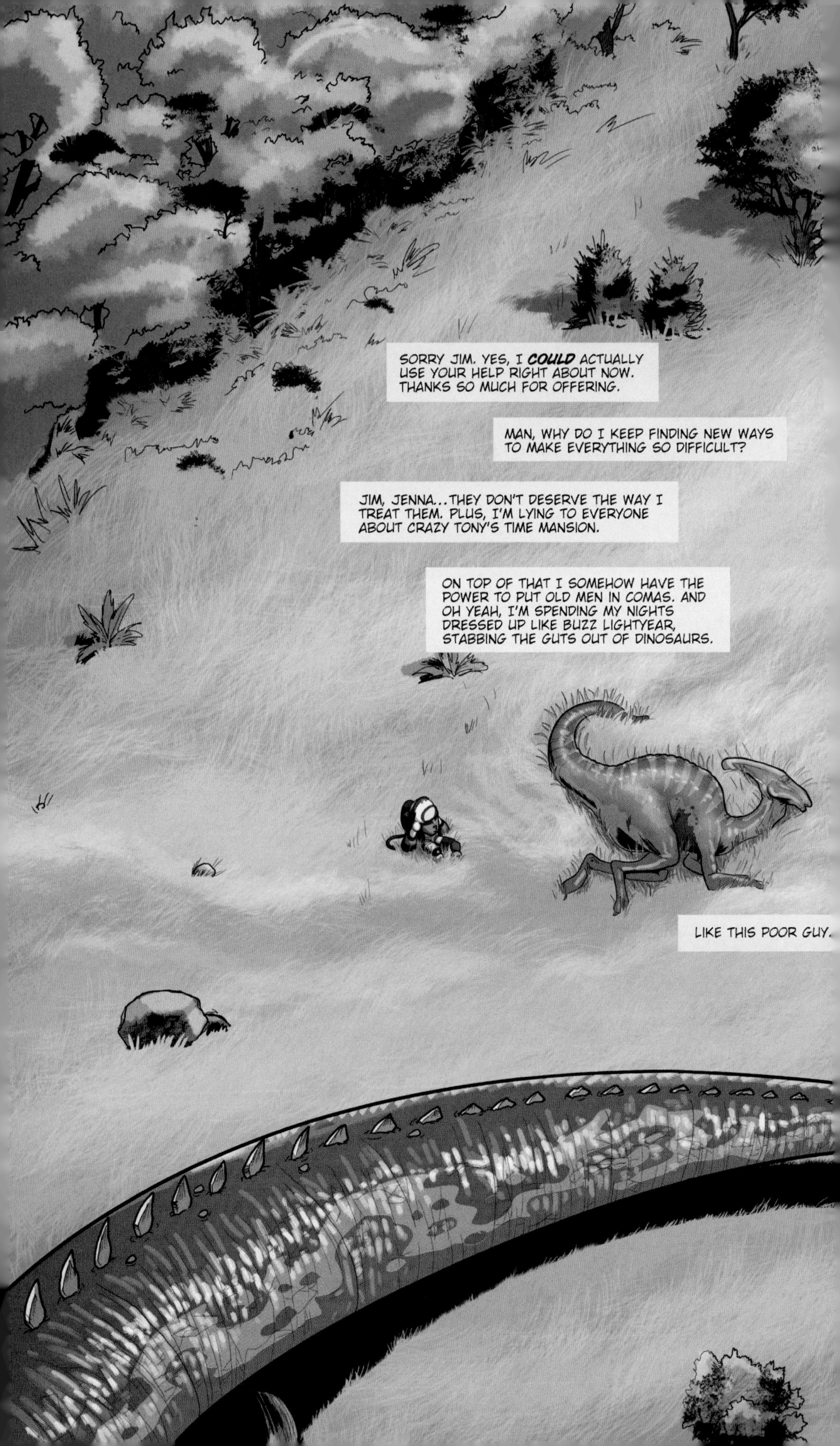
SORRY JIM. YES, I **COULD** ACTUALLY USE YOUR HELP RIGHT ABOUT NOW. THANKS SO MUCH FOR OFFERING.
MAN, WHY DO I KEEP FINDING NEW WAYS TO MAKE EVERYTHING SO DIFFICULT?
JIM, JENNA...THEY DON'T DESERVE THE WAY I TREAT THEM. PLUS, I'M LYING TO EVERYONE ABOUT CRAZY TONY'S TIME MANSION.
ON TOP OF THAT I SOMEHOW HAVE THE POWER TO PUT OLD MEN IN COMAS. AND OH YEAH, I'M SPENDING MY NIGHTS DRESSED UP LIKE BUZZ LIGHTYEAR, STABBING THE GUTS OUT OF DINOSAURS.
LIKE THIS POOR GUY.

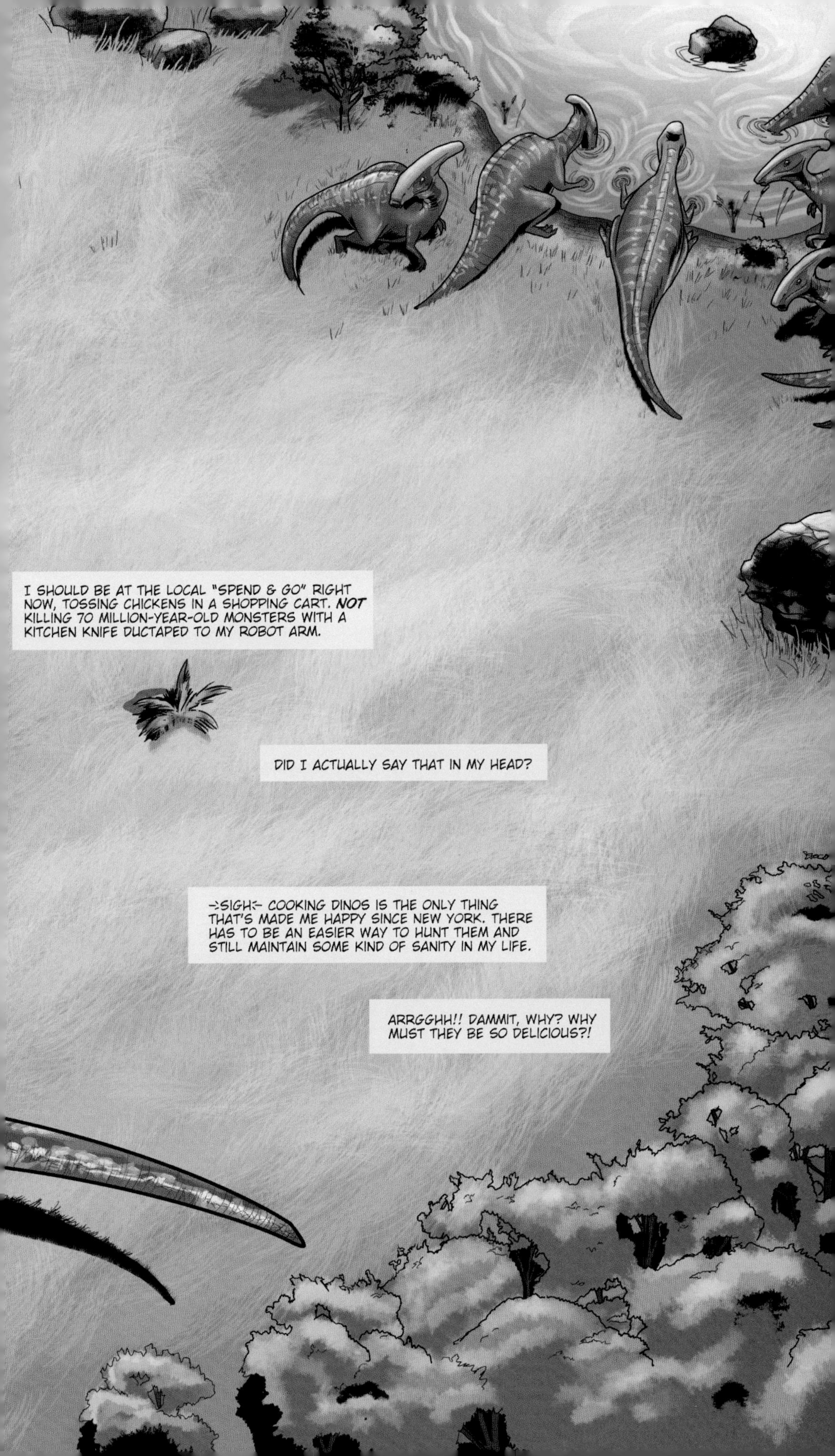
I SHOULD BE AT THE LOCAL "SPEND & GO" RIGHT NOW, TOSSING CHICKENS IN A SHOPPING CART. NOT KILLING 70 MILLION-YEAR-OLD MONSTERS WITH A KITCHEN KNIFE DUCTAPED TO MY ROBOT ARM.
DID I ACTUALLY SAY THAT IN MY HEAD?
-SIGH- COOKING DINOS IS THE ONLY THING THAT'S MADE ME HAPPY SINCE NEW YORK. THERE HAS TO BE AN EASIER WAY TO HUNT THEM AND STILL MAINTAIN SOME KIND OF SANITY IN MY LIFE.
ARRGGHH!! DAMMIT, WHY? WHY MUST THEY BE SO DELICIOUS?!

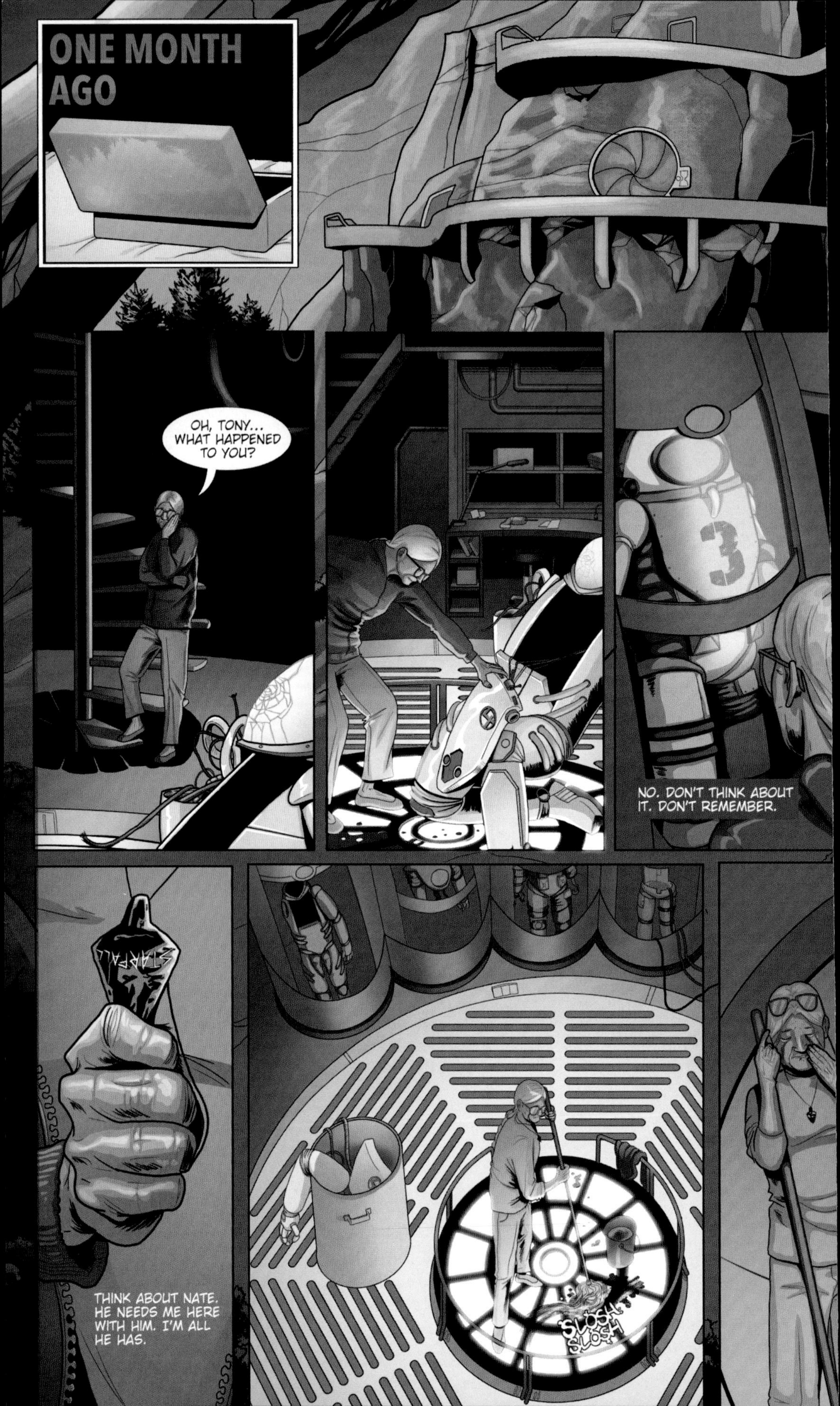
ONE MONTH AGO
OH, TONY... WHAT HAPPENED TO YOU?
3
NO. DON'T THINK ABOUT IT. DON'T REMEMBER.
STARFALL
THINK ABOUT NATE. HE NEEDS ME HERE WITH HIM. I'M ALL HE HAS.
SLOSH SLOSH

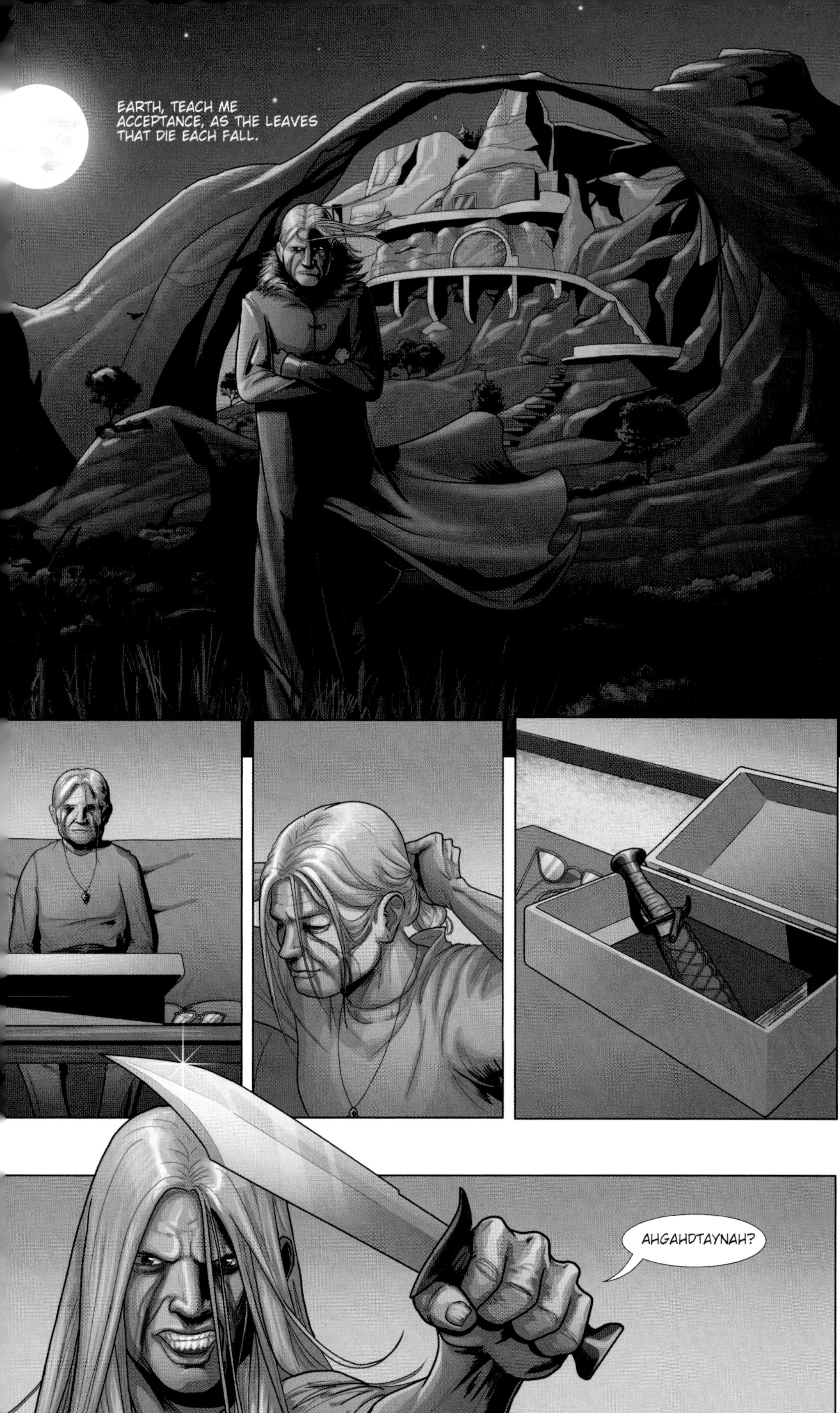
EARTH, TEACH ME ACCEPTANCE, AS THE LEAVES THAT DIE EACH FALL.
AHGAHDTAYNAH?

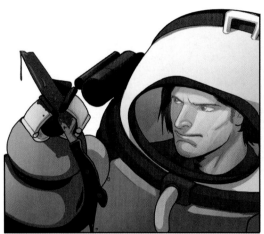

AFTER EVERYTHING THAT'S HAPPENED IN MY LIFE, I NEED TO MAKE THIS WORK.

I THINK I HAVE TO LEARN MORE ABOUT THE SUIT. AND MY UNCLE.

AND **GUNS**. GUNS WOULD BE FANTASTIC.

WARNING: DANGER DETECTED.

End of **CHAPTER 2**
THE LEAVES THAT DIE EACH FALL

Writer **MARKISAN NASO**
Artist & Letterer **JASON MUHR**
Colorist **ANDREI TABACARU**

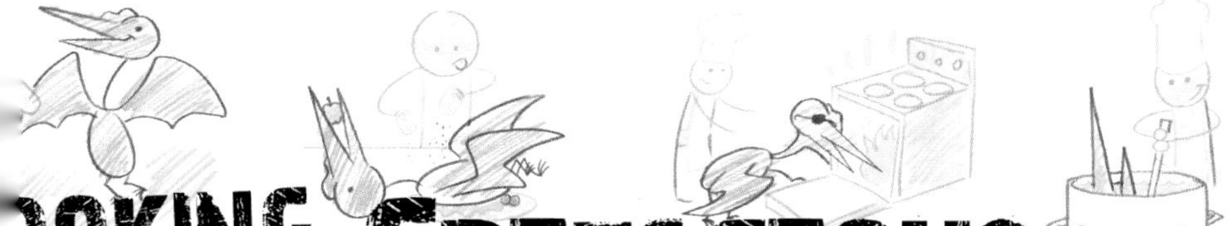

OOKING CRETACEOUS

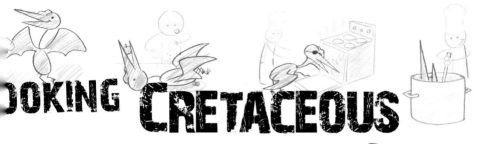

ne to the extra-sized first issue of VORACIOUS! Jason, Andrei really can't thank you enough for taking a chance on us. ly. Thank you.

a for VORACIOUS first came to me at a party when a friend hat age-old geek question, "If you could have any superpower, ould it be?" I said I would take all the powers. She scoffed. But said I'd choose complete mastery over time and space to that goal, she started to listen. I told her that time/space lation would not only allow me to visit legendary places and it would allow me to acquire pretty much any gear or powers d from the future. I'd pop into 3097 for a thermonuclear flight ightsaber and a personal cloaking device. I'd casually win the a week from now and use the cash to build an army of robot to do my bidding. I'd get myself a sweet spaceship shaped cobra. And then I'd use all that swag to go back 70 million years Cretaceous and fix myself a dinosaur sandwich.

e we are, years after I accidentally planned how to get the lunch. I had no idea that crazy answer to a simple question turn into a comic book series, but Jason, Andrei and I are so t's in your hands now. There's a smorgasbord of dinosaur crazy e for Nate and company. Mystery, romance, tomahawks, nosauruses and the most delicious meals ever in comics await anks again for checking out VORACIOUS. Time to get back to and turn the Pterodactyl.

an
15

FOSSIL FACTS

What was that strange word Maribel spoke at the end of the book? It's Ute for: "Who are you?"

Learn more about Ute culture at http://utahindians.org/archives/ute.html

Voraciouscomic@gmail.com
VoraciousComic
@VoraciousComic
voraciouscomic.tumblr

Throughout this series we will be featuring dinosaur recipes based on real meals by family, friends and maybe even actual chefs! The one below is by Markisan. You gave this issue a go, now try this recipe and let us know what you think about both!

etzalcoatlus Saltimbocca

mbocca means "jumps in the mouth" in Italian. Buon appetito!

REDIENTS

- Quetzalcoatlus breast (Note: If you don't have y Quetzalcoatlus on hand, you may substitute chicken breasts)
- hin slices of prosciutto ham
- ablespoon fresh sage
- ounces olive oil
- unce all-purpose flour
- ounces artichoke hearts, quartered
- unce capers
- cup of Chardonnay
- cup fresh lemon juice
- cup heavy cream
- 1 tablespoon butter
- 1 tablespoon salt
- 1 tablespoon black pepper

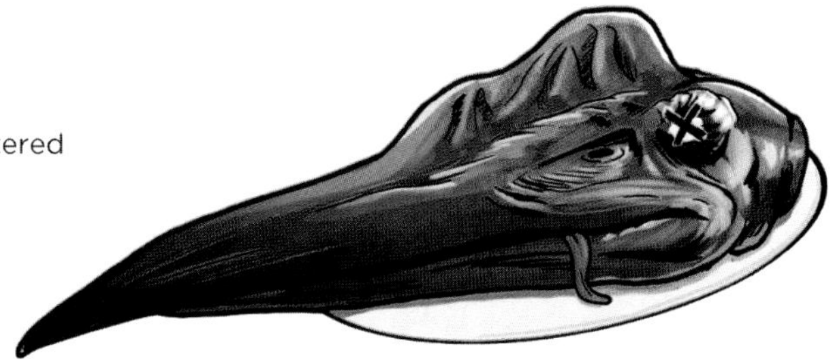

ECTIONS

ut your hunk of Quetzalcoatlus into 24 even breast pieces (or just use 4 chicken breasts).
ghtly salt and pepper Quetzalcoatlus.
prinkle chopped sage evenly on each piece of breast.
lace sliced prosciutto on top of breast pieces.
ound prosciutto into breast pieces with meat hammer until thickness measures 3/8 inch.
eat olive oil in a sauté pan.
ghtly flour pounded Quetzalcoatlus (Note: Dip Quetzalcoatlus in beaten egg first before flouring r a richer crust).
ace in heated oil, prosciutto side down.
rown one side, turn and brown other side.
emove Quetzalcoatlus from pan and drain off excess oil. Set aside on platter.
eglaze pan with white wine.
Add artichokes, fresh lemon juice, cream and butter and cook until sauce is thickened.
Pour sauce over the top of Quetzalcoatlus.
Garnish with additional capers.

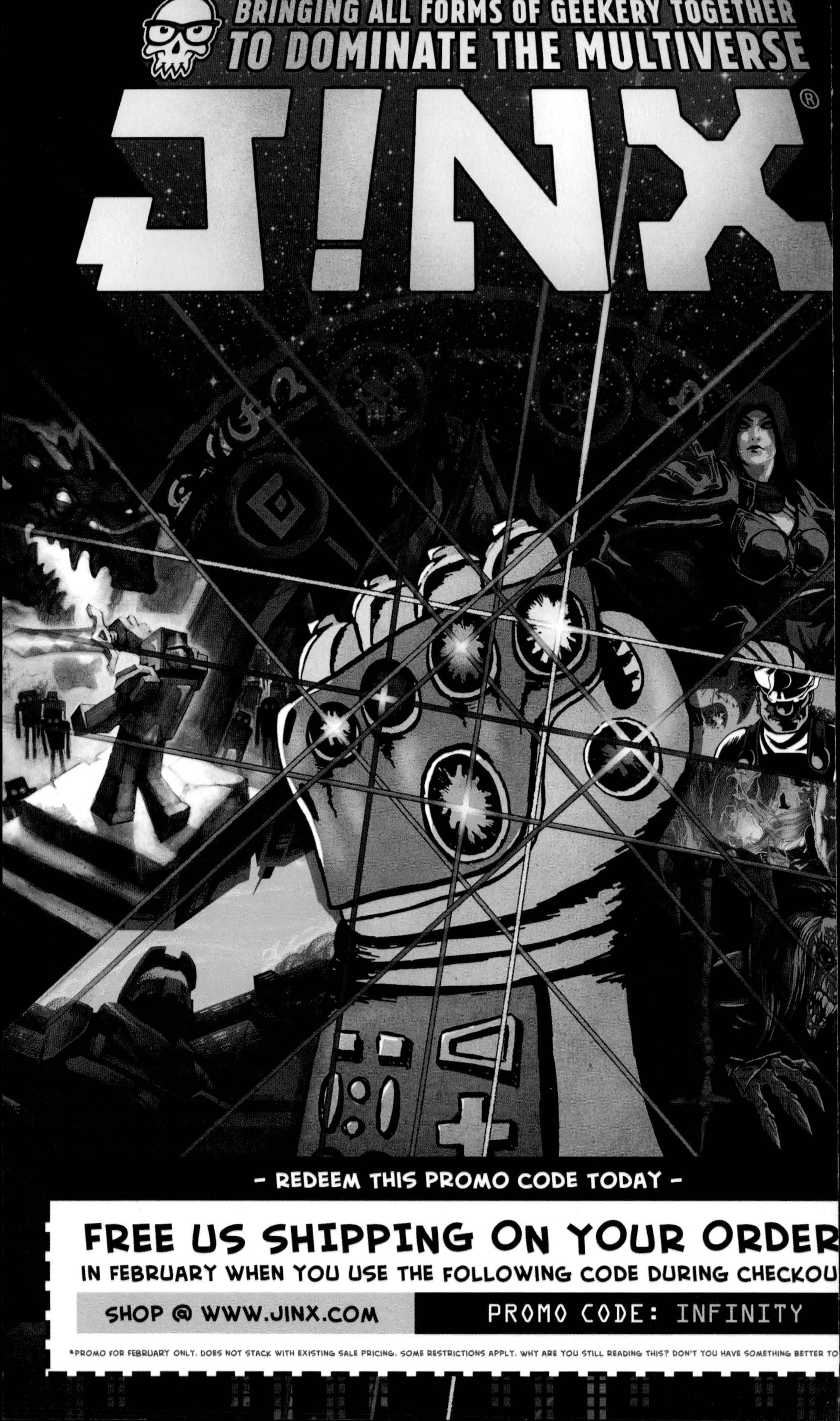
BRINGING ALL FORMS OF GEEKERY TOGETHER
TO DOMINATE THE MULTIVERSE
J!NX®
- REDEEM THIS PROMO CODE TODAY -
FREE US SHIPPING ON YOUR ORDER
IN FEBRUARY WHEN YOU USE THE FOLLOWING CODE DURING CHECKOU
SHOP @ WWW.JINX.COM
PROMO CODE: INFINITY
*PROMO FOR FEBRUARY ONLY. DOES NOT STACK WITH EXISTING SALE PRICING. SOME RESTRICTIONS APPLY. WHY ARE YOU STILL READING THIS? DON'T YOU HAVE SOMETHING BETTER TO

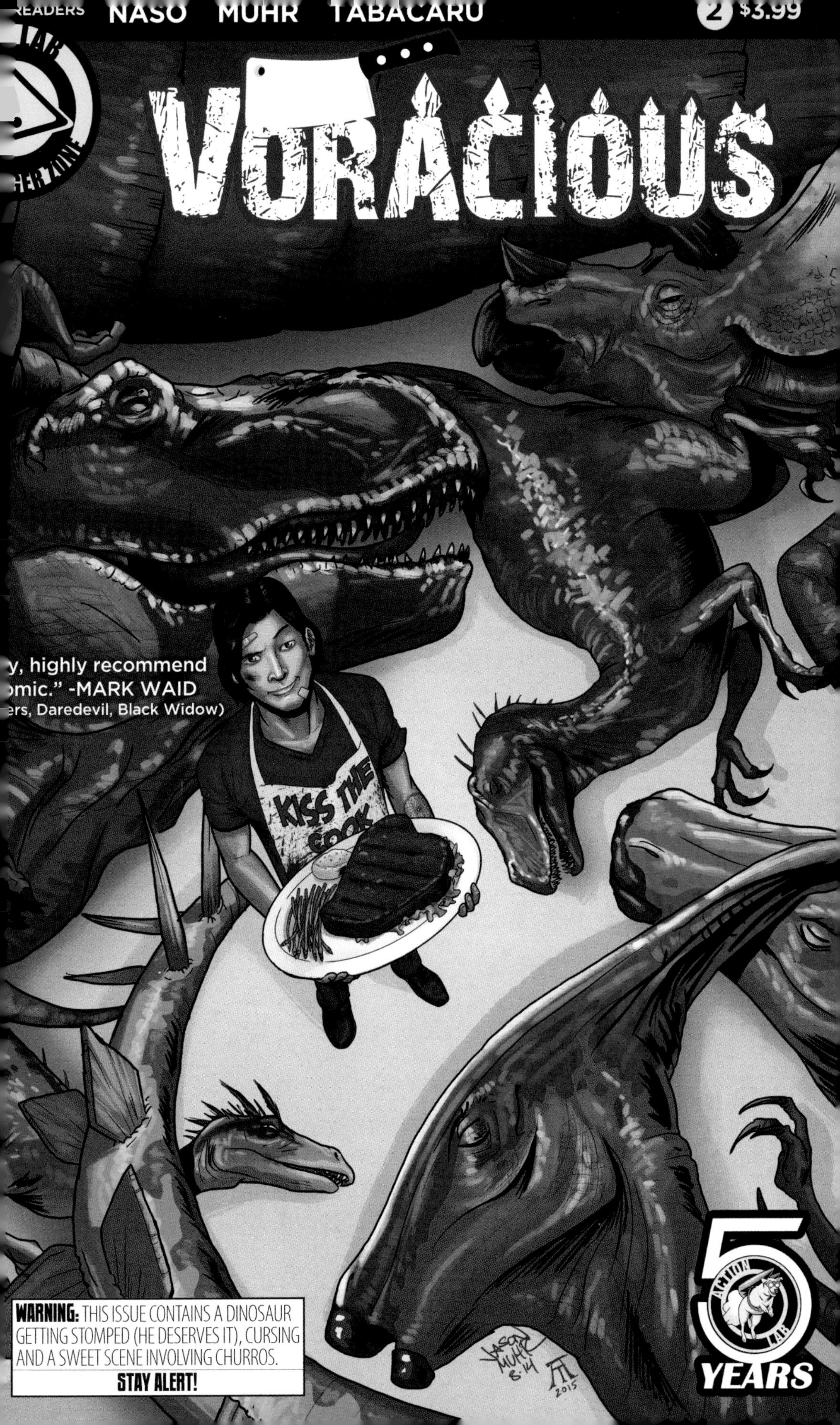

READERS NASO MUHR TABACARU
2 $3.99
VORACIOUS
y, highly recommend
omic." -MARK WAID
ers, Daredevil, Black Widow)
KISS THE COOK
WARNING: THIS ISSUE CONTAINS A DINOSAUR GETTING STOMPED (HE DESERVES IT), CURSING AND A SWEET SCENE INVOLVING CHURROS.
STAY ALERT!
5 YEARS

PREVIOUSLY...

Nate Willner, a chef in NYC, was forced to move back to his tiny hometown of Blackfossil, Utah, after his restaurant exploded, killing his sister and leaving him unmotivated and hollow. After months of living with his grandmother, Maribel, and working at the Javarado Café with childhood friend, Starlee, it looks like Nate's life has become a dead end. But when he unexpectedly inherits a time travel suit from his Great Uncle Tony, he is transported back to the era of the dinosaurs. In order to survive, Nate has to kill a Quetzalcoatlus in self-defense with the suit's blowtorch. The smell of the roasted beast makes Nate wonder what it tastes like. He eats some of the meat and discovers it's the greatest meal he's ever had. Nate drags the carcass back to his time and decides to open a restaurant in the present using ancient meat from the past!

Using his inheritance Nate purchases the Javarado and makes plans to open the restaurant with Starlee as his business partner. Meanwhile, Tony's death has started to take a mental toll on Maribel, who had some kind of secret relationship with him in the past. Nate, unaware of the connection, tries to figure out how to get his life on track and not get killed by dinosaurs. As he heads back home with his latest kill, a pack of vicious predators prepare to attack.

CHAPTER 3
FORK & FOSSIL

Written by
MARKISAN NASO

Art, Lettering & Design by
JASON MUHR

Color Art by
ANDREI TABACARU

VORACIOUS created by
NASO & MUHR

"Private Parts" variant cover
(LTD to 1500) by
JASON MUHR

JASON MARTIN - PUBLISHER
DAVE DWONCH - PRESIDENT
SHAWN GABBORIN - EDITOR IN CHIEF
JAMAL IGLE - V.P. OF MARKETING
JIM DIETZ - SOCIAL MEDIA DIRECTOR
KEVIN FREEMAN - EDITOR
COLLEEN BOYD - ASSOCIATE EDITOR

Find Markisan Naso at www.markisan.com.
Find Jason Muhr at www.jasonmuhr.com.

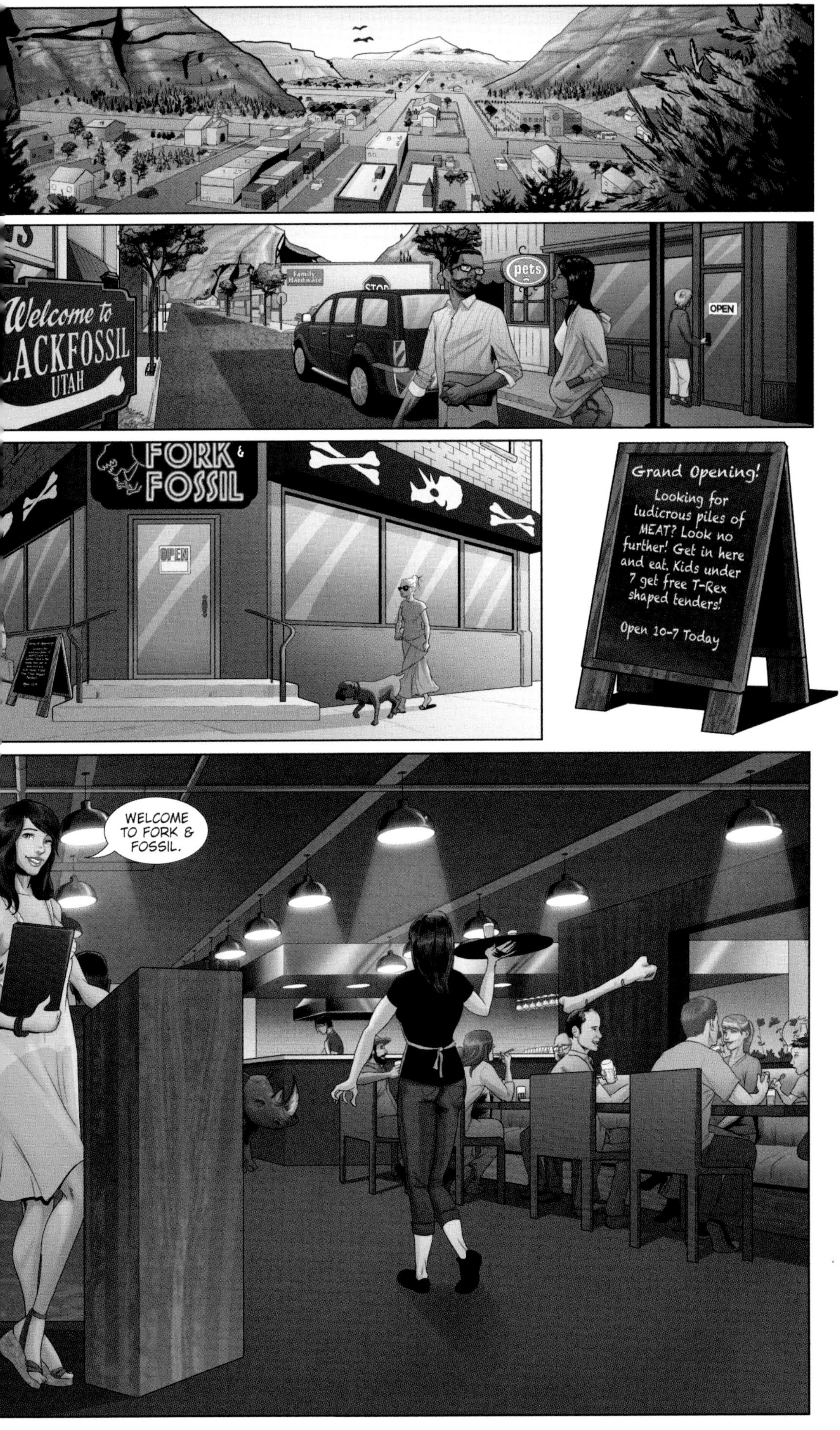
Welcome to
LACKFOSSIL
UTAH
Family Hardware
STOP
pets
OPEN
FORK & FOSSIL
OPEN
Grand Opening!
Looking for ludicrous piles of MEAT? Look no further! Get in here and eat. Kids under 7 get free T-Rex shaped tenders!
Open 10-7 Today
WELCOME TO FORK & FOSSIL.

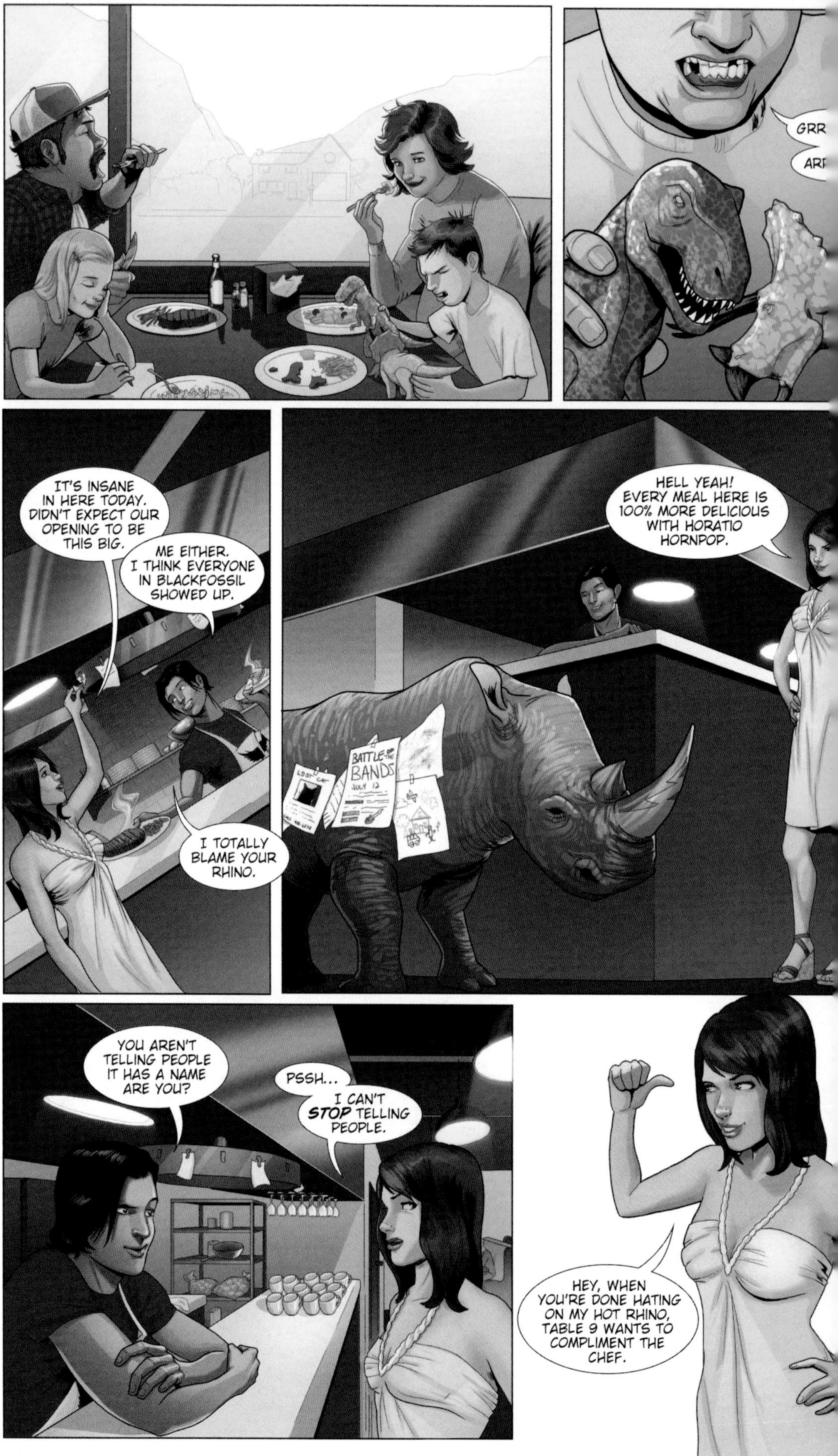
GRR
IT'S INSANE IN HERE TODAY. DIDN'T EXPECT OUR OPENING TO BE THIS BIG.
ME EITHER. I THINK EVERYONE IN BLACKFOSSIL SHOWED UP.
I TOTALLY BLAME YOUR RHINO.
HELL YEAH! EVERY MEAL HERE IS 100% MORE DELICIOUS WITH HORATIO HORNPOP.
LOST CAT
BATTLE OF THE BANDS
JULY 12
YOU AREN'T TELLING PEOPLE IT HAS A NAME ARE YOU?
PSSH... I CAN'T *STOP* TELLING PEOPLE.
HEY, WHEN YOU'RE DONE HATING ON MY HOT RHINO, TABLE 9 WANTS TO COMPLIMENT THE CHEF.

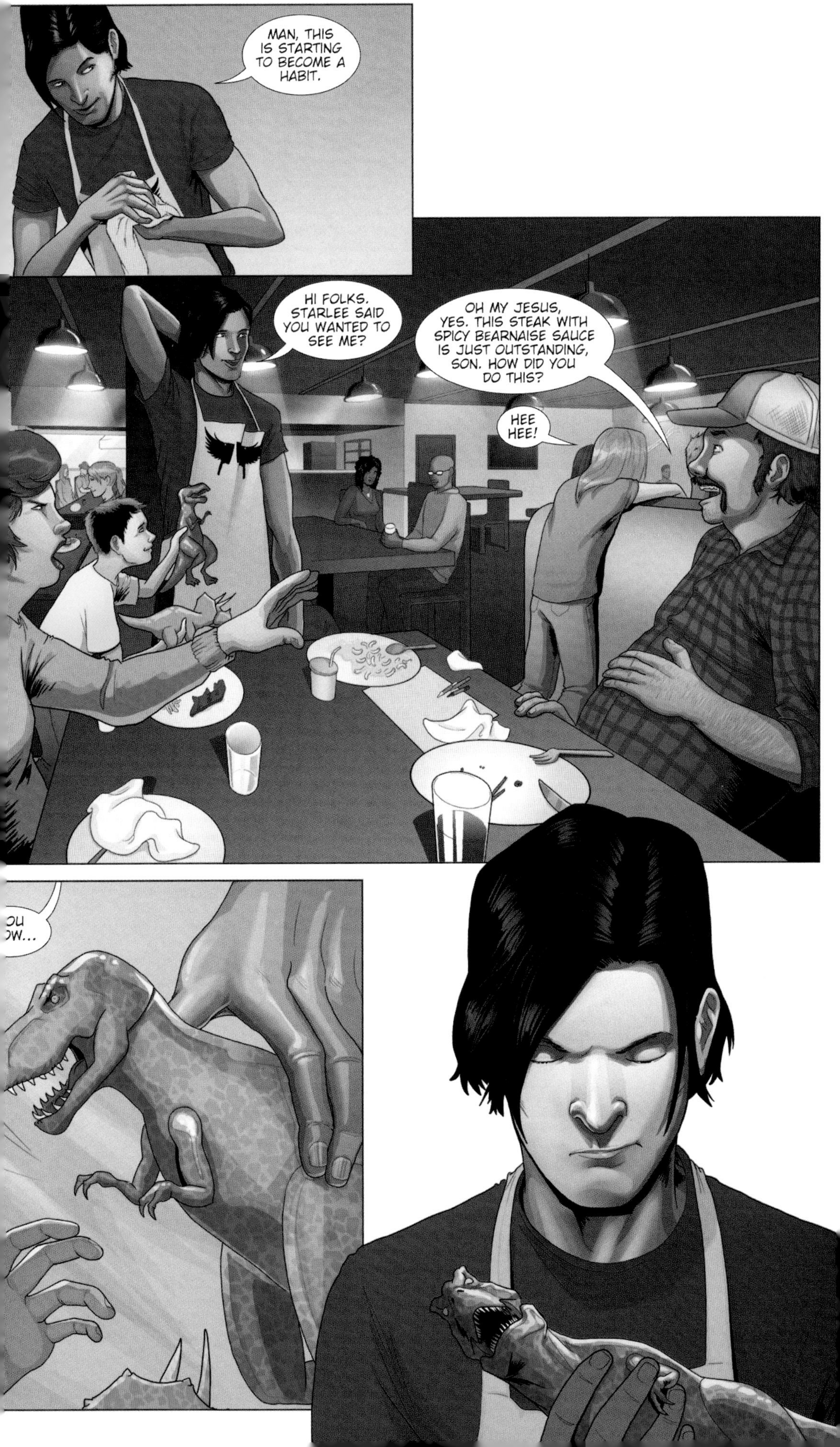
MAN, THIS IS STARTING TO BECOME A HABIT.
HI FOLKS. STARLEE SAID YOU WANTED TO SEE ME?
OH MY JESUS, YES. THIS STEAK WITH SPICY BEARNAISE SAUCE IS JUST OUTSTANDING, SON. HOW DID YOU DO THIS?
HEE HEE!

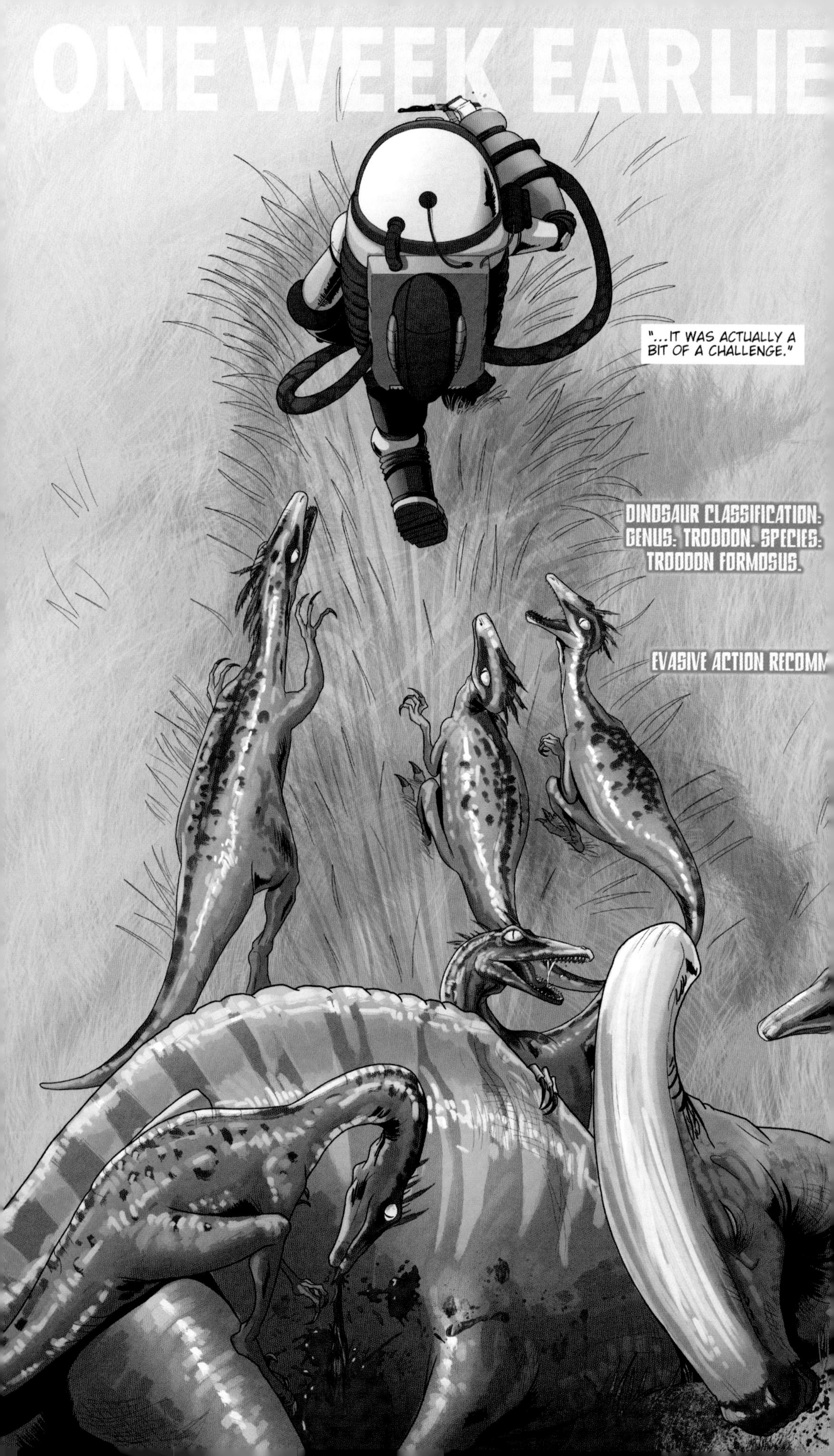
ONE WEEK EARLIE
"...IT WAS ACTUALLY A BIT OF A CHALLENGE."
DINOSAUR CLASSIFICATION: GENUS: TROODON. SPECIES: TROODON FORMOSUS.
EVASIVE ACTION RECOMM

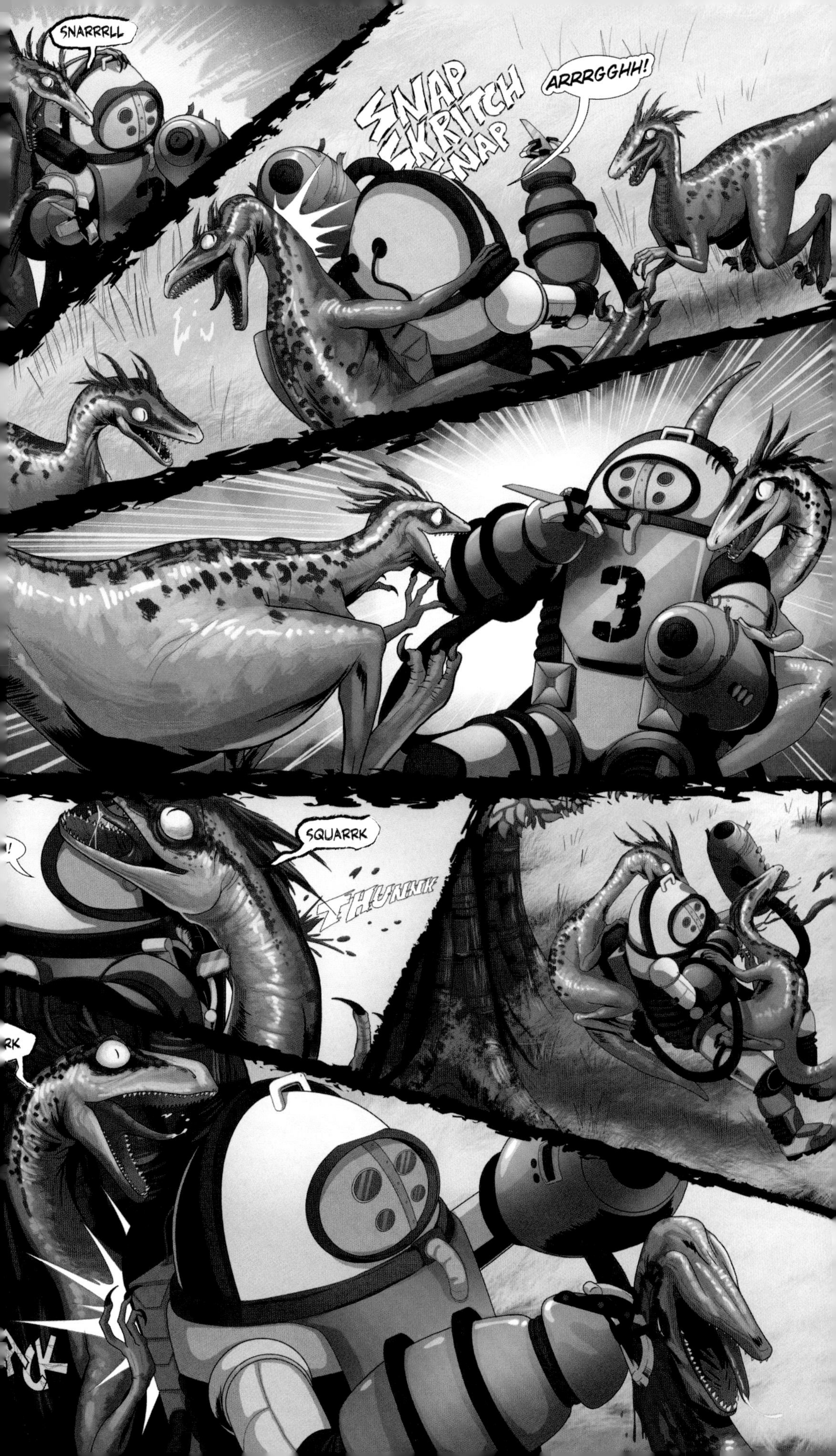
SNARRRLL
SNAP
KRITCH
SNAP
ARRRGGHH!
SQUARRK
THUNNK
RK
UK

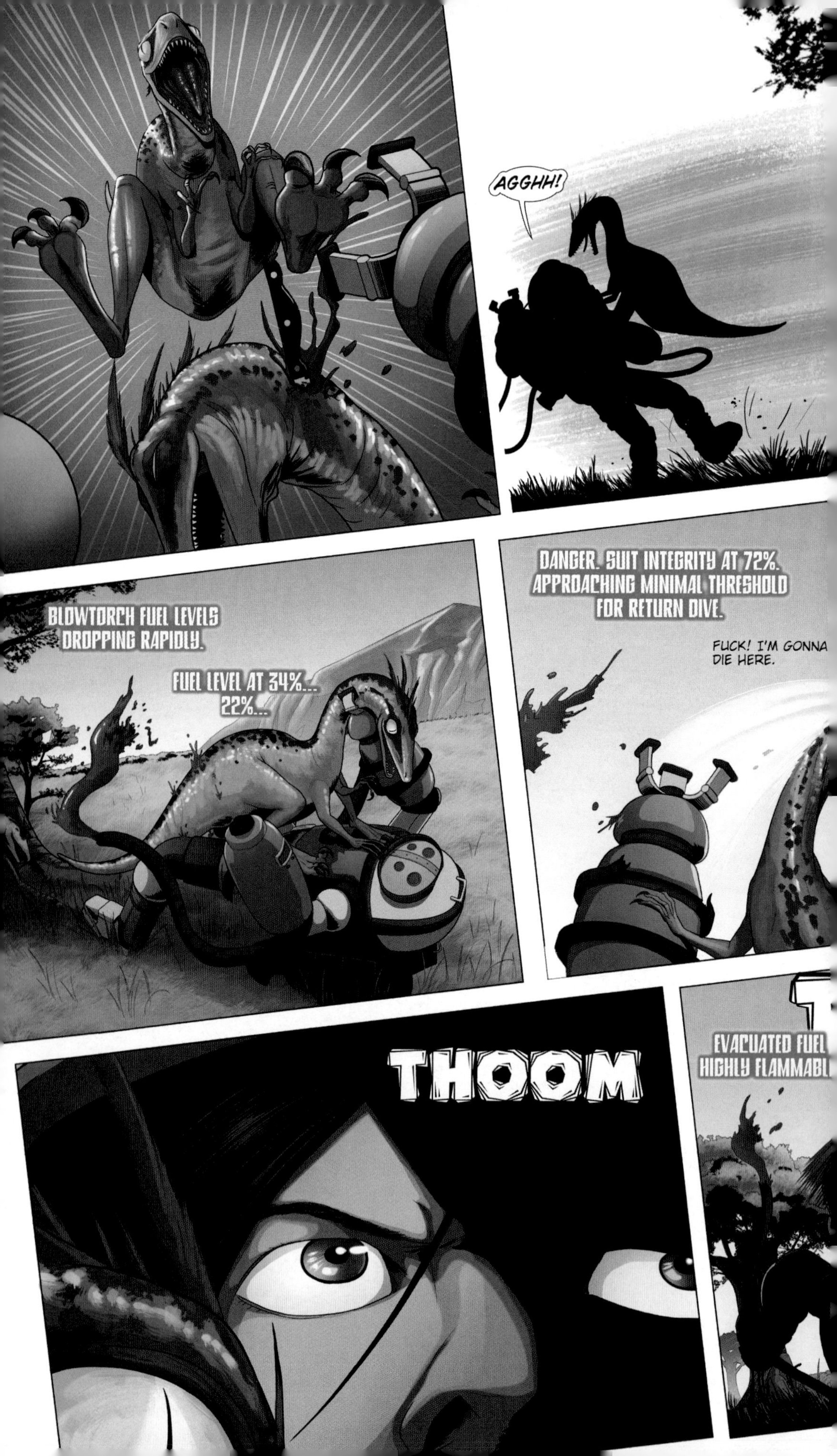
AGGHH!
BLOWTORCH FUEL LEVELS DROPPING RAPIDLY.
FUEL LEVEL AT 34%... 22%...
DANGER. SUIT INTEGRITY AT 72%. APPROACHING MINIMAL THRESHOLD FOR RETURN DIVE.
FUCK! I'M GONNA DIE HERE.
THOOM
EVACUATED FUEL HIGHLY FLAMMABL

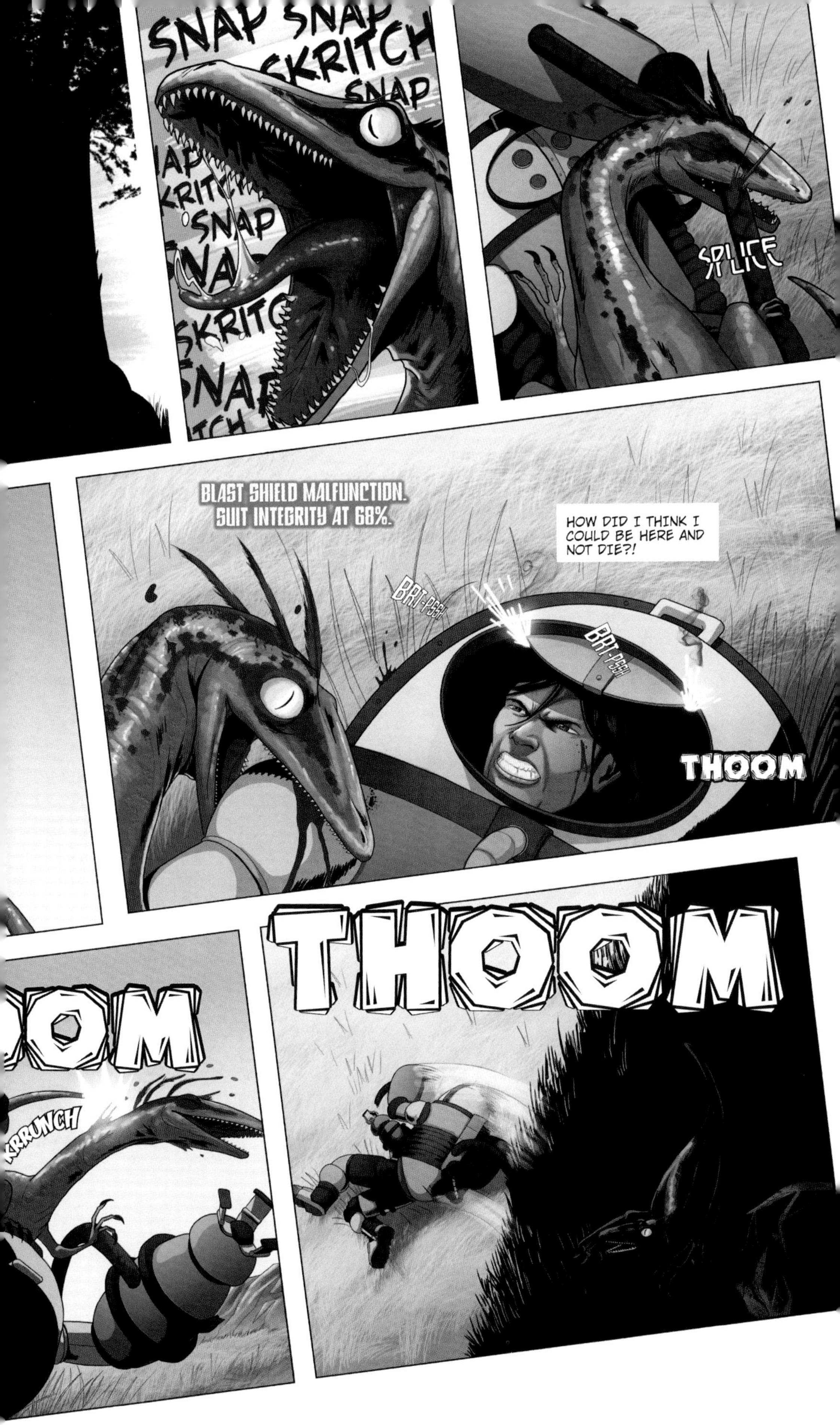
SNAP SNAP
SKRITCH
SNAP
SNAP
SPLICE
BLAST SHIELD MALFUNCTION.
SUIT INTEGRITY AT 68%.
HOW DID I THINK I COULD BE HERE AND NOT DIE?!
BRT-PSSH
BRT-PSSH
THOOM
KRRUNCH
THOOM

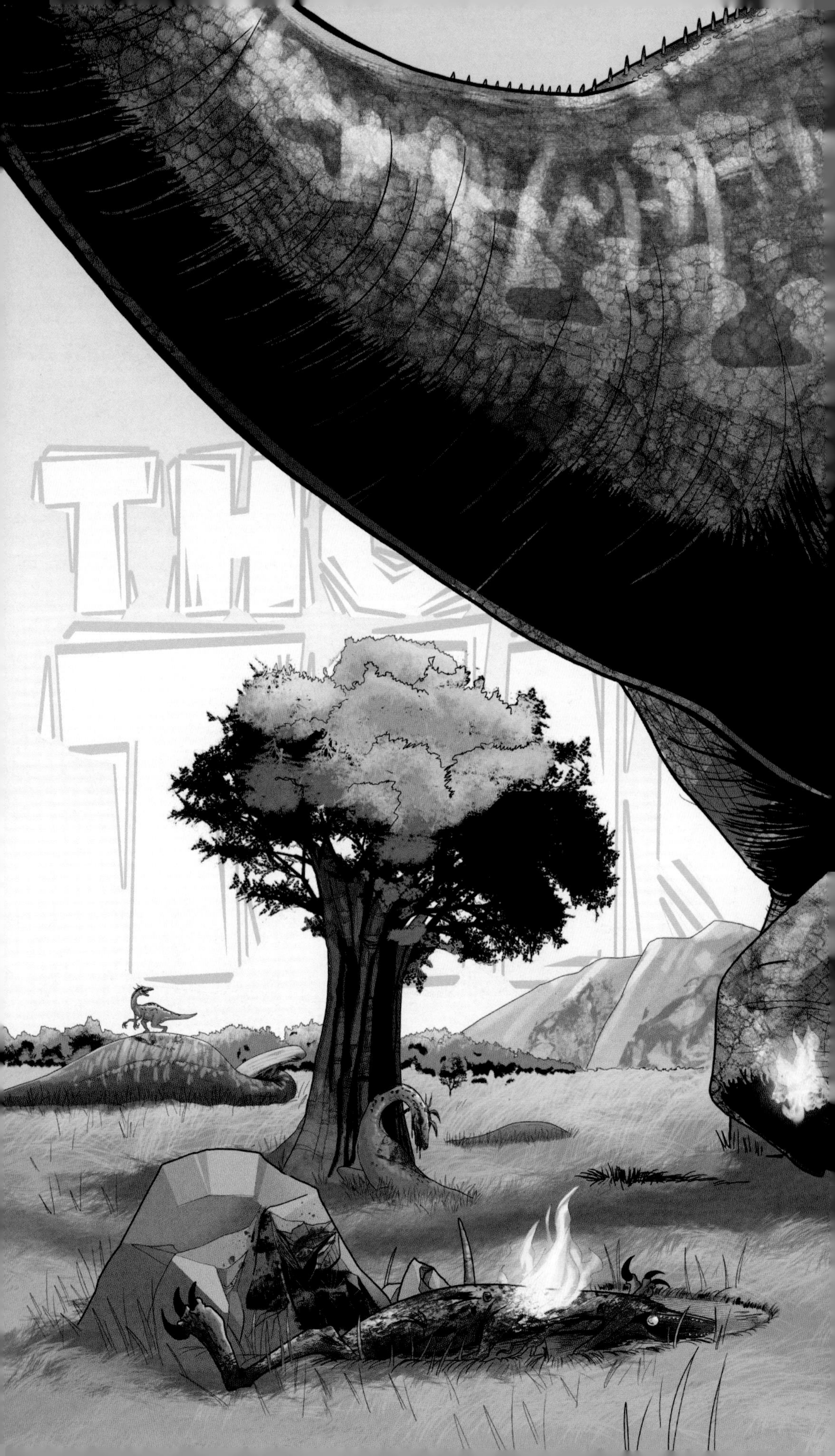

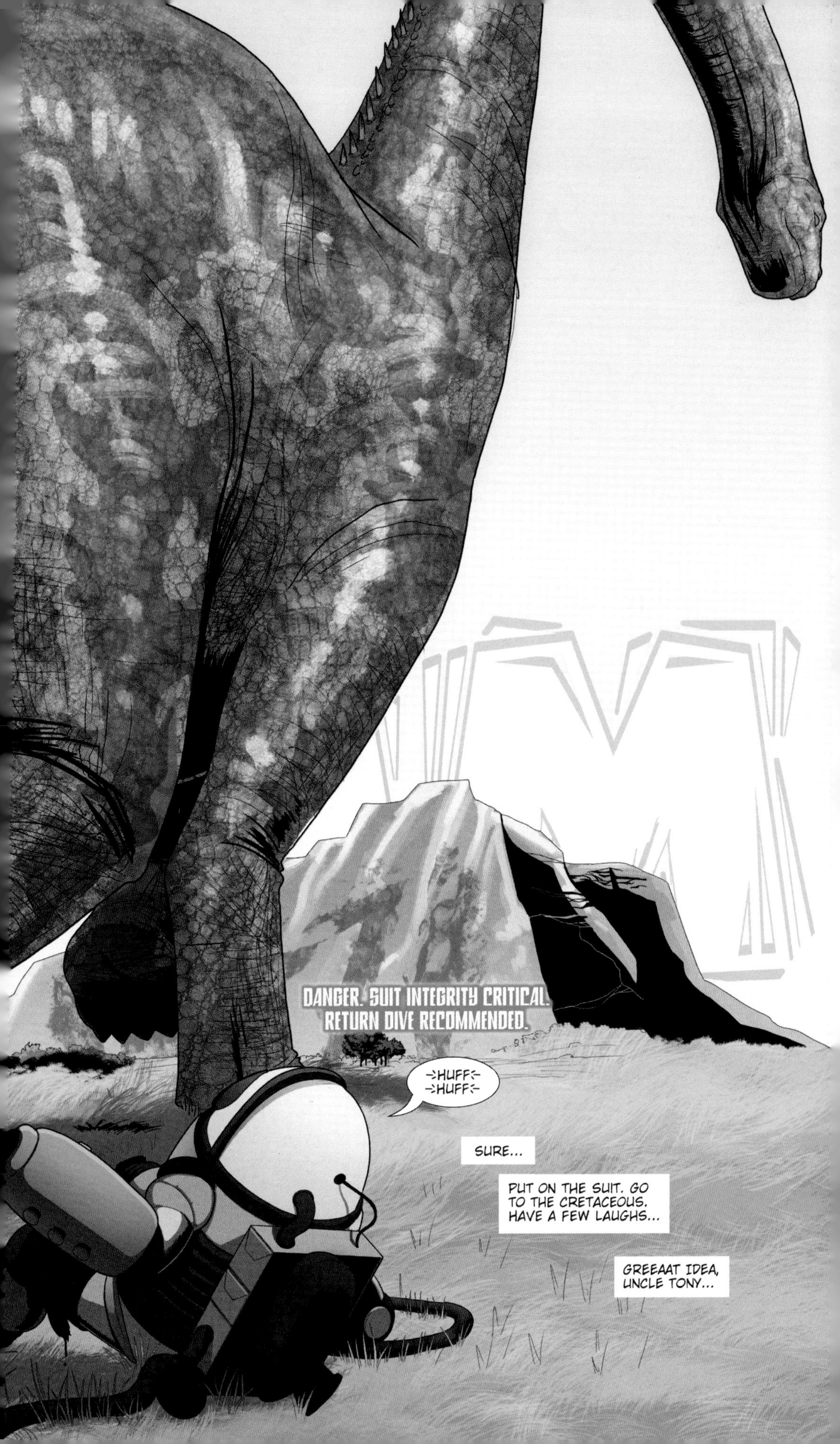
DANGER. SUIT INTEGRITY CRITICAL.
RETURN DIVE RECOMMENDED.
HUFF HUFF
SURE...
PUT ON THE SUIT. GO TO THE CRETACEOUS. HAVE A FEW LAUGHS...
GREEAAT IDEA, UNCLE TONY...

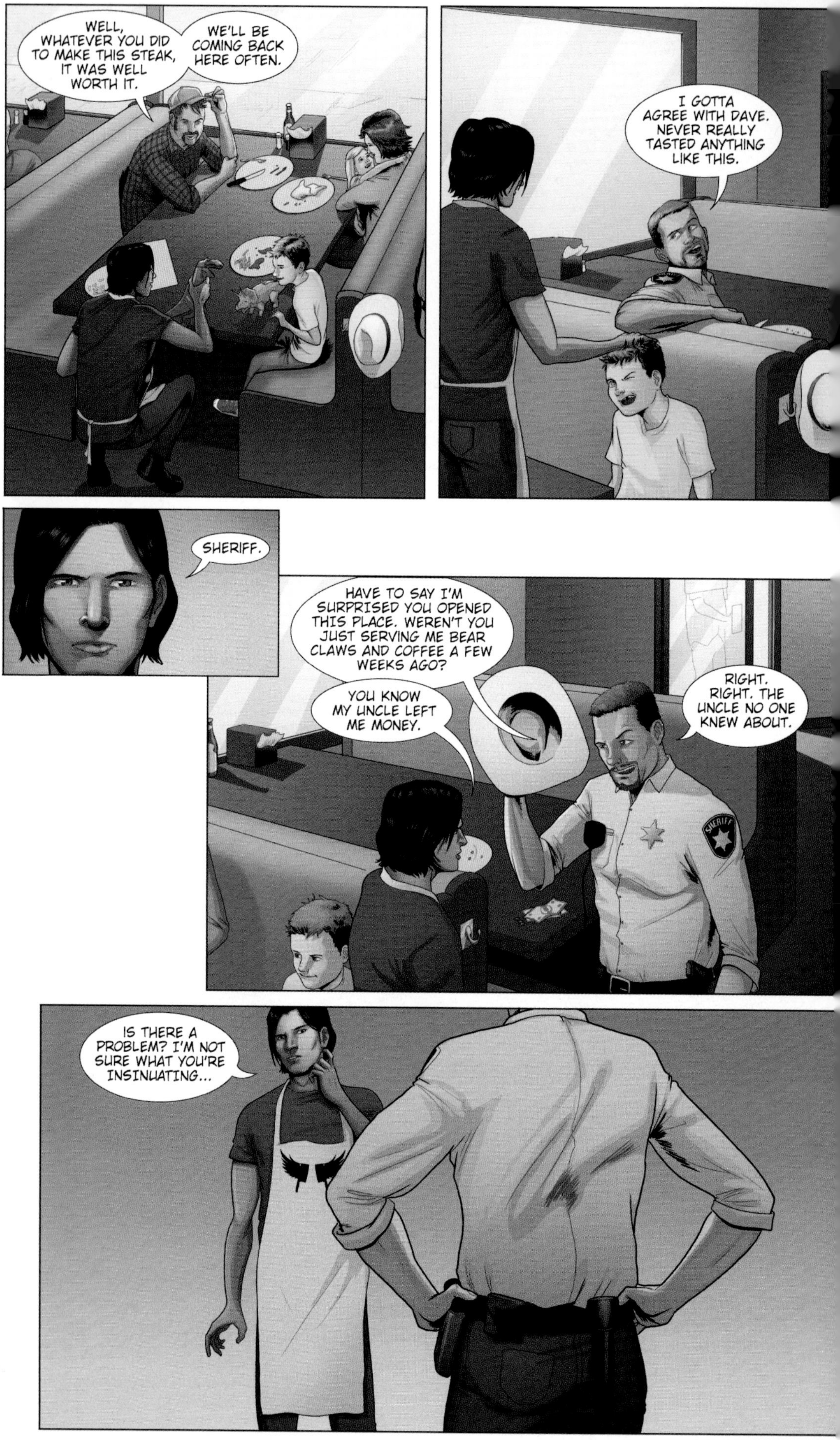
WELL, WHATEVER YOU DID TO MAKE THIS STEAK, IT WAS WELL WORTH IT.
WE'LL BE COMING BACK HERE OFTEN.
I GOTTA AGREE WITH DAVE. NEVER REALLY TASTED ANYTHING LIKE THIS.
SHERIFF.
HAVE TO SAY I'M SURPRISED YOU OPENED THIS PLACE. WEREN'T YOU JUST SERVING ME BEAR CLAWS AND COFFEE A FEW WEEKS AGO?
YOU KNOW MY UNCLE LEFT ME MONEY.
RIGHT. RIGHT. THE UNCLE NO ONE KNEW ABOUT.
IS THERE A PROBLEM? I'M NOT SURE WHAT YOU'RE INSINUATING...

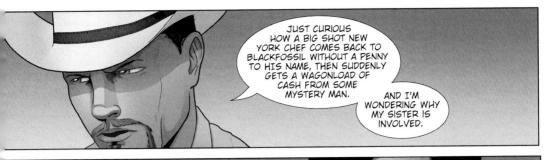

JUST CURIOUS HOW A BIG SHOT NEW YORK CHEF COMES BACK TO BLACKFOSSIL WITHOUT A PENNY TO HIS NAME, THEN SUDDENLY GETS A WAGONLOAD OF CASH FROM SOME MYSTERY MAN.

AND I'M WONDERING WHY MY SISTER IS INVOLVED.

DON... I ADMIT IT DOES SEEM A LITTLE SHADY. BUT THIS IS ON THE LEVEL. YOU CAN CHECK WITH MR. PEARSON IF YOU WANT.

AND I WOULD NEVER DO ANYTHING TO HURT STARLEE. YOU SHOULD KNOW THAT.

RIGHT. LIKE THAT TIME YOU KNOCKED HER INTO A DRESSER AND SHE GOT 12 STICHES?

THAT WAS AN ACCIDENT! YOU'RE THE ONE WHO TRIPPED ME INTO HER!

AND WE WERE EIGHT!

NOTHING BAD BETTER HAPPEN TO MY SIS, NATE. BECAUSE IF SHE GETS HURT IN ANY WAY, I PROMISE SOMETHING WILL DEFINITELY HAPPEN TO YOU.

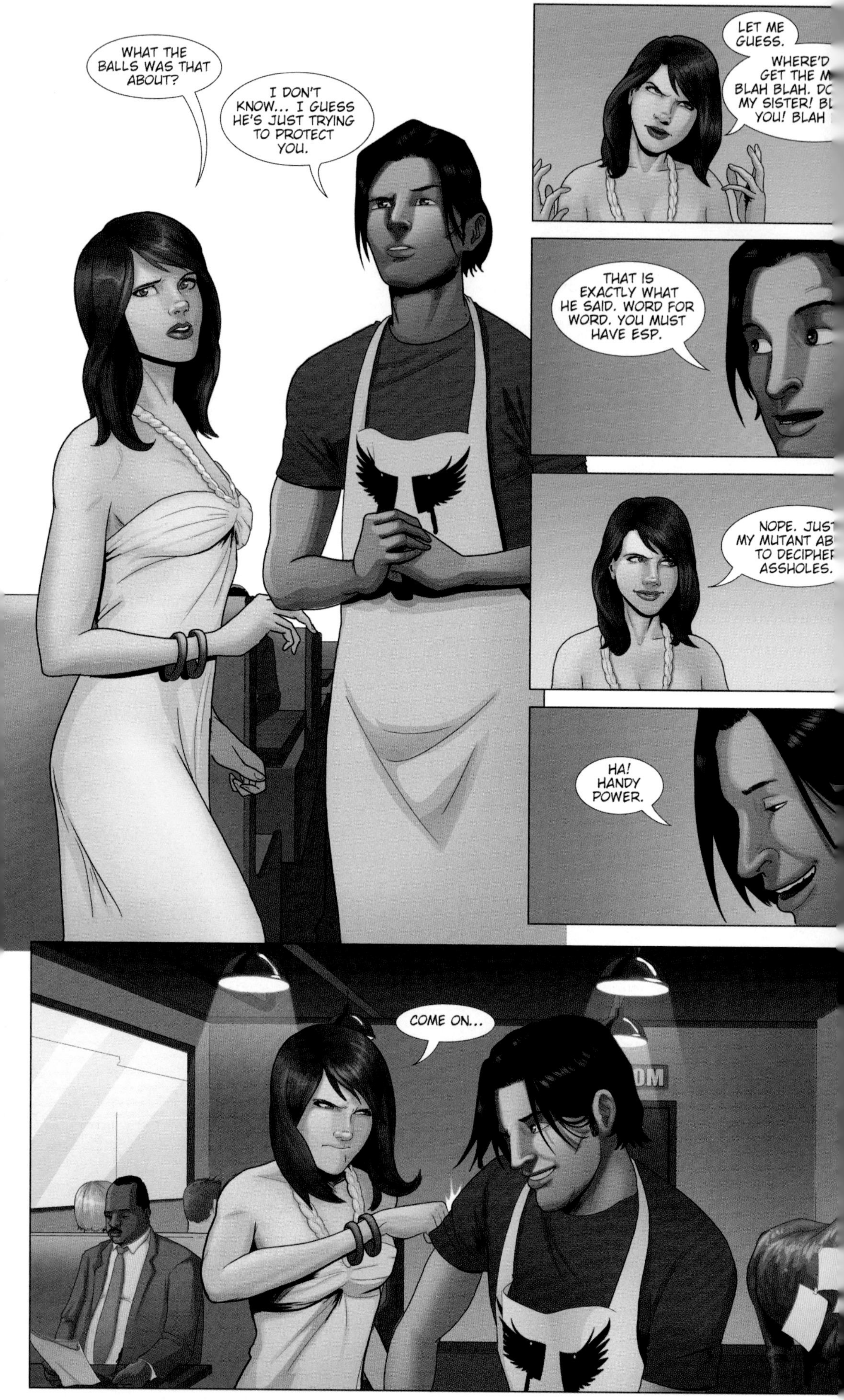
WHAT THE BALLS WAS THAT ABOUT?
I DON'T KNOW... I GUESS HE'S JUST TRYING TO PROTECT YOU.
LET ME GUESS.
WHERE'D GET THE
BLAH BLAH.
MY SISTER!
YOU! BLAH
THAT IS EXACTLY WHAT HE SAID. WORD FOR WORD. YOU MUST HAVE ESP.
NOPE. JUST MY MUTANT
TO DECIPHER
ASSHOLES.
HA! HANDY POWER.
COME ON...

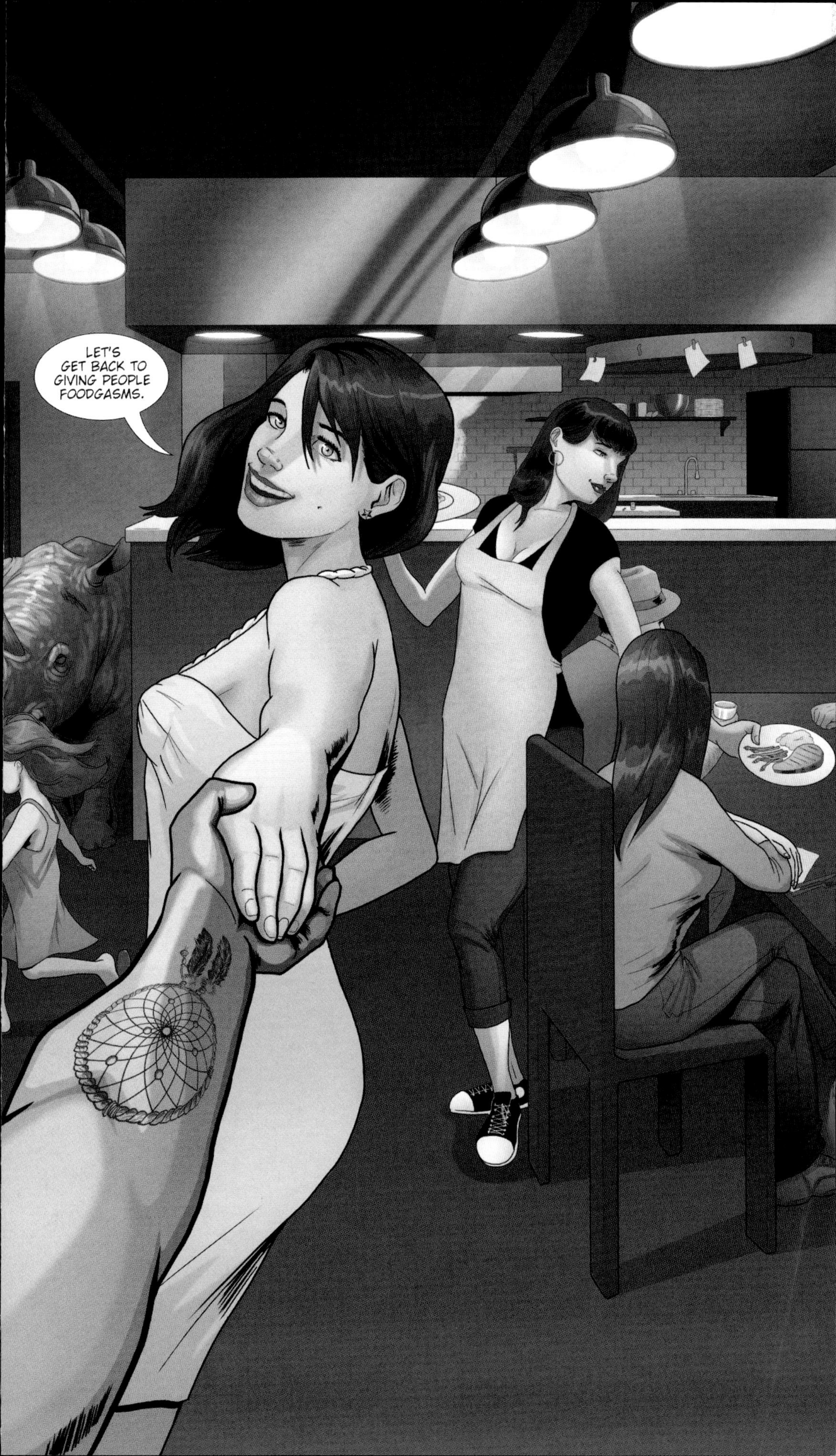
LET'S GET BACK TO GIVING PEOPLE FOODGASMS.

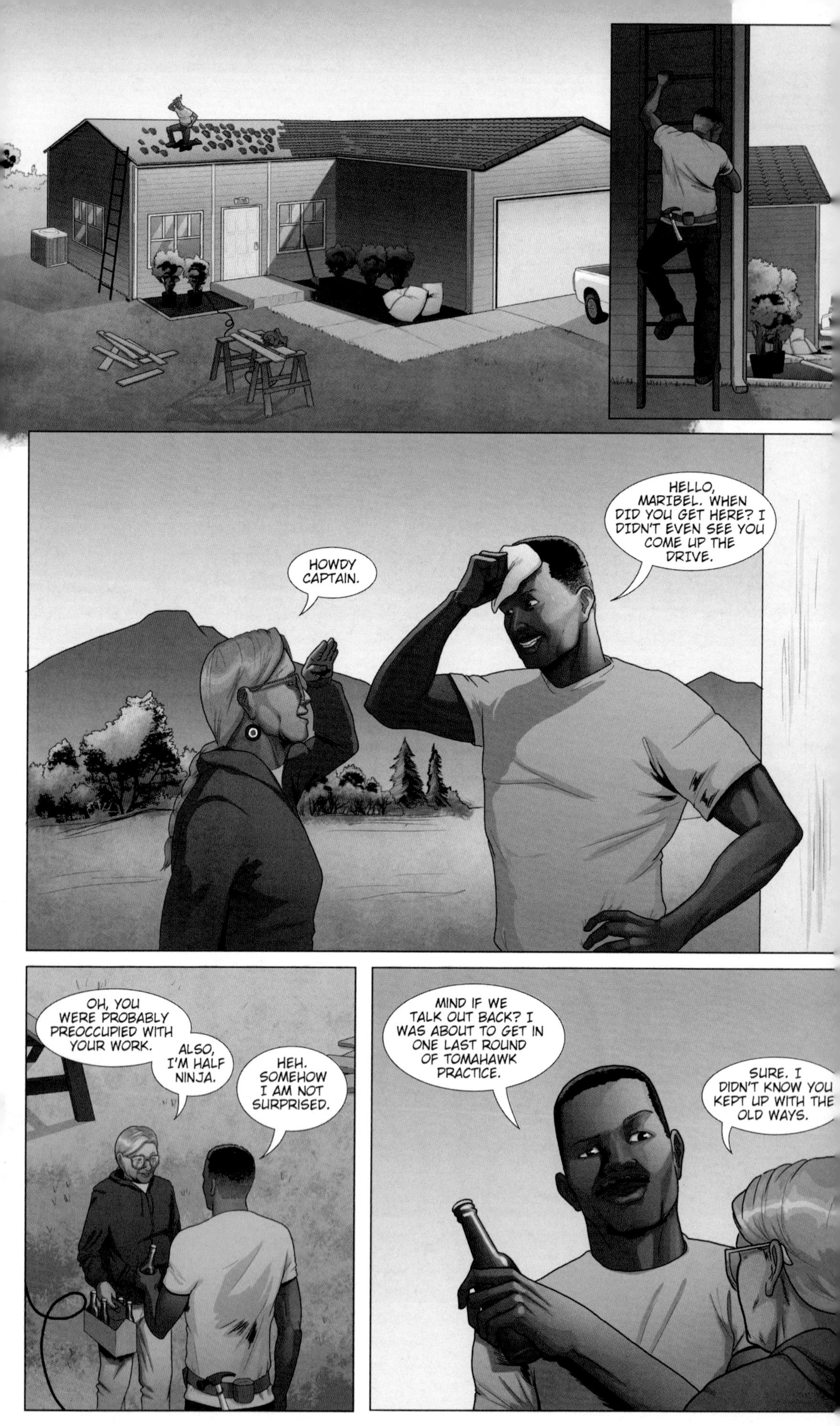
HOWDY CAPTAIN.
HELLO, MARIBEL. WHEN DID YOU GET HERE? I DIDN'T EVEN SEE YOU COME UP THE DRIVE.
OH, YOU WERE PROBABLY PREOCCUPIED WITH YOUR WORK.
ALSO, I'M HALF NINJA.
HEH. SOMEHOW I AM NOT SURPRISED.
MIND IF WE TALK OUT BACK? I WAS ABOUT TO GET IN ONE LAST ROUND OF TOMAHAWK PRACTICE.
SURE. I DIDN'T KNOW YOU KEPT UP WITH THE OLD WAYS.

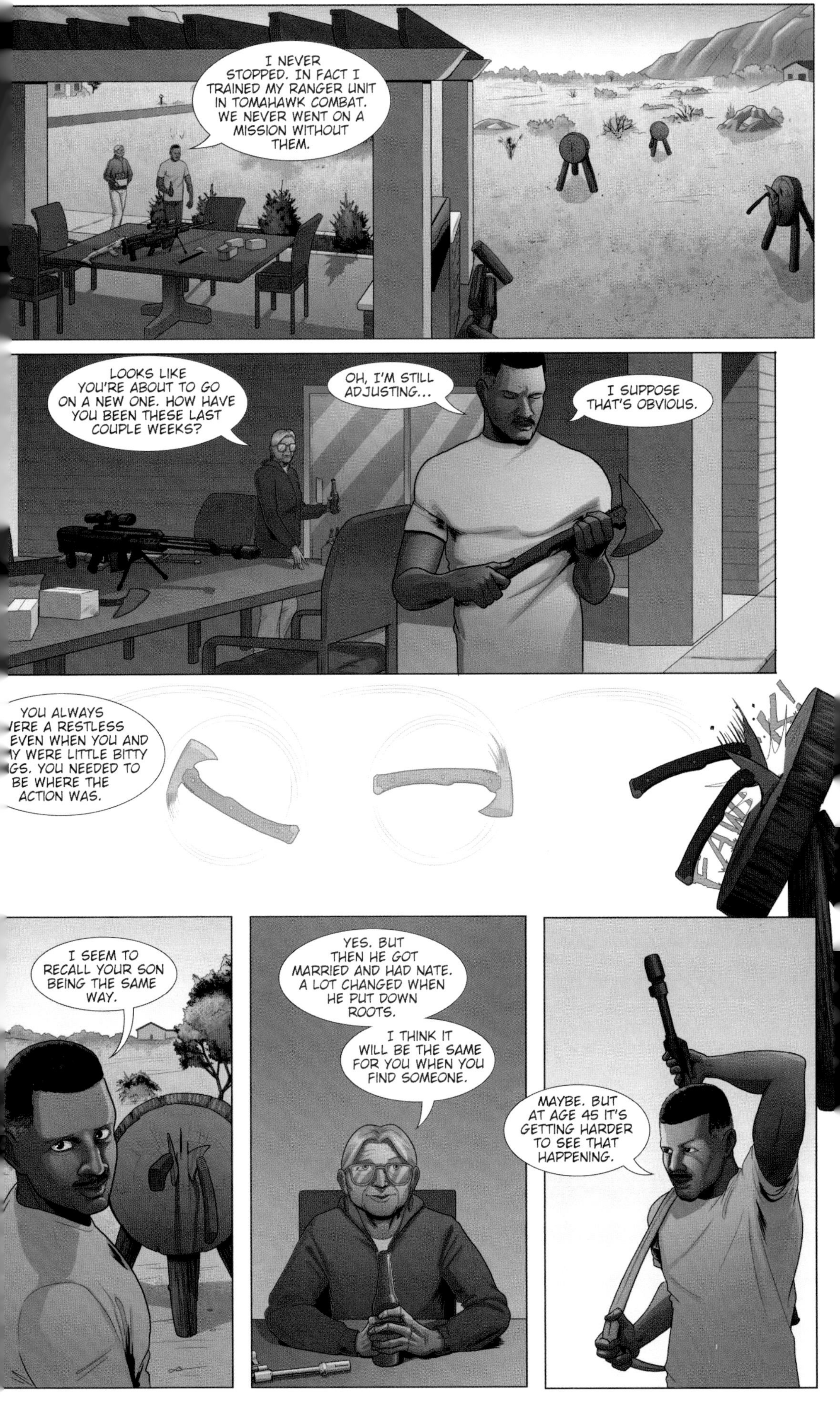
I NEVER STOPPED. IN FACT I TRAINED MY RANGER UNIT IN TOMAHAWK COMBAT. WE NEVER WENT ON A MISSION WITHOUT THEM.
LOOKS LIKE YOU'RE ABOUT TO GO ON A NEW ONE. HOW HAVE YOU BEEN THESE LAST COUPLE WEEKS?
OH, I'M STILL ADJUSTING...
I SUPPOSE THAT'S OBVIOUS.
YOU ALWAYS ERE A RESTLESS EVEN WHEN YOU AND Y WERE LITTLE BITTY GS. YOU NEEDED TO BE WHERE THE ACTION WAS.
I SEEM TO RECALL YOUR SON BEING THE SAME WAY.
YES. BUT THEN HE GOT MARRIED AND HAD NATE. A LOT CHANGED WHEN HE PUT DOWN ROOTS.
I THINK IT WILL BE THE SAME FOR YOU WHEN YOU FIND SOMEONE.
MAYBE. BUT AT AGE 45 IT'S GETTING HARDER TO SEE THAT HAPPENING.

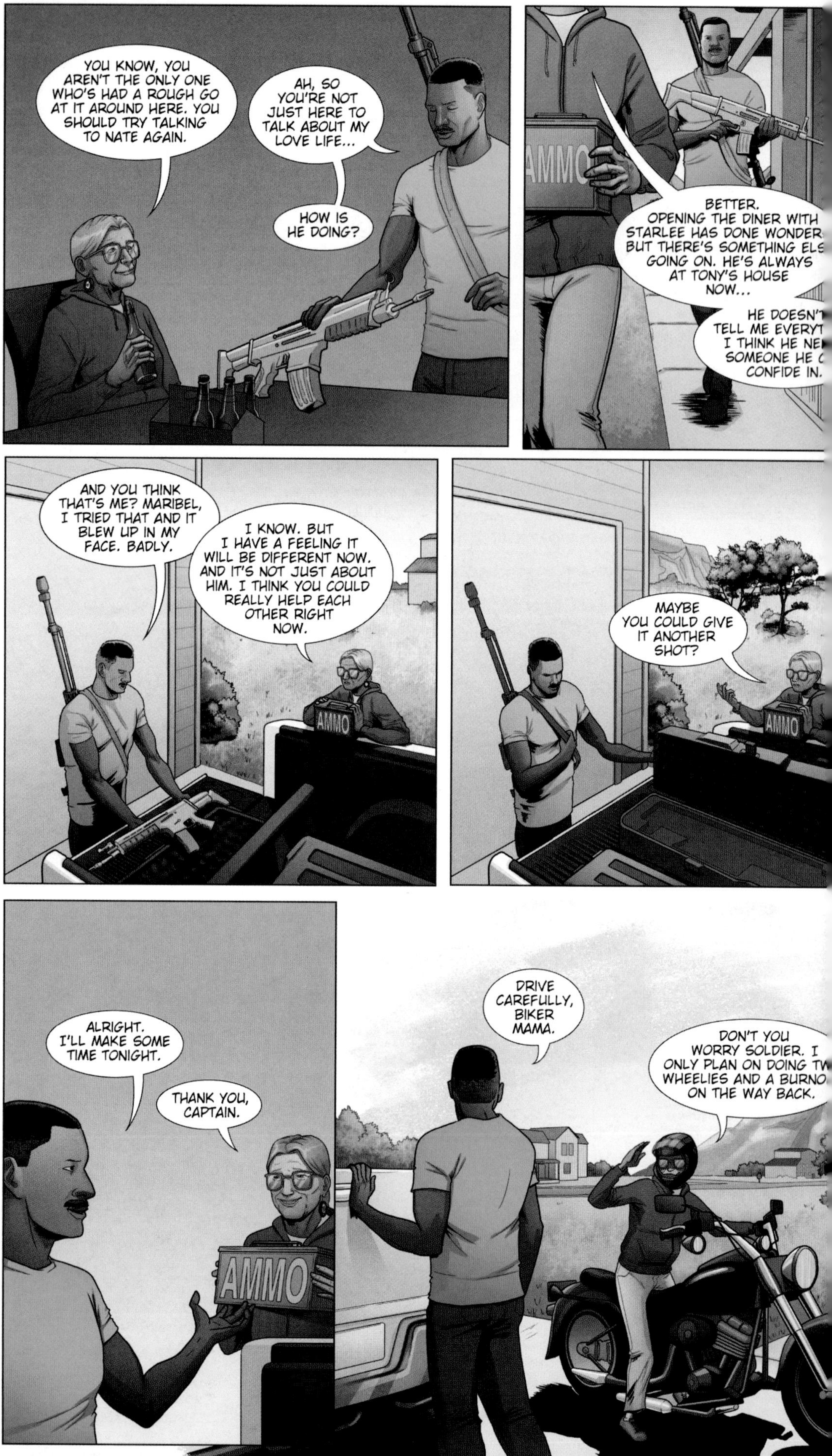
YOU KNOW, YOU AREN'T THE ONLY ONE WHO'S HAD A ROUGH GO AT IT AROUND HERE. YOU SHOULD TRY TALKING TO NATE AGAIN.
AH, SO YOU'RE NOT JUST HERE TO TALK ABOUT MY LOVE LIFE...
HOW IS HE DOING?
BETTER. OPENING THE DINER WITH STARLEE HAS DONE WONDER BUT THERE'S SOMETHING ELS GOING ON. HE'S ALWAYS AT TONY'S HOUSE NOW...
HE DOESN' TELL ME EVERY I THINK HE NE SOMEONE HE CONFIDE IN.
AMMO
AND YOU THINK THAT'S ME? MARIBEL, I TRIED THAT AND IT BLEW UP IN MY FACE. BADLY.
I KNOW. BUT I HAVE A FEELING IT WILL BE DIFFERENT NOW. AND IT'S NOT JUST ABOUT HIM. I THINK YOU COULD REALLY HELP EACH OTHER RIGHT NOW.
AMMO
MAYBE YOU COULD GIVE IT ANOTHER SHOT?
AMMO
ALRIGHT. I'LL MAKE SOME TIME TONIGHT.
THANK YOU, CAPTAIN.
AMMO
DRIVE CAREFULLY, BIKER MAMA.
DON'T YOU WORRY SOLDIER. I ONLY PLAN ON DOING T WHEELIES AND A BURN ON THE WAY BACK.

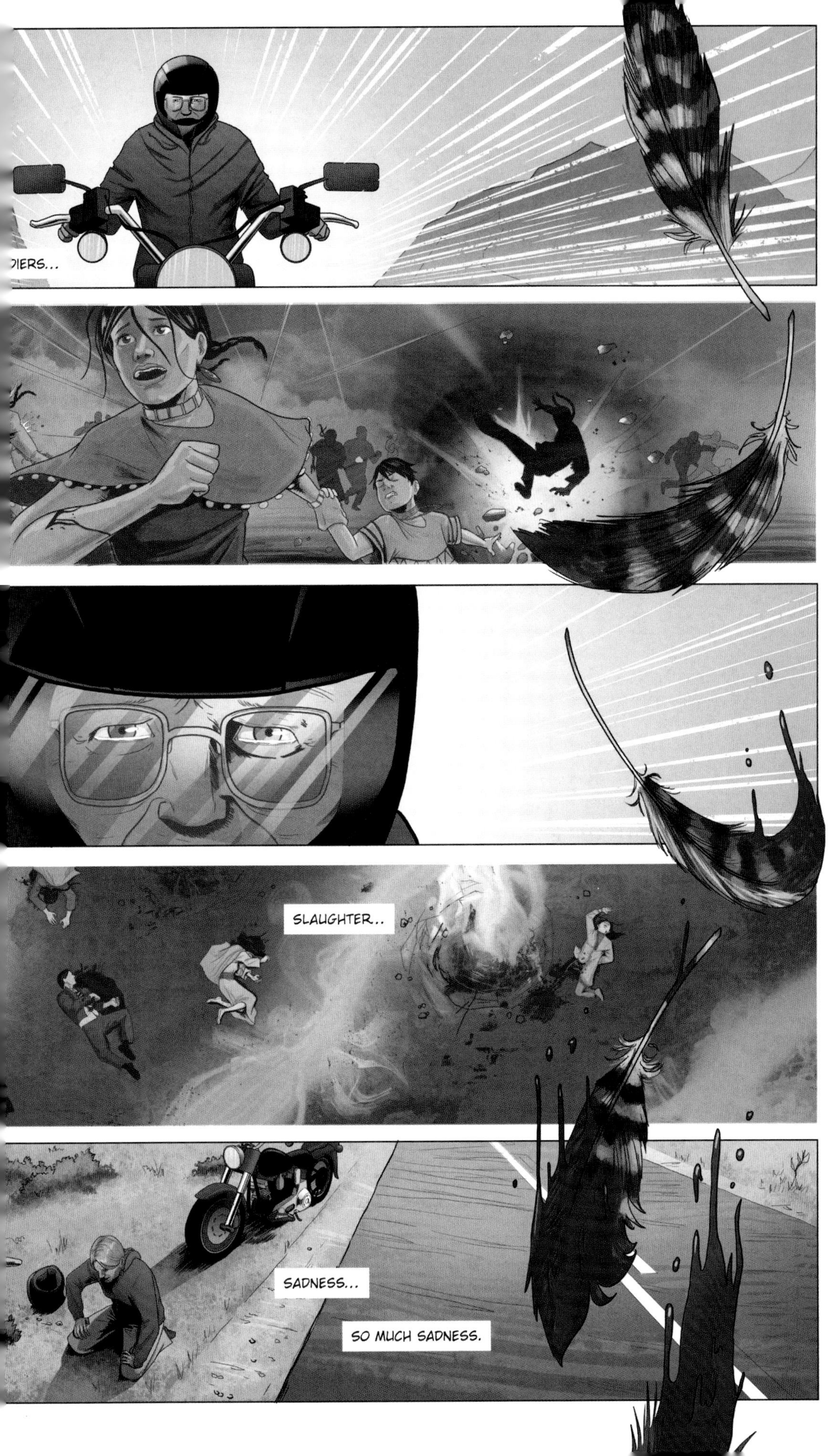

DIERS...
SLAUGHTER..
SADNESS...
SO MUCH SADNESS.

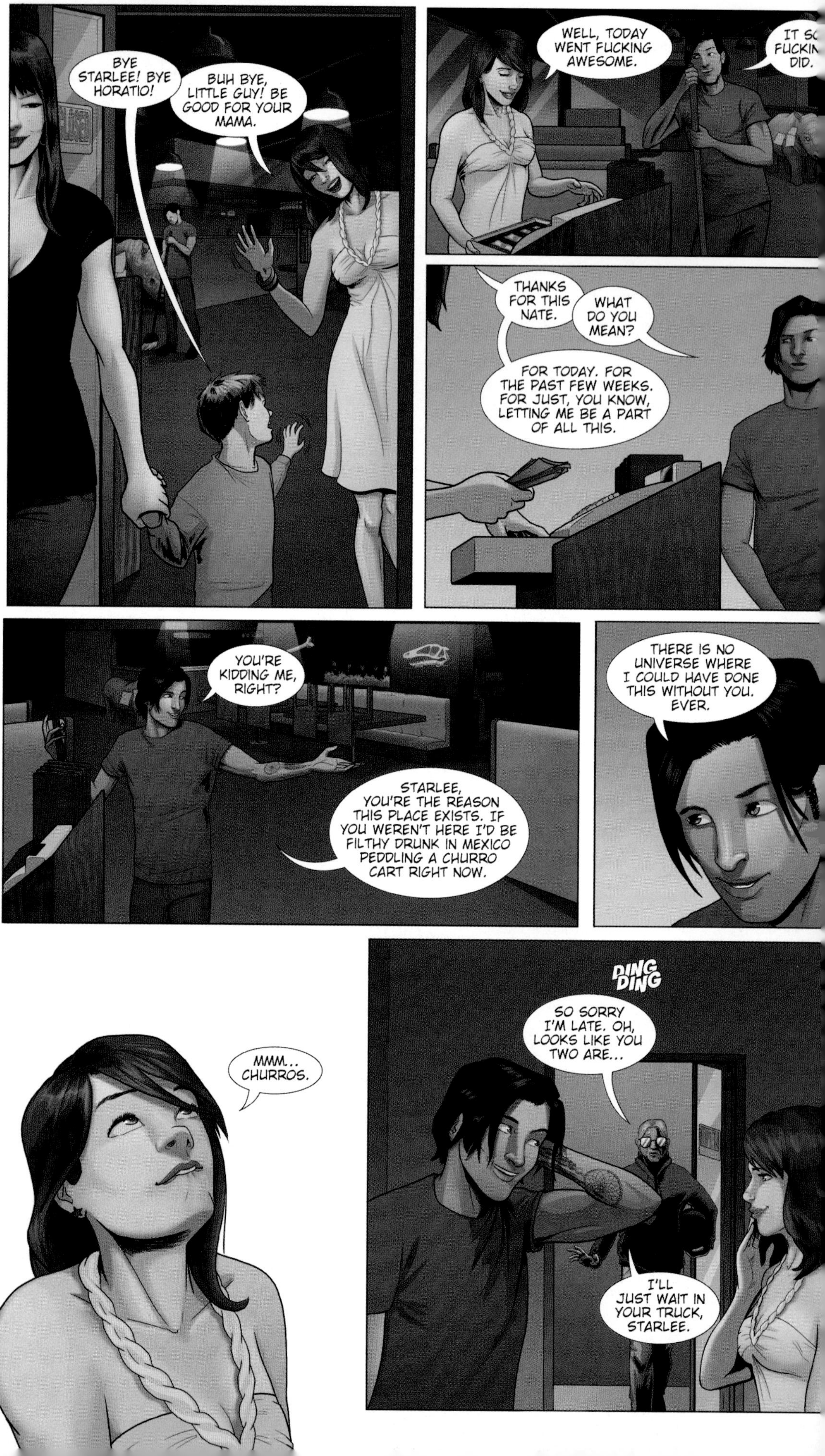
BYE STARLEE! BYE HORATIO!
BUH BYE, LITTLE GUY! BE GOOD FOR YOUR MAMA.
WELL, TODAY WENT FUCKING AWESOME.
THANKS FOR THIS NATE.
WHAT DO YOU MEAN?
FOR TODAY. FOR THE PAST FEW WEEKS. FOR JUST, YOU KNOW, LETTING ME BE A PART OF ALL THIS.
YOU'RE KIDDING ME, RIGHT?
STARLEE, YOU'RE THE REASON THIS PLACE EXISTS. IF YOU WEREN'T HERE I'D BE FILTHY DRUNK IN MEXICO PEDDLING A CHURRO CART RIGHT NOW.
THERE IS NO UNIVERSE WHERE I COULD HAVE DONE THIS WITHOUT YOU. EVER.
MMM... CHURROS.
DING DING
SO SORRY I'M LATE. OH, LOOKS LIKE YOU TWO ARE...
I'LL JUST WAIT IN YOUR TRUCK, STARLEE.

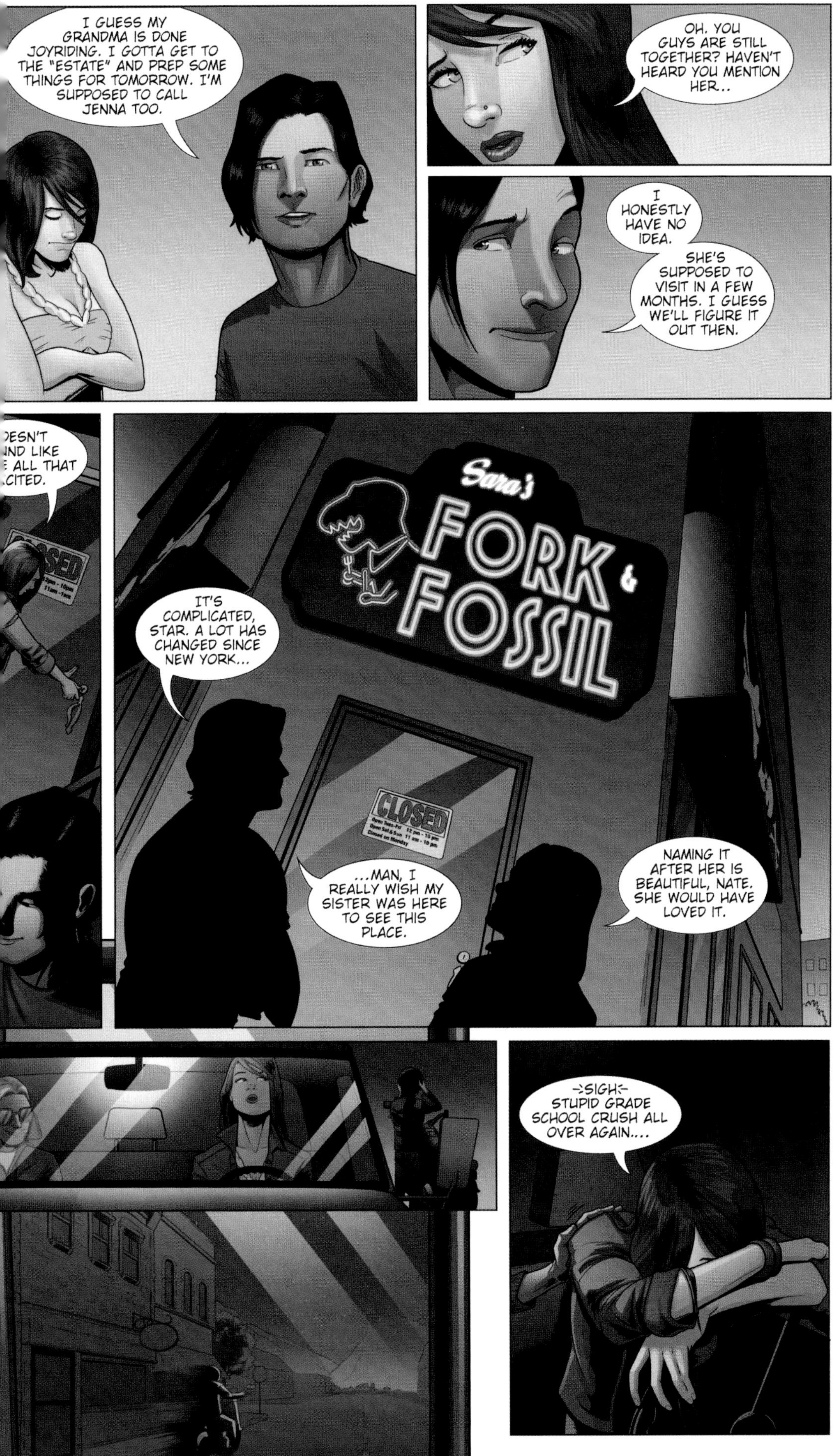
I GUESS MY GRANDMA IS DONE JOYRIDING. I GOTTA GET TO THE "ESTATE" AND PREP SOME THINGS FOR TOMORROW. I'M SUPPOSED TO CALL JENNA TOO.
OH. YOU GUYS ARE STILL TOGETHER? HAVEN'T HEARD YOU MENTION HER...
I HONESTLY HAVE NO IDEA.
SHE'S SUPPOSED TO VISIT IN A FEW MONTHS. I GUESS WE'LL FIGURE IT OUT THEN.
DESN'T
ND LIKE
E ALL THAT
CITED.
Sara's
FORK & FOSSIL
IT'S COMPLICATED, STAR. A LOT HAS CHANGED SINCE NEW YORK...
CLOSED
...MAN, I REALLY WISH MY SISTER WAS HERE TO SEE THIS PLACE.
NAMING IT AFTER HER IS BEAUTIFUL, NATE. SHE WOULD HAVE LOVED IT.
-SIGH-
STUPID GRADE SCHOOL CRUSH ALL OVER AGAIN....

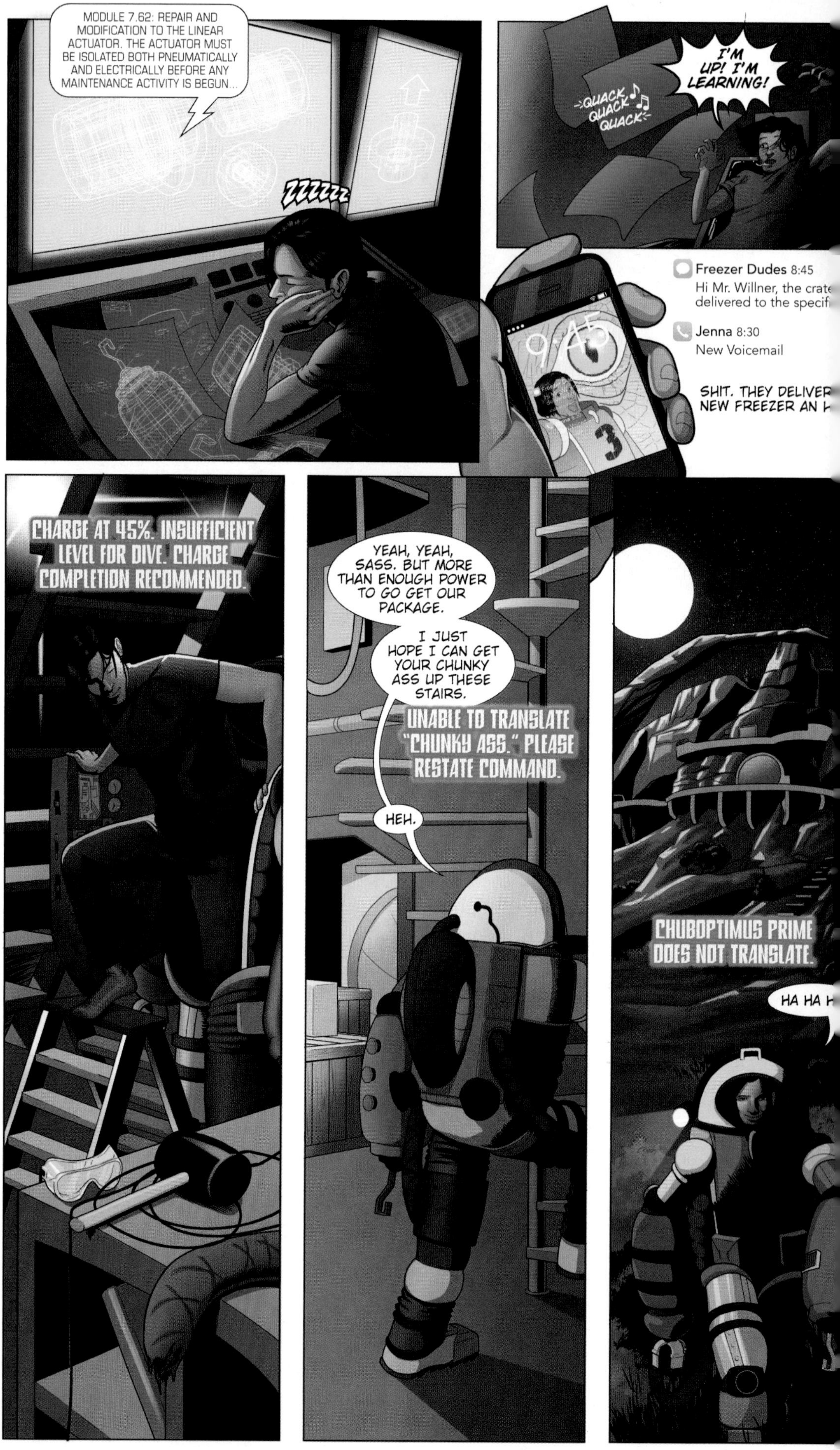
MODULE 7.62: REPAIR AND MODIFICATION TO THE LINEAR ACTUATOR. THE ACTUATOR MUST BE ISOLATED BOTH PNEUMATICALLY AND ELECTRICALLY BEFORE ANY MAINTENANCE ACTIVITY IS BEGUN...
ZZZZZZ
QUACK QUACK QUACK
I'M UP! I'M LEARNING!
9:45
Freezer Dudes 8:45
Hi Mr. Willner, the crate
delivered to the specifi
Jenna 8:30
New Voicemail
SHIT. THEY DELIVER
NEW FREEZER AN H
CHARGE AT 45%. INSUFFICIENT LEVEL FOR DIVE. CHARGE COMPLETION RECOMMENDED.
YEAH, YEAH, SASS. BUT MORE THAN ENOUGH POWER TO GO GET OUR PACKAGE.
I JUST HOPE I CAN GET YOUR CHUNKY ASS UP THESE STAIRS.
UNABLE TO TRANSLATE "CHUNKY ASS." PLEASE RESTATE COMMAND.
HEH.
CHUBOPTIMUS PRIME DOES NOT TRANSLATE.
HA HA H

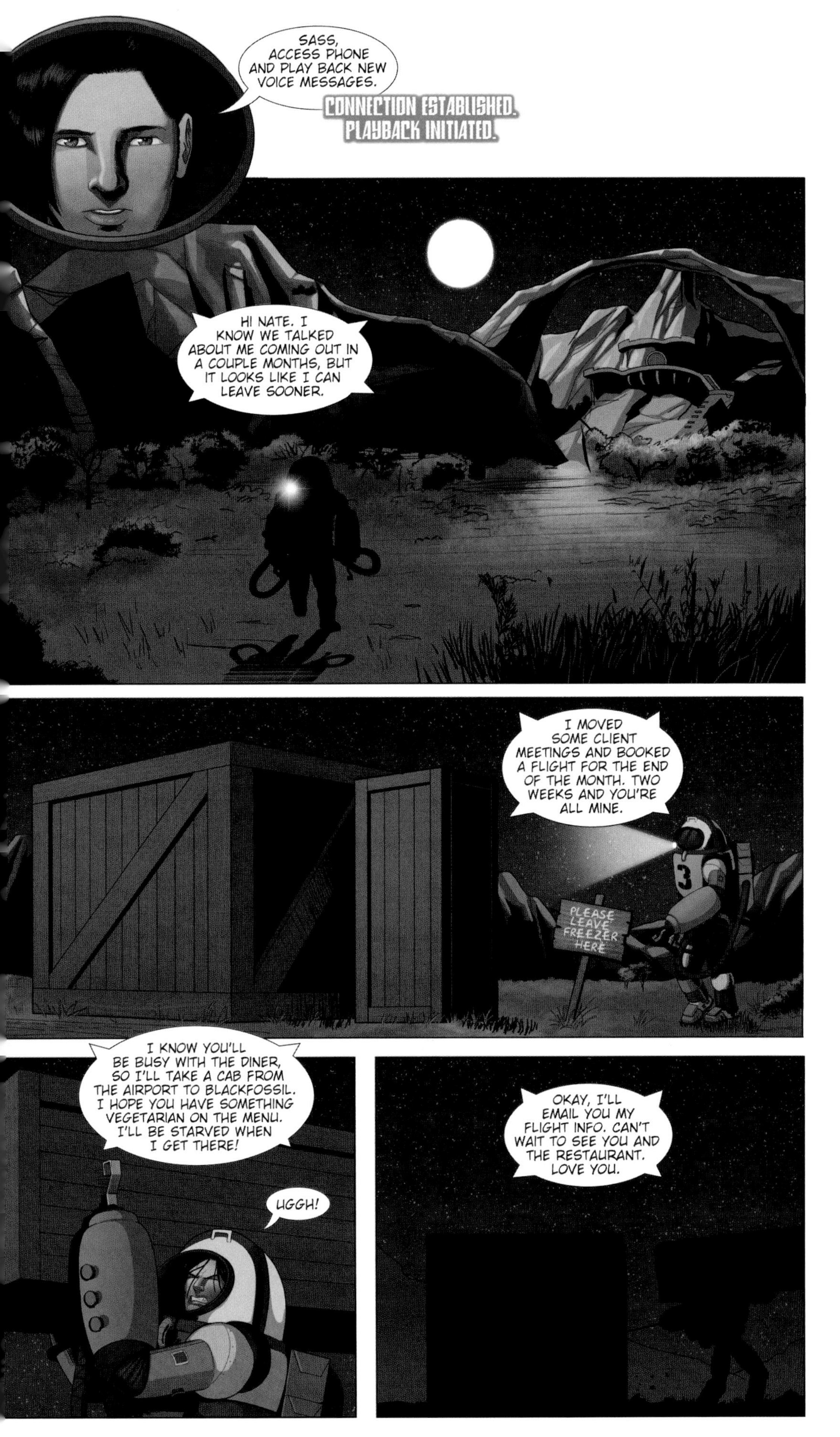
SASS, ACCESS PHONE AND PLAY BACK NEW VOICE MESSAGES.
CONNECTION ESTABLISHED. PLAYBACK INITIATED.
HI NATE. I KNOW WE TALKED ABOUT ME COMING OUT IN A COUPLE MONTHS, BUT IT LOOKS LIKE I CAN LEAVE SOONER.
I MOVED SOME CLIENT MEETINGS AND BOOKED A FLIGHT FOR THE END OF THE MONTH. TWO WEEKS AND YOU'RE ALL MINE.
PLEASE LEAVE FREEZER HERE
I KNOW YOU'LL BE BUSY WITH THE DINER, SO I'LL TAKE A CAB FROM THE AIRPORT TO BLACKFOSSIL. I HOPE YOU HAVE SOMETHING VEGETARIAN ON THE MENU. I'LL BE STARVED WHEN I GET THERE!
UGGH!
OKAY, I'LL EMAIL YOU MY FLIGHT INFO. CAN'T WAIT TO SEE YOU AND THE RESTAURANT. LOVE YOU.

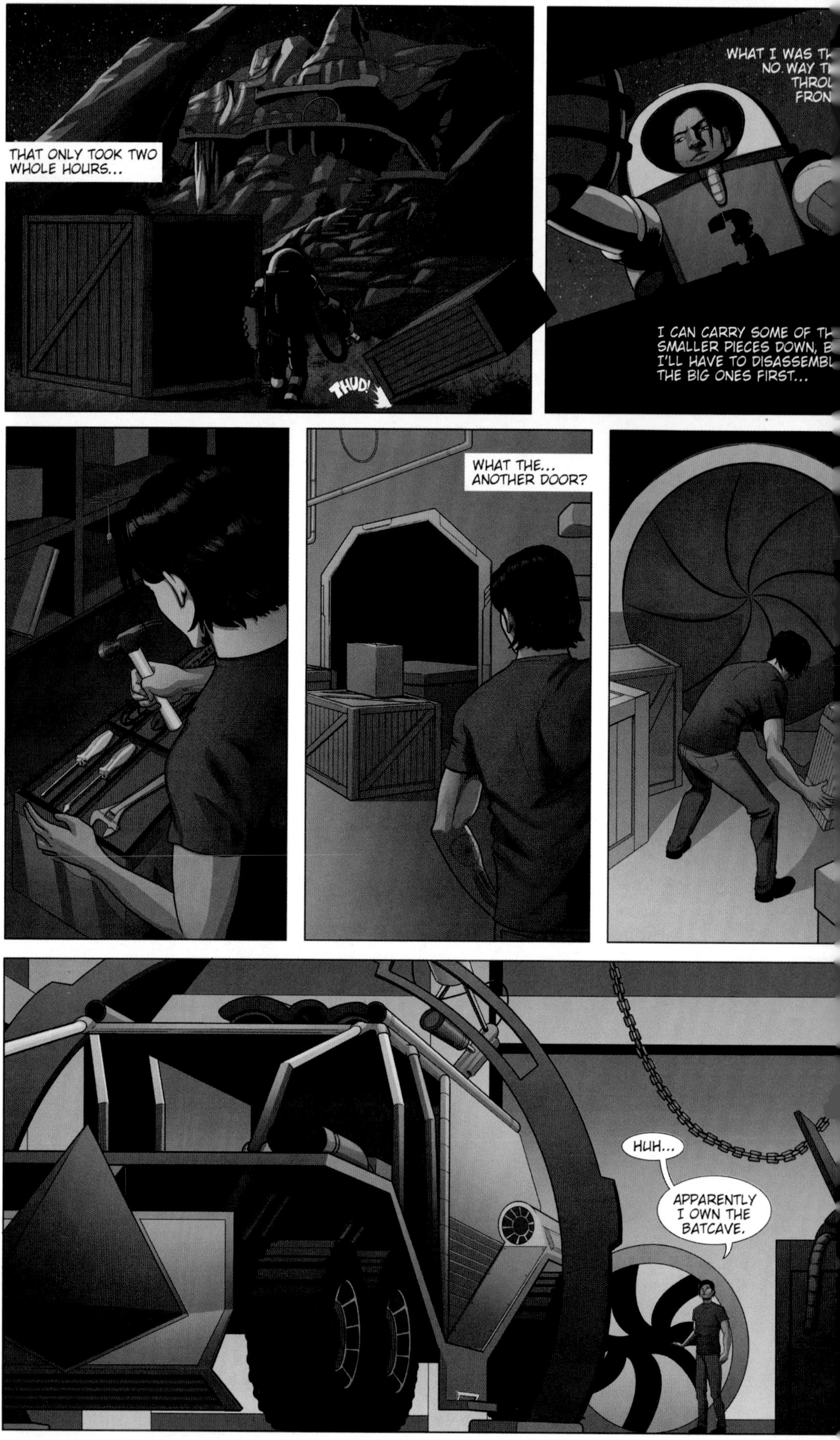
THAT ONLY TOOK TWO WHOLE HOURS...
THUD!
WHAT I WAS T
NO. WAY T
THRO
FRON
I CAN CARRY SOME OF TH
SMALLER PIECES DOWN, B
I'LL HAVE TO DISASSEMBL
THE BIG ONES FIRST...
WHAT THE... ANOTHER DOOR?
HUH...
APPARENTLY I OWN THE BATCAVE.

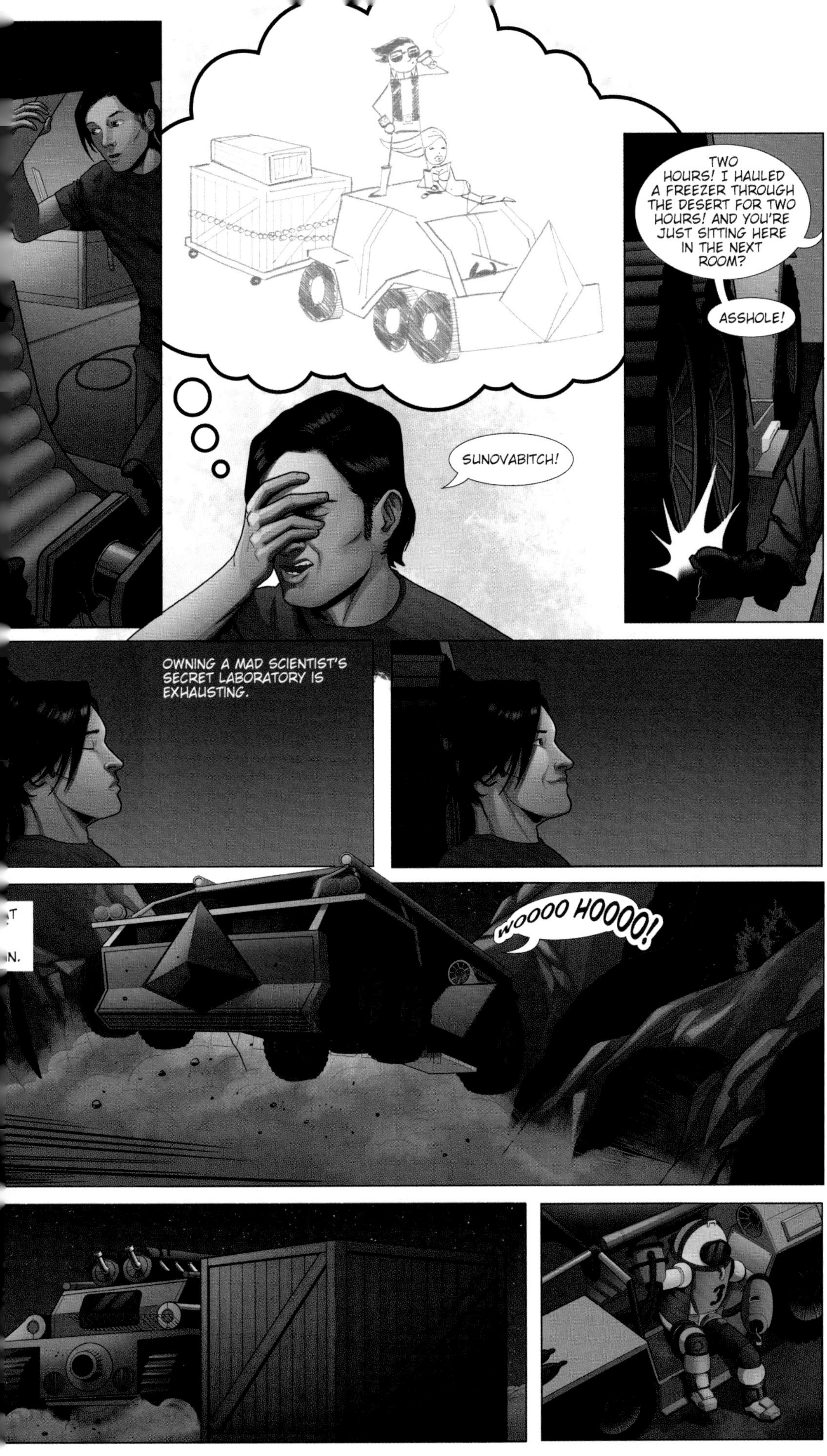
SUNOVABITCH!
TWO HOURS! I HAULED A FREEZER THROUGH THE DESERT FOR TWO HOURS! AND YOU'RE JUST SITTING HERE IN THE NEXT ROOM?
ASSHOLE!
OWNING A MAD SCIENTIST'S SECRET LABORATORY IS EXHAUSTING.
WOOOO HOOOO!

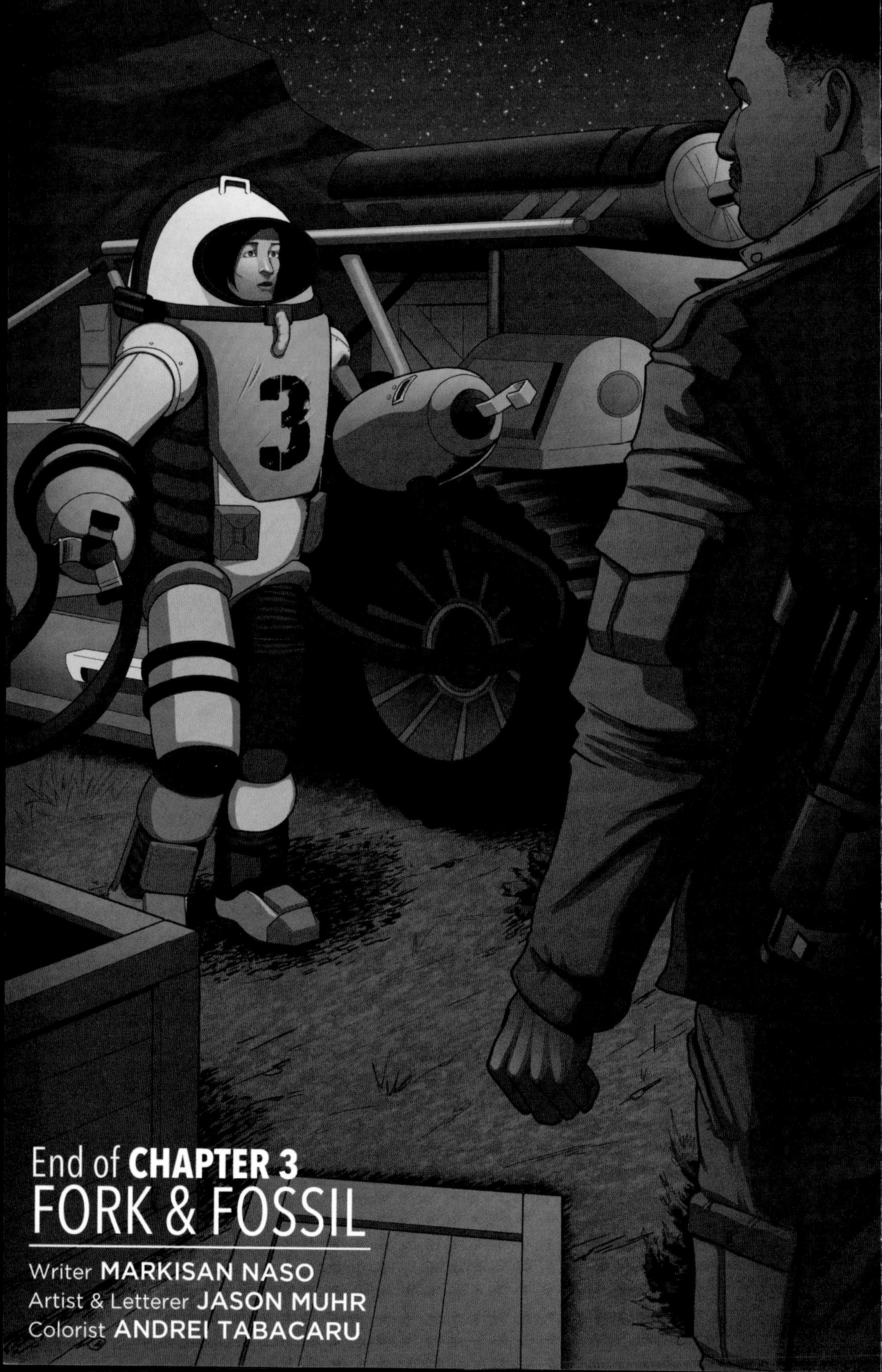
3
End of CHAPTER 3
FORK & FOSSIL
Writer MARKISAN NASO
Artist & Letterer JASON MUHR
Colorist ANDREI TABACARU

COOKING CRETACEOUS

#2! Or, as I like to call it, the issue that made me realize I'm really writing a romance comic. But
stand that it's all Jason's fault. In the early days when we were discussing the book, he mentioned I
 have a young woman work at Nate's diner to create some sexual tension and challenge Nate's
nship with Jenna. So I created Starlee. Now she's my favorite character to write. She's smart, sassy
pable, but like most of our characters there's something in her past that she just can't seem to let go
n though she knows she should. Maybe she'll end up with Nate and maybe she won't, but in the end
ush won't define her. There is a lot more to come for Miss Starlee.

ing of sassy smart girls, this issue's recipe is by my dear friend, Dr. Karilyn Lesperance, wife of my old
 Josh. He married waaaay up nearly 10 years ago. Not only is Kay a beautiful physician, she also cooks
the most delicious meals I've ever had. She gave me this stuffing recipe for Thanksgiving last year
se I simply had to have it. After I tasted her meattastic version of the classic holiday dish, no other
g will do.

san

oraciouscomic@gmail.com   **f** VoraciousComic

VoraciousComic   **t** voraciouscomic.tumblr

Kay's Troodon Sausage Stuffing

REDIENTS

oll of savory sage Troodon sausage (or pork sage sausage)
cup chopped onion
cup chopped celery
cup chopped/peeled apple (optional)
teaspoons chopped garlic
loaves stale bread (usually combine white/wheat)
 fresh you can leave out overnight to dry up, or dry
ut in the oven at low temp, then rip/cut up into chunks
quart turkey or chicken stock
tablespoons fresh chopped sage
tablespoon chopped fresh rosemary
tablespoon chopped fresh thyme (you can used dried spices or even poultry seasoning
ut you'll use more like 1-2 teaspoons)
alt and pepper to taste

RECTIONS

Brown sausage in small chunks in large saucepan, then put cooked pieces aside.
Add celery/onion/apple/garlic and sauté in same pan with sausage drippings until tender.
Add chicken/turkey stock and chopped herbs, add back sausage.
Add salt and pepper to taste.
Start adding bread chunks, while mixing, until the stuffing has absorbed all of the liquid.
Transfer from sauté pan to a buttered baking dish.
Bake at 350 until top is crunchy (30-45 minutes).

FROM M. GOODWIN, THE VISI
ORIGINAL ARTIST OF PRIN

TOMBOY

AVAILABLE IN FINER STORES EVERYWH

Wherever she goes, death is sure to follow. Four months after the funeral of her be
friend, Addison has embraced her new life as a vigilante, but trouble is on the horiz
as Detective Tico closes in on his suspect and the notorious Irene Trent finally ste
out of the shadows.

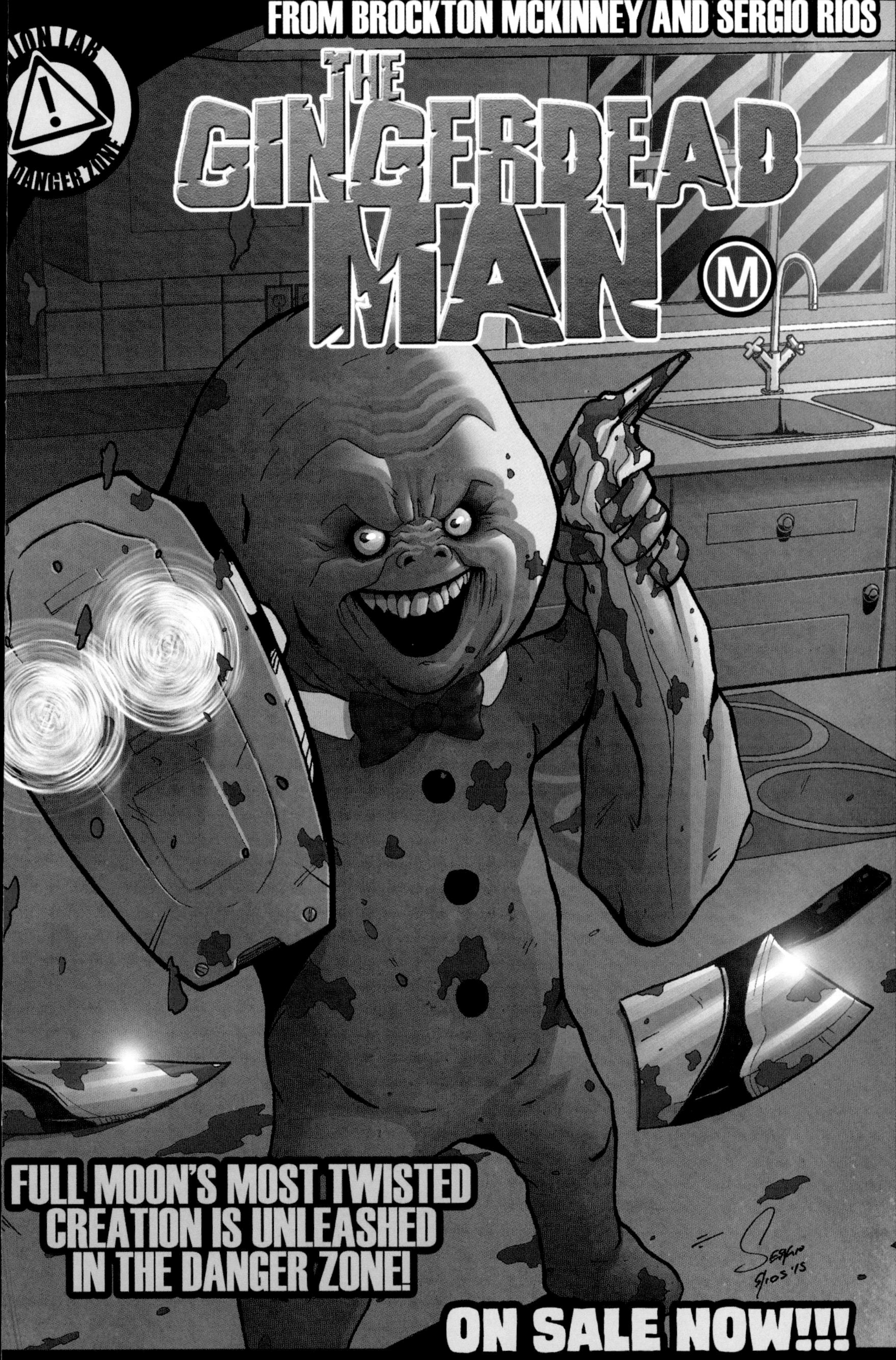
FROM BROCKTON MCKINNEY AND SERGIO RIOS
DANGER ZONE
THE GINGERDEAD MAN
M
FULL MOON'S MOST TWISTED CREATION IS UNLEASHED IN THE DANGER ZONE!
ON SALE NOW!!!

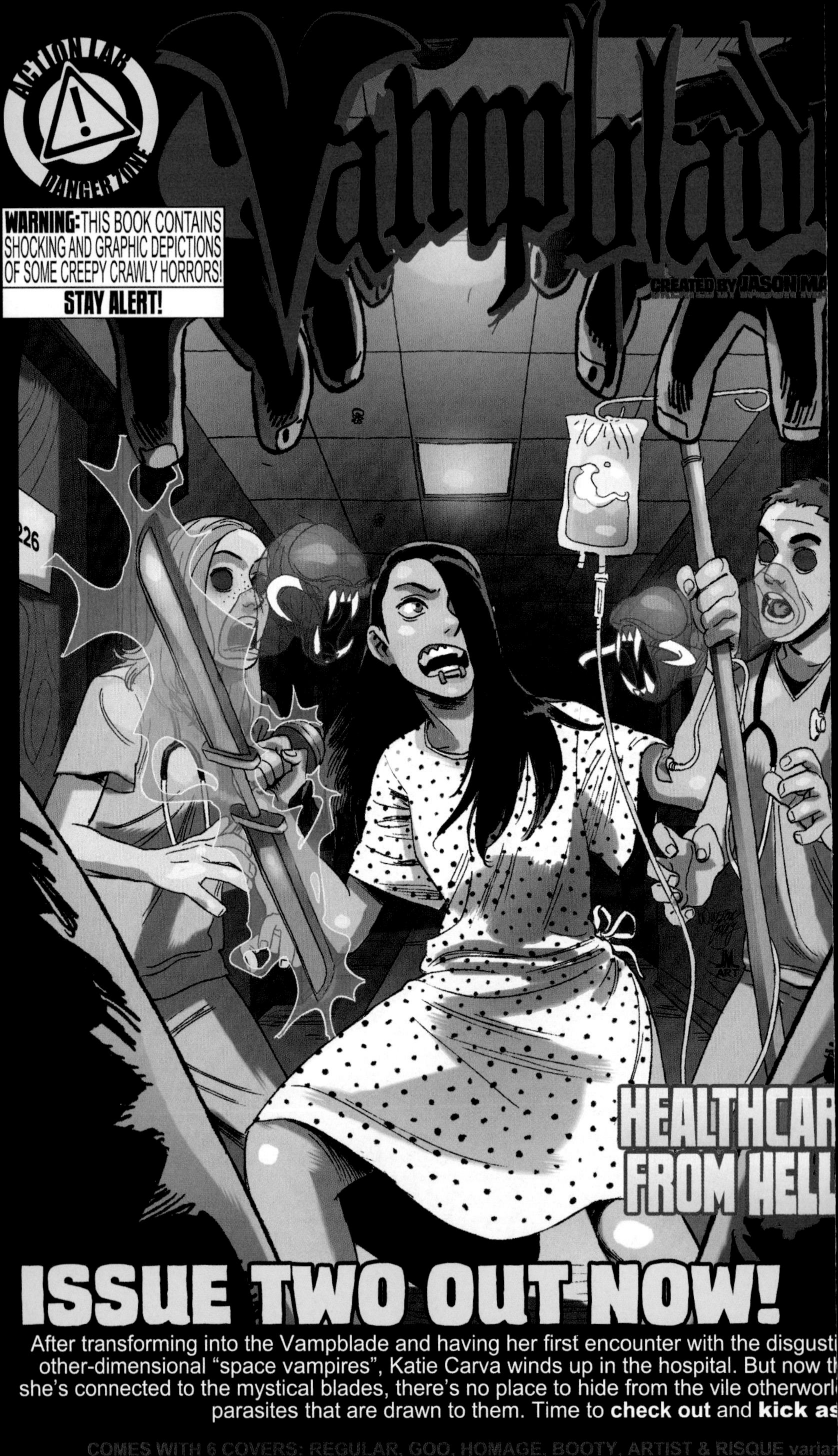
ACTION LAB
DANGER ZONE
Vampblade
WARNING: THIS BOOK CONTAINS SHOCKING AND GRAPHIC DEPICTIONS OF SOME CREEPY CRAWLY HORRORS!
STAY ALERT!
CREATED BY JASON MA
226
HEALTHCAR
FROM HELL
ISSUE TWO OUT NOW!
After transforming into the Vampblade and having her first encounter with the disgusti
other-dimensional "space vampires", Katie Carva winds up in the hospital. But now t
she's connected to the mystical blades, there's no place to hide from the vile otherworl
parasites that are drawn to them. Time to **check out** and **kick as**
COMES WITH 6 COVERS: REGULAR, GOO, HOMAGE, BOOTY, ARTIST & RISQUE varia

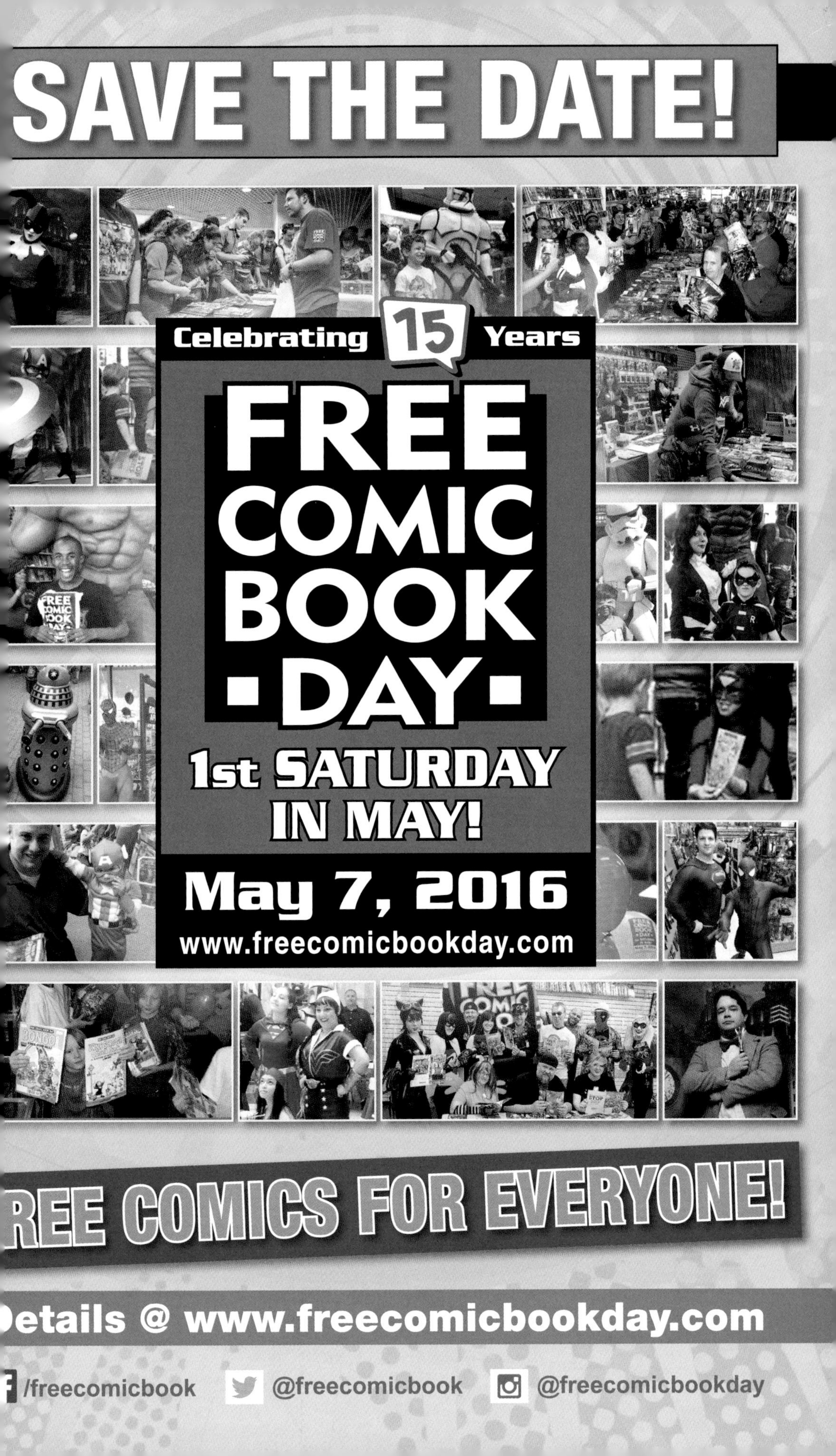
SAVE THE DATE!
Celebrating 15 Years
FREE COMIC BOOK DAY
1st SATURDAY IN MAY!
May 7, 2016
www.freecomicbookday.com
REE COMICS FOR EVERYONE!
etails @ www.freecomicbookday.com
/freecomicbook
@freecomicbook
@freecomicbookday

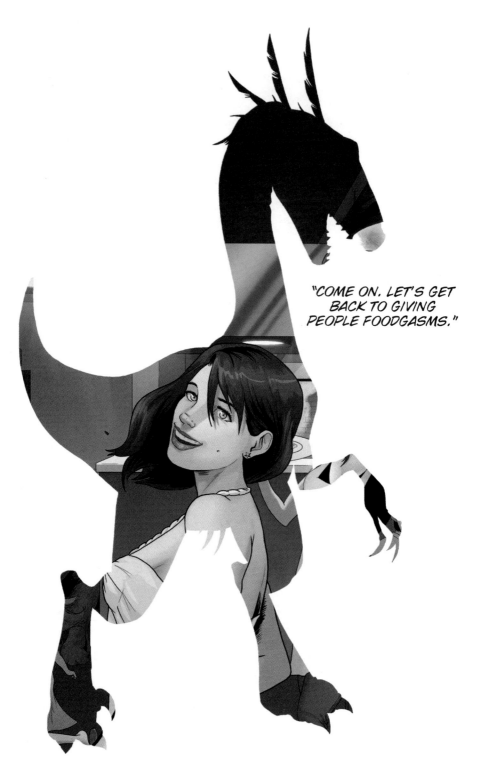

"COME ON. LET'S GET BACK TO GIVING PEOPLE FOODGASMS."

Voracious - Danger Zone
www.actionlabcomics.com
00211
7 02382 69123 3

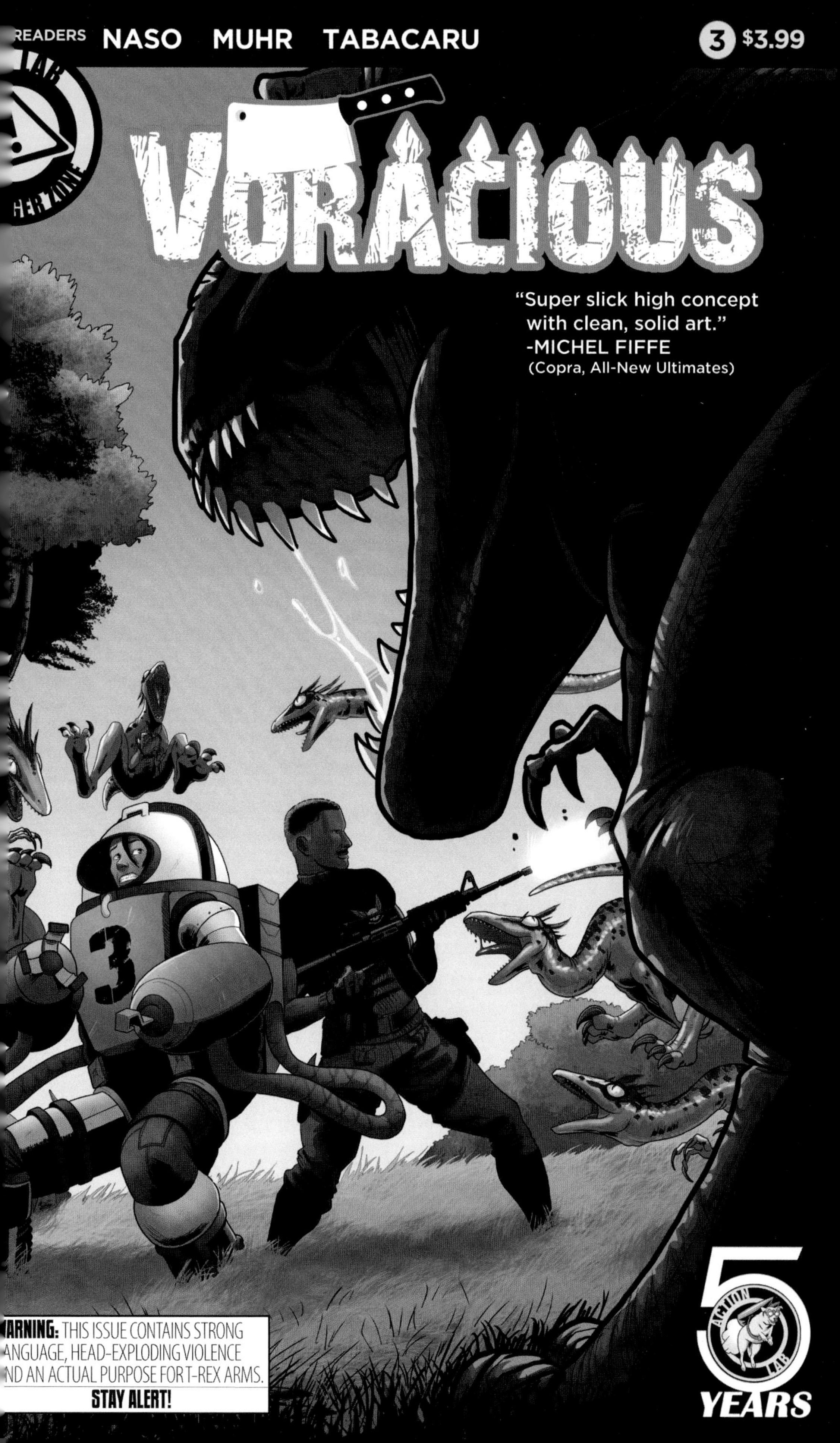
READERS
NASO MUHR TABACARU
3 $3.99
VORACIOUS
"Super slick high concept with clean, solid art."
-MICHEL FIFFE
(Copra, All-New Ultimates)
3
ARNING: THIS ISSUE CONTAINS STRONG
ANGUAGE, HEAD-EXPLODING VIOLENCE
ND AN ACTUAL PURPOSE FOR T-REX ARMS.
STAY ALERT!
5 YEARS

VORACIOUS

PREVIOUSLY...

Nate Willner, a chef in NYC, was forced to move back to Utah, after his restaurant exploded, killing his sister and leaving him unmotivated and hollow. Working at the Javarado Café, it seems Nate's life has become a dead end. But when he unexpectedly inherits a time travel suit from his Great Uncle Tony that can take him to the time of the dinosaurs, his passion for cooking is renewed. Dinosaurs are so delicious that Nate decides to open a restaurant in the present that serves secret meat from the past!

Using his inheritance Nate purchases the Javarado and names it after his sister. In the weeks leading up to the debut of Sara's Fork & Fossil, Nate and Starlee (now his business partner) ha grown closer. Meanwhile, Tony's death has taken a mental toll on Nate's grandmother, Maribel who had some kind of secret relationship with him in the past. Nate is unaware of the connection, but he has bigger problems. He's nearly been killed by dinosaurs several times. His NYC girlfriend, Jenna, is on her way to Blackfossil. Starlee's brother, Sheriff Don Parker, is high suspicious of him. And oh yeah, family friend, Captain Jim Hand, just discovered Nate's secret.

CHAPTER 4
GIVE IT MEANING

Written by
MARKISAN NASO

Art, Lettering & Design by
JASON MUHR

Color Art by
ANDREI TABACARU

VORACIOUS created by
NASO & MUHR

"Happy Meal" variant cover
(LTD to 1500) by
JEFFREY VEREGGE

JASON MARTIN - PUBLISHER
DAVE DWONCH - PRESIDENT
SHAWN GABBORIN - EDITOR IN CHIEF
JAMAL IGLE - V.P. OF MARKETING
JIM DIETZ - SOCIAL MEDIA DIRECTOR
KEVIN FREEMAN - EDITOR
COLLEEN BOYD - ASSOCIATE EDITOR

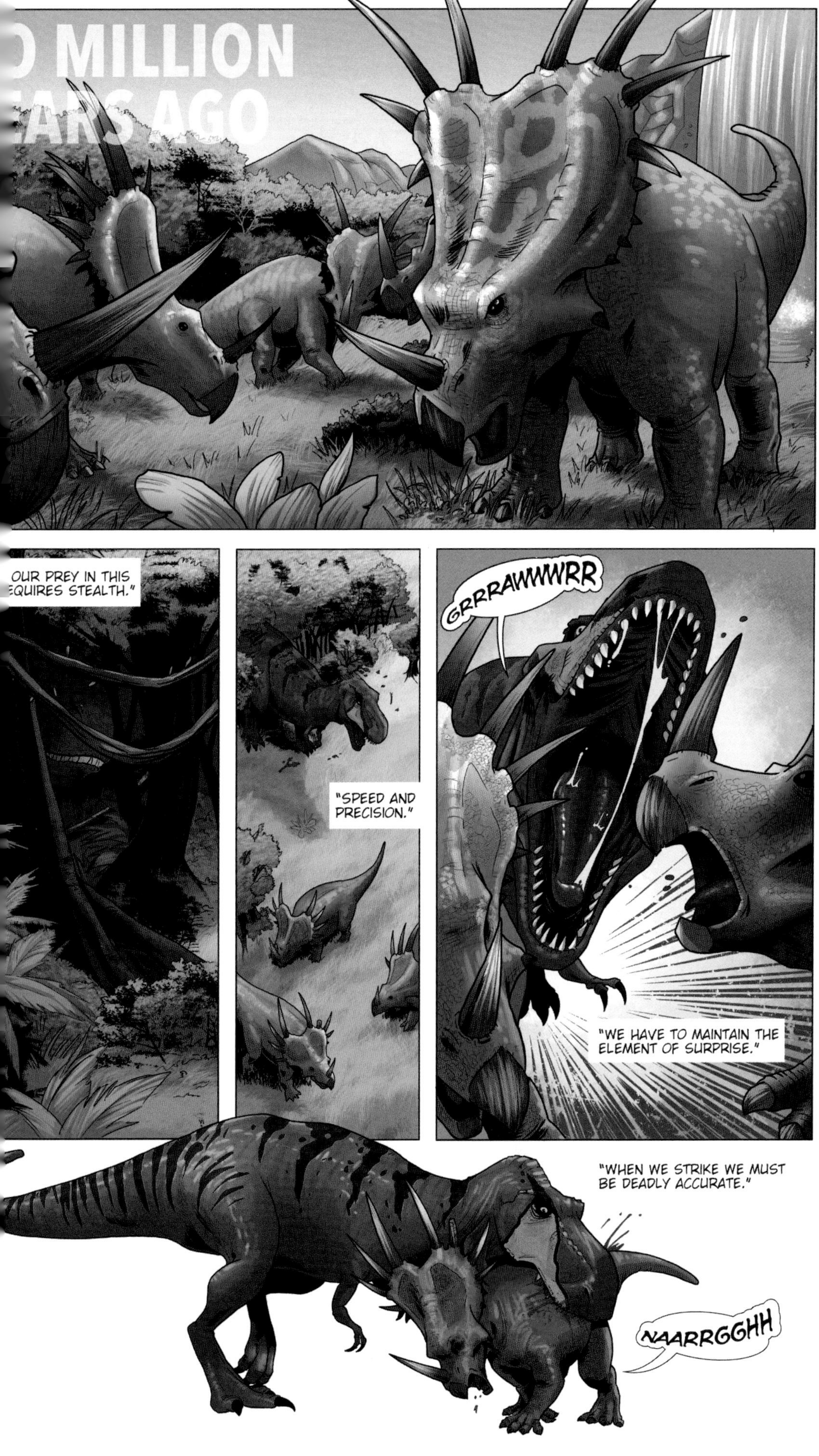
O MILLION
EARS AGO
OUR PREY IN THIS
EQUIRES STEALTH."
"SPEED AND
PRECISION."
GRRRAWWWRR
"WE HAVE TO MAINTAIN THE
ELEMENT OF SURPRISE."
"WHEN WE STRIKE WE MUST
BE DEADLY ACCURATE."
NAARRGGHH

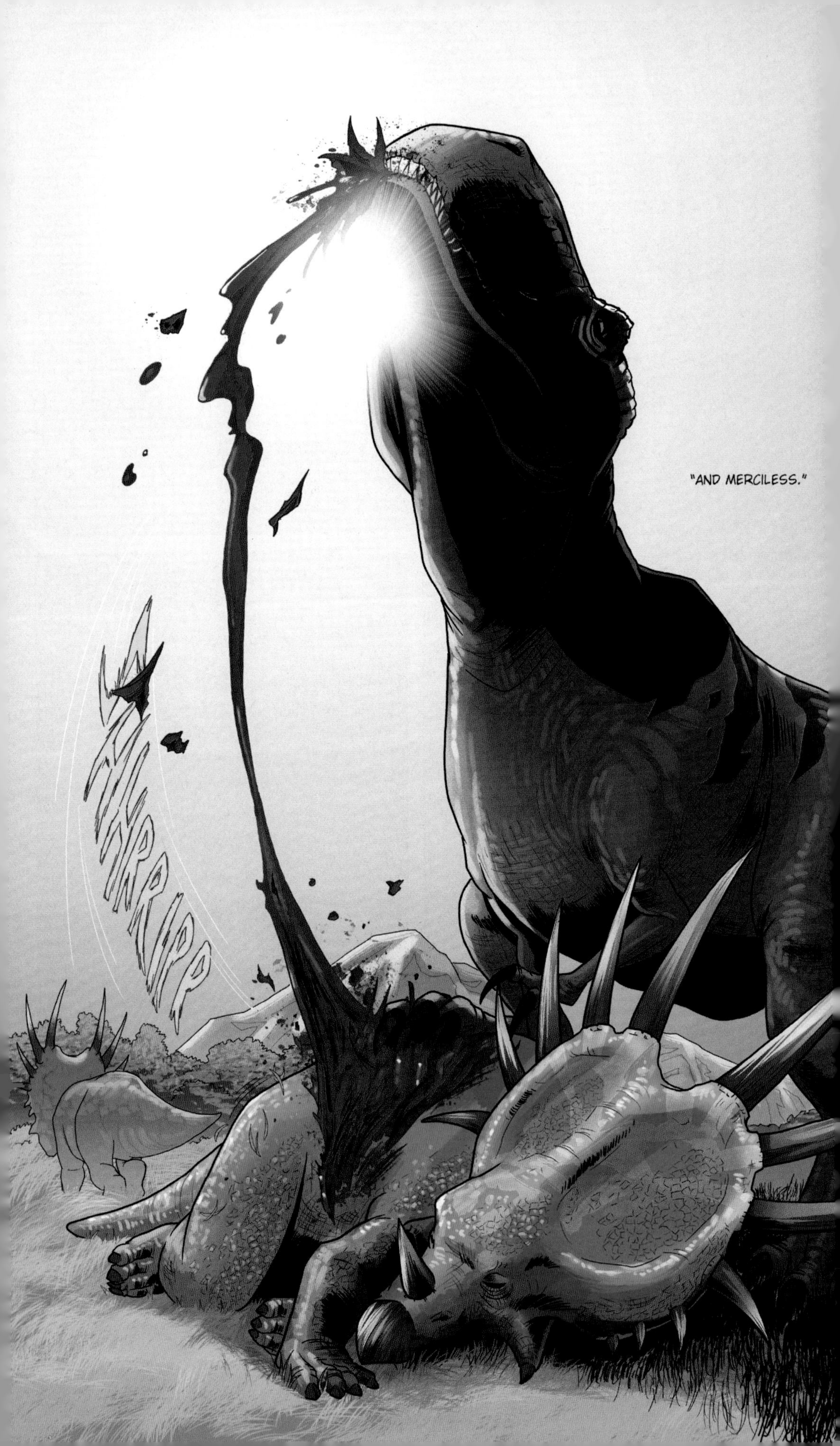
"AND MERCILESS."

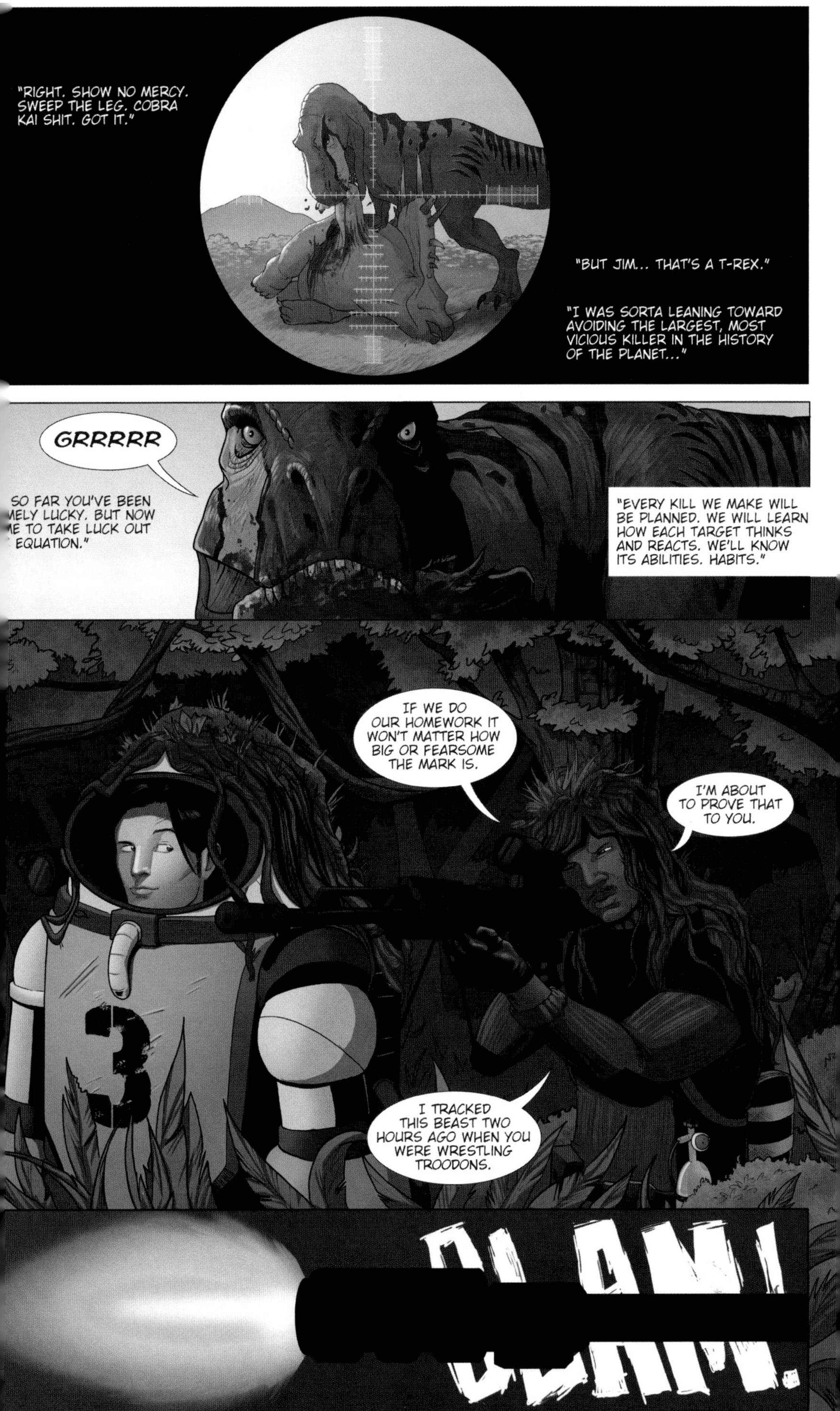
"RIGHT. SHOW NO MERCY. SWEEP THE LEG. COBRA KAI SHIT. GOT IT."
"BUT JIM... THAT'S A T-REX."
"I WAS SORTA LEANING TOWARD AVOIDING THE LARGEST, MOST VICIOUS KILLER IN THE HISTORY OF THE PLANET..."
GRRRRR
SO FAR YOU'VE BEEN MELY LUCKY. BUT NOW E TO TAKE LUCK OUT EQUATION."
"EVERY KILL WE MAKE WILL BE PLANNED. WE WILL LEARN HOW EACH TARGET THINKS AND REACTS. WE'LL KNOW ITS ABILITIES. HABITS."
IF WE DO OUR HOMEWORK IT WON'T MATTER HOW BIG OR FEARSOME THE MARK IS.
I'M ABOUT TO PROVE THAT TO YOU.
I TRACKED THIS BEAST TWO HOURS AGO WHEN YOU WERE WRESTLING TROODONS.

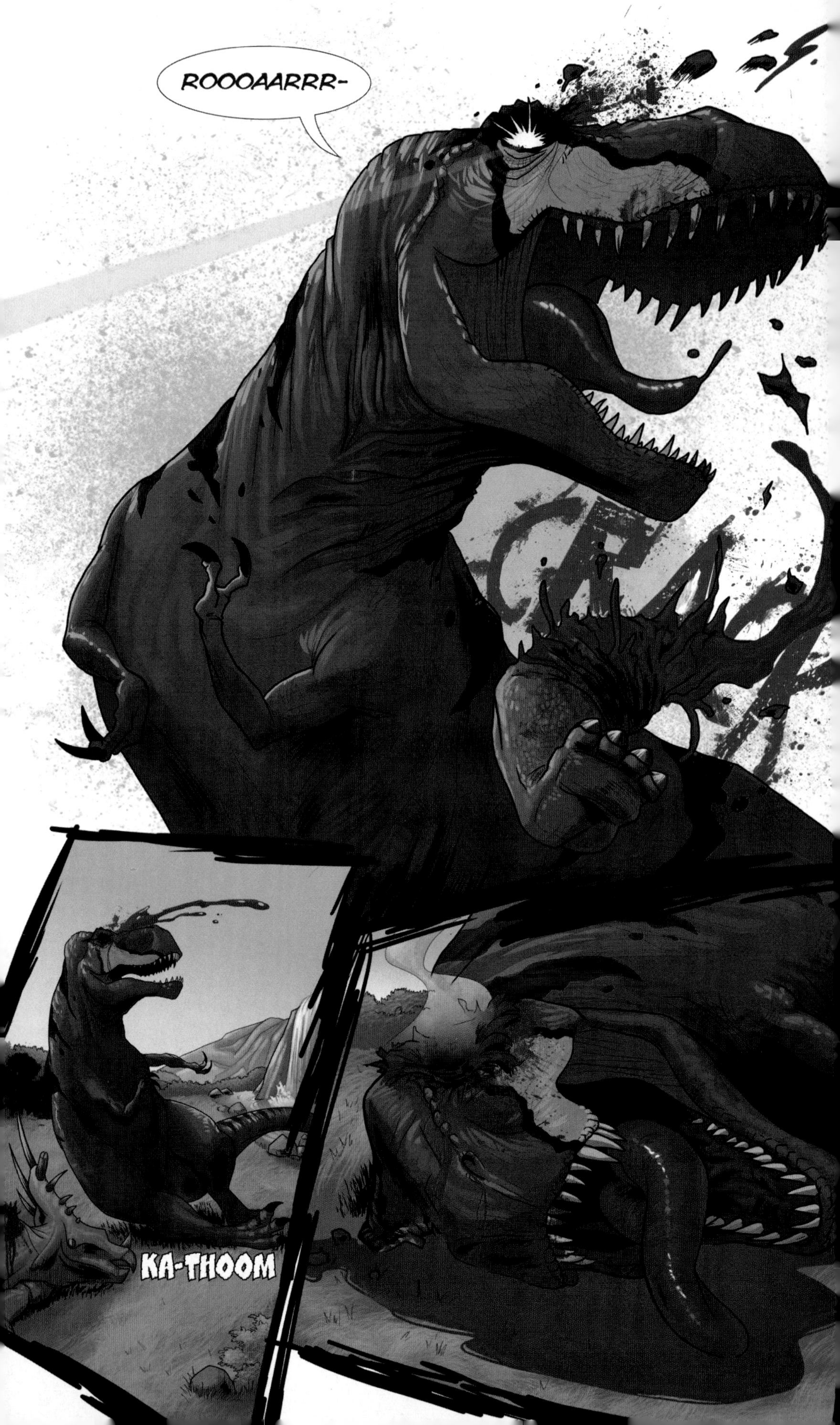
ROOOAARRR-
KA-THOOM

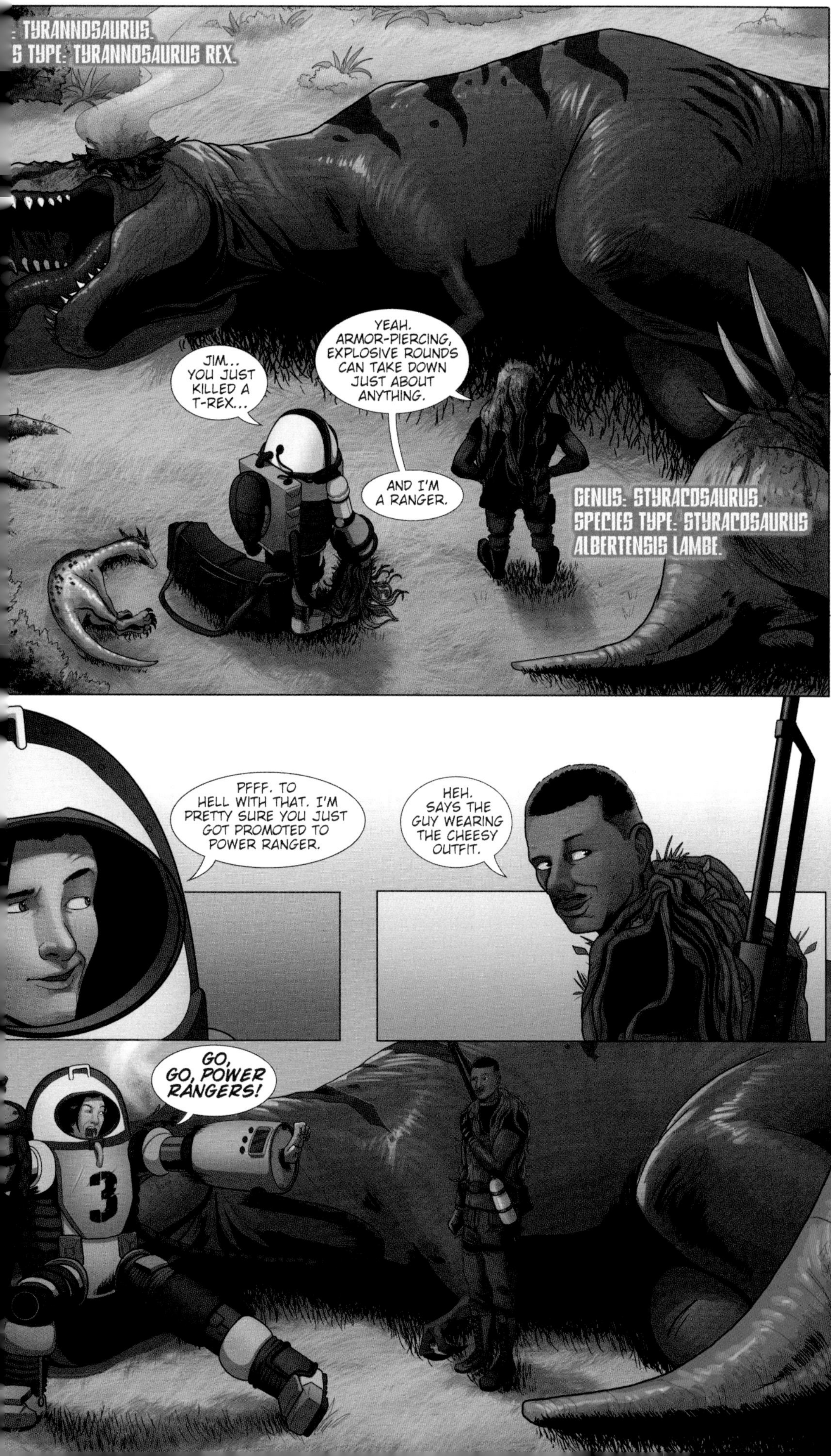
: TYRANNOSAURUS.
S TYPE: TYRANNOSAURUS REX.
JIM... YOU JUST KILLED A T-REX...
YEAH. ARMOR-PIERCING, EXPLOSIVE ROUNDS CAN TAKE DOWN JUST ABOUT ANYTHING.
AND I'M A RANGER.
GENUS: STYRACOSAURUS.
SPECIES TYPE: STYRACOSAURUS ALBERTENSIS LAMBE.
PFFF. TO HELL WITH THAT. I'M PRETTY SURE YOU JUST GOT PROMOTED TO POWER RANGER.
HEH. SAYS THE GUY WEARING THE CHEESY OUTFIT.
GO, GO, POWER RANGERS!
3

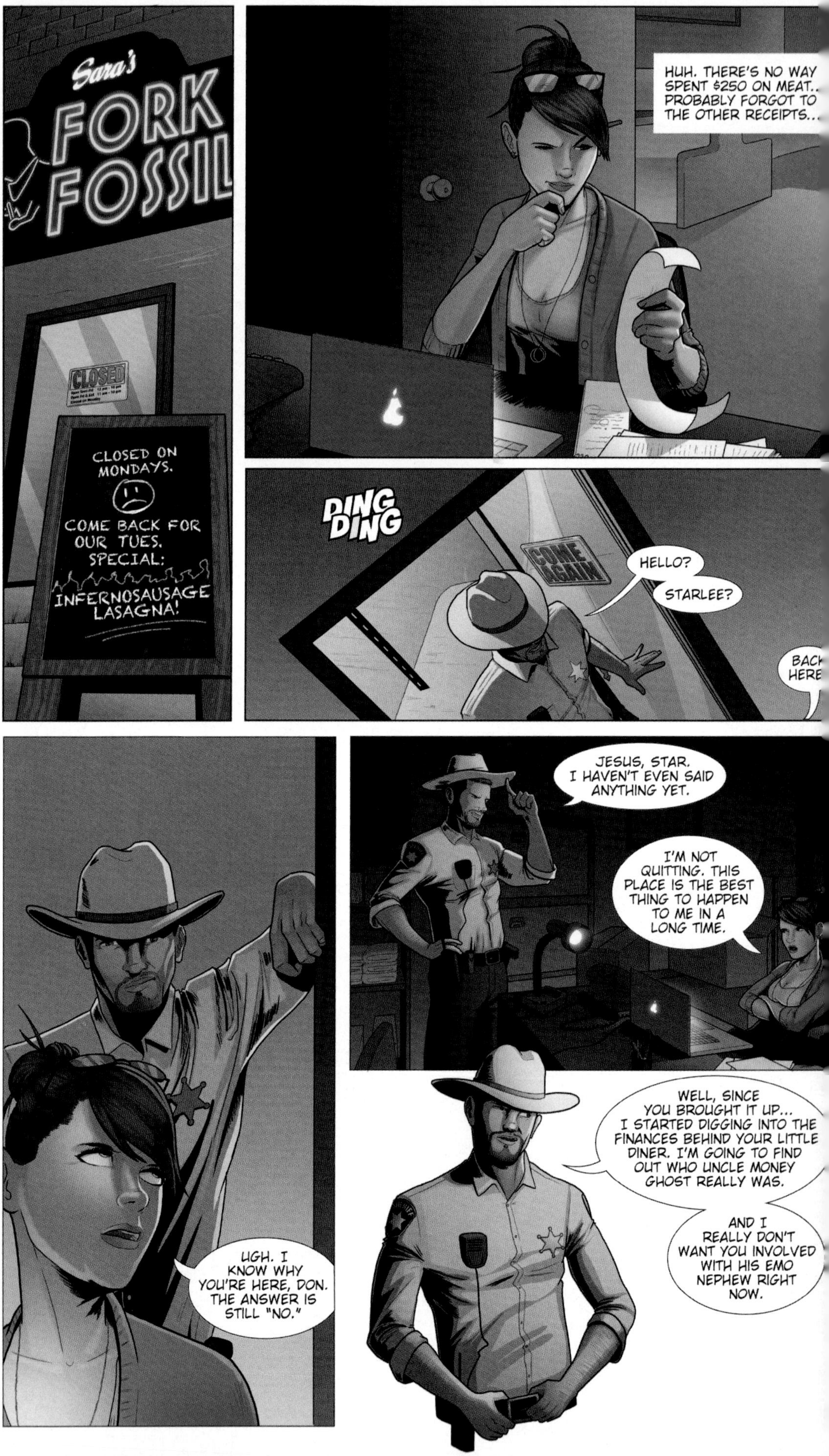
Sara's
FORK
FOSSIL
CLOSED
CLOSED ON MONDAYS.
COME BACK FOR OUR TUES. SPECIAL:
INFERNOSAUSAGE LASAGNA!
HUH. THERE'S NO WAY SPENT $250 ON MEAT... PROBABLY FORGOT TO THE OTHER RECEIPTS...
DING DING
COME AGAIN
HELLO?
STARLEE?
BACK HERE
UGH. I KNOW WHY YOU'RE HERE, DON. THE ANSWER IS STILL "NO."
JESUS, STAR. I HAVEN'T EVEN SAID ANYTHING YET.
I'M NOT QUITTING. THIS PLACE IS THE BEST THING TO HAPPEN TO ME IN A LONG TIME.
WELL, SINCE YOU BROUGHT IT UP... I STARTED DIGGING INTO THE FINANCES BEHIND YOUR LITTLE DINER. I'M GOING TO FIND OUT WHO UNCLE MONEY GHOST REALLY WAS.
AND I REALLY DON'T WANT YOU INVOLVED WITH HIS EMO NEPHEW RIGHT NOW.

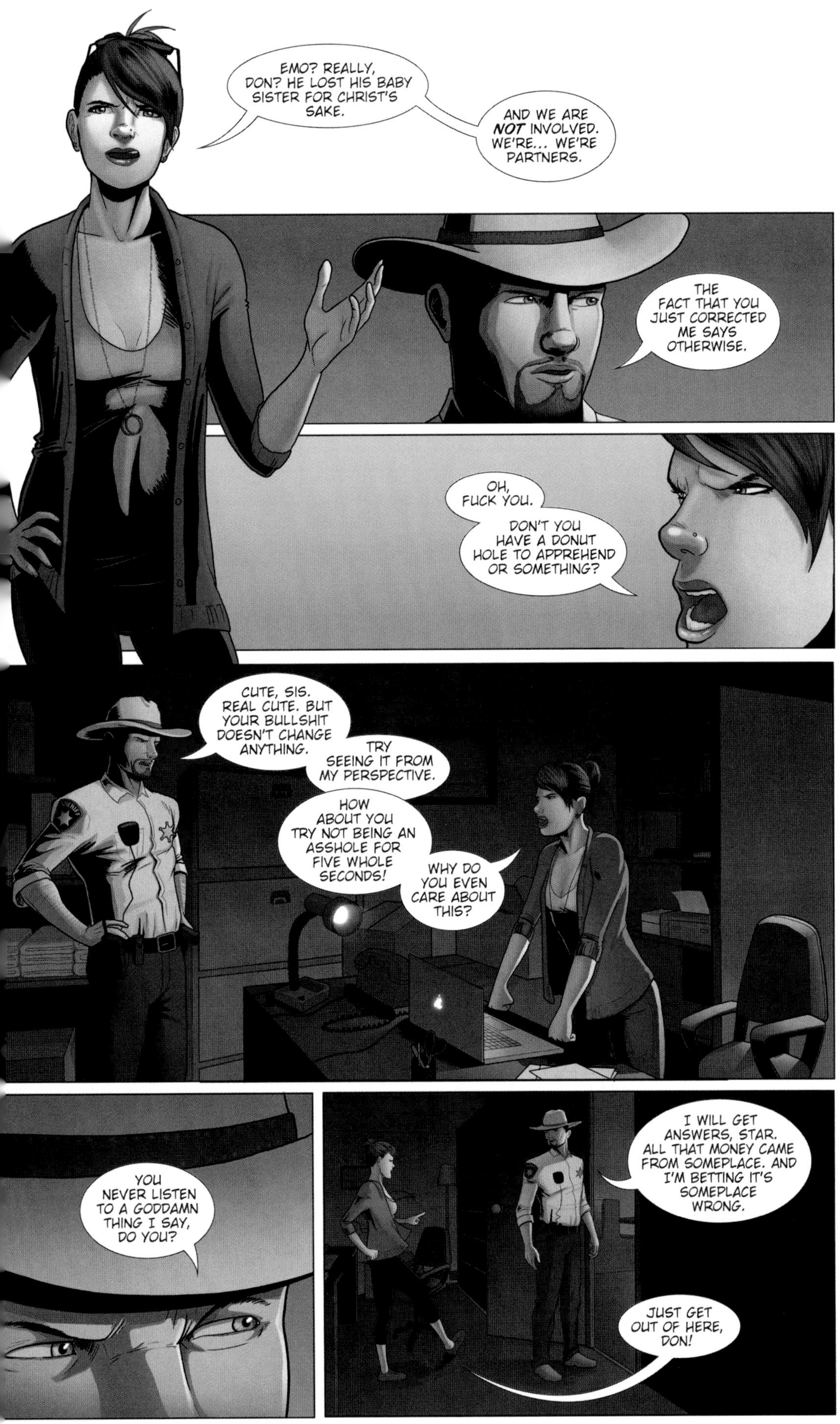
EMO? REALLY, DON? HE LOST HIS BABY SISTER FOR CHRIST'S SAKE.
AND WE ARE ***NOT*** INVOLVED. WE'RE... WE'RE PARTNERS.
THE FACT THAT YOU JUST CORRECTED ME SAYS OTHERWISE.
OH, FUCK YOU.
DON'T YOU HAVE A DONUT HOLE TO APPREHEND OR SOMETHING?
CUTE, SIS. REAL CUTE. BUT YOUR BULLSHIT DOESN'T CHANGE ANYTHING.
TRY SEEING IT FROM MY PERSPECTIVE.
HOW ABOUT YOU TRY NOT BEING AN ASSHOLE FOR FIVE WHOLE SECONDS!
WHY DO YOU EVEN CARE ABOUT THIS?
YOU NEVER LISTEN TO A GODDAMN THING I SAY, DO YOU?
I WILL GET ANSWERS, STAR. ALL THAT MONEY CAME FROM SOMEPLACE. AND I'M BETTING IT'S SOMEPLACE WRONG.
JUST GET OUT OF HERE, DON!

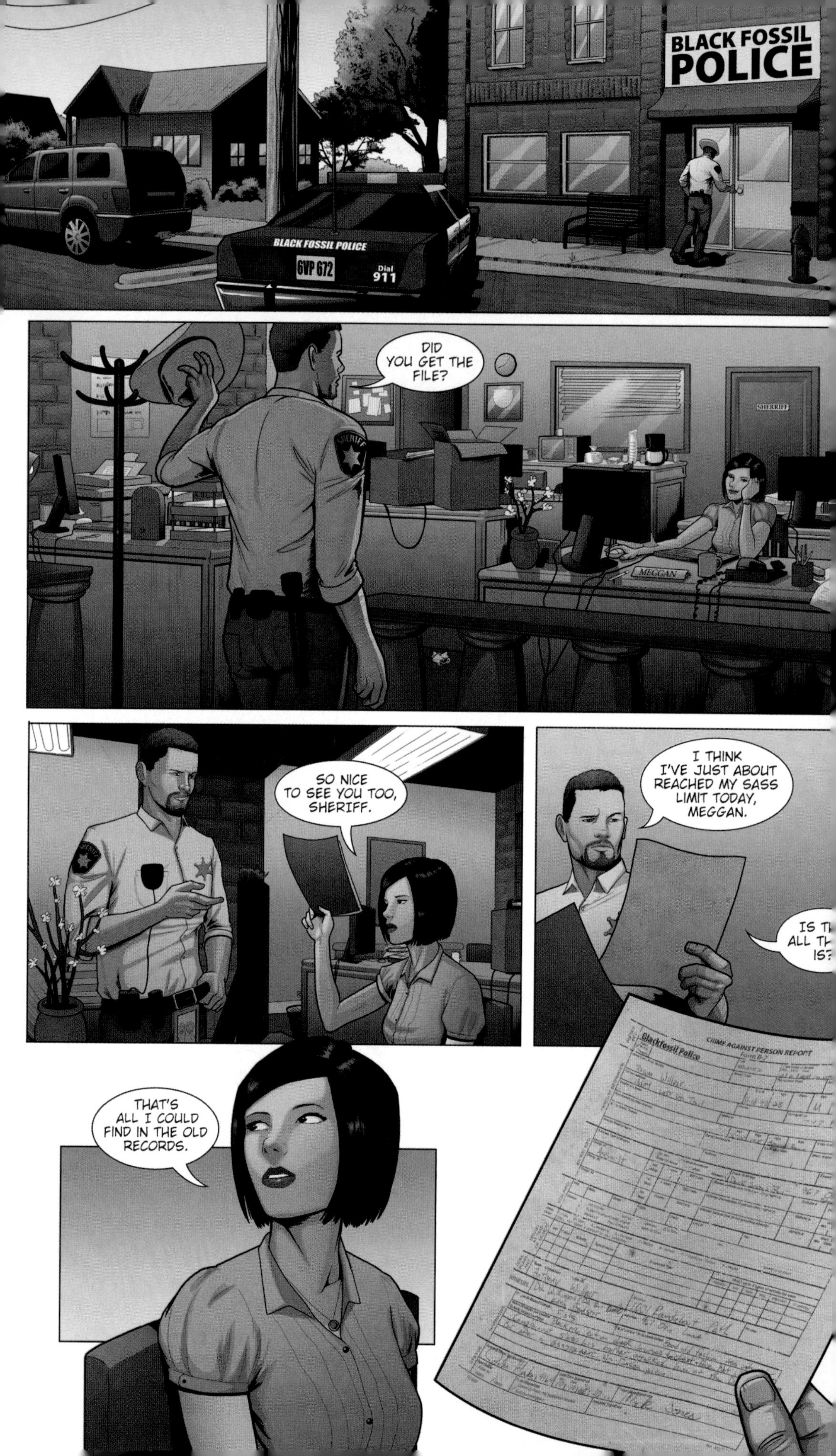
BLACK FOSSIL
POLICE
BLACK FOSSIL POLICE
6VP 672
Dial
911
DID YOU GET THE FILE?
SHERRIFF
MEGGAN
SO NICE TO SEE YOU TOO, SHERIFF.
I THINK I'VE JUST ABOUT REACHED MY SASS LIMIT TODAY, MEGGAN.
THAT'S ALL I COULD FIND IN THE OLD RECORDS.
Blackfossil Police
CRIME AGAINST PERSON REPORT

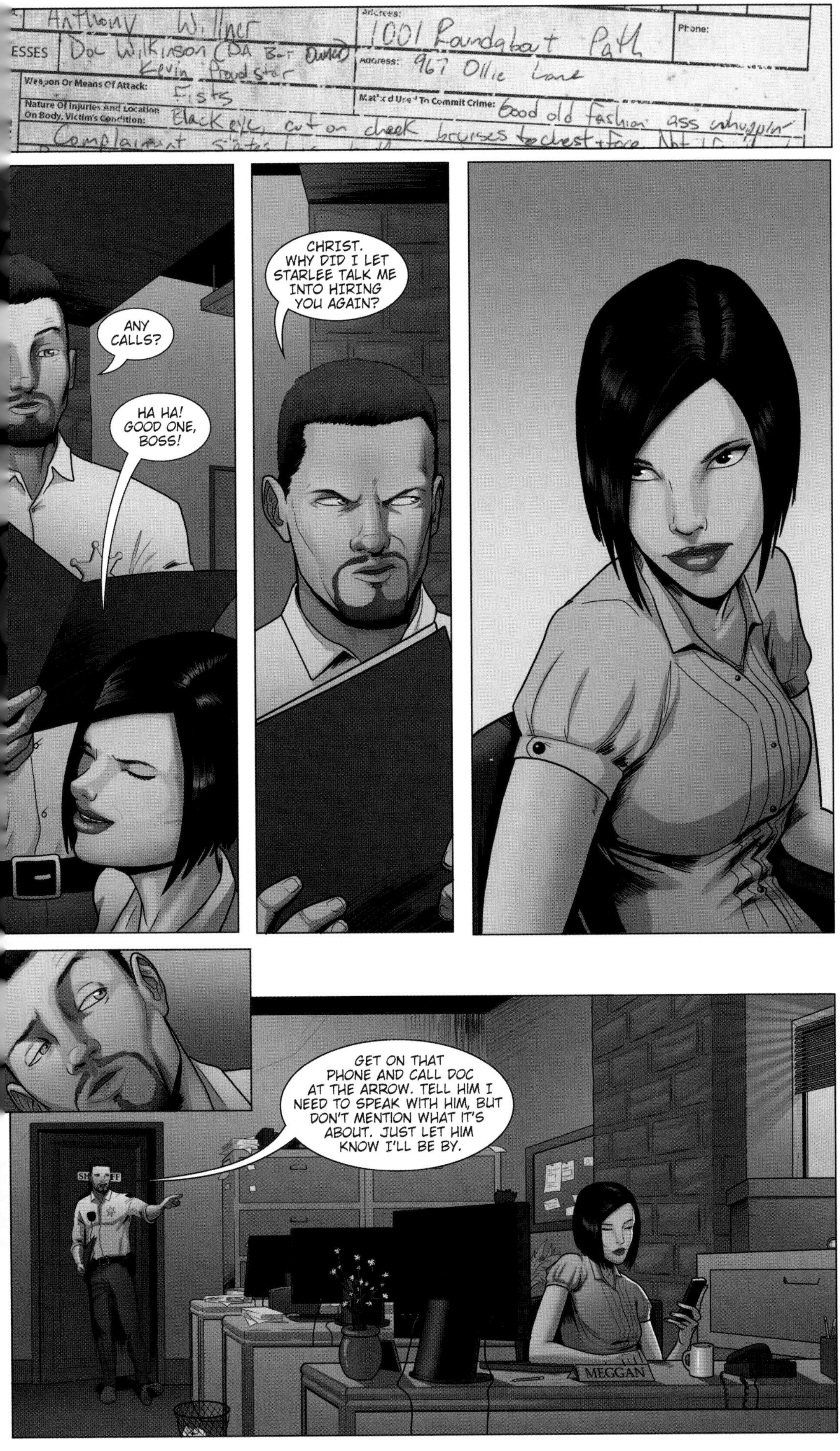

Anthony Willner
Address: 1001 Roundabout Path
Phone:
Doc Wilkinson (DA Bar Owner)
Kevin Proudstar
Address: 967 Ollie Lane
Weapon Or Means Of Attack: Fists
Nature Of Injuries And Location On Body, Victim's Condition: Black eye, cut on cheek bruises to chest + face.
Good old fashion ass whuppin'
ANY CALLS?
HA HA! GOOD ONE, BOSS!
CHRIST. WHY DID I LET STARLEE TALK ME INTO HIRING YOU AGAIN?
GET ON THAT PHONE AND CALL DOC AT THE ARROW. TELL HIM I NEED TO SPEAK WITH HIM, BUT DON'T MENTION WHAT IT'S ABOUT. JUST LET HIM KNOW I'LL BE BY.
MEGGAN

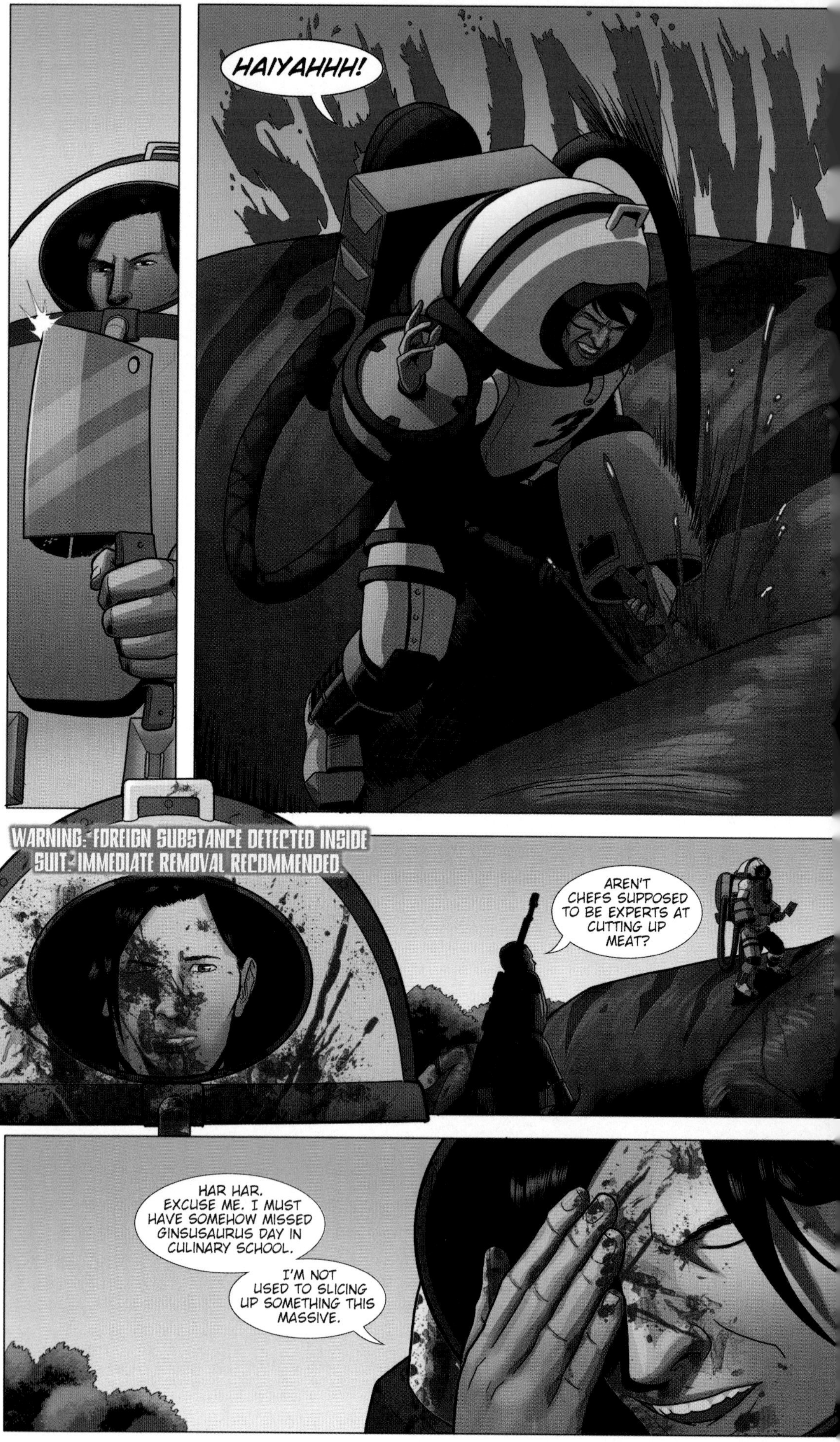
HAIYAHHH!
WARNING: FOREIGN SUBSTANCE DETECTED INSIDE SUIT. IMMEDIATE REMOVAL RECOMMENDED.
AREN'T CHEFS SUPPOSED TO BE EXPERTS AT CUTTING UP MEAT?
HAR HAR. EXCUSE ME. I MUST HAVE SOMEHOW MISSED GINSUSAURUS DAY IN CULINARY SCHOOL.
I'M NOT USED TO SLICING UP SOMETHING THIS MASSIVE.

WELL, GOOD THING I BROUGHT THIS FOR YOU THEN.

A WELLSAW? AWW... IT'S NOT EVEN MY BIRTHDAY.

JUST GONNA TAKE ONE LEG. WE CAN GET THE REST LATER.

WRRRRR

MMMM

WE 'D TAKE ARMS 'OO.

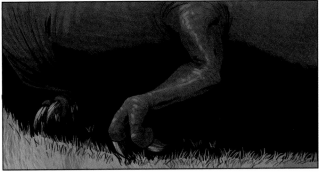

SURE, WHY NOT.

WE'LL GET MORE USE OUT OF THEM THAN THIS GUY EVER DID.

VVVRRRRRRMMMMM

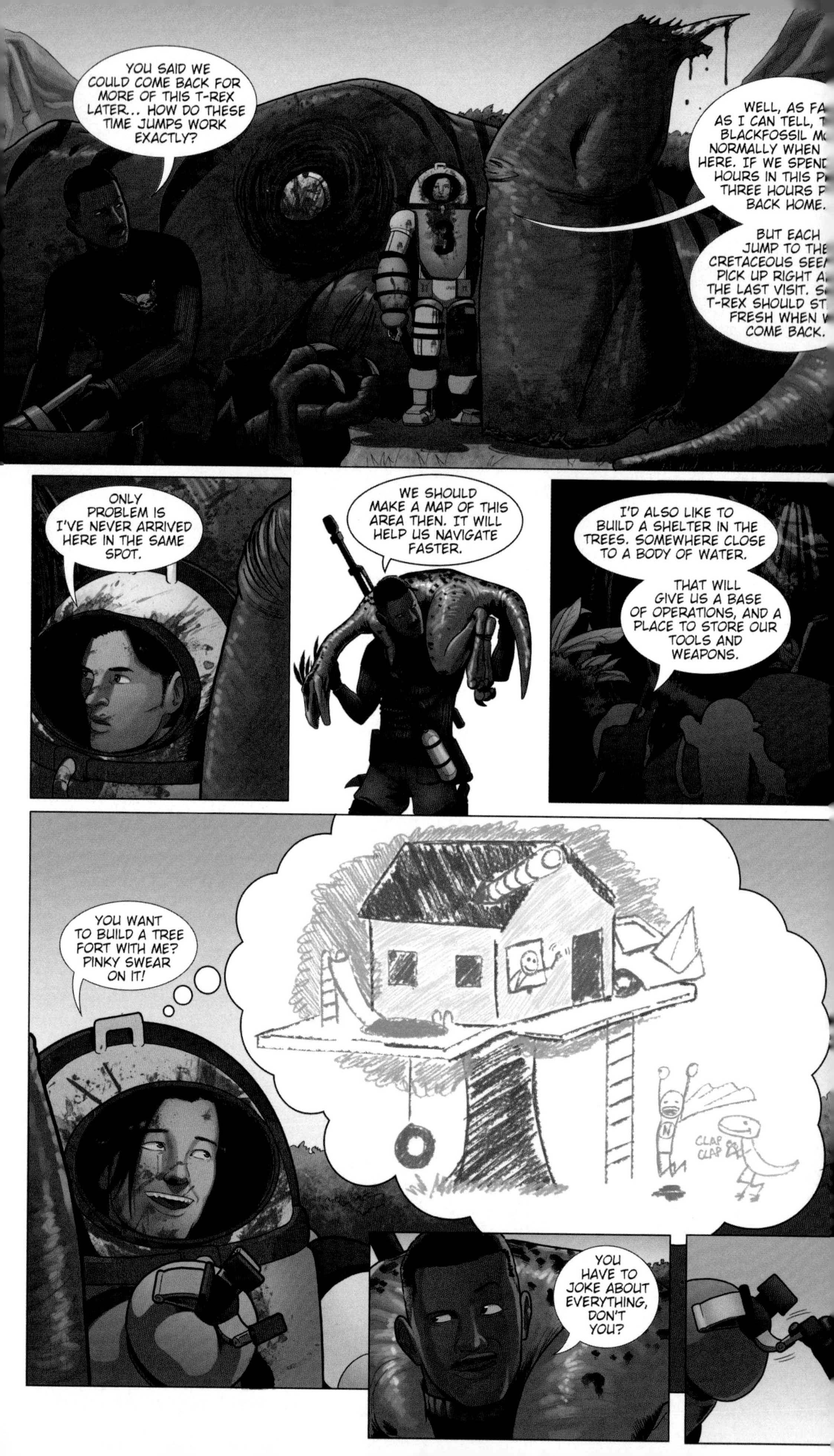
YOU SAID WE COULD COME BACK FOR MORE OF THIS T-REX LATER... HOW DO THESE TIME JUMPS WORK EXACTLY?
WELL, AS FA AS I CAN TELL, T BLACKFOSSIL M NORMALLY WHEN HERE. IF WE SPEND HOURS IN THIS P THREE HOURS P BACK HOME.
BUT EACH JUMP TO THE CRETACEOUS SEE PICK UP RIGHT A THE LAST VISIT. S T-REX SHOULD ST FRESH WHEN W COME BACK.
ONLY PROBLEM IS I'VE NEVER ARRIVED HERE IN THE SAME SPOT.
WE SHOULD MAKE A MAP OF THIS AREA THEN. IT WILL HELP US NAVIGATE FASTER.
I'D ALSO LIKE TO BUILD A SHELTER IN THE TREES. SOMEWHERE CLOSE TO A BODY OF WATER.
THAT WILL GIVE US A BASE OF OPERATIONS, AND A PLACE TO STORE OUR TOOLS AND WEAPONS.
YOU WANT TO BUILD A TREE FORT WITH ME? PINKY SWEAR ON IT!
CLAP CLAP
YOU HAVE TO JOKE ABOUT EVERYTHING, DON'T YOU?

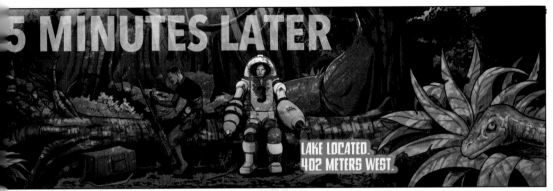

5 MINUTES LATER

LAKE LOCATED.
402 METERS WEST.

IM...
KIDDING
... THANK
'OU.

HEN I SAW
OUTSIDE THE
E LAST WEEK,
LLY THOUGHT
THIS WOULD
BE OVER.

YOU KNOW, WHEN YOUR PARENTS TOLD ME YOU'D DO GREAT THINGS, THIS ISN'T EXACTLY WHAT I HAD IN MIND.

MAN, FOR A LONG TIME AFTER SARA DIED I WAS THE FURTHEST THING FROM GREAT. I WAS... EMPTY. THEN I CAME HERE AND EVERYTHING CHANGED.

I KNOW IT'S CRAZY... BUT THIS PLACE, THESE DINOSAURS... THEY MAKE ME FEEL LIKE I MATTER AGAIN.

HM. I
EFINITELY GET THAT.
METIMES SOMETHING
RAORDINARY HAS TO
HAPPEN IN YOUR
LIFE TO GIVE IT
MEANING.

FOR ME IT WAS BECOMING A RANGER. FOR YOU... I GUESS ITS HUNTING DINOSAURS.

YEAH... AND THIS IS THE FIRST TIME I HAVEN'T ALMOST DIED DOING IT.

HEH. YOU'RE WELCOME.

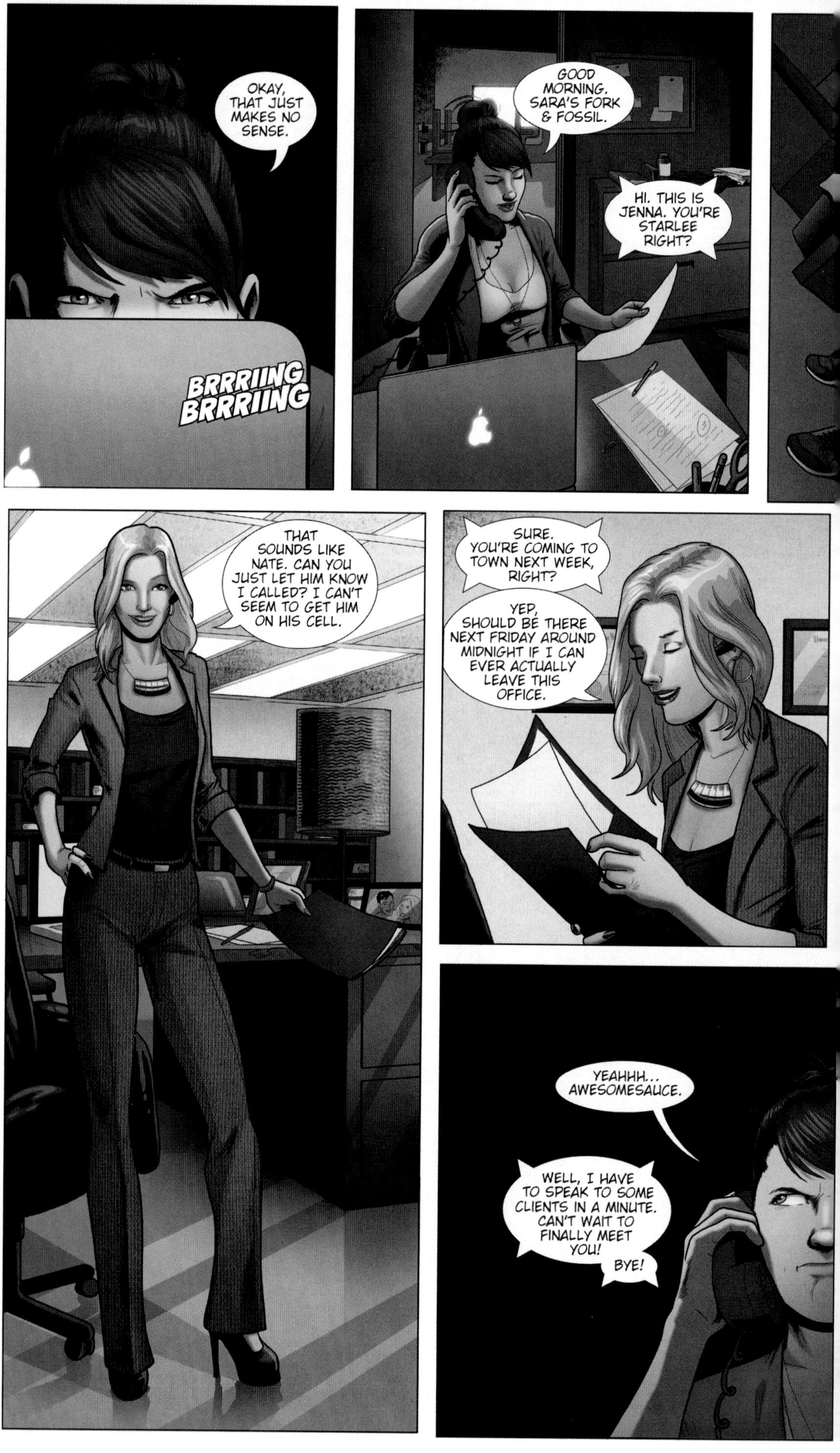
OKAY, THAT JUST MAKES NO SENSE.
BRRRIING BRRRIING
GOOD MORNING. SARA'S FORK & FOSSIL.
HI. THIS IS JENNA. YOU'RE STARLEE RIGHT?
THAT SOUNDS LIKE NATE. CAN YOU JUST LET HIM KNOW I CALLED? I CAN'T SEEM TO GET HIM ON HIS CELL.
SURE. YOU'RE COMING TO TOWN NEXT WEEK, RIGHT?
YEP, SHOULD BE THERE NEXT FRIDAY AROUND MIDNIGHT IF I CAN EVER ACTUALLY LEAVE THIS OFFICE.
YEAHHH... AWESOMESAUCE.
WELL, I HAVE TO SPEAK TO SOME CLIENTS IN A MINUTE. CAN'T WAIT TO FINALLY MEET YOU!
BYE!

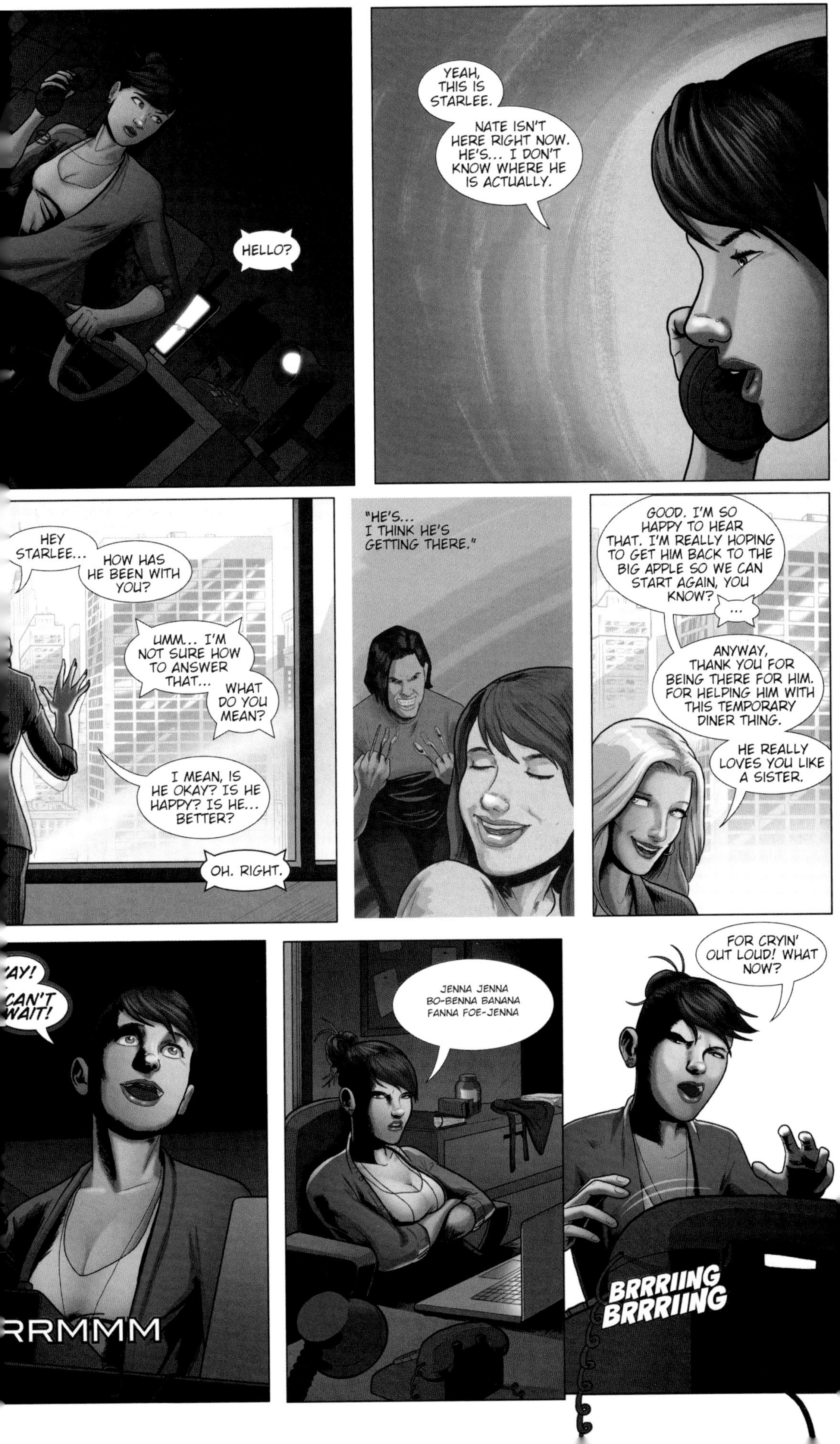

HELLO?
YEAH, THIS IS STARLEE.
NATE ISN'T HERE RIGHT NOW. HE'S... I DON'T KNOW WHERE HE IS ACTUALLY.
HEY STARLEE...
HOW HAS HE BEEN WITH YOU?
UMM... I'M NOT SURE HOW TO ANSWER THAT...
WHAT DO YOU MEAN?
I MEAN, IS HE OKAY? IS HE HAPPY? IS HE... BETTER?
OH. RIGHT.
"HE'S... I THINK HE'S GETTING THERE."
GOOD. I'M SO HAPPY TO HEAR THAT. I'M REALLY HOPING TO GET HIM BACK TO THE BIG APPLE SO WE CAN START AGAIN, YOU KNOW?
...
ANYWAY, THANK YOU FOR BEING THERE FOR HIM. FOR HELPING HIM WITH THIS TEMPORARY DINER THING.
HE REALLY LOVES YOU LIKE A SISTER.
AY!
CAN'T WAIT!
RRMMM
JENNA JENNA BO-BENNA BANANA FANNA FOE-JENNA
FOR CRYIN' OUT LOUD! WHAT NOW?
BRRRIING BRRRIING

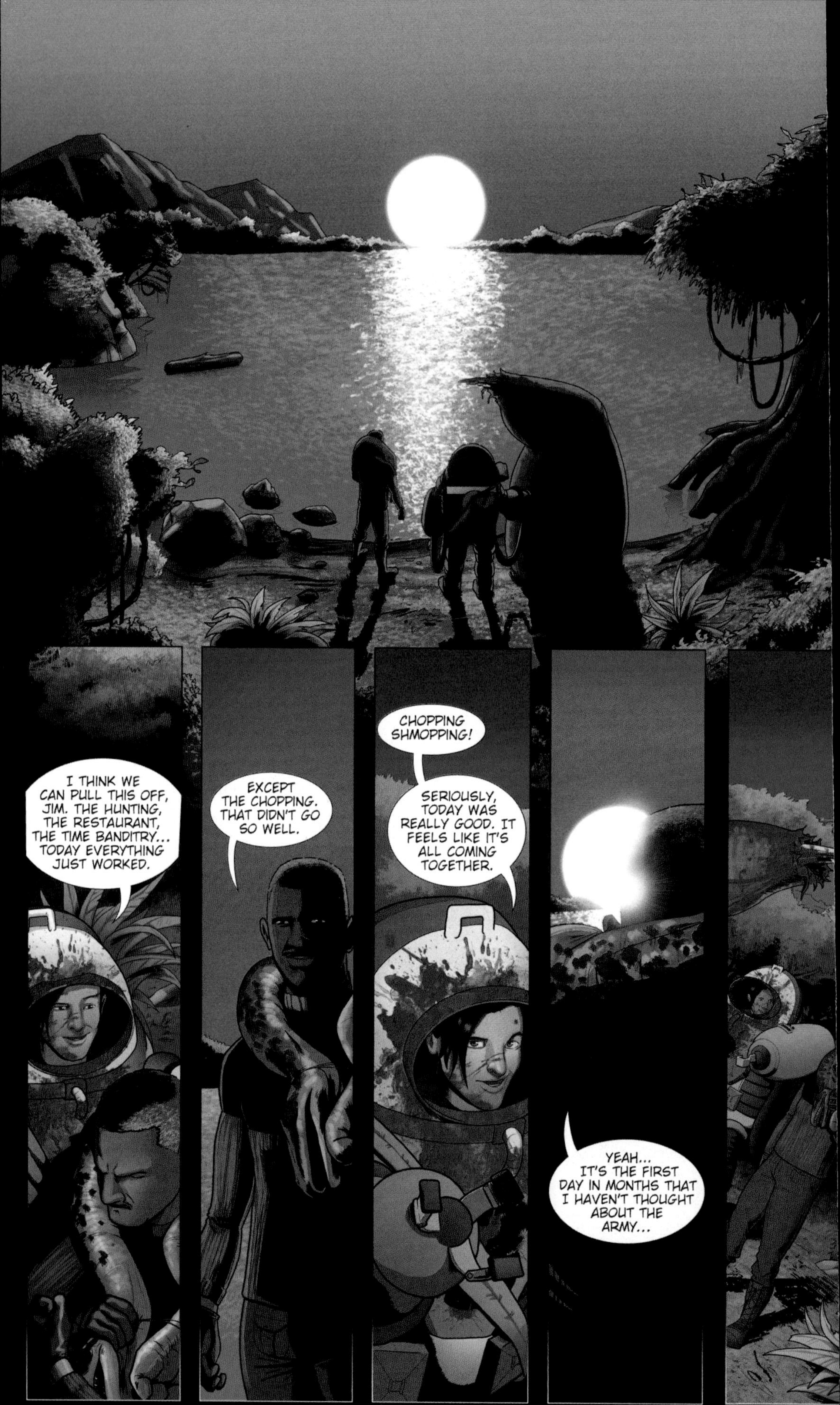
I THINK WE CAN PULL THIS OFF, JIM. THE HUNTING, THE RESTAURANT, THE TIME BANDITRY... TODAY EVERYTHING JUST WORKED.
EXCEPT THE CHOPPING. THAT DIDN'T GO SO WELL.
CHOPPING SHMOPPING!
SERIOUSLY, TODAY WAS REALLY GOOD. IT FEELS LIKE IT'S ALL COMING TOGETHER.
YEAH... IT'S THE FIRST DAY IN MONTHS THAT I HAVEN'T THOUGHT ABOUT THE ARMY...

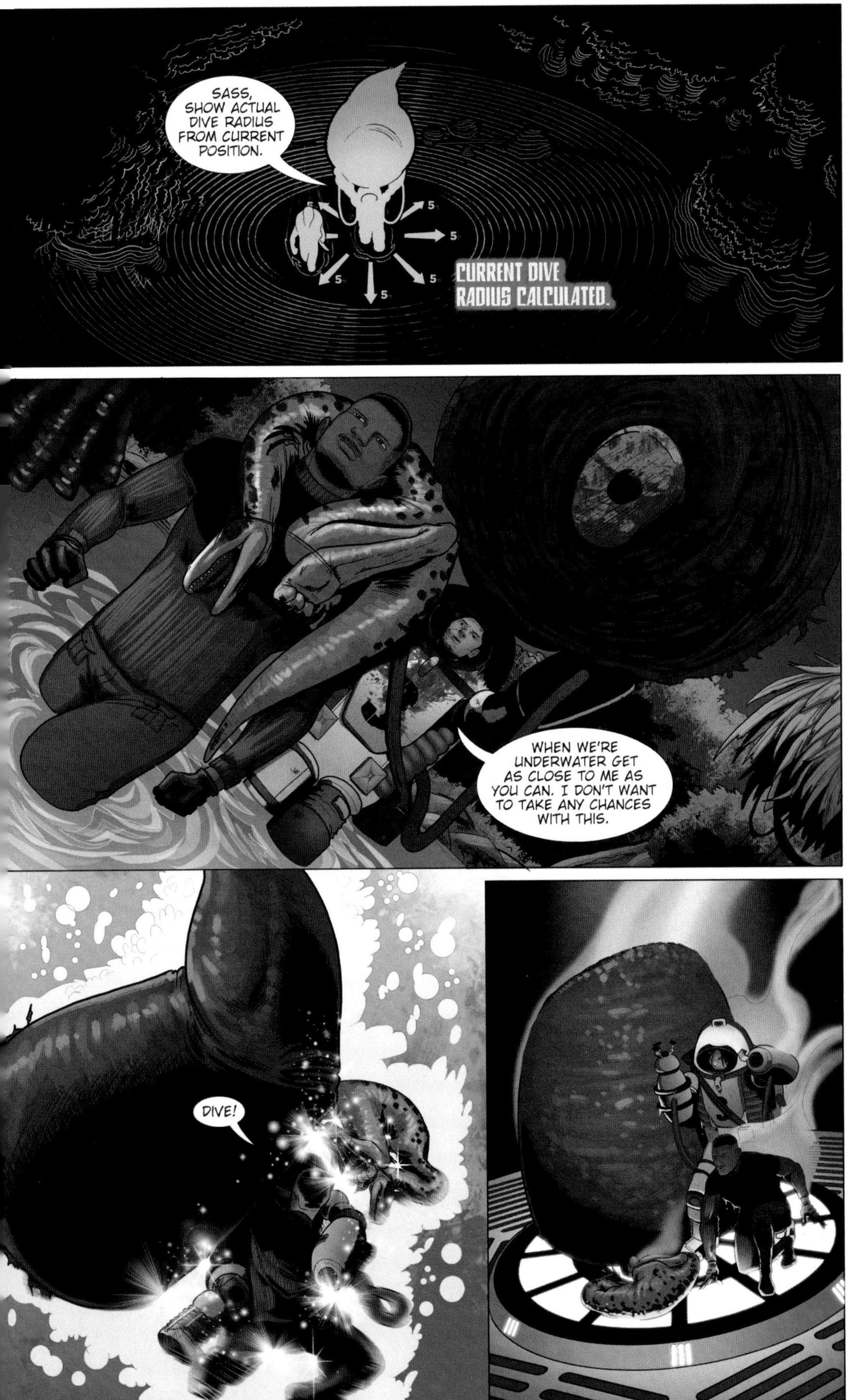
SASS, SHOW ACTUAL DIVE RADIUS FROM CURRENT POSITION.
CURRENT DIVE RADIUS CALCULATED.
WHEN WE'RE UNDERWATER GET AS CLOSE TO ME AS YOU CAN. I DON'T WANT TO TAKE ANY CHANCES WITH THIS.
DIVE!

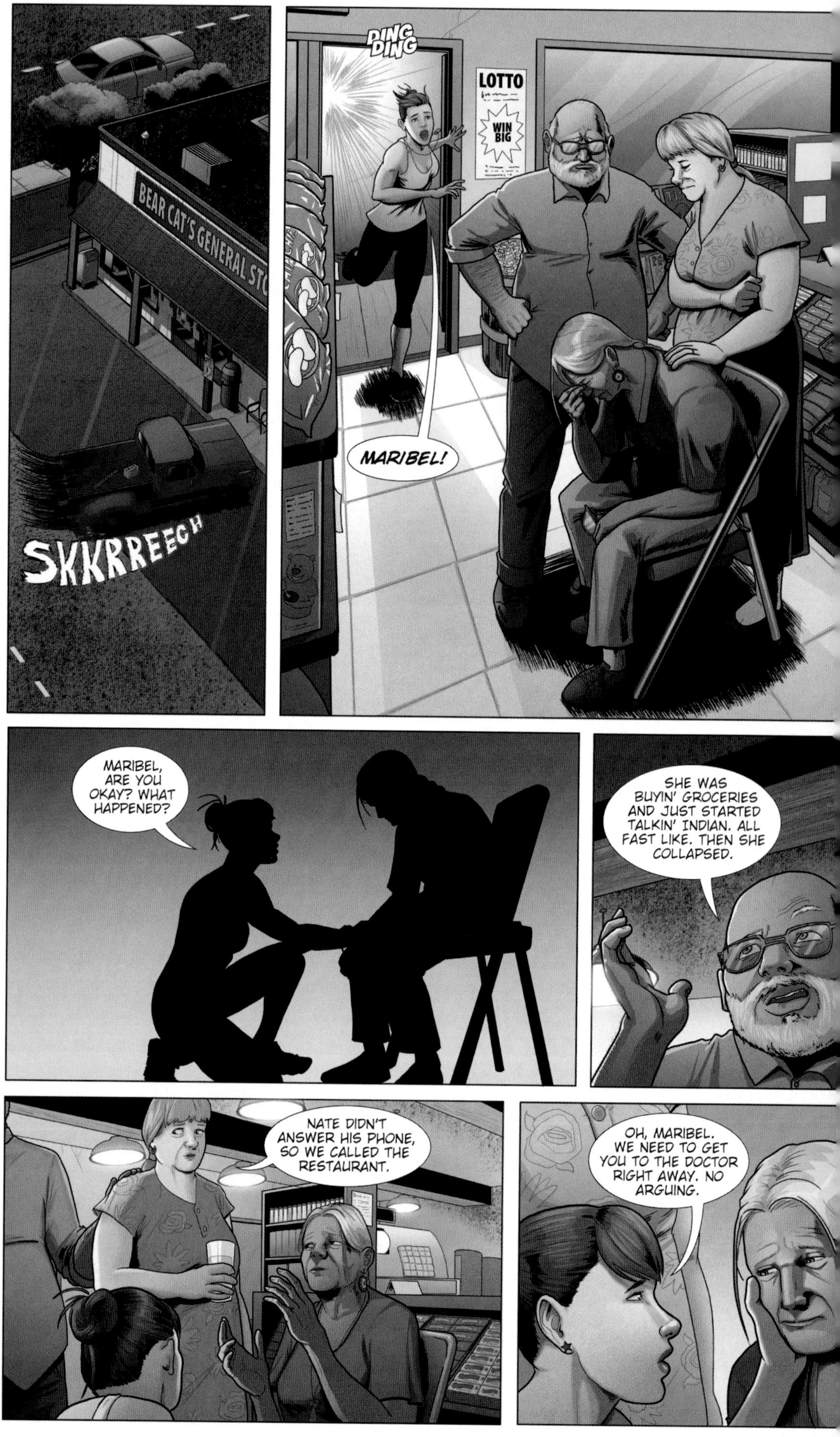
SKKRREECH
DING DING
LOTTO
WIN BIG
BEAR CAT'S GENERAL STO
MARIBEL!
MARIBEL, ARE YOU OKAY? WHAT HAPPENED?
SHE WAS BUYIN' GROCERIES AND JUST STARTED TALKIN' INDIAN. ALL FAST LIKE. THEN SHE COLLAPSED.
NATE DIDN'T ANSWER HIS PHONE, SO WE CALLED THE RESTAURANT.
OH, MARIBEL. WE NEED TO GET YOU TO THE DOCTOR RIGHT AWAY. NO ARGUING.

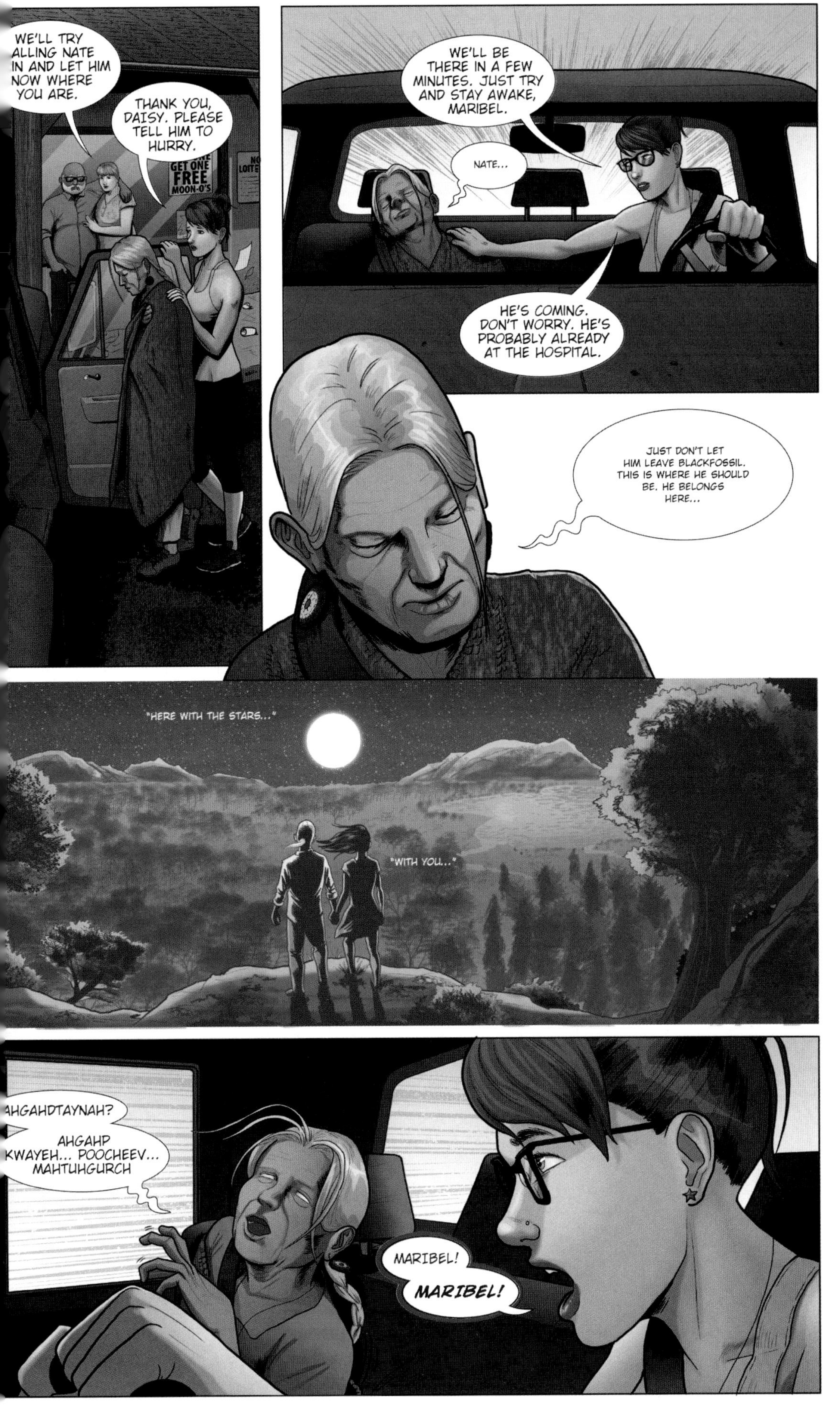
WE'LL TRY
ALLING NATE
IN AND LET HIM
NOW WHERE
YOU ARE.
THANK YOU, DAISY. PLEASE TELL HIM TO HURRY.
GET ONE FREE MOON-O'S
WE'LL BE THERE IN A FEW MINUTES. JUST TRY AND STAY AWAKE, MARIBEL.
NATE...
HE'S COMING. DON'T WORRY. HE'S PROBABLY ALREADY AT THE HOSPITAL.
JUST DON'T LET HIM LEAVE BLACKFOSSIL. THIS IS WHERE HE SHOULD BE. HE BELONGS HERE...
"HERE WITH THE STARS..."
"WITH YOU..."
AHGAHDTAYNAH?
AHGAHP KWAYEH... POOCHEEV... MAHTUHGURCH
MARIBEL!
MARIBEL!

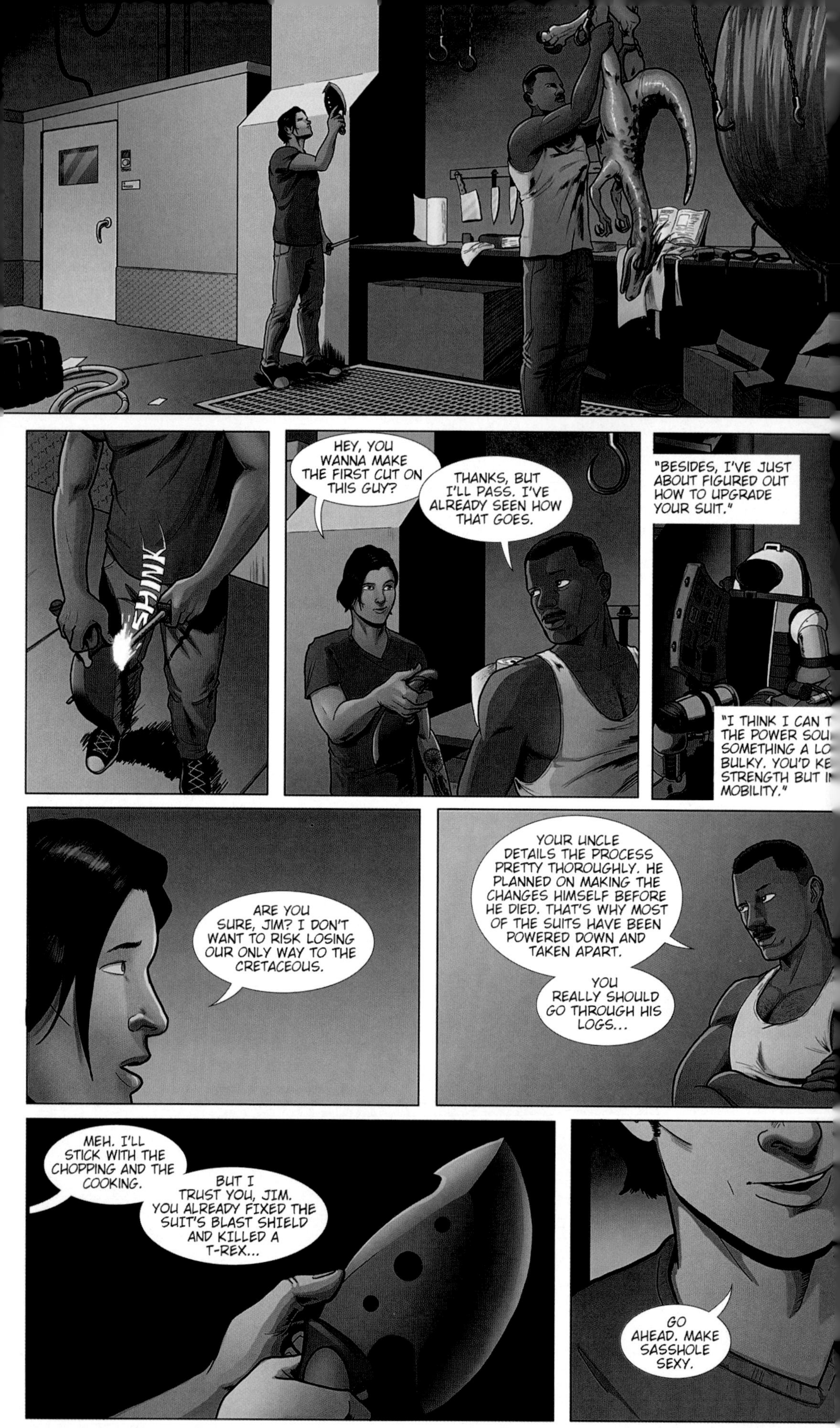
SHINK
HEY, YOU WANNA MAKE THE FIRST CUT ON THIS GUY?
THANKS, BUT I'LL PASS. I'VE ALREADY SEEN HOW THAT GOES.
"BESIDES, I'VE JUST ABOUT FIGURED OUT HOW TO UPGRADE YOUR SUIT."
"I THINK I CAN T
THE POWER SOU
SOMETHING A LO
BULKY. YOU'D KE
STRENGTH BUT IN
MOBILITY."
ARE YOU SURE, JIM? I DON'T WANT TO RISK LOSING OUR ONLY WAY TO THE CRETACEOUS.
YOUR UNCLE DETAILS THE PROCESS PRETTY THOROUGHLY. HE PLANNED ON MAKING THE CHANGES HIMSELF BEFORE HE DIED. THAT'S WHY MOST OF THE SUITS HAVE BEEN POWERED DOWN AND TAKEN APART.
YOU REALLY SHOULD GO THROUGH HIS LOGS...
MEH. I'LL STICK WITH THE CHOPPING AND THE COOKING.
BUT I TRUST YOU, JIM. YOU ALREADY FIXED THE SUIT'S BLAST SHIELD AND KILLED A T-REX...
GO AHEAD. MAKE SASSHOLE SEXY.

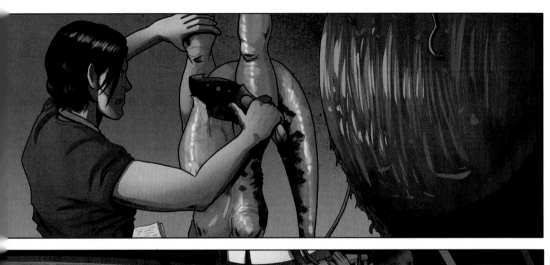

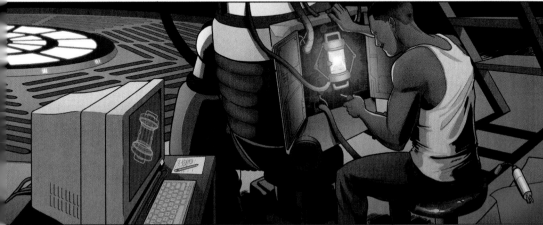

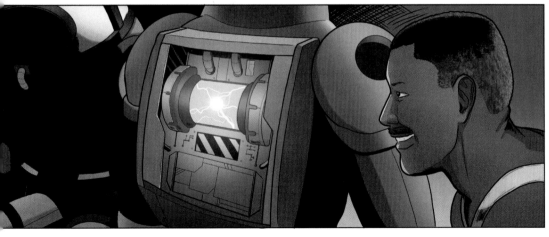

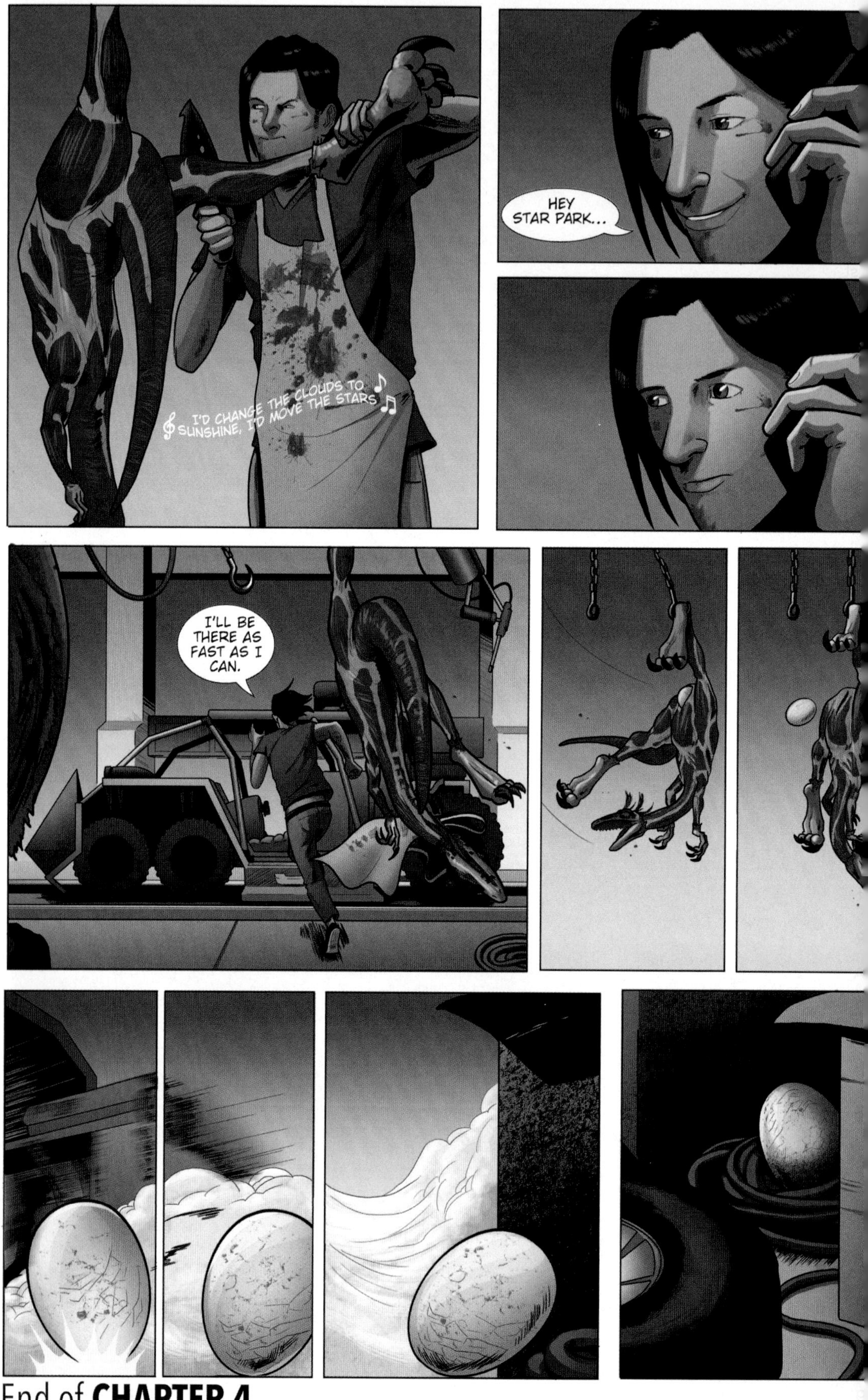
I'D CHANGE THE CLOUDS TO SUNSHINE, I'D MOVE THE STARS
HEY STAR PARK...
I'LL BE THERE AS FAST AS I CAN.

End of **CHAPTER 4**

GIVE IT MEANING

Writer **MARKISAN NASO** • Artist & Letterer **JASON MUHR** • Colorist **ANDREI TABAC**

COOKING CRETACEOUS

...by. That double cliffhanger was a doozy for me and I'm the writer! Hope everyone enjoyed this issue. Next... Our first arc concludes and everything changes. You think Nate and company have a lot to deal with... ...st wait until you read the final pages of issue #4...

...fore that, try cooking up this insane, Creole concoction from my best buddy, Jim Parker - AKA The Captain!

...an

...oraciouscomic@gmail.com   [f] VoraciousComic

...VoraciousComic   [t] voraciouscomic.tumblr

...e Captain's Red Beans and Rice

...AN INGREDIENTS
- ...b dry red kidney beans
- ...qts water
- ...qt Archaeopteryx stock (or chicken stock)
- ...onion diced
- ...ribs celery stalk (with leafy green tops)
- ...green bell pepper
- ...cloves garlic
- ...2 lb good-quality smoked T-Rex thigh ...or ham), diced
- ...b smoked T-Rex knuckles (or ham hocks)
- ...bay leaf
- ...tbsp Creole seasoning (I make my own, ...ut you can use the store version)
- ...tbsp Worcestershire sauce
- ...tsp Tabasco sauce

- A dozen turns of ground black pepper
- 3 tsp coarse salt

RICE GRITS INGREDIENTS
- 1 cup long-grain white rice
- 4 cups water
- 1 tsp salt
- 3 tbsp unsalted butter

HAVE READY TO SERVE
- 6 poached or loose sunnyside up eggs
- 2 links of grilled Troodon sausage (or Andouille)
- ½ cup chopped green scallions

...RECTIONS

...ANS INSTRUCTIONS
...Place the beans and 2 qt water in a small stockpot over high heat and bring to a boil.
...Remove from heat and cover for 30 minutes.
...Drain the water from the beans and add 2 qt fresh water and the stock along with all other ingredients except the salt.
...Bring to a boil and reduce to a simmer and cook for 90 minutes.
...Add the salt and crush some of the beans with a potato masher. Continue to simmer for another 30 minutes.
...Remove T-Rex knuckles (strip off and return any meat to the pot) and keep beans warm.
...At this point, you can remove half the red beans, cool, and freeze for future use.

...CE INSTRUCTIONS
...n a clean coffee grinder or small food processor, grind the rice into a meal.
...Bring the water to a boil with the salt and 1 tbsp of the butter.
...Slowly whisk the rice meal into the boiling water and continue to whisk until the mixture begins to thicken and spit at you.
...Lower the heat and continue to stir for about three minutes. Cover and reduce heat to low, cooking until thick and creamy, about 15 minutes. Stir in the remaining butter.

...SERVE: Ladle about 1 cup beans into a bowl and top with about 1/2 cup rice grits. Top the grits with ...gs and serve with Troodon sausage and some freshly chopped scallions.

...rves 6 hearty eaters.

SKETCHBOOK

Hey! Jason here. I draw all the exploding dinosaur heads. I thought I'd share some behind-the-scenes stuff.

My first attempt at the time-travel suit. I went a little Mr. Freeze-y with it, more form-fitting, with a mix of metal and some kind of durable cloth material. Markisan thought it should be a lot more retro and clunky, to better suit the mismatched metal materials Tony had available when he created it, and also to make Nate's journey to the Cretaceous more challenging and ripe for physical comedy.

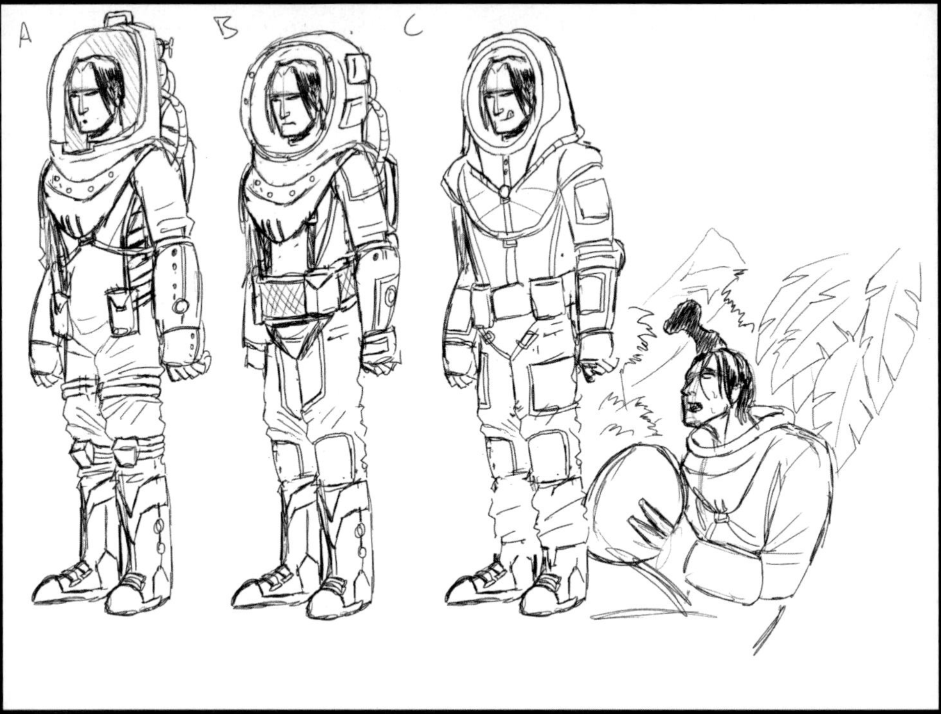
A
B
C

My second shot at it was a lot closer to what Markisan envisioned. Though, as an artist, I do have to say designing a suit with tons of rivets and mismatched materials is quite the headache to draw page after page. Maybe someday Nate might get an upgraded suit...hmm...

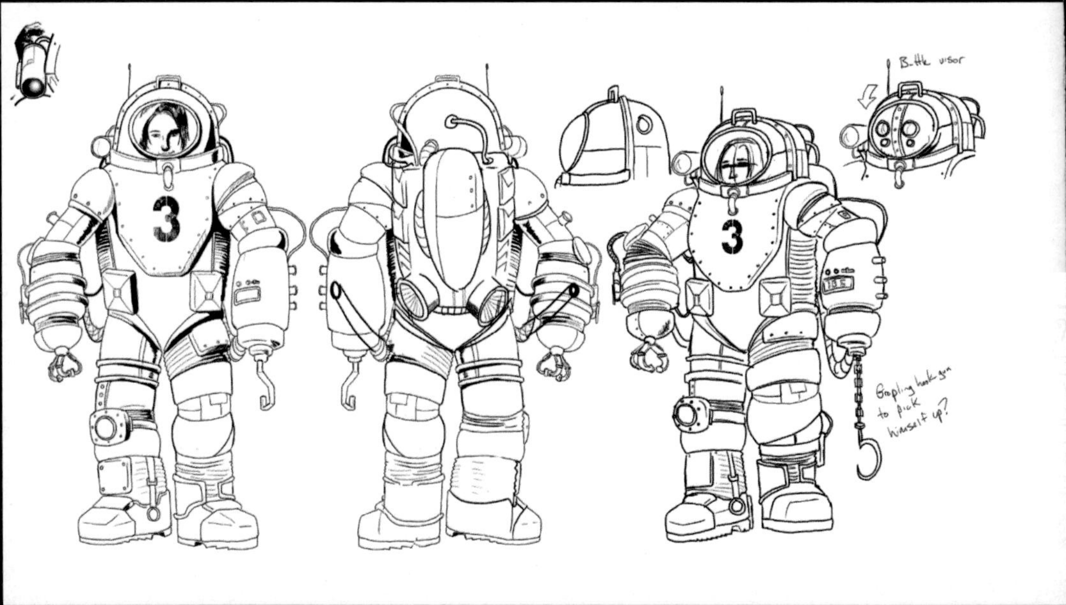
3
3
Grapling hook gun to pick himself up?

ETCHBOOK

time-travel tank to better explain the idea to me.

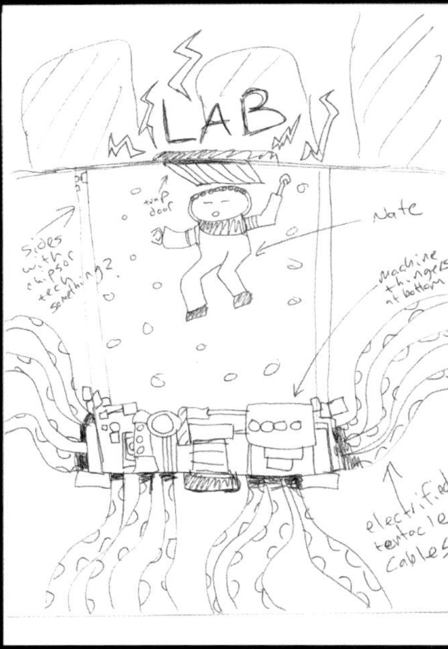
LAB
trap door
Sides with chips or tech something?
Nate
machine thingers at bottom
electrified tentacle cables

tudies.

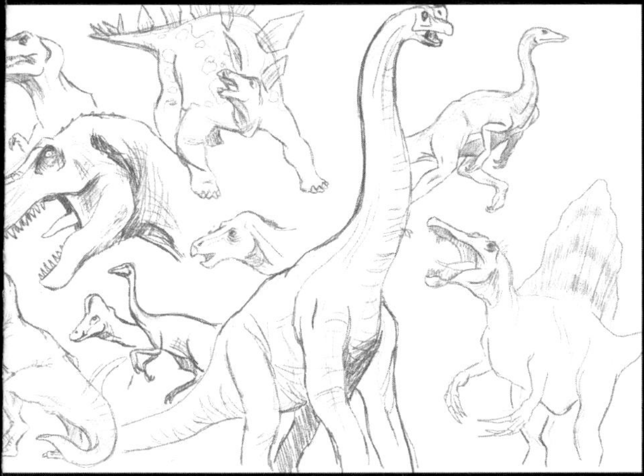

I sketched out some rough floor plans for Tony's lab and the Fork & Fossil to keep track of where everything is located while drawing and moving the camera around.

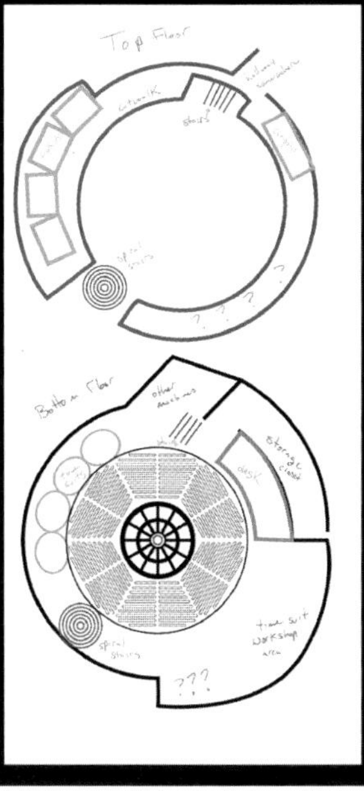
Top Floor
Bottom Floor
storage closet
time suit workshop area
spiral stairs
???

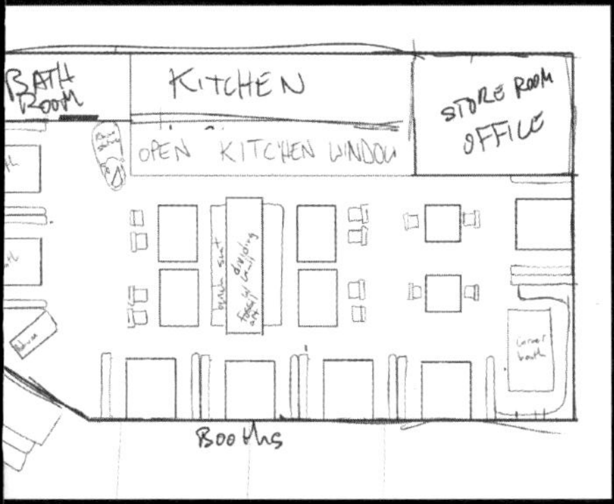
BATH ROOM
KITCHEN
OPEN KITCHEN WINDOW
STORE ROOM
OFFICE
Booths

Cover concepts. Some might be used in the future or as variants.

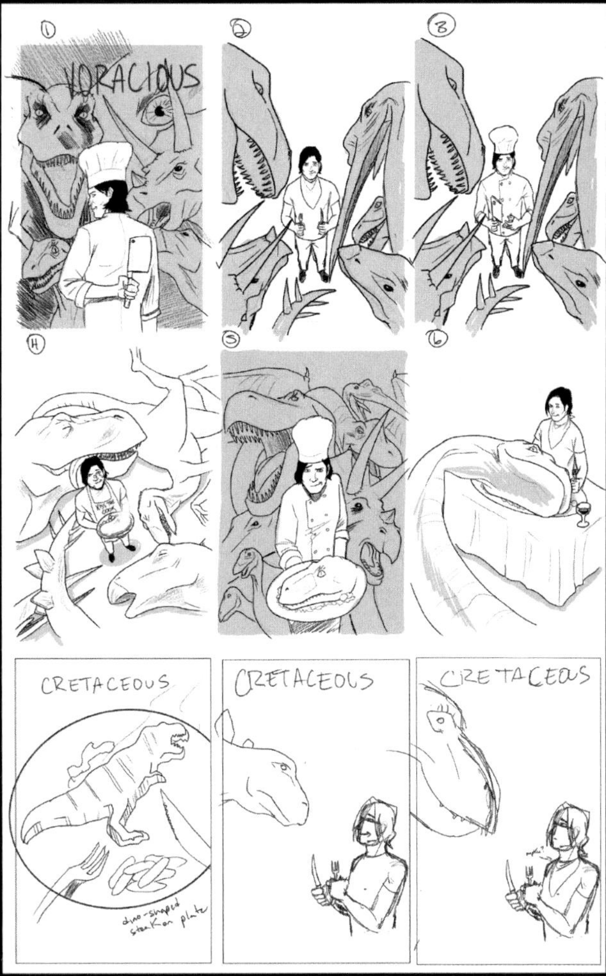
1
2
3
VORACIOUS
4
5
6
CRETACEOUS
dino-shaped steak on plate
CRETACEOUS
CRETACEOUS

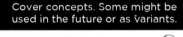

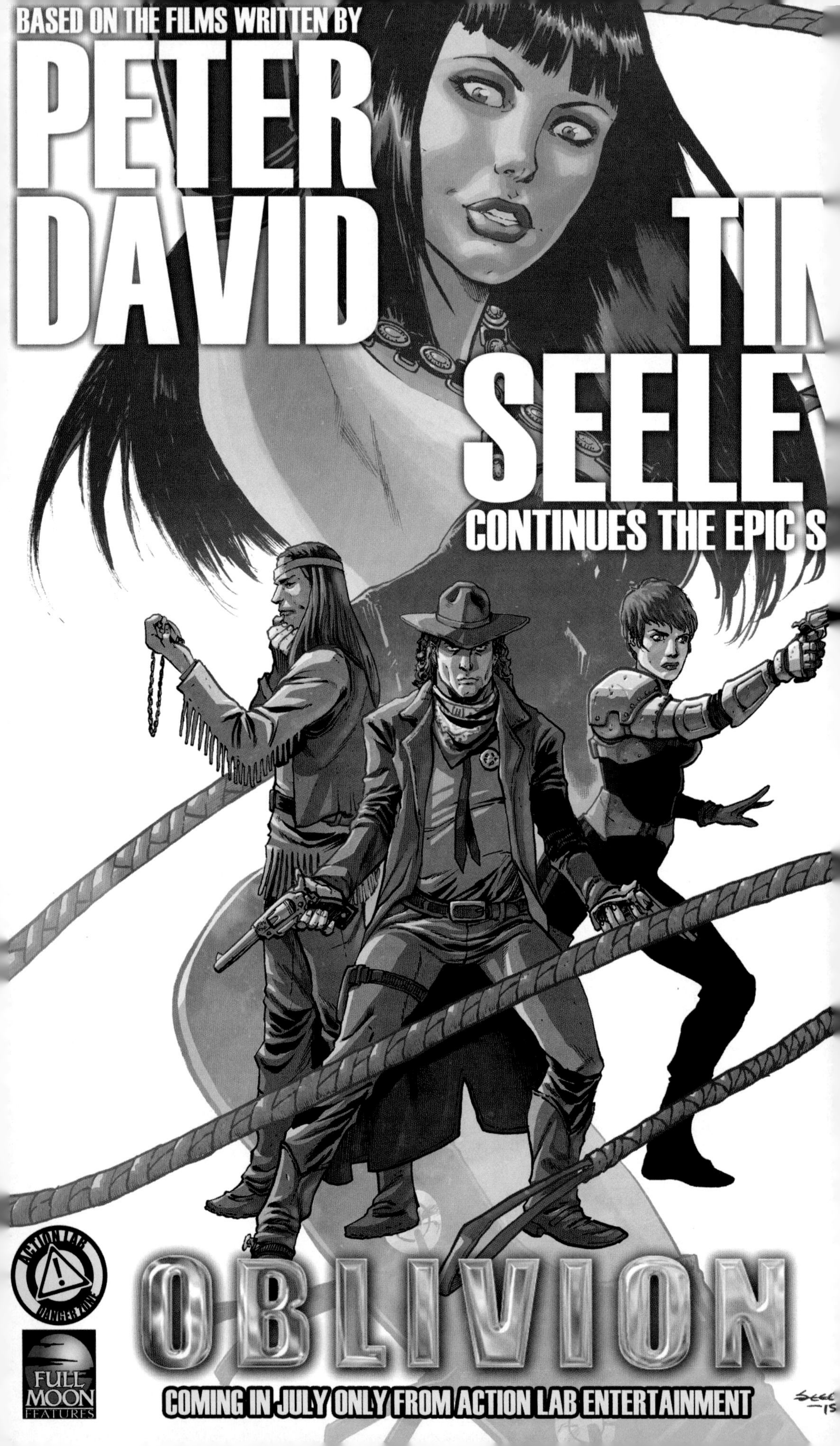
BASED ON THE FILMS WRITTEN BY
PETER DAVID
TI
SEELE
CONTINUES THE EPIC S
ACTION LAB
DANGER ZONE
FULL MOON FEATURES
OBLIVION
COMING IN JULY ONLY FROM ACTION LAB ENTERTAINMENT

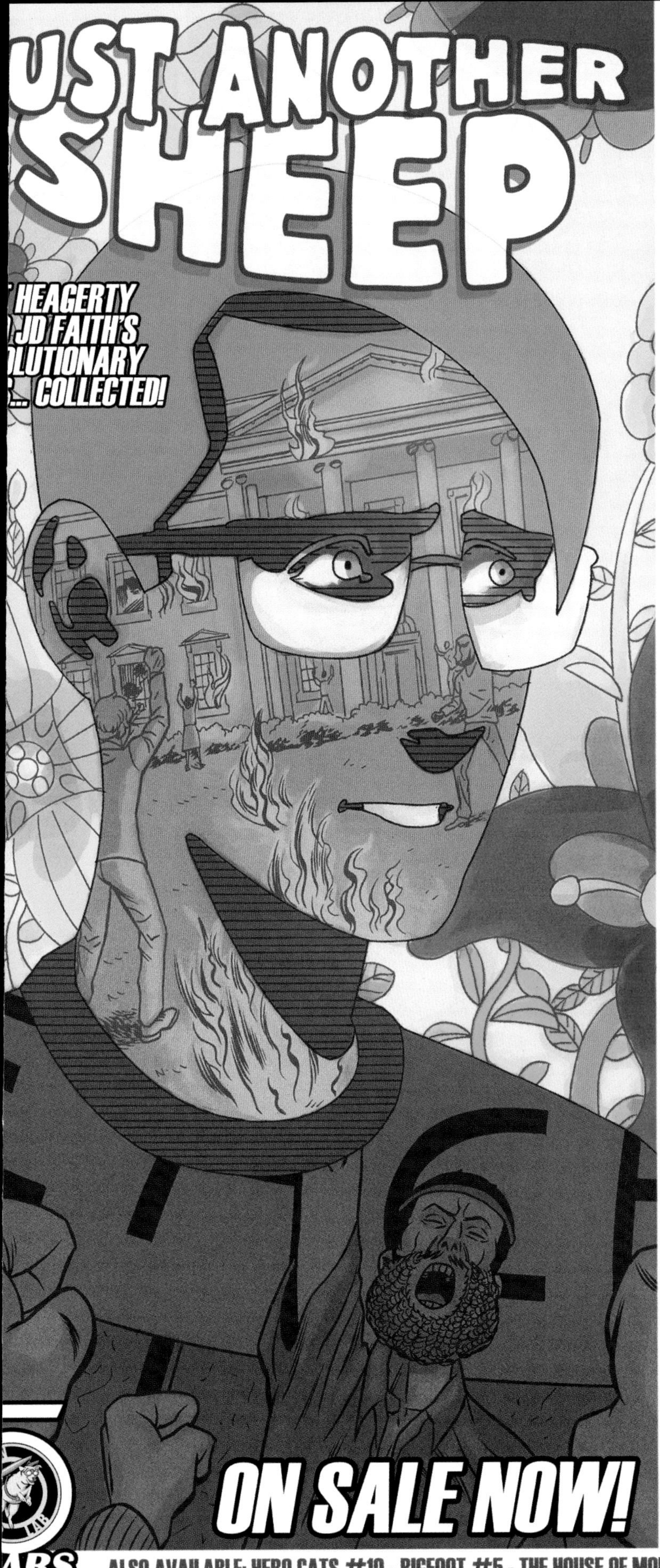
UST ANOTHER
SHEEP
HEAGERTY
JD FAITH'S
OLUTIONARY
... COLLECTED!
ON SALE NOW!
ARS

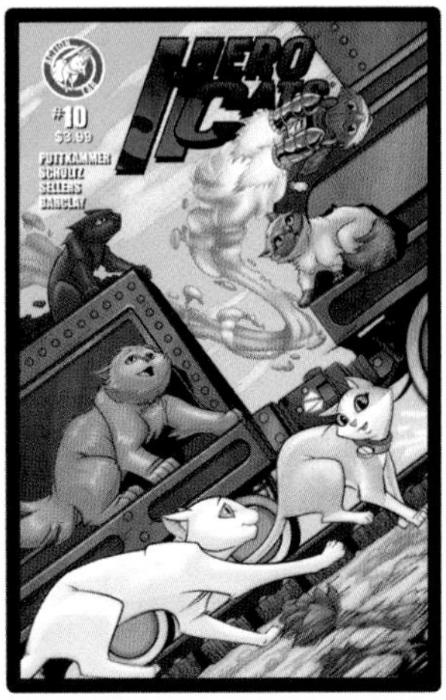
HERO CATS
#10
$3.99
PUTTKAMMER
SCHULTZ
SELLERS
BARCLAY

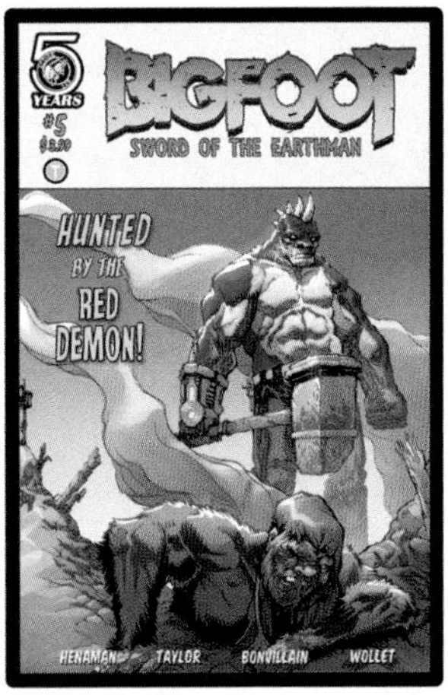
5 YEARS
BIGFOOT
SWORD OF THE EARTHMAN
#5
HUNTED BY THE RED DEMON!
HENAMAN TAYLOR BONVILLAIN WOLLET

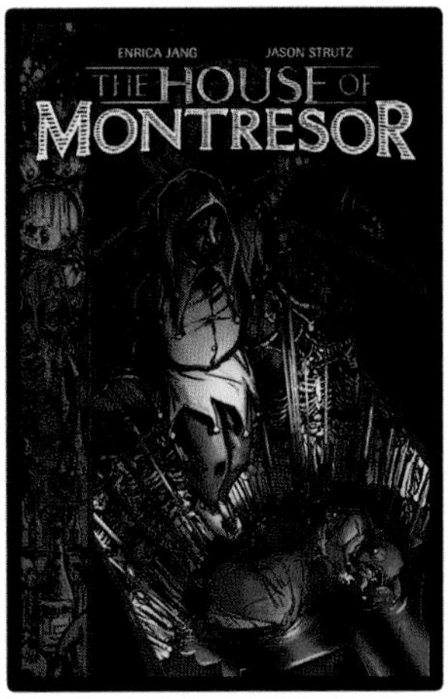
ENRICA JANG
JASON STRUTZ
THE HOUSE OF MONTRESOR

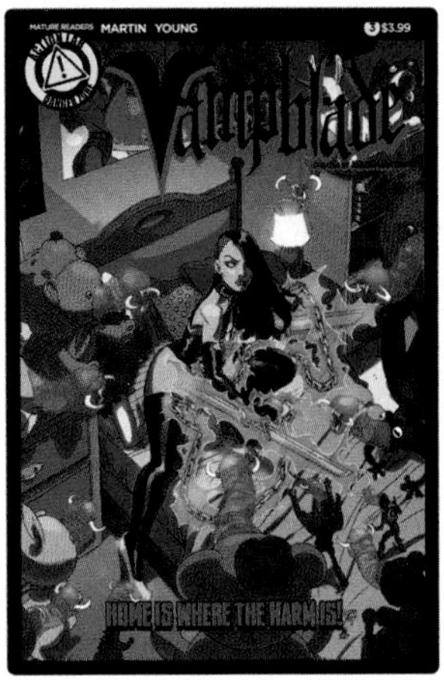
MATURE READERS
MARTIN YOUNG
$3.99
Vampblade
HOME IS WHERE THE WARM IS!

ALSO AVAILABLE: HERO CATS #10 - BIGFOOT #5 - THE HOUSE OF MONTRESOR #3 - VAMPBLADE #3

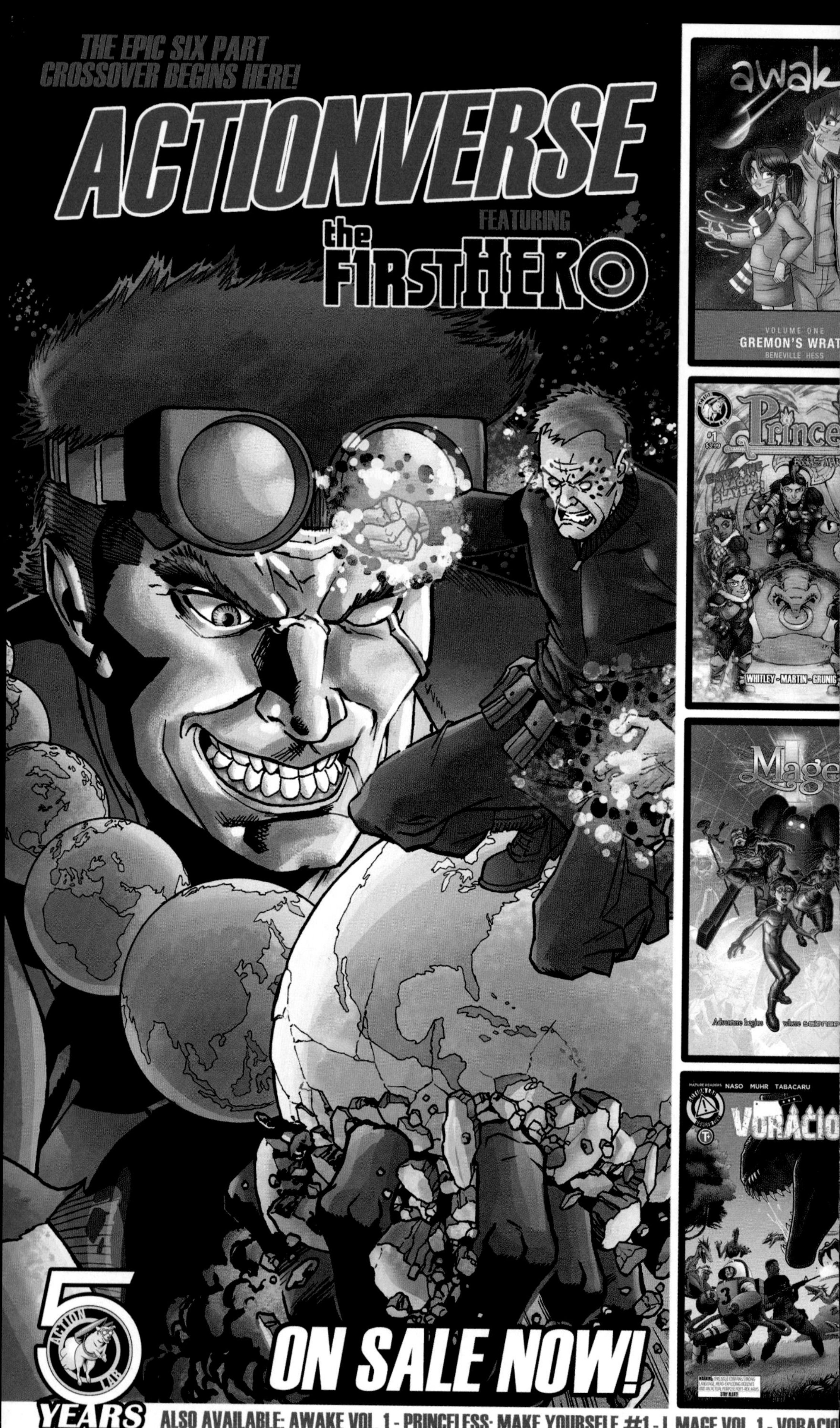
THE EPIC SIX PART
CROSSOVER BEGINS HERE!
ACTIONVERSE
FEATURING
the FIRSTHERO
ON SALE NOW!
5 YEARS
ACTION LAB
awak
VOLUME ONE
GREMON'S WRAT
BENEVILLE HESS
#1
$3.99
Prince
WHITLEY - MARTIN - GRUNIG
Mage
Adventure begins where science
MATURE READERS
NASO MUHR TABACARU
VORACIO
ALSO AVAILABLE: AWAKE VOL. 1 - PRINCELESS: MAKE YOURSELF #1 - I, MAGE VOL. 1 - VORACIO

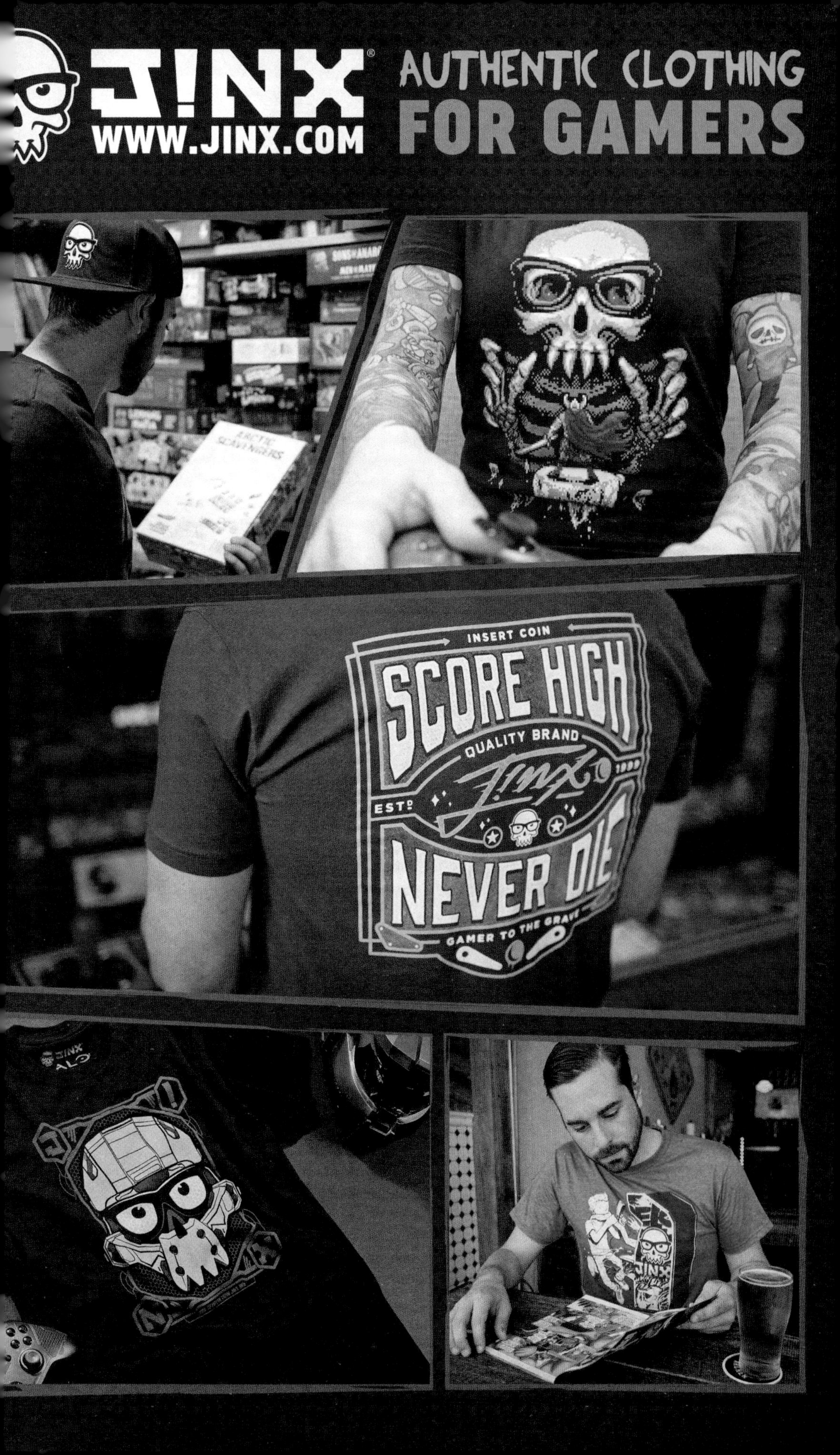
ARCTIC SCAVENGERS
INSERT COIN
SCORE HIGH
QUALITY BRAND
EST'D
NEVER DIE
GAMER TO THE GRAVE

"WHEN WE STRIKE WE MUST BE DEAD
ACCURATE. AND MERCILESS."

Voracious - Danger Zone
www.actionlabcomics.com

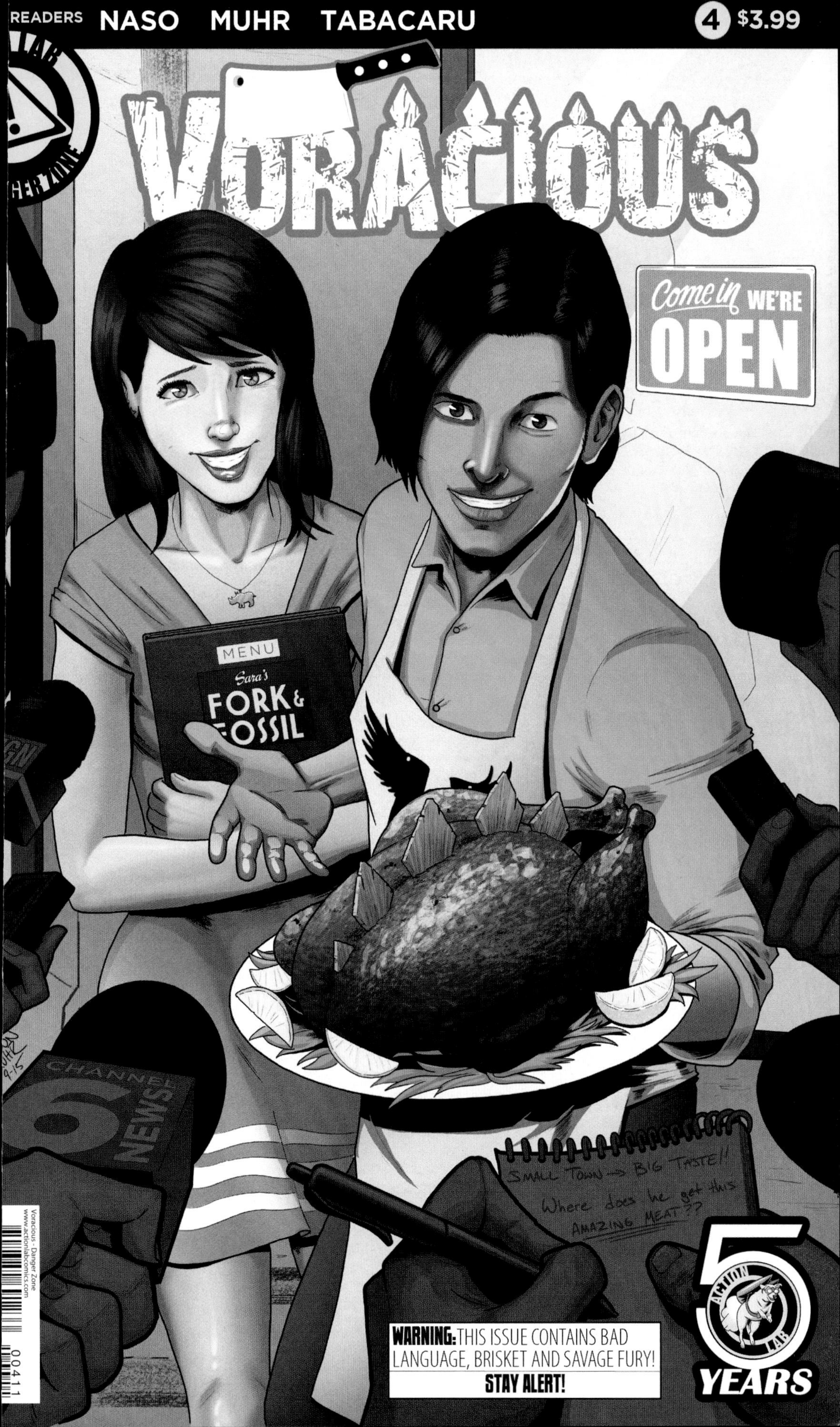
READERS NASO MUHR TABACARU
4 $3.99
VORACIOUS
Come in WE'RE OPEN
MENU
Sara's FORK & FOSSIL
CHANNEL 6 NEWS
SMALL TOWN → BIG TASTE!!
Where does he get this AMAZING MEAT??
WARNING: THIS ISSUE CONTAINS BAD LANGUAGE, BRISKET AND SAVAGE FURY!
STAY ALERT!
5 ACTION LAB YEARS

PREVIOUSLY...

Nate Willner, a chef in NYC, was forced to move back to Utah, after his restaurant exploded, killing his sister and leaving him unmotivated and hollow. Working at the Javarado Café, it seems Nate's life has become a dead end. But when he unexpectedly inherits a time travel suit from his Great Uncle Tony that can take him to the time of the dinosaurs, his passion for cooking is renewed. Dinosaurs are so delicious that Nate decides to open a restaurant in the present that serves secret meat from the past!

Using his inheritance Nate purchases the Javarado and names it Sara's Fork & Fossil, after his sister. In the weeks since the restaurant opened, Nate and his childhood friend, Starlee (now his business partner), have grown closer. Meanwhile, Nate's grandmother, Maribel, collapsed after a series of old memories triggered a psychological blowback. Her past is somehow linked to Uncle Tony's, but Nate is unaware of the connection. He's also unaware that the town Sheriff has started looking into his finances. Nate's been too preoccupied with running the diner and hunting dinosaurs with his friend, Jim Hand. Jim's skills as an ex-Army Ranger have been invaluable. He took down a T-Rex last issue! He's also been improving the time dive suit.

Now that Nate has a handle on hunting and the diner is off to a great start, he needs to make sure his Grandma is okay and figure out his feelings for former NYC flame, Jenna, who's on her way to visit.

CHAPTER 5
VANISHING POINT

Written by
MARKISAN NASO

Art, Lettering & Design by
JASON MUHR

Color Art by
ANDREI TABACARU

VORACIOUS created by
NASO & MUHR

"Meat Grinder" variant cover
(LTD to 1500) by
JOHN MCCREA

with colors by **MIKE SPICER**

JASON MARTIN - PUBLISHER
DAVE DWONCH - PRESIDENT
SHAWN GABBORIN - EDITOR IN CHIEF
JAMAL IGLE - V.P. OF MARKETING
JIM DIETZ - SOCIAL MEDIA DIRECTOR
KEVIN FREEMAN - EDITOR
COLLEEN BOYD - ASSOCIATE EDITOR

Find Markisan Naso at www.markisan.com.
Find Jason Muhr at www.jasonmuhr.com.

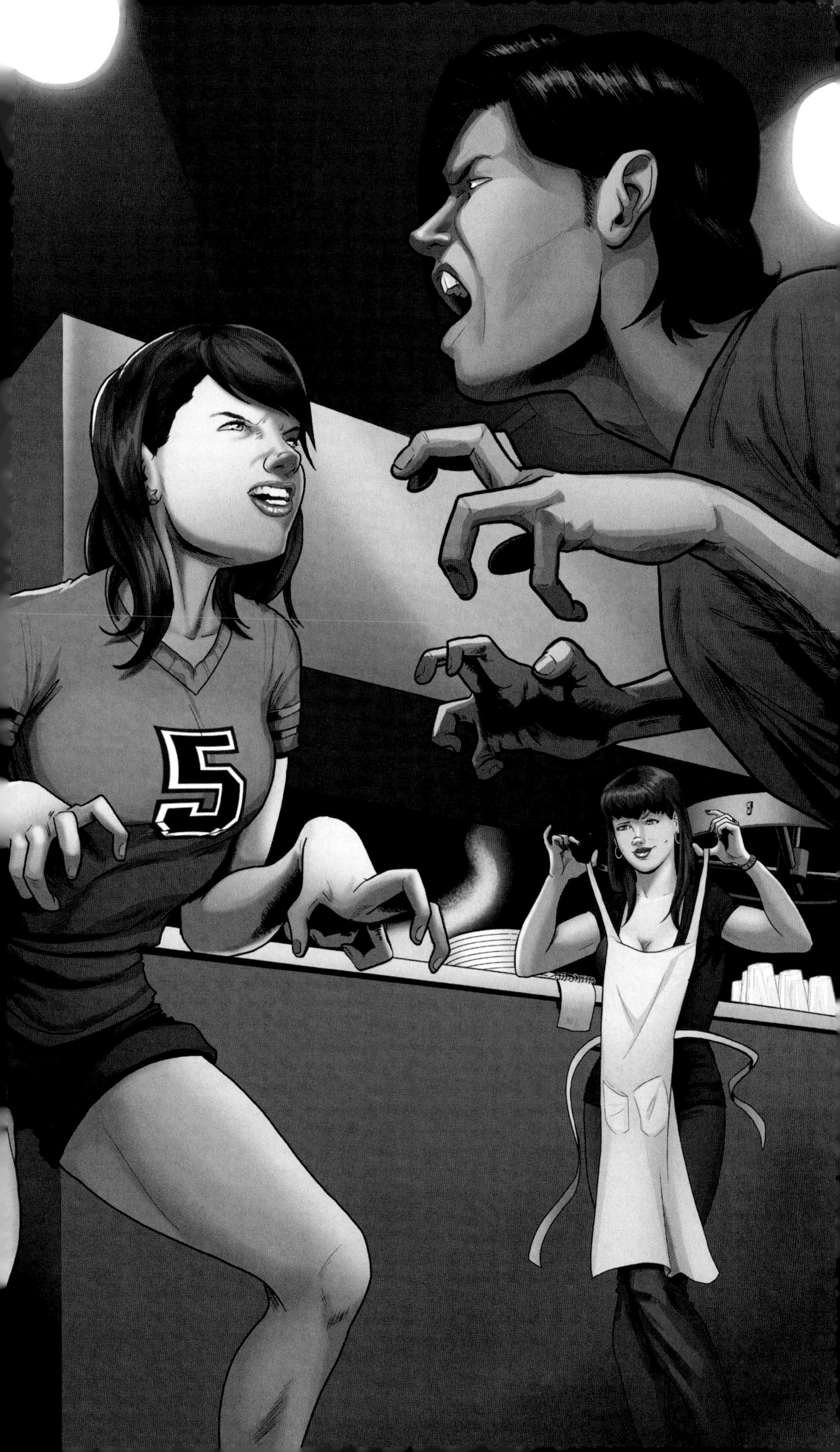

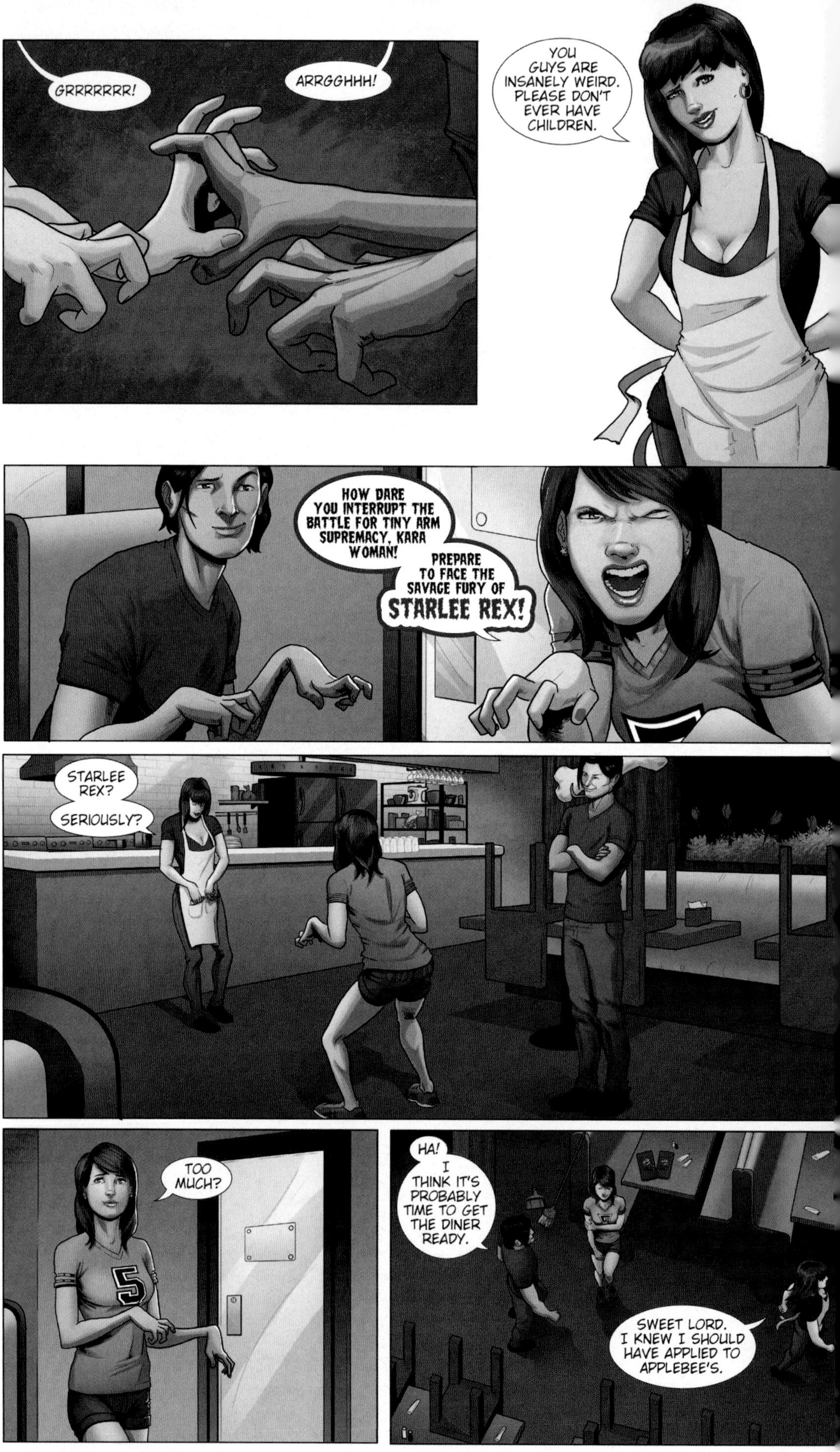
GRRRRRRR!
ARRGGHHH!
YOU GUYS ARE INSANELY WEIRD. PLEASE DON'T EVER HAVE CHILDREN.
HOW DARE YOU INTERRUPT THE BATTLE FOR TINY ARM SUPREMACY, KARA WOMAN!
PREPARE TO FACE THE SAVAGE FURY OF STARLEE REX!
STARLEE REX?
SERIOUSLY?
TOO MUCH?
HA!
I THINK IT'S PROBABLY TIME TO GET THE DINER READY.
SWEET LORD. I KNEW I SHOULD HAVE APPLIED TO APPLEBEE'S.

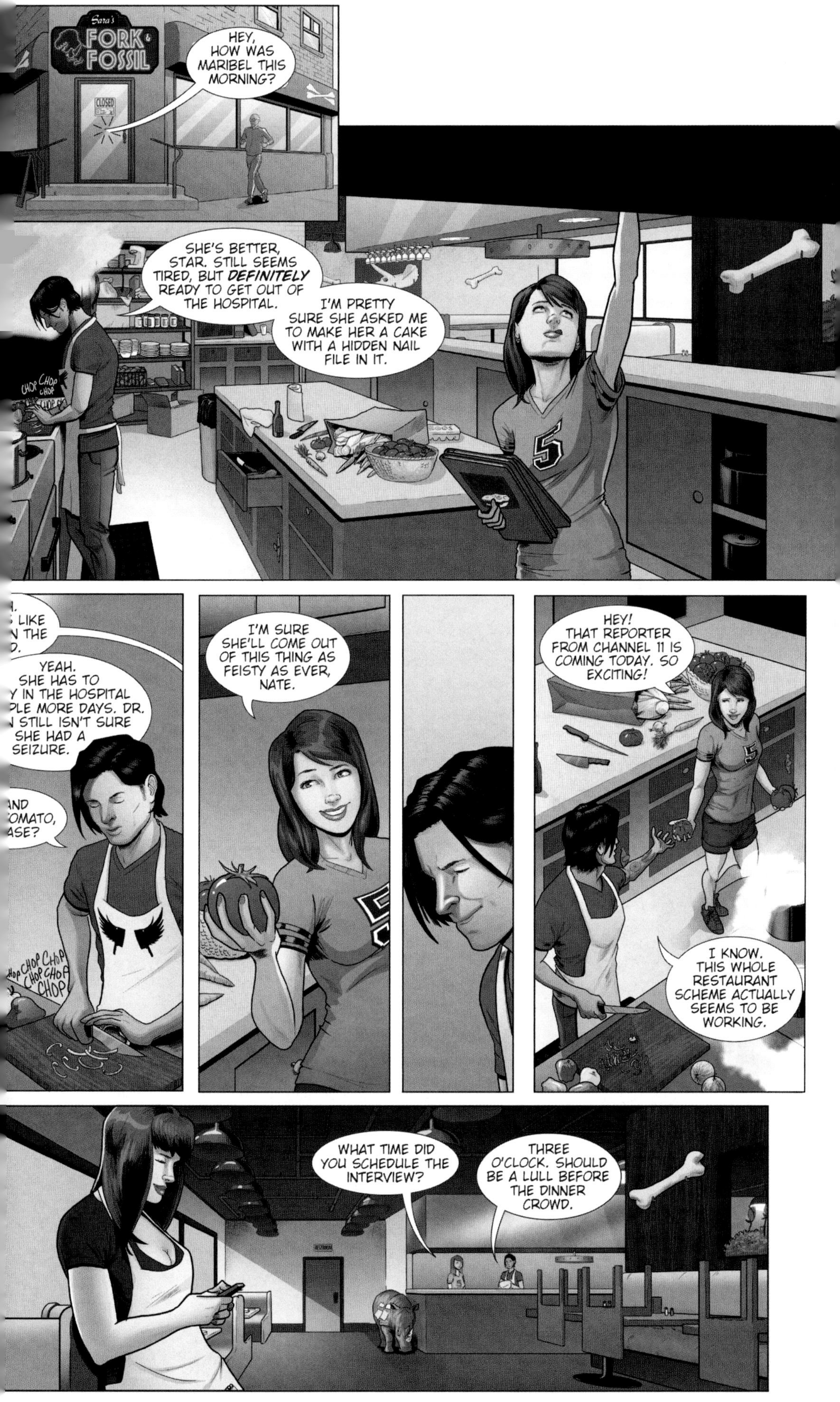
Sara's
FORK & FOSSIL
CLOSED
HEY, HOW WAS MARIBEL THIS MORNING?
SHE'S BETTER, STAR. STILL SEEMS TIRED, BUT *DEFINITELY* READY TO GET OUT OF THE HOSPITAL.
I'M PRETTY SURE SHE ASKED ME TO MAKE HER A CAKE WITH A HIDDEN NAIL FILE IN IT.
CHOP CHOP CHOP
S LIKE N THE
YEAH. SHE HAS TO Y IN THE HOSPITAL PLE MORE DAYS. DR. N STILL ISN'T SURE SHE HAD A SEIZURE.
AND OMATO, ASE?
CHOP CHOP CHOP CHOP CHOP
I'M SURE SHE'LL *COME OUT* OF THIS THING AS FEISTY AS EVER, NATE.
HEY! THAT REPORTER FROM CHANNEL 11 IS COMING TODAY. SO EXCITING!
I KNOW. THIS WHOLE RESTAURANT SCHEME ACTUALLY SEEMS TO BE WORKING.
WHAT TIME DID YOU SCHEDULE THE INTERVIEW?
THREE O'CLOCK. SHOULD BE A LULL BEFORE THE DINNER CROWD.

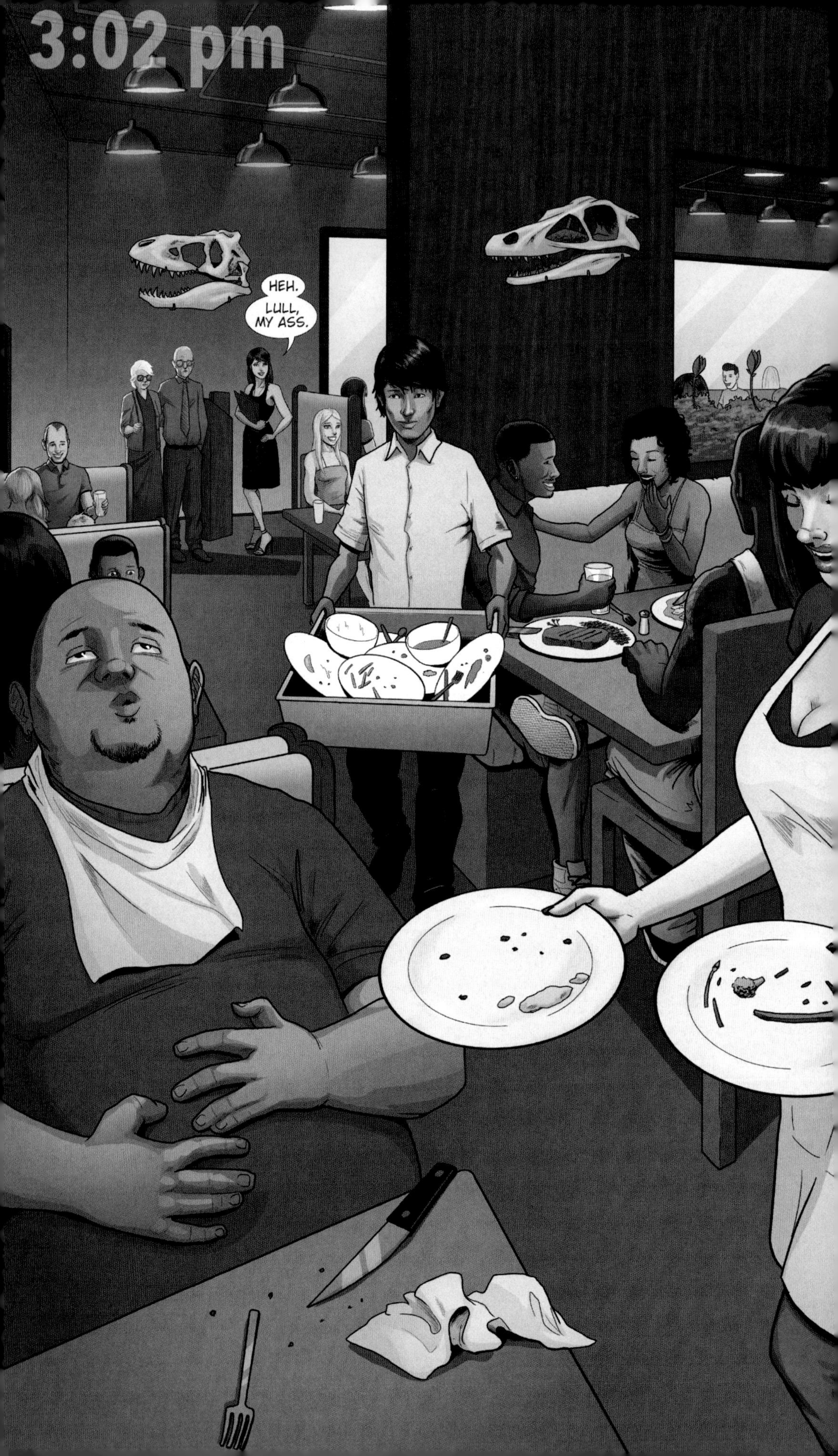
3:02 pm
HEH. LULL, MY ASS.

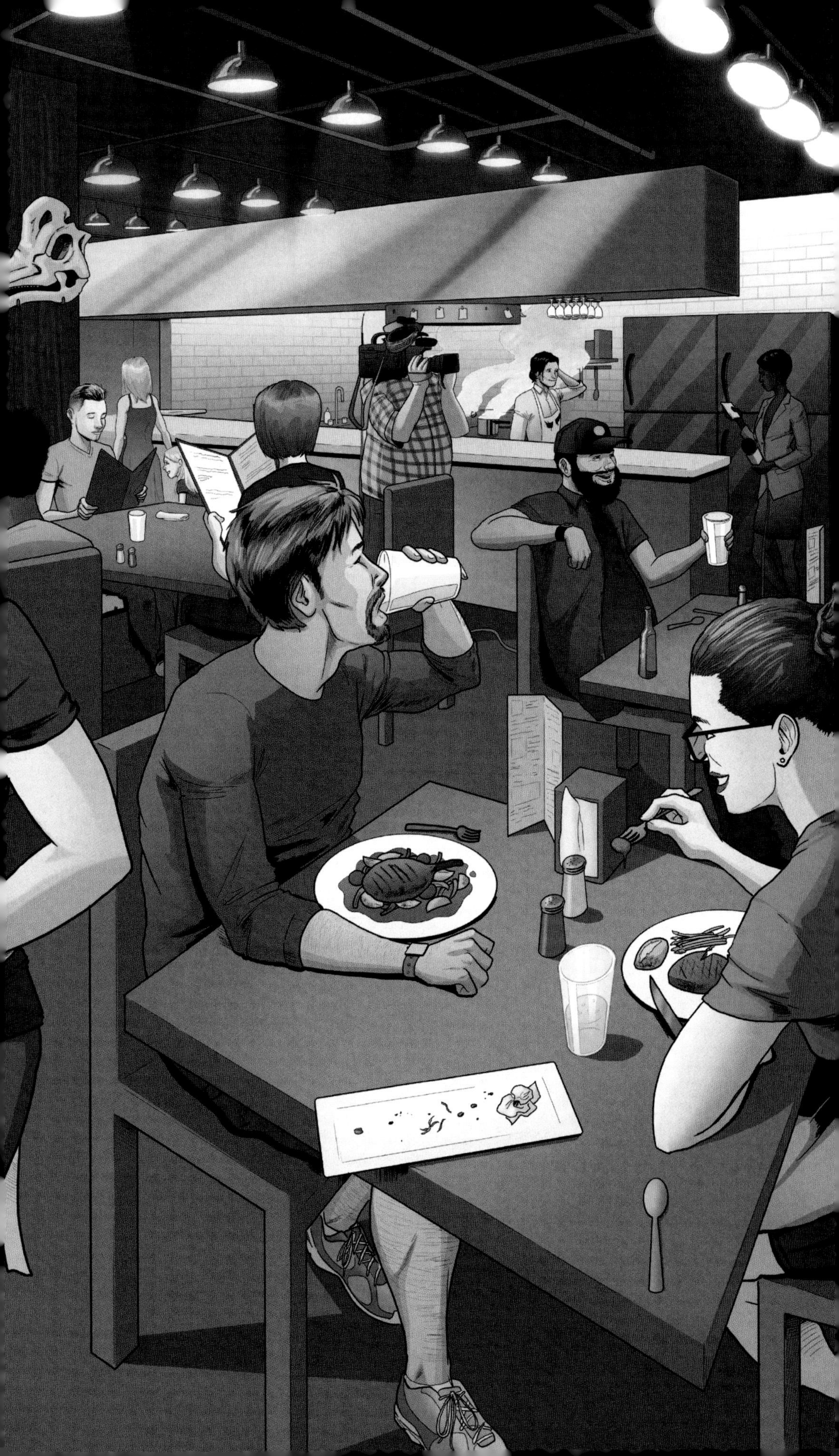

SYSTEM SCAN COMPLETE.

SUIT INTEGRITY AT 100%. INTERDIMENSIONAL DIVE CAPABILITY NOW 100%

ALRIGH

WAIT... INTERDIMENSI WHAT DOES MEAN?

COMPUTER, I INTERDIMENS DIVE.

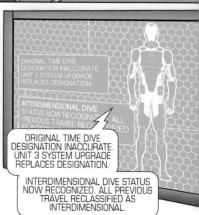

ORIGINAL TIME DIVE DESIGNATION INACCURATE. UNIT 3 SYSTEM UPGRADE REPLACES DESIGNATION.

INTERDIMENSIONAL DIVE STATUS NOW RECOGNIZED. ALL PREVIOUS TRAVEL RECLASSIFIED AS INTERDIMENSIONAL.

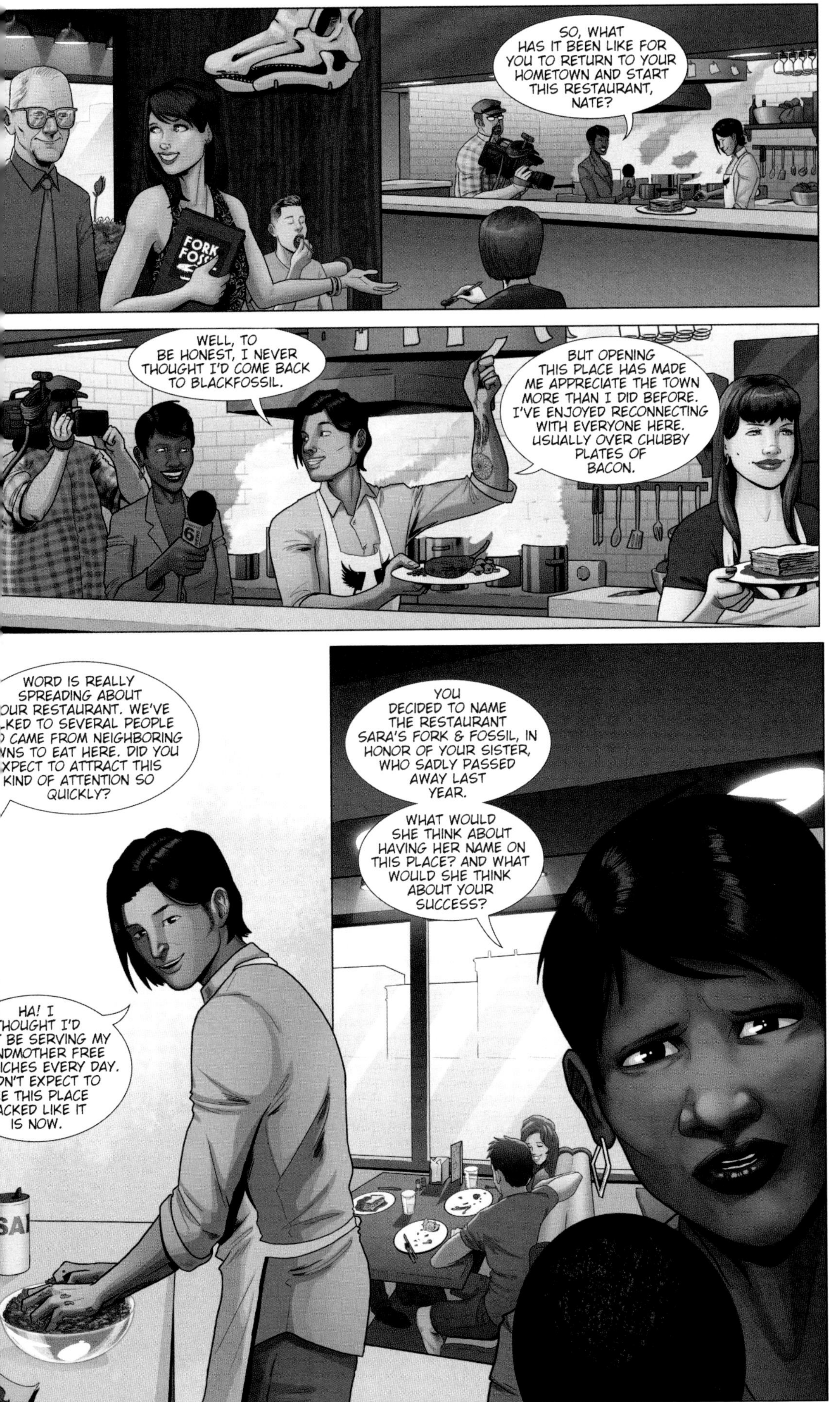
FORK FOSS
SO, WHAT HAS IT BEEN LIKE FOR YOU TO RETURN TO YOUR HOMETOWN AND START THIS RESTAURANT, NATE?
WELL, TO BE HONEST, I NEVER THOUGHT I'D COME BACK TO BLACKFOSSIL.
BUT OPENING THIS PLACE HAS MADE ME APPRECIATE THE TOWN MORE THAN I DID BEFORE. I'VE ENJOYED RECONNECTING WITH EVERYONE HERE. USUALLY OVER CHUBBY PLATES OF BACON.
WORD IS REALLY SPREADING ABOUT OUR RESTAURANT. WE'VE LKED TO SEVERAL PEOPLE CAME FROM NEIGHBORING WNS TO EAT HERE. DID YOU XPECT TO ATTRACT THIS KIND OF ATTENTION SO QUICKLY?
HA! I THOUGHT I'D BE SERVING MY NDMOTHER FREE ICHES EVERY DAY. ON'T EXPECT TO E THIS PLACE ACKED LIKE IT IS NOW.
YOU DECIDED TO NAME THE RESTAURANT SARA'S FORK & FOSSIL, IN HONOR OF YOUR SISTER, WHO SADLY PASSED AWAY LAST YEAR.
WHAT WOULD SHE THINK ABOUT HAVING HER NAME ON THIS PLACE? AND WHAT WOULD SHE THINK ABOUT YOUR SUCCESS?

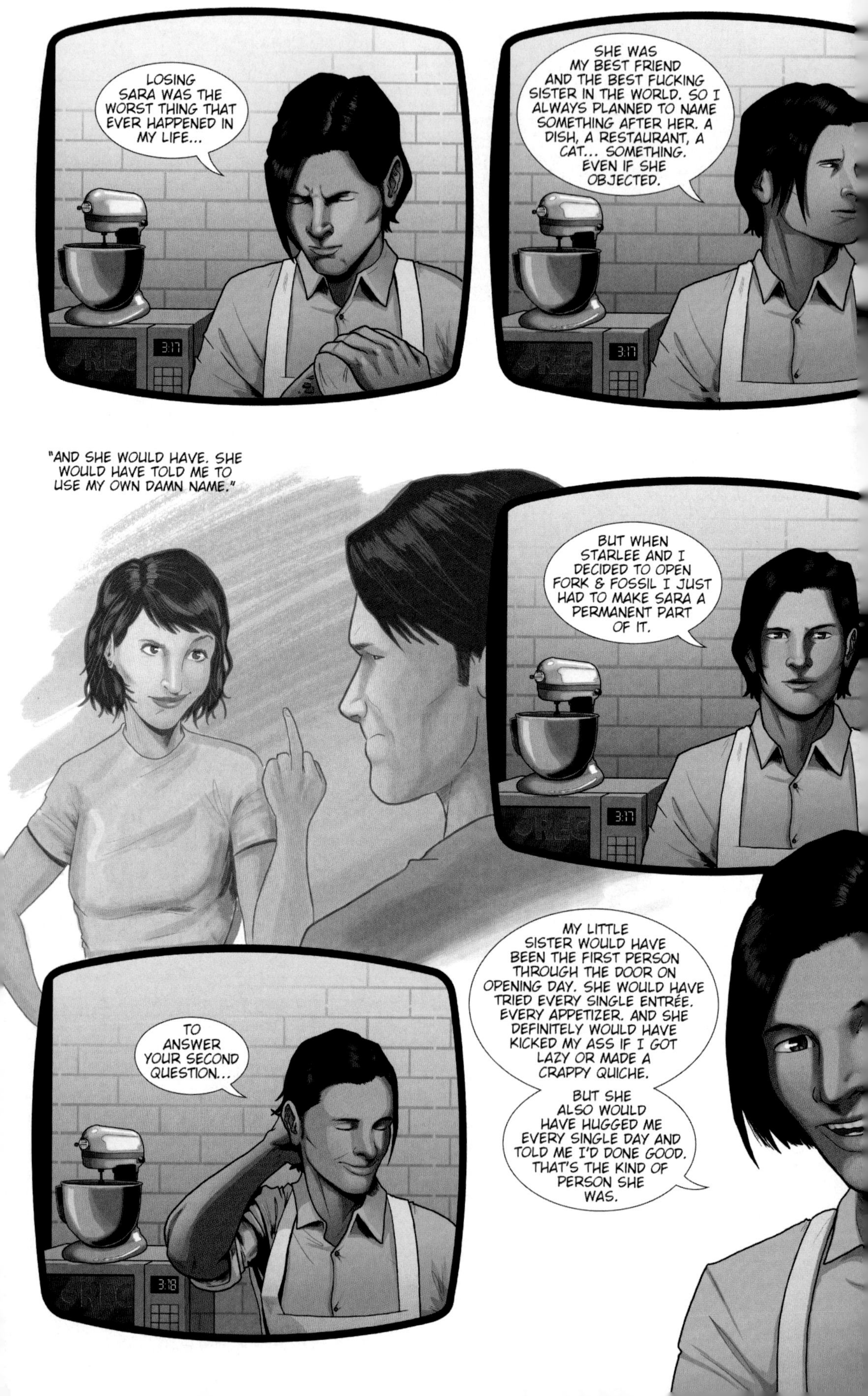
LOSING SARA WAS THE WORST THING THAT EVER HAPPENED IN MY LIFE...
SHE WAS MY BEST FRIEND AND THE BEST FUCKING SISTER IN THE WORLD. SO I ALWAYS PLANNED TO NAME SOMETHING AFTER HER. A DISH, A RESTAURANT, A CAT... SOMETHING. EVEN IF SHE OBJECTED.
"AND SHE WOULD HAVE. SHE WOULD HAVE TOLD ME TO USE MY OWN DAMN NAME."
BUT WHEN STARLEE AND I DECIDED TO OPEN FORK & FOSSIL I JUST HAD TO MAKE SARA A PERMANENT PART OF IT.
TO ANSWER YOUR SECOND QUESTION...
MY LITTLE SISTER WOULD HAVE BEEN THE FIRST PERSON THROUGH THE DOOR ON OPENING DAY. SHE WOULD HAVE TRIED EVERY SINGLE ENTRÉE. EVERY APPETIZER. AND SHE DEFINITELY WOULD HAVE KICKED MY ASS IF I GOT LAZY OR MADE A CRAPPY QUICHE.
BUT SHE ALSO WOULD HAVE HUGGED ME EVERY SINGLE DAY AND TOLD ME I'D DONE GOOD. THAT'S THE KIND OF PERSON SHE WAS.

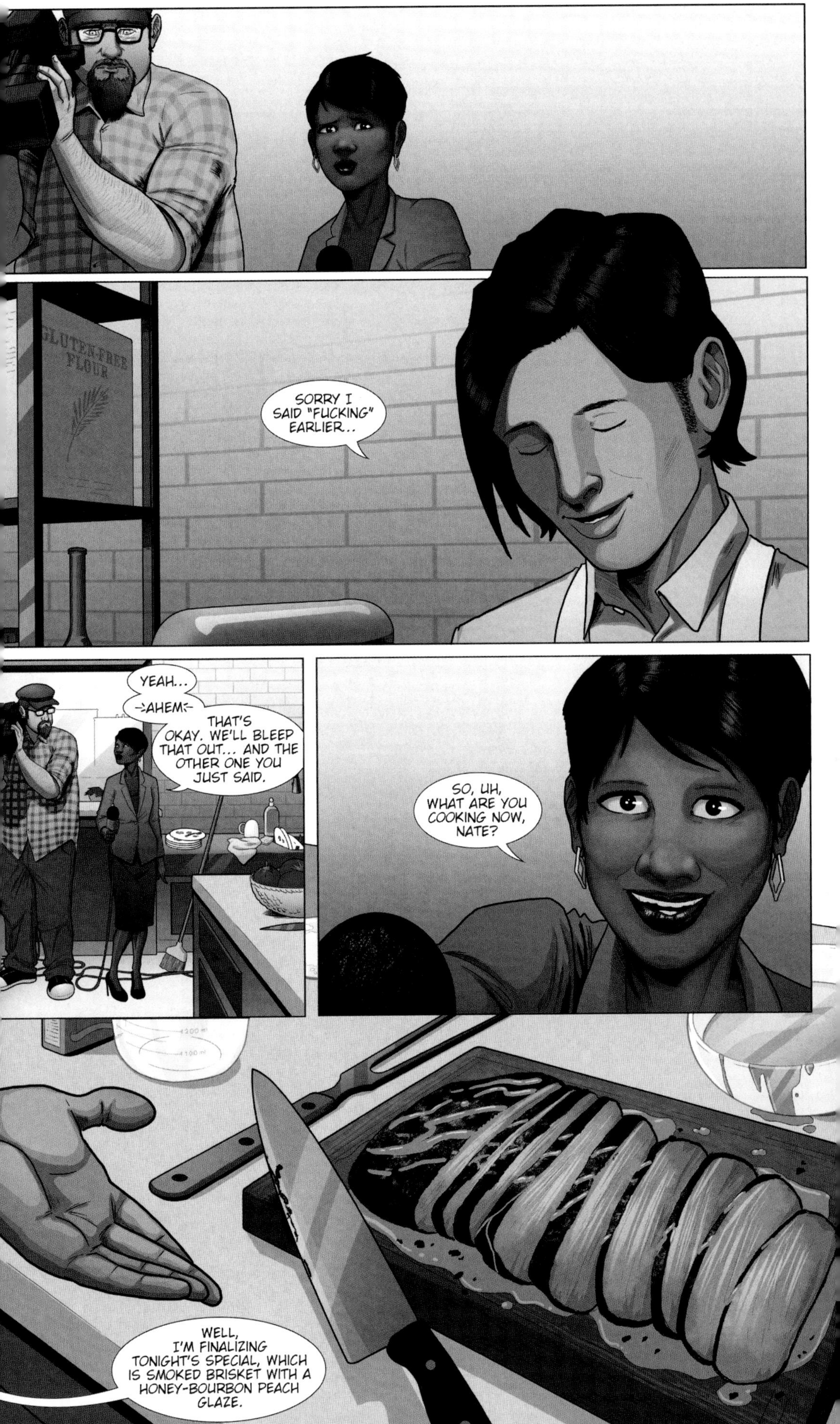

GLUTEN-FREE FLOUR
SORRY I SAID "FUCKING" EARLIER...
YEAH...
-AHEM-
THAT'S OKAY. WE'LL BLEEP THAT OUT... AND THE OTHER ONE YOU JUST SAID.
SO, UH, WHAT ARE YOU COOKING NOW, NATE?
WELL, I'M FINALIZING TONIGHT'S SPECIAL, WHICH IS SMOKED BRISKET WITH A HONEY-BOURBON PEACH GLAZE.

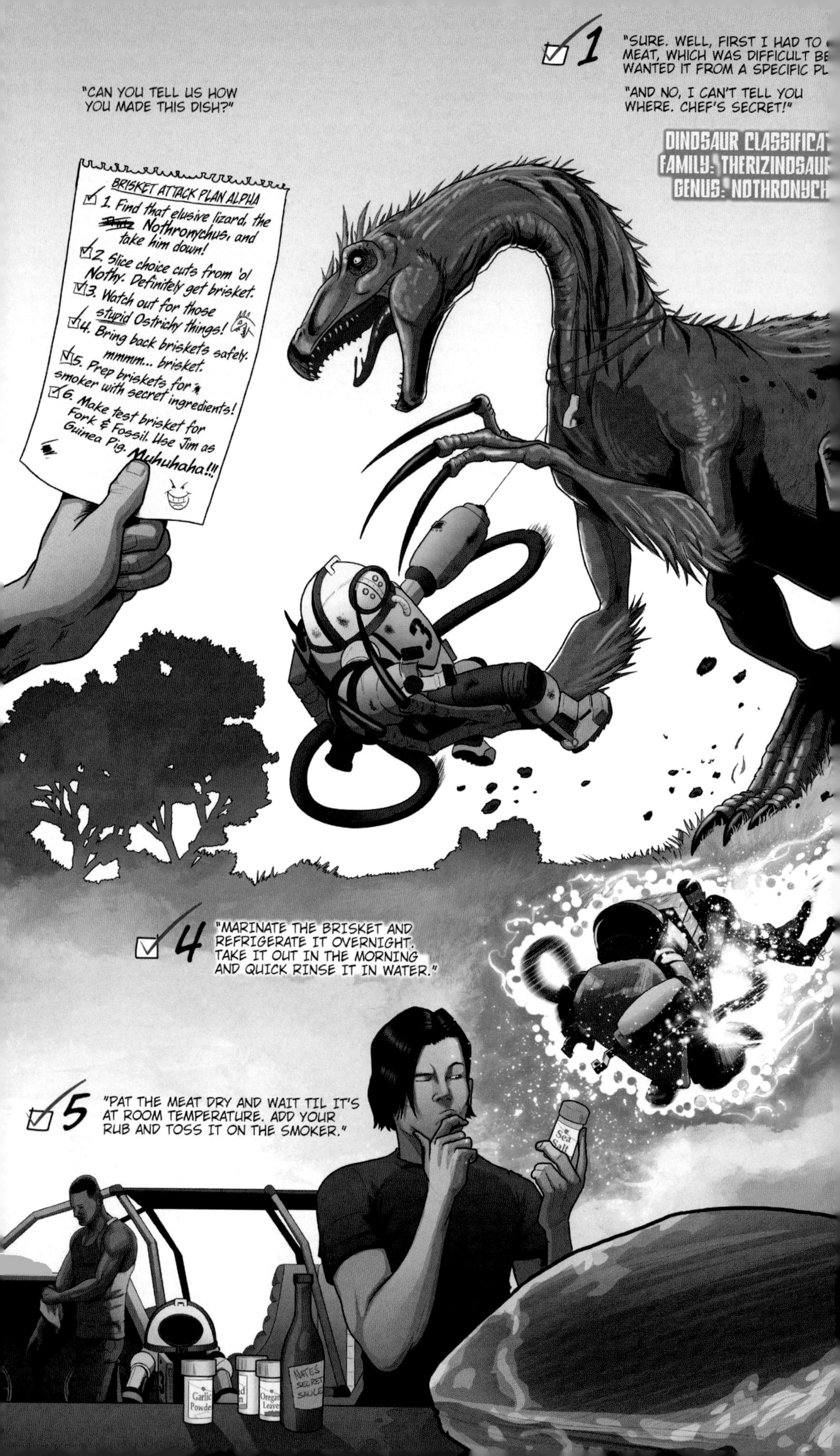
"CAN YOU TELL US HOW YOU MADE THIS DISH?"
1
"SURE. WELL, FIRST I HAD TO
MEAT, WHICH WAS DIFFICULT BE
WANTED IT FROM A SPECIFIC PL
"AND NO, I CAN'T TELL YOU WHERE. CHEF'S SECRET!"
DINOSAUR CLASSIFICAT
FAMILY: THERIZINOSAUR
GENUS: NOTHRONYCH
BRISKET ATTACK PLAN ALPHA
1. Find that elusive lizard, the Nothronychus, and take him down!
2. Slice choice cuts from 'ol Nothy. Definitely get brisket.
3. Watch out for those stupid Ostrichy things!
4. Bring back briskets safely. mmmm... brisket.
5. Prep briskets for smoker with secret ingredients!
6. Make test brisket for Fork & Fossil. Use Jim as Guinea Pig. Muhuhaha!!!
4
"MARINATE THE BRISKET AND REFRIGERATE IT OVERNIGHT. TAKE IT OUT IN THE MORNING AND QUICK RINSE IT IN WATER."
5
"PAT THE MEAT DRY AND WAIT TIL IT'S AT ROOM TEMPERATURE. ADD YOUR RUB AND TOSS IT ON THE SMOKER."
Sea Salt
Garlic Powder
Oregano Leaves
NATE'S SECRET SAUCE

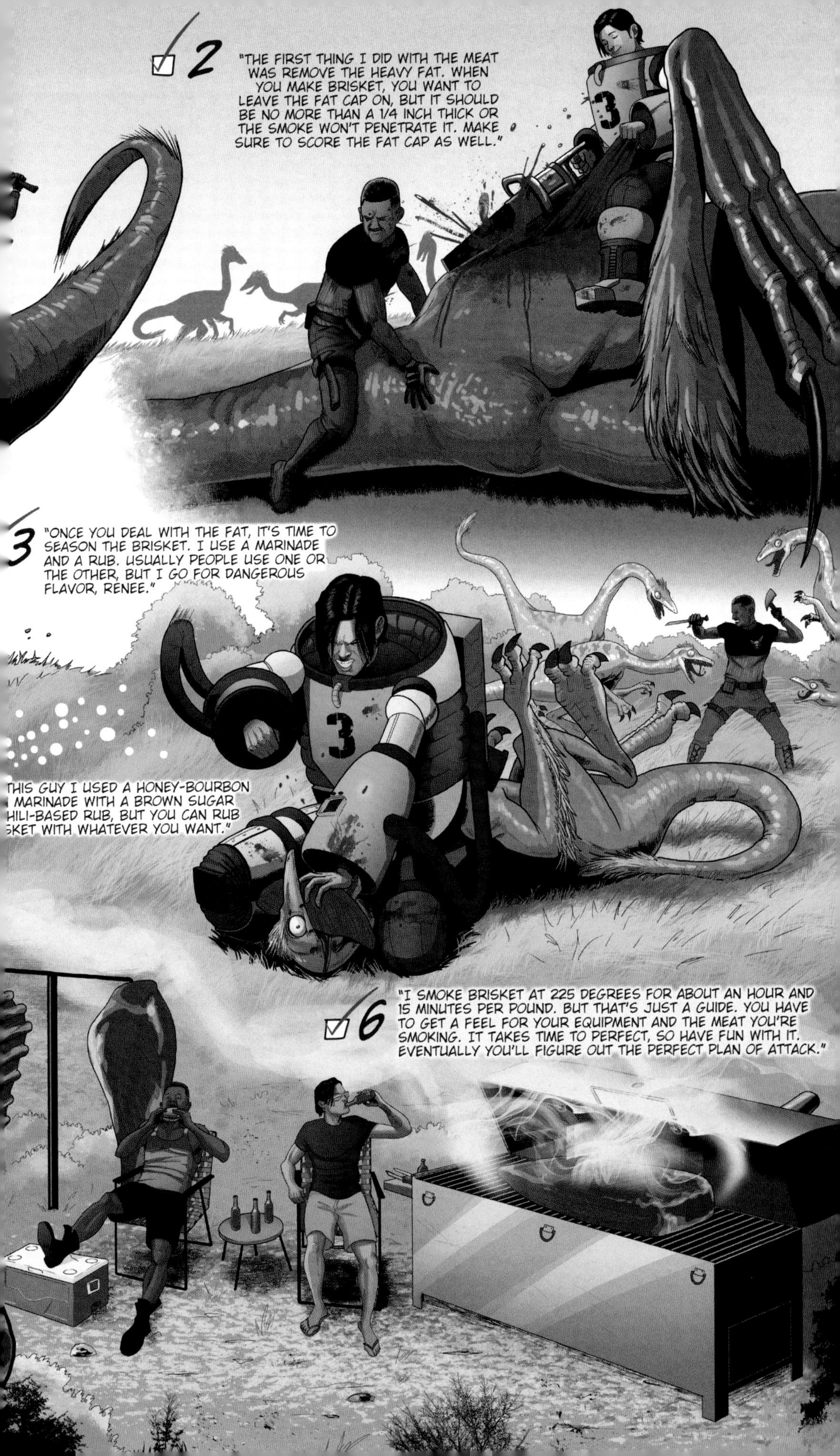
2
"THE FIRST THING I DID WITH THE MEAT WAS REMOVE THE HEAVY FAT. WHEN YOU MAKE BRISKET, YOU WANT TO LEAVE THE FAT CAP ON, BUT IT SHOULD BE NO MORE THAN A 1/4 INCH THICK OR THE SMOKE WON'T PENETRATE IT. MAKE SURE TO SCORE THE FAT CAP AS WELL."
3
"ONCE YOU DEAL WITH THE FAT, IT'S TIME TO SEASON THE BRISKET. I USE A MARINADE AND A RUB. USUALLY PEOPLE USE ONE OR THE OTHER, BUT I GO FOR DANGEROUS FLAVOR, RENEE."
THIS GUY I USED A HONEY-BOURBON MARINADE WITH A BROWN SUGAR HILI-BASED RUB, BUT YOU CAN RUB SKET WITH WHATEVER YOU WANT."
3
3
6
"I SMOKE BRISKET AT 225 DEGREES FOR ABOUT AN HOUR AND 15 MINUTES PER POUND. BUT THAT'S JUST A GUIDE. YOU HAVE TO GET A FEEL FOR YOUR EQUIPMENT AND THE MEAT YOU'RE SMOKING. IT TAKES TIME TO PERFECT, SO HAVE FUN WITH IT. EVENTUALLY YOU'LL FIGURE OUT THE PERFECT PLAN OF ATTACK."

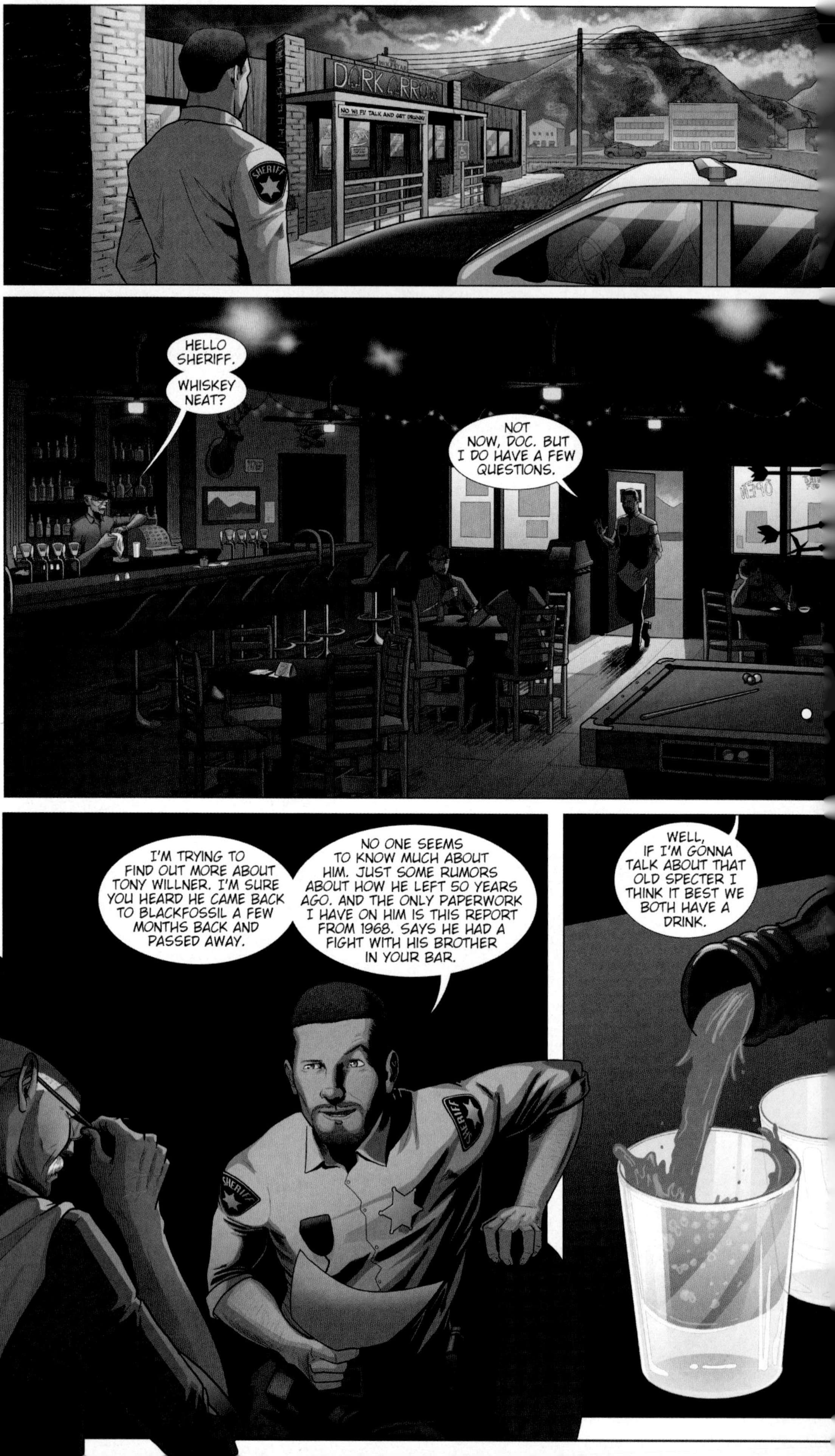

HELLO SHERIFF.
WHISKEY NEAT?
NOT NOW, DOC. BUT I DO HAVE A FEW QUESTIONS.
I'M TRYING TO FIND OUT MORE ABOUT TONY WILLNER. I'M SURE YOU HEARD HE CAME BACK TO BLACKFOSSIL A FEW MONTHS BACK AND PASSED AWAY.
NO ONE SEEMS TO KNOW MUCH ABOUT HIM. JUST SOME RUMORS ABOUT HOW HE LEFT 50 YEARS AGO. AND THE ONLY PAPERWORK I HAVE ON HIM IS THIS REPORT FROM 1968. SAYS HE HAD A FIGHT WITH HIS BROTHER IN YOUR BAR.
WELL, IF I'M GONNA TALK ABOUT THAT OLD SPECTER I THINK IT BEST WE BOTH HAVE A DRINK.

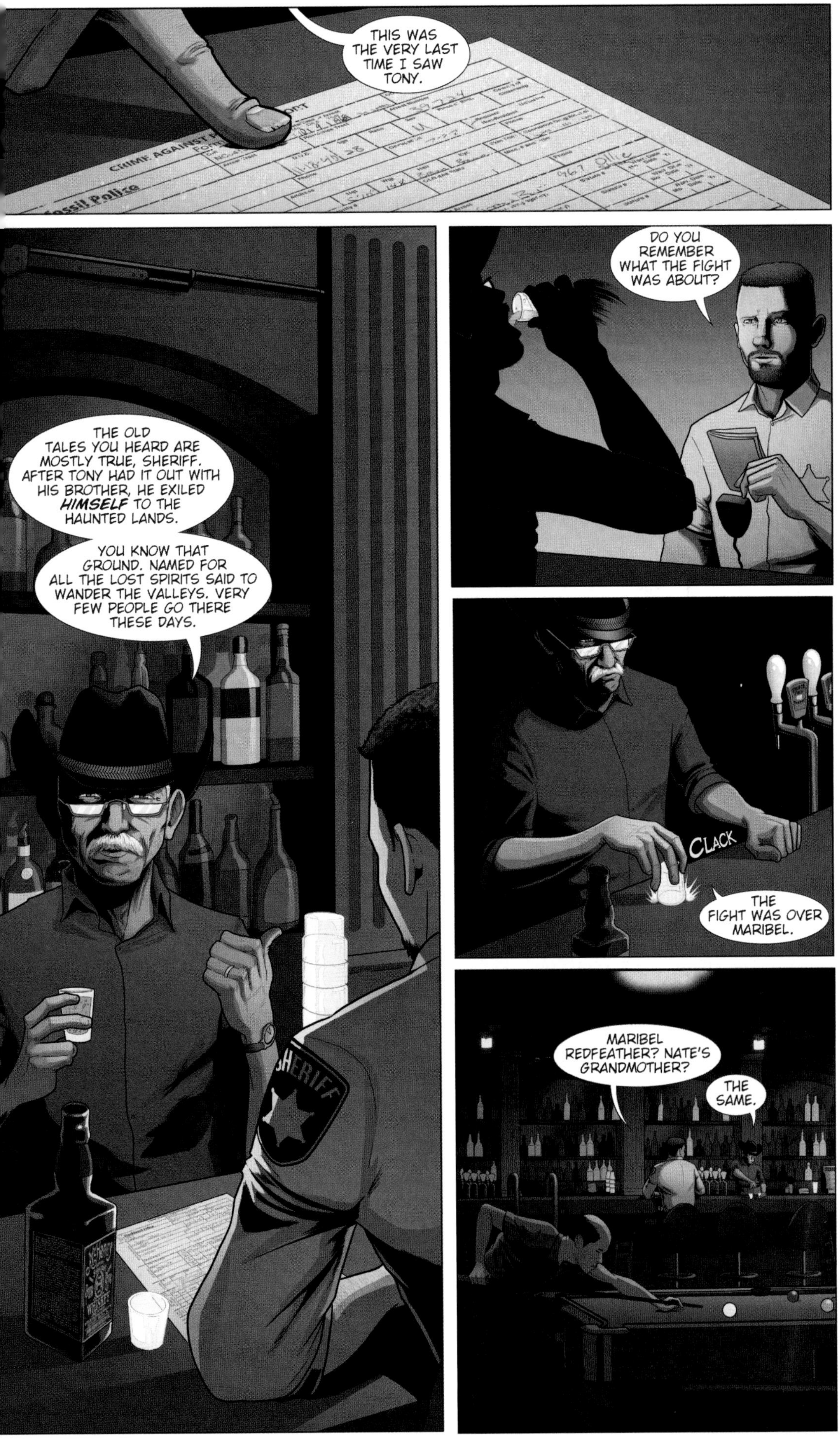
THIS WAS THE VERY LAST TIME I SAW TONY.
CRIME AGAINST P
Fossil Police
THE OLD TALES YOU HEARD ARE MOSTLY TRUE, SHERIFF. AFTER TONY HAD IT OUT WITH HIS BROTHER, HE EXILED *HIMSELF* TO THE HAUNTED LANDS.
YOU KNOW THAT GROUND. NAMED FOR ALL THE LOST SPIRITS SAID TO WANDER THE VALLEYS. VERY FEW PEOPLE GO THERE THESE DAYS.
SHERIFF
DO YOU REMEMBER WHAT THE FIGHT WAS ABOUT?
CLACK
THE FIGHT WAS OVER MARIBEL.
MARIBEL REDFEATHER? NATE'S GRANDMOTHER?
THE SAME.

"AS I REMEMBER IT, TONY BROUGHT MARIBEL TO BLACKFOSSIL. THEY LIVED TOGETHER FOR A TIME."

"HE LOVED THAT GIRL MORE THAN LIFE AND WAS P[...] MARRYING HER. BUT SHE DIDN'T QUITE FEEL THE[...]"

"TONY WAS SOME KIND OF ENGINEER. SMART AS HELL. SPENT A LOT OF TIME WORKING IN THE HILLS FOR THE GOVERNMENT, BUILDING AND TESTING STRANGE DEVICES."

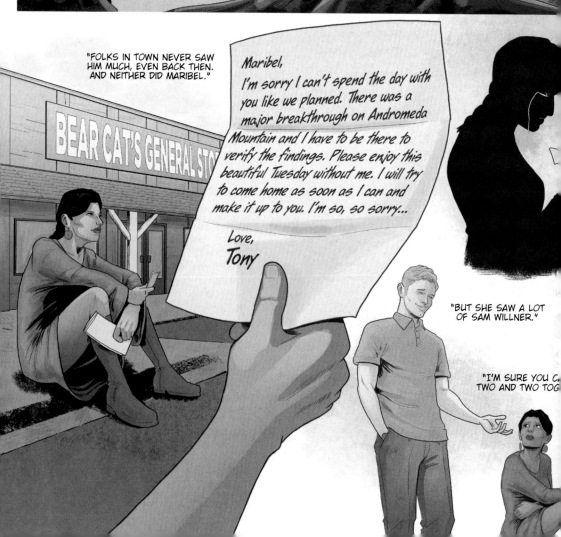

"FOLKS IN TOWN NEVER SAW HIM MUCH, EVEN BACK THEN. AND NEITHER DID MARIBEL."

BEAR CAT'S GENERAL STO[...]

Maribel,

I'm sorry I can't spend the day with you like we planned. There was a major breakthrough on Andromeda Mountain and I have to be there to verify the findings. Please enjoy this beautiful Tuesday without me. I will try to come home as soon as I can and make it up to you. I'm so, so sorry...

Love,
Tony

"BUT SHE SAW A LOT OF SAM WILLNER."

"I'M SURE YOU C[...] TWO AND TWO TOG[...]"

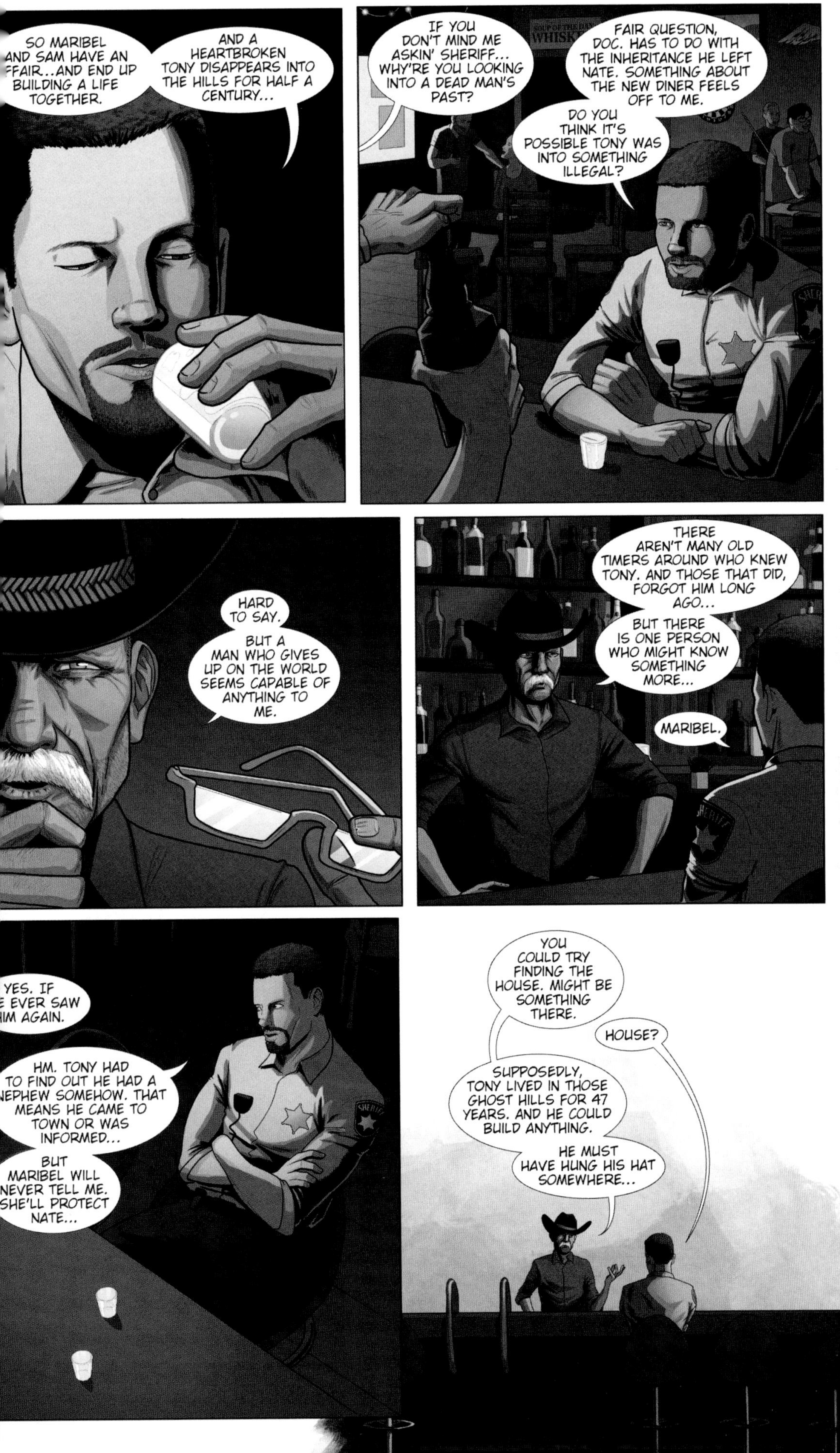

SO MARIBEL AND SAM HAVE AN FFAIR...AND END UP BUILDING A LIFE TOGETHER.
AND A HEARTBROKEN TONY DISAPPEARS INTO THE HILLS FOR HALF A CENTURY...
IF YOU DON'T MIND ME ASKIN' SHERIFF... WHY'RE YOU LOOKING INTO A DEAD MAN'S PAST?
FAIR QUESTION, DOC. HAS TO DO WITH THE INHERITANCE HE LEFT NATE. SOMETHING ABOUT THE NEW DINER FEELS OFF TO ME.
DO YOU THINK IT'S POSSIBLE TONY WAS INTO SOMETHING ILLEGAL?
HARD TO SAY.
BUT A MAN WHO GIVES UP ON THE WORLD SEEMS CAPABLE OF ANYTHING TO ME.
THERE AREN'T MANY OLD TIMERS AROUND WHO KNEW TONY. AND THOSE THAT DID, FORGOT HIM LONG AGO...
BUT THERE IS ONE PERSON WHO MIGHT KNOW SOMETHING MORE...
MARIBEL.
YES. IF E EVER SAW IM AGAIN.
HM. TONY HAD TO FIND OUT HE HAD A EPHEW SOMEHOW. THAT MEANS HE CAME TO TOWN OR WAS INFORMED...
BUT MARIBEL WILL NEVER TELL ME. SHE'LL PROTECT NATE...
YOU COULD TRY FINDING THE HOUSE. MIGHT BE SOMETHING THERE.
HOUSE?
SUPPOSEDLY, TONY LIVED IN THOSE GHOST HILLS FOR 47 YEARS. AND HE COULD BUILD ANYTHING.
HE MUST HAVE HUNG HIS HAT SOMEWHERE...

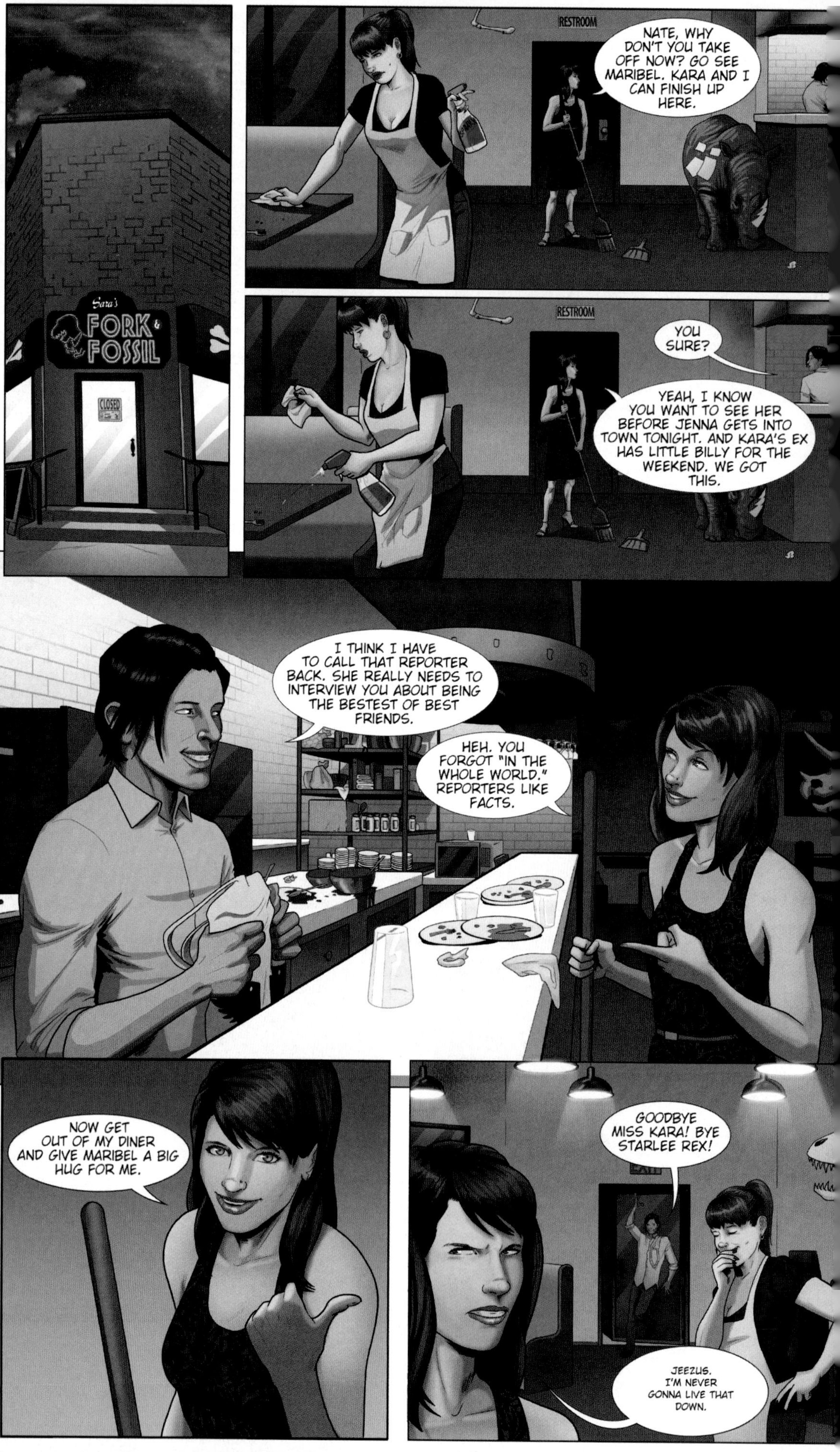
Sara's
FORK & FOSSIL
CLOSED
RESTROOM
NATE, WHY DON'T YOU TAKE OFF NOW? GO SEE MARIBEL. KARA AND I CAN FINISH UP HERE.
RESTROOM
YOU SURE?
YEAH, I KNOW YOU WANT TO SEE HER BEFORE JENNA GETS INTO TOWN TONIGHT. AND KARA'S EX HAS LITTLE BILLY FOR THE WEEKEND. WE GOT THIS.
I THINK I HAVE TO CALL THAT REPORTER BACK. SHE REALLY NEEDS TO INTERVIEW YOU ABOUT BEING THE BESTEST OF BEST FRIENDS.
HEH. YOU FORGOT "IN THE WHOLE WORLD." REPORTERS LIKE FACTS.
NOW GET OUT OF MY DINER AND GIVE MARIBEL A BIG HUG FOR ME.
GOODBYE MISS KARA! BYE STARLEE REX!
JEEZUS. I'M NEVER GONNA LIVE THAT DOWN.

BLACKFOSSIL MEDICAL CENTER

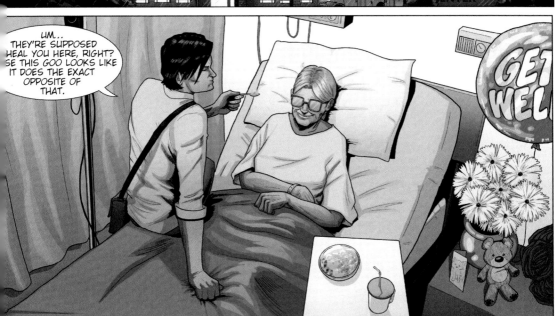

UM...
THEY'RE SUPPOSED [TO] HEAL YOU HERE, RIGHT? [BECAU]SE THIS GOO LOOKS LIKE IT DOES THE EXACT OPPOSITE OF THAT.

GOOD THING I BROUGHT YOU SOME HOMEMADE MEDICINE.

OH, THANK THE SPIRITS.

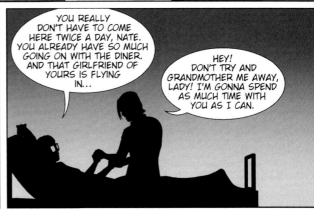

YOU REALLY DON'T HAVE TO COME HERE TWICE A DAY, NATE. YOU ALREADY HAVE SO MUCH GOING ON WITH THE DINER. AND THAT GIRLFRIEND OF YOURS IS FLYING IN...

HEY! DON'T TRY AND GRANDMOTHER ME AWAY, LADY! I'M GONNA SPEND AS MUCH TIME WITH YOU AS I CAN.

I [WORRY] NOW. I JUST WORRY...

I NEED TO MAKE SURE YOU'RE GOING TO BE OKAY. AND HAPPY.

I... I FEEL MYSELF WINDING DOWN, NATE. I KNOW THAT'S NOT SOMETHING EITHER OF US WANT TO DISCUSS...

BUT JUST PROMISE ME YOU'LL LET JIM AND STARLEE BE THERE FOR YOU. THAT YOU'LL TREAT THEM LIKE BLOOD FROM NOW ON.

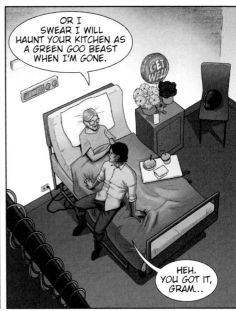

OR I SWEAR I WILL HAUNT YOUR KITCHEN AS A GREEN GOO BEAST WHEN I'M GONE.

HEH. YOU GOT IT, GRAM...

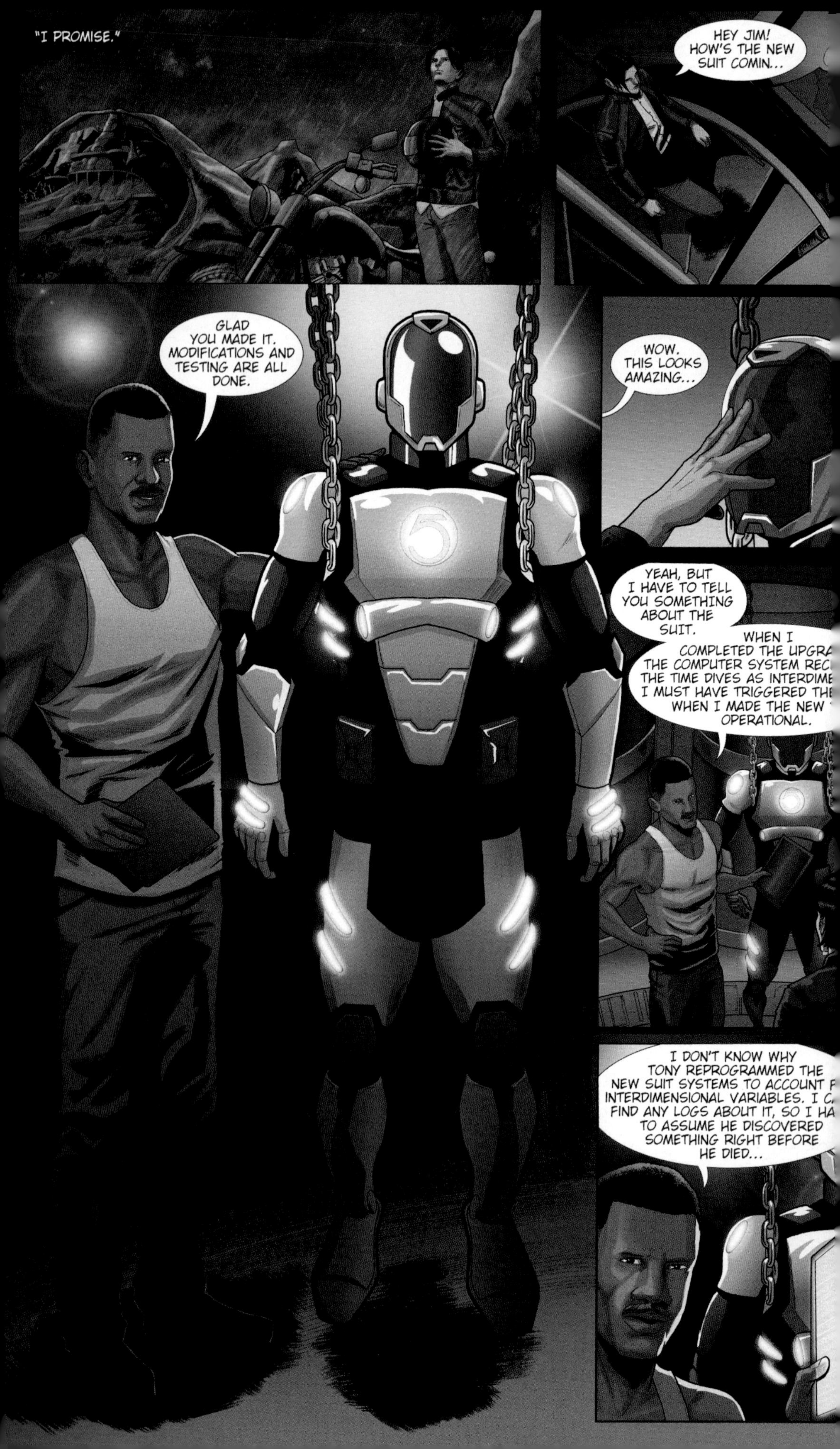
"I PROMISE."
HEY JIM! HOW'S THE NEW SUIT COMIN...
GLAD YOU MADE IT. MODIFICATIONS AND TESTING ARE ALL DONE.
WOW. THIS LOOKS AMAZING...
YEAH, BUT I HAVE TO TELL YOU SOMETHING ABOUT THE SUIT.
WHEN I COMPLETED THE UPGRA THE COMPUTER SYSTEM REC THE TIME DIVES AS INTERDIME I MUST HAVE TRIGGERED THE WHEN I MADE THE NEW OPERATIONAL.
I DON'T KNOW WHY TONY REPROGRAMMED THE NEW SUIT SYSTEMS TO ACCOUNT F INTERDIMENSIONAL VARIABLES. I C FIND ANY LOGS ABOUT IT, SO I HA TO ASSUME HE DISCOVERED SOMETHING RIGHT BEFORE HE DIED...

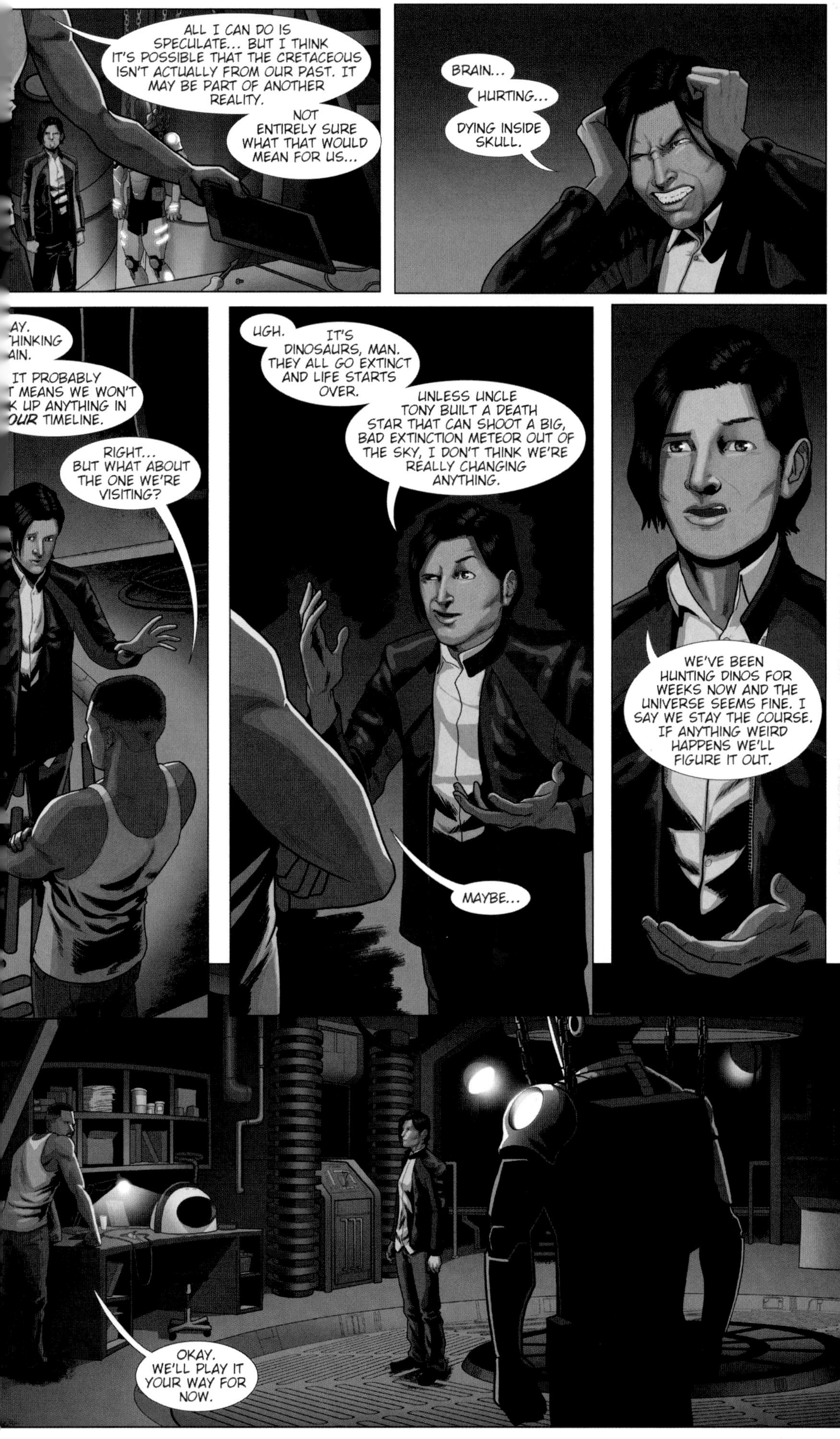
ALL I CAN DO IS SPECULATE... BUT I THINK IT'S POSSIBLE THAT THE CRETACEOUS ISN'T ACTUALLY FROM OUR PAST. IT MAY BE PART OF ANOTHER REALITY.
NOT ENTIRELY SURE WHAT THAT WOULD MEAN FOR US...
BRAIN...
HURTING...
DYING INSIDE SKULL.
AY. THINKING AIN.
IT PROBABLY T MEANS WE WON'T K UP ANYTHING IN OUR TIMELINE.
RIGHT... BUT WHAT ABOUT THE ONE WE'RE VISITING?
UGH.
IT'S DINOSAURS, MAN. THEY ALL GO EXTINCT AND LIFE STARTS OVER.
UNLESS UNCLE TONY BUILT A DEATH STAR THAT CAN SHOOT A BIG, BAD EXTINCTION METEOR OUT OF THE SKY, I DON'T THINK WE'RE REALLY CHANGING ANYTHING.
MAYBE...
WE'VE BEEN HUNTING DINOS FOR WEEKS NOW AND THE UNIVERSE SEEMS FINE. I SAY WE STAY THE COURSE. IF ANYTHING WEIRD HAPPENS WE'LL FIGURE IT OUT.
OKAY. WE'LL PLAY IT YOUR WAY FOR NOW.

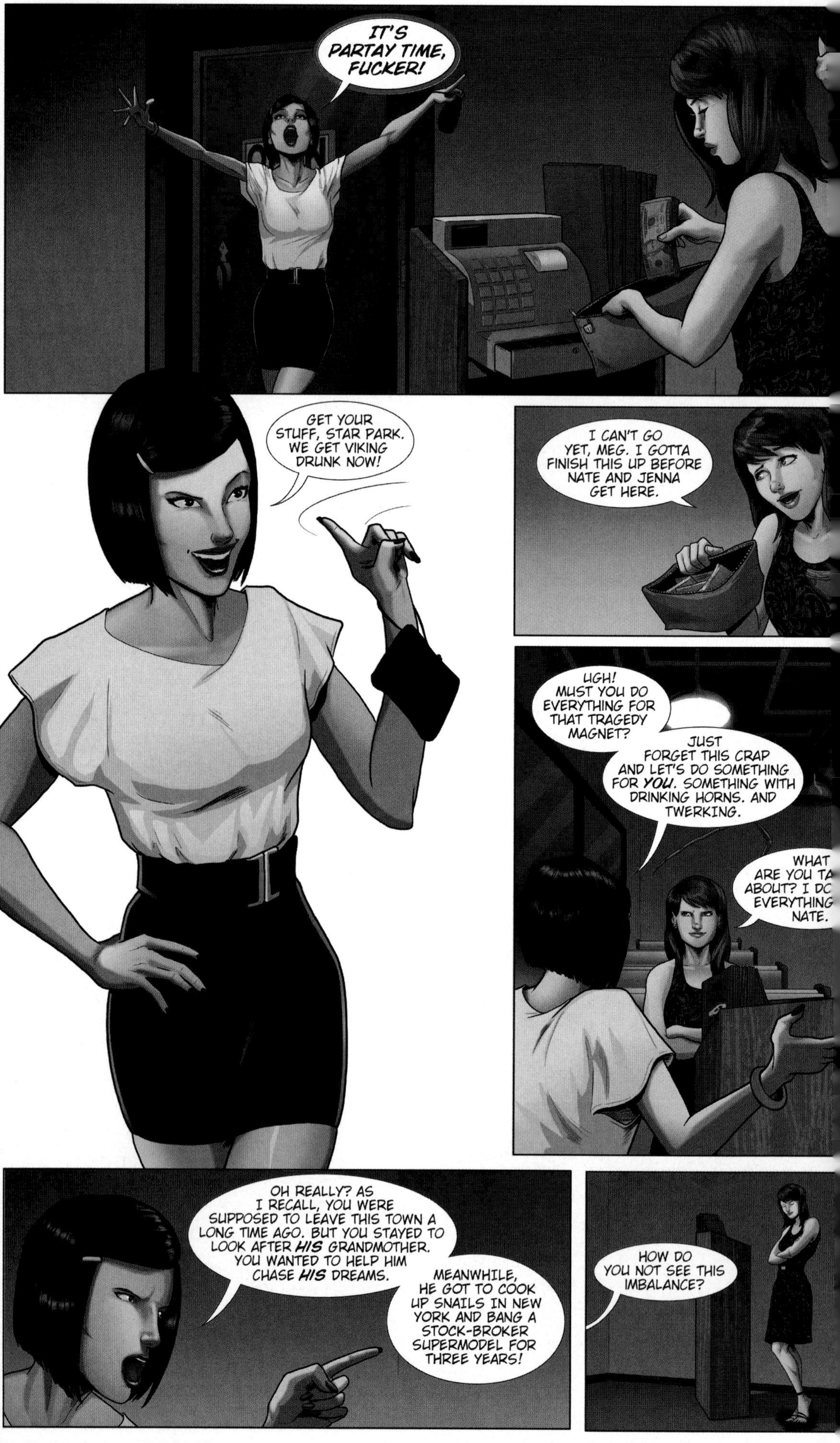

IT'S PARTAY TIME, FUCKER!
GET YOUR STUFF, STAR PARK. WE GET VIKING DRUNK NOW!
I CAN'T GO YET, MEG. I GOTTA FINISH THIS UP BEFORE NATE AND JENNA GET HERE.
UGH! MUST YOU DO EVERYTHING FOR THAT TRAGEDY MAGNET?
JUST FORGET THIS CRAP AND LET'S DO SOMETHING FOR YOU. SOMETHING WITH DRINKING HORNS. AND TWERKING.
WHAT ARE YOU TA ABOUT? I DO EVERYTHING NATE.
OH REALLY? AS I RECALL, YOU WERE SUPPOSED TO LEAVE THIS TOWN A LONG TIME AGO. BUT YOU STAYED TO LOOK AFTER HIS GRANDMOTHER. YOU WANTED TO HELP HIM CHASE HIS DREAMS.
MEANWHILE, HE GOT TO COOK UP SNAILS IN NEW YORK AND BANG A STOCK-BROKER SUPERMODEL FOR THREE YEARS!
HOW DO YOU NOT SEE THIS IMBALANCE?

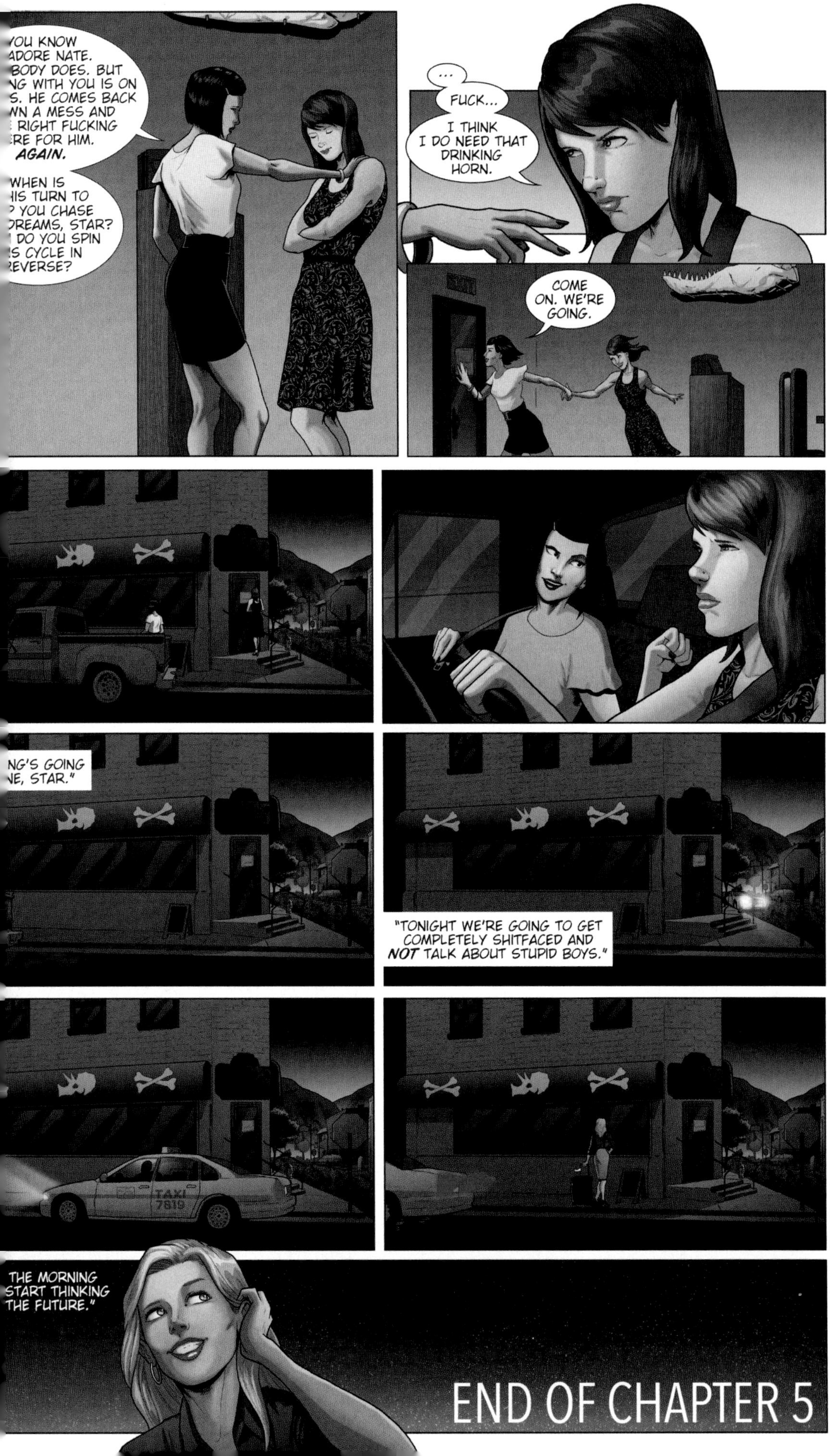

YOU KNOW
ADORE NATE.
BODY DOES. BUT
NG WITH YOU IS ON
S. HE COMES BACK
WN A MESS AND
RIGHT FUCKING
RE FOR HIM.
AGAIN.
WHEN IS
HIS TURN TO
YOU CHASE
DREAMS, STAR?
DO YOU SPIN
S CYCLE IN
REVERSE?
...
FUCK...
I THINK I DO NEED THAT DRINKING HORN.
COME ON. WE'RE GOING.
NG'S GOING
NE, STAR."
"TONIGHT WE'RE GOING TO GET COMPLETELY SHITFACED AND NOT TALK ABOUT STUPID BOYS."
TAXI
7819
THE MORNING
START THINKING
THE FUTURE."
END OF CHAPTER 5

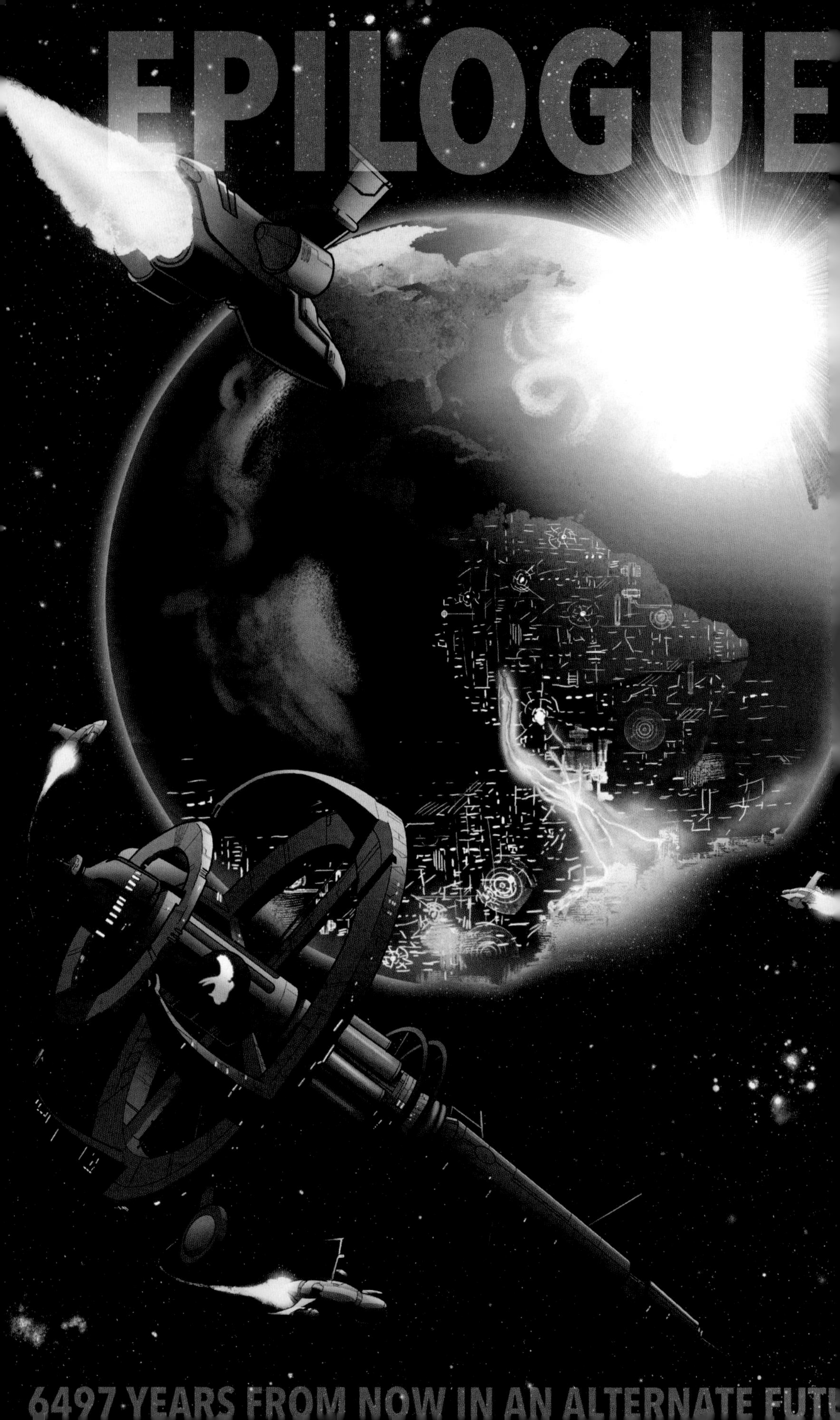
EPILOGUE
6497 YEARS FROM NOW IN AN ALTERNATE FUTU

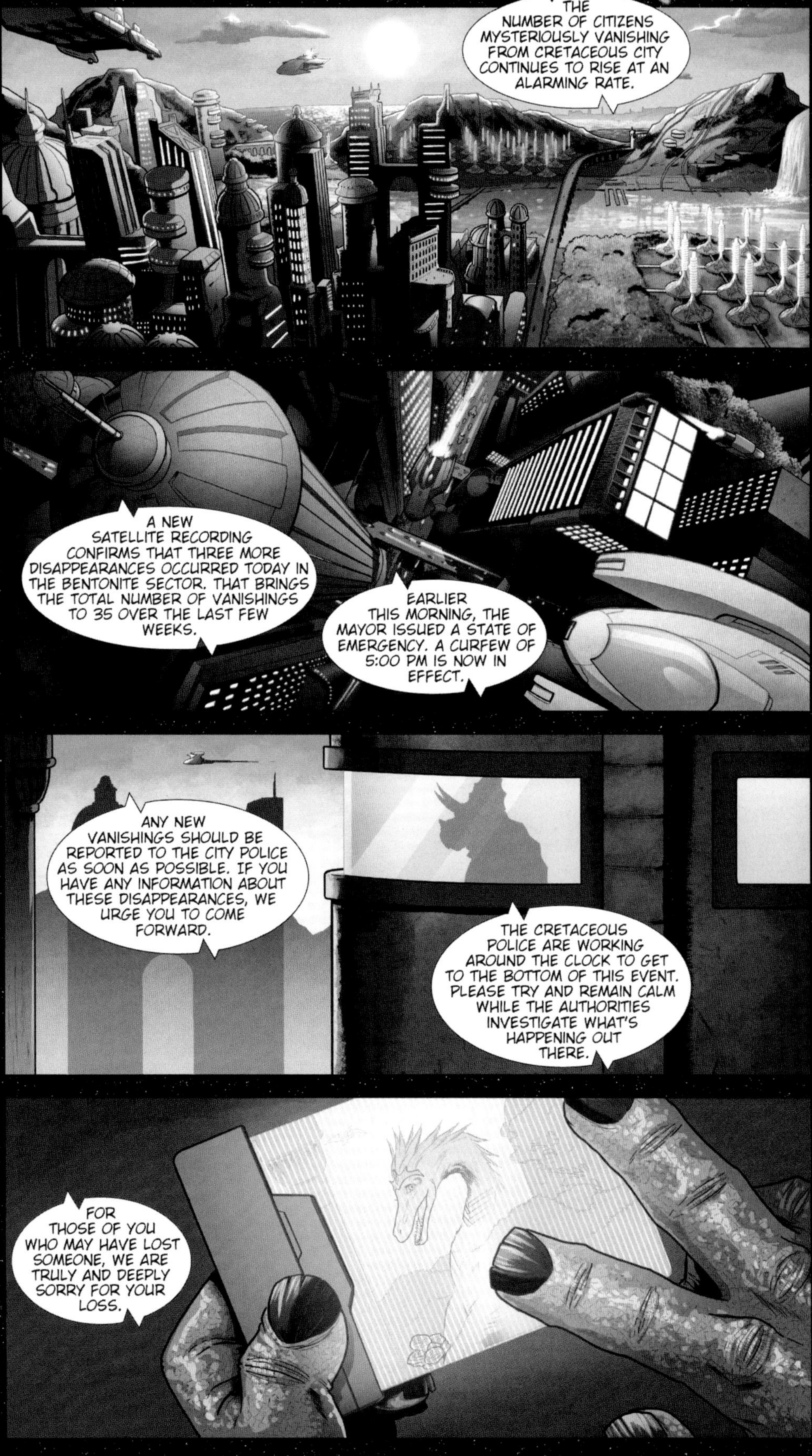
THE NUMBER OF CITIZENS MYSTERIOUSLY VANISHING FROM CRETACEOUS CITY CONTINUES TO RISE AT AN ALARMING RATE.
A NEW SATELLITE RECORDING CONFIRMS THAT THREE MORE DISAPPEARANCES OCCURRED TODAY IN THE BENTONITE SECTOR. THAT BRINGS THE TOTAL NUMBER OF VANISHINGS TO 35 OVER THE LAST FEW WEEKS.
EARLIER THIS MORNING, THE MAYOR ISSUED A STATE OF EMERGENCY. A CURFEW OF 5:00 PM IS NOW IN EFFECT.
ANY NEW VANISHINGS SHOULD BE REPORTED TO THE CITY POLICE AS SOON AS POSSIBLE. IF YOU HAVE ANY INFORMATION ABOUT THESE DISAPPEARANCES, WE URGE YOU TO COME FORWARD.
THE CRETACEOUS POLICE ARE WORKING AROUND THE CLOCK TO GET TO THE BOTTOM OF THIS EVENT. PLEASE TRY AND REMAIN CALM WHILE THE AUTHORITIES INVESTIGATE WHAT'S HAPPENING OUT THERE.
FOR THOSE OF YOU WHO MAY HAVE LOST SOMEONE, WE ARE TRULY AND DEEPLY SORRY FOR YOUR LOSS.

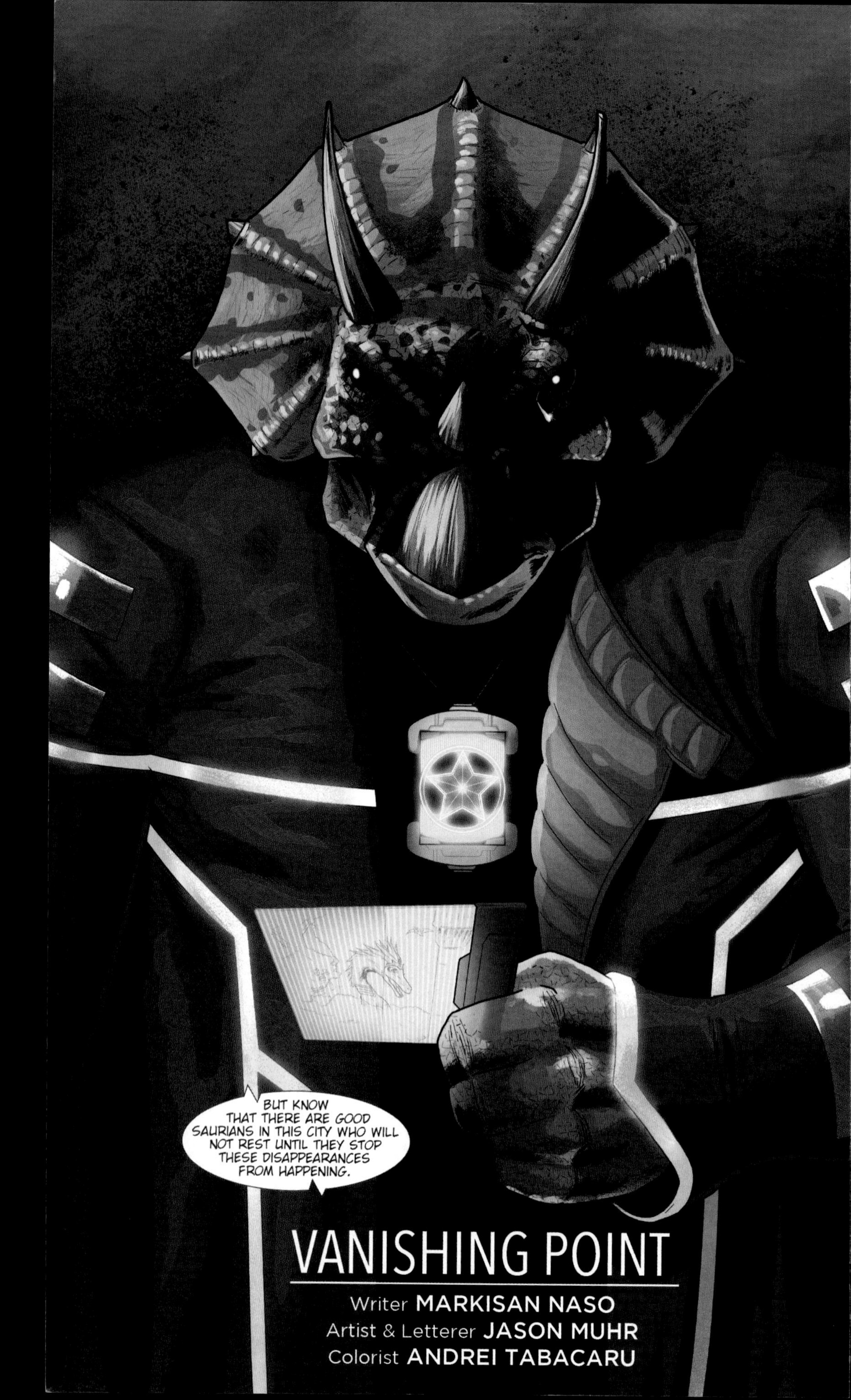
BUT KNOW THAT THERE ARE GOOD SAURIANS IN THIS CITY WHO WILL NOT REST UNTIL THEY STOP THESE DISAPPEARANCES FROM HAPPENING.

VANISHING POINT

Writer **MARKISAN NASO**
Artist & Letterer **JASON MUHR**
Colorist **ANDREI TABACARU**

COOKING CRETACEOUS

IOUS #4! This is the issue we most wanted to get into your little hands. With time travel there are always
uences. As those last few pages indicate, the consequences for Nate and Jim are going to be pretty
g huge. And starting this Winter you'll get to see those consequences unfold in our second mini-series,
IOUS: Feeding Time!

ext series you'll learn a lot more about the future Cretaceous. You'll also meet some new characters who
ome regulars in our story, as we take a turn toward a much bigger epic. Check out the preview on the
o pages!

ou for all the tweets, messages and kind words. It really means the world to the whole team that you
DRACIOUS a shot and that you continue to support our strange little saga so strongly. We hope to see
ome conventions this year, where Jason and I will gladly take T-Rex battle photos with you and sign any
ou bring us. In the meantime, get out your best silverware and throw on a sexy bib, because the second
s being prepared for you right now. Can't wait to show you what we've got cookin' for our next arc. It's
be even more hearty and delicious than the first.

an

aking of hearty, try making my favorite chili in the world, hand-crafted in a man kitchen of love by my
um, Mark Kedziora!

aciouscomic@gmail.com   @VoraciousComic   VoraciousComic   voraciouscomic.tumblr

:le Marko's Nothronychus Chili

REDIENTS

ounds Hot Italian sausage (sans the casing)
ounds Nothronychus meat (or substitute beef stew meat)
up chili powder (I make my own but you can use the store version)
ontainers beef stock (Kitchen Basics unsalted Beef Stock ... 32 fl oz)
rge can crushed or stewed tomatoes
rge onion
alapeños
loves garlic
or 2 regular Bass Ale
orcestershire sauce
r 3 large cans dark red kidney beans

*: My big secret is the pot I use. I have a cast iron dutch oven that I have had for around 20 years now
will not cook chili without it.*

ECTIONS

art by tossing the stew meat in a little Worcestershire sauce and dusting it with about a TBS of your
ili powder.

ld a little oil to the pot and sear the stew meat in small batches. Remove to a separate bowl when
ne. Once you finish the stew meat, brown up the Italian sausage. You should season this with a TBS of
ili powder. Make sure to break up all the clumps. You want this to be the base of the chili. When done
move to same bowl as stew meat.

ere will be all kinds of brown bits at the bottom of the pot which is real good for you! You're gonna
ed to deglaze that stuff. I do it with the onions. Add your onions and another TSB of chili powder and
them cook down slow. Stir a lot, keep them moving. Once they get pretty brown and soft, add the
opped jalapeños and garlic. Cook that out until the peppers and garlic get soft.

nce you have your mash done, add your can of tomatoes and another TBS of chili powder, and let
at cook so everything gets gooey. Time to add the beer! Cook that for another 10 minutes so it all
xes nice.

ump the meat back in the pool with all the juices that collected at the bottom of the bowl and mix
ell. Now you're gonna add the stock. Add a whole container and 4 TBS of chili powder. Check your
ix before you do this for heat. You may want to cut back.

ow cook this down for around 3-4 hours - be patient! Add the beans the last hour. I drain my beans. If
u want, a little of the bean juice can be used to thicken the pot.

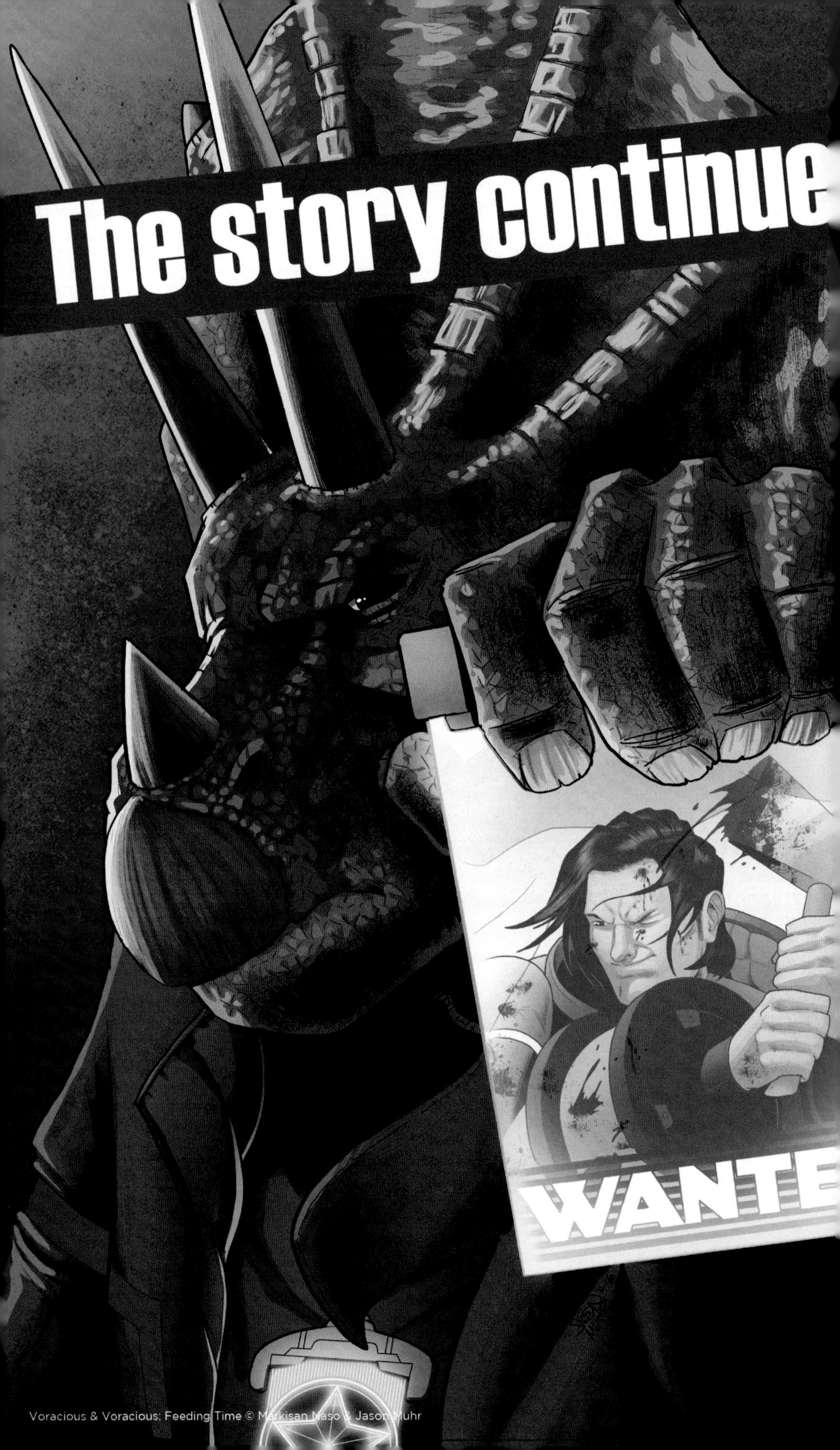
The story continue
WANTE

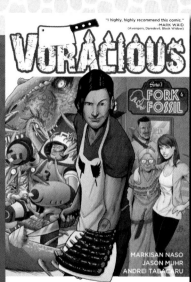

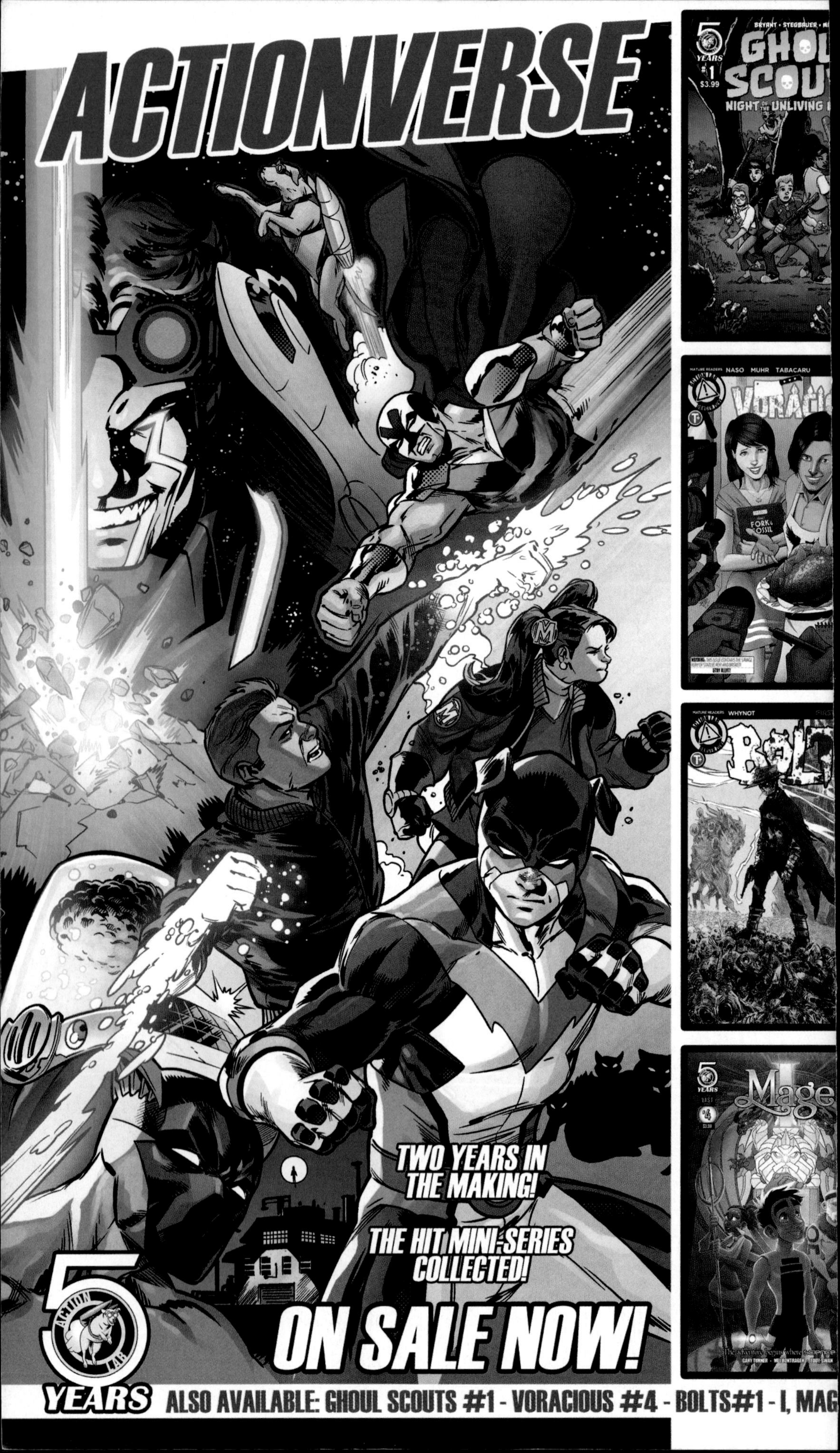

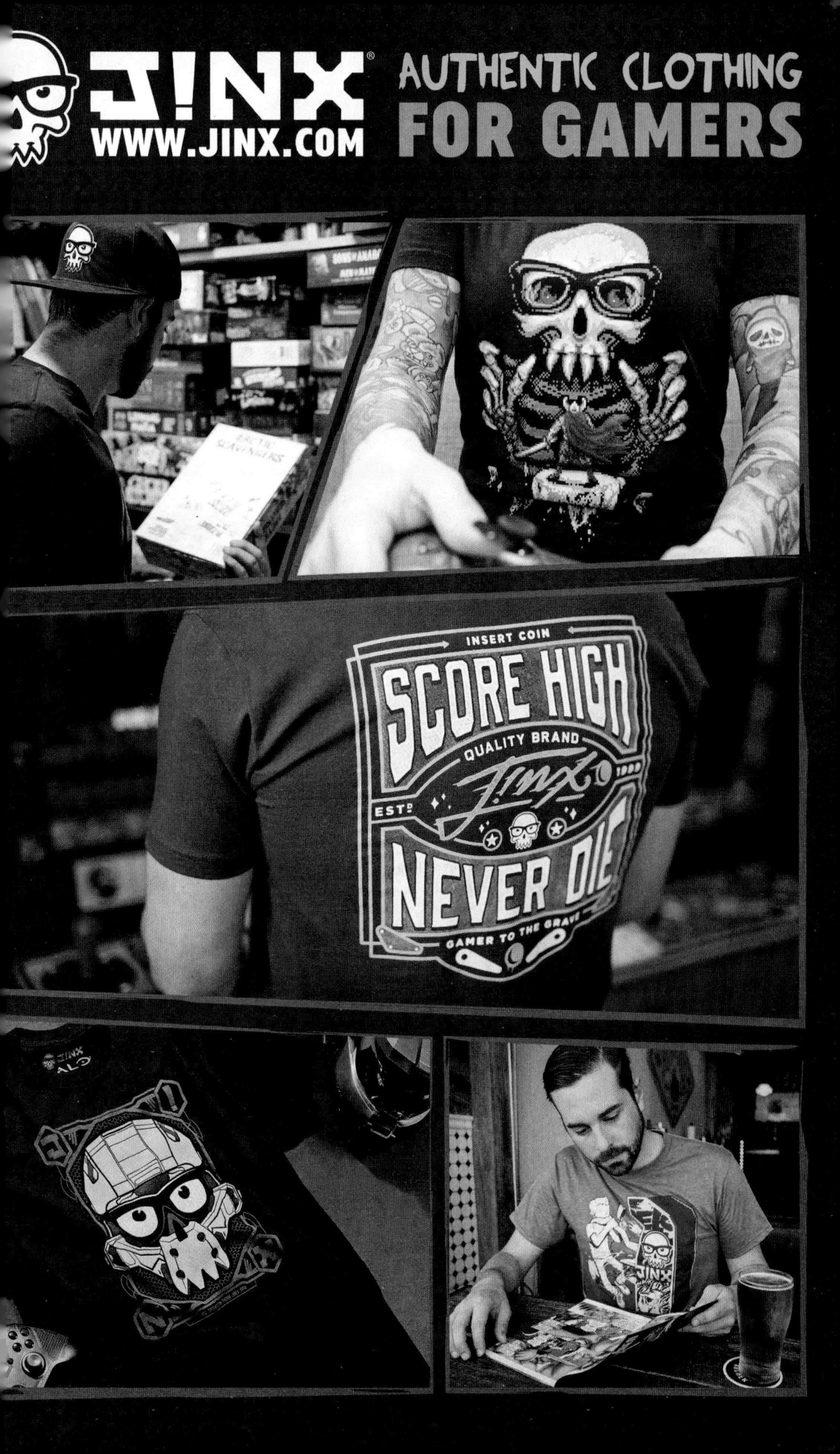
J!NX®
WWW.JINX.COM
AUTHENTIC CLOTHING
FOR GAMERS
INSERT COIN
SCORE HIGH
QUALITY BRAND
J!NX
ESTD
NEVER DIE
GAMER TO THE GRAVE

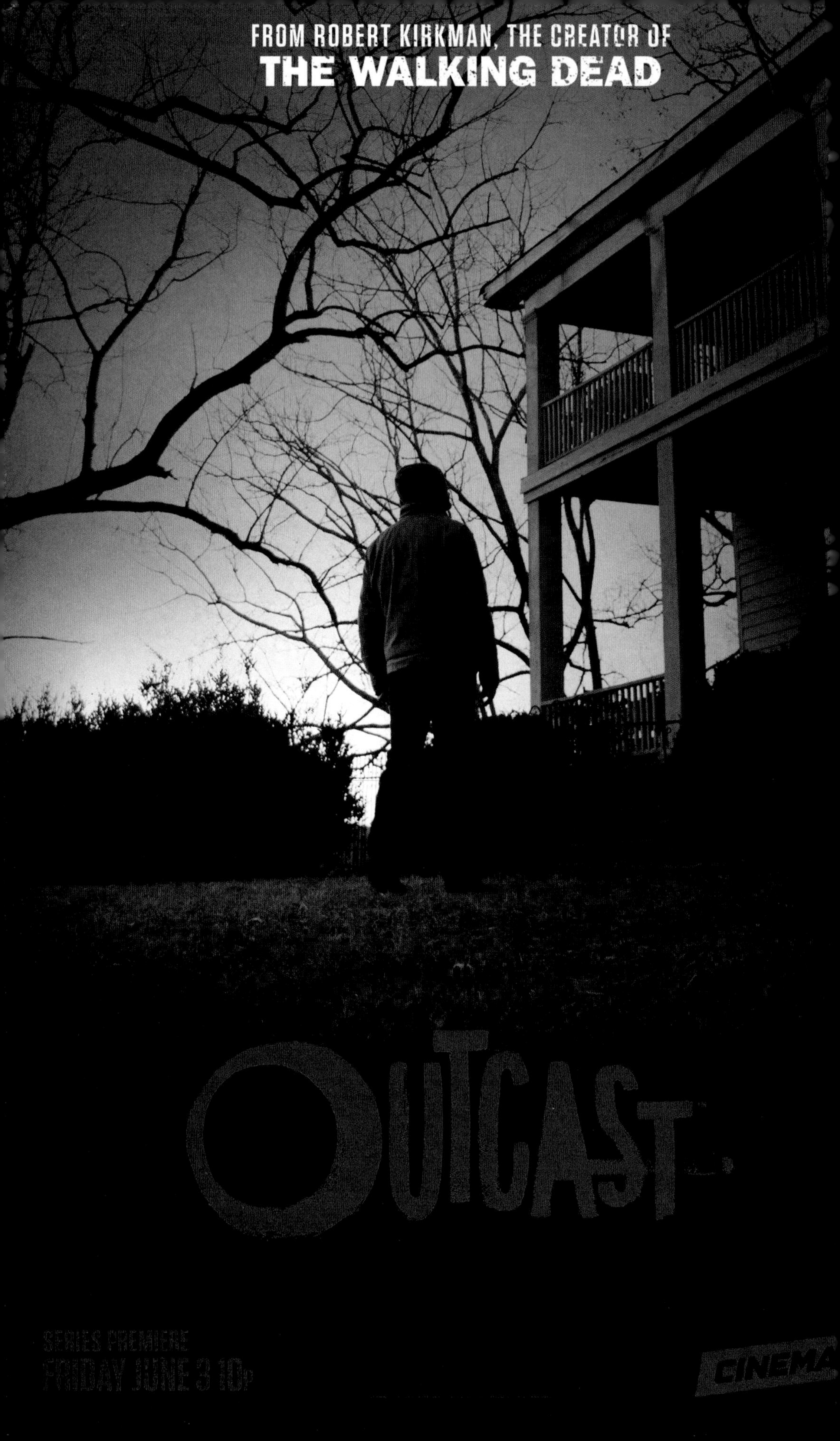

FROM ROBERT KIRKMAN, THE CREATOR OF
THE WALKING DEAD
OUTCAST
SERIES PREMIERE
FRIDAY JUNE 3 10p
CINEMA